HOMINY CORNERS

By

O. RAY DODSON

ISBN: 1-4033-1447-0 (e-book)
ISBN: 1-4033-1448-9 (Paperback)
ISBN: 1-4033-1449-7 (Hardcover)

Library of Congress Control Number: 2002091067

This book is printed on acid free paper.

Printed in the United States of America
Bloomington, IN

Cover Artwork by: Kathleen W. Dodson

1stBooks – rev. 07/12/02

CHAPTER I

Lillie wasn't sure of her ability to withstand the cold weather. Unable to control the shuddering at times, she rubbed her hands together as best she could. Her breath appeared as white frost against the clear, blue air. Ever so slowly the ache left her slender fingers but not without a struggle. She could have worn gloves, but too often they were in the way, especially when trying to hold matches. Lighting the fire under the cast-iron pot of water would surely generate heat, but igniting the kindling was not easily done. Bending over was not readily accomplished, either, and more than once she dropped the match as her grip betrayed her. When she finally did manage to hold onto the small, wooden stick with a sulfur tip, the stiff breeze often blew out the ensuing flame.

Eventually, though, success rewarded her diligent efforts. Instead of curling lazily to the sky, however, the smoke fled upward as if in fright. Clearly, the climate was frigid for this time of year. Generally such cold weather was reserved for after "Indian Summer," a desirable season typically lingering until around New Year's Day.

Pulling her bonnet strings tighter, Lillie surveyed her surroundings. There wasn't a bird to be seen in the sky, and the blue canopy over her world possessed few clouds. At least an infrequent squirrel could be seen scurrying for an elongated hole several feet above the ground in the trunk of a nearby pecan tree. Perhaps the long-tailed creatures were storing their last food supplies while the weather was somewhat cooperative. Pecans were especially plentiful this year. Lillie had worked hard to insure that she had her fair share of these nuts before the furry creatures hid them all for future use.

The wind's force kept the branches swaying continuously, and a rare cloud occasionally blanked out what little warmth the sun could muster. The chill went to the bone. Even worse, it was the kind of cold that hurt your lungs if you breathed too deeply. A woman's outer clothing could be mighty thin; it just wasn't made for spending long periods of time outside of the cabin on wintry days. Human beings should have been inside sitting on the hearth by a warm fire on a day like this.

What made the weather somewhat bearable was the look of Indian Summer now visible when Lillie scanned the countryside trying to catch a glimpse of her beloved Samuel. The oak trees still had a few hardy leaves surviving the harsh December winds. All of the fall colors, crimson red, golden yellow, moon orange, and burnt brown, were still in evidence among the darkened boughs, though the hanging leaves possessing such exquisite coats were rare in number. Their colors, reminiscent of a patchwork quilt, were especially prominent when viewed against a backdrop of pine trees and a royal blue sky the color of fine china seen in the best restaurants back in Kentucky. Yes, this just might be a beautiful day if the sun would remain in view, and the wind would cease and desist from its incessant blowing. Perhaps her sense of smell might even return if she could clear the congestion.

Lillie couldn't seem to keep her mind on hanging out the clothes to dry on the single hemp rope Samuel had strung between their tiny abode and the closest willow tree on the south side. A continual reminder, though, was the water not sufficiently wrung from an item of clothing running down upstretched arms as she attached clothespins.

Hesitating long enough to pull the threadbare shawl tighter around her thin shoulders, Lillie paused to consider her current state of affairs. She wasn't worried about Christmas, which was only two weeks away. It would be a meager holiday as usual for her and Samuel. No, her being anxious was due to the pending birth of their first child. She had turned seventeen earlier in October, and there were so many things she didn't know about having a baby. She was proud of her approaching motherhood and didn't want Samuel to know of her apprehension. Oh, she knew that she was as grownup as most women her age, and it was not unusual for women to bear children at seventeen. Why, she had been a housewife for over three years now. But in these days so many children died during childbirth that one had to worry. Then, even if the baby survived the many difficulties of birth, a mother had no assurances the infant would ever reach adulthood. No question about it, she had every reason to be concerned.

Doing laundry was lonely and hard work. It meant soaking clothes in a pot of boiling water heated over an open fire. Care was required to not drop wet clothes, as the pulverized dirt yard was generally bare of the necessary vegetation to protect the fallen clothes from being dirtier than ever. Scrubbing the garments out one at a time on a scrub board with a brush was an all day job, and no one wanted to unnecessarily repeat the task. It was not essential to sort the clothes by color or any other arbitrary system. Actually, clothes might be unrecognizable as male or female or for work or church, as even these differences were not easily noted at times. Each moment you began to think that you were making progress on the task at hand it was necessary to halt the clothes washing to stoke the fire with more wood, while trying to not get ashes into the water. Or, the laundress stopped to add replacement water for that liquid absorbed by the dry clothes.

It was hard for Lillie to even take time out for cooking meals and cleaning the cabin on wash day, as the washing routine was so time consuming. Besides that, the swirling heat rising from the pot of boiling water, along with the strong, caustic odor of the lye soap used, often took away her desire for eating. Samuel was seldom seen around the house during the middle of the day because outside work continually needed his attention. Often, then, Lillie saw no need to cook a meal at noontime.

Currently Samuel was out taking care of their few livestock. Lillie was especially proud of their brindle cow, which had recently delivered a new calf. “Bossy” well earned her name from her cantankerous disposition. The typical settler often named his livestock, as the four-legged critters frequently afforded the opportunity for discussion at mealtimes. The calf had not been named at this point, though, as it was too early to determine its individual personality. The awkward bovine had the colors of a calico cat, just like its mother. This new calf meant the cow was once again fresh, so they would have ample milk when the baby was born. Of course Lillie would nurse the infant, but the fresh cow's milk would help her body meet her child's need for milk. Just as important, the calf was a heifer. The birth of a female meant that you could continue expanding your holdings in livestock as the new addition was in due course bred for reproduction. Of course a heifer also meant a bull calf was not available for butchering for meat for the family table.

It had been hard for Lillie and her parents to leave Owensboro in western Kentucky where she was born to live in the unsettled wilderness of Indian Territory. Friends and family alike had always been close by, and generally there would be someone with whom you could play while still a child. Owensboro would always find a special place in her thoughts, as it was so scenic along the river near their earlier home. It was an old town with its many dirty, coal-burning mills and factories processing cloth goods and making steel products. Still it possessed a character that brought detailed memories of happy events to her mind when she felt alone. Often were the times she had leisurely swung in their store-bought porch swing and looked across the river at the thick, lush forests of Indiana and wondered if there were Indians lurking in the shadows. Surely with the name of Indiana there must be Indians hiding everywhere.

She was now pleased, though, that they had moved west, but the decision to move from Owensboro was most troubling for her at the time it occurred. The thought of leaving her many friends and a home she loved found no experience to guide her. Perhaps it would have been easier if she had had a brother or sister sharing the westward journey.

"Why do we have to go, Ma?" she asked.

"We've already sold this place, Honey, and a family doesn't back out on its offer to sell a place."

"But why did we have ta sell it in the first place?" Lillie asked.

"Well you know how Pa gits when there are too many people around, don't you?"

"Yes, but..."

"No buts, there're just too many people here in Owensboro. Pa's been gittin' awful restless. He doesn't sleep well at night knowin' that he's surrounded by all of these here people and he doesn't even know many of their names. Anyway, the Civil War's been over for twenty odd years now, and they're a openin' up new land all of the time. Pa ain't getting' any younger, and he figures this will be the last major move like this that we will ever make."

"But couldn't we git a place outside of town?" asked Lillie.

"We've tried, Honey, but the closest land like that is twenty miles away. Besides, we've moved before, and each time the town has slowly caught up with us. Pa says if we're a goin' to move twenty miles we might as well keep on a goin' to the Territory."

"What territory?" asked Lillie.

"Indian Territory," answered Mrs. Shaughnessy.

"That's in Indiana, ain't it?" asked Lillie. "Just 'cross the river? That might be real excitin'."

"No, it's out west on the other side of Arkansas," replied her mother. "Now we ain't a goin' to be movin' for another month. That'll give you plenty of time to settle up with your friends and say your good-byes. And you might as well know now, we can't be takin' all of your dolls and stuff with us. Besides, you're a gittin' too grownup for such things. We'll have room for a trunk full of your stuff, and that includes yer clothes. You know that green trunk on the back porch? That's all the room we'll have for your stuff. We'll need all of the space we can find in the wagon for furniture and Pa's tools. Anything that doesn't fit in the wagon or can't be tied on somewhere else will be sold. If it don't sell, we'll give it to the church. They're always a wantin' things for the needy."

"Will Pa be a blacksmith out there?"

"No, Pa wants to try his hand at farmin'. It's somethin' he's always wanted to do. Farmin' uses lots of equipment, and Lord knows he's the man to see about fixin' equipment. Why, he can make most anything people need around here. I reckon he can do the same for us. He's takin' his forge and tools with us. If nothin' else, he can do blacksmith work for others to help make ends meet."

"Do we have to move, Ma?"

"Yes, that matter has already been settled. Now you best be a decidin' what you'll be a movin' out west with us."

"Can we take that china cabinet Pa built for you before I was born? I've always a been right partial to that cabinet. Pa made it look right purty."

"I reckon so, Honey. It is right purty and some things you just don't leave behind. I'd walk beside the wagon all of the way to the territory before I'd leave that behind."

"Is it a long ways, Ma?"

"More than five hundred miles, I reckon."

"Is that a long ways?"

"Yes, child. It's a long ways."

Here in the territory Lillie had emerged into womanhood much like a butterfly emerging from a caterpillar. Actually the process had occurred fairly rapidly. What little schooling she had acquired in the territory was received from her mother in spare moments found throughout the day. Otherwise, she worked alongside her mother doing many household tasks without questioning the responsibilities given her.

Soon after arriving in the territory, Lillie's parents had settled in the vicinity of Caddo, a community near Durant. For the time being they were living in a soddy. This meant that the walls and even the roof were made of prairie grasses bound together by the sod in which they originally grew. Actually, with sufficient rainfall the grass could still be growing. A special plow was used to turn the soil in such a way that a twelve-inch strip of sod was overturned. This strip could be stacked as blocks or in long layers. As soon as the wall was sufficiently tall, however, the job could only be done with the blocks.

The luxury associated with big rooms or high ceilings was out of the question. Poles placed side-by-side to span the walls supported the sod for the roof. Ma had asked for two luxuries, however. She wanted at least one window overlooking the prairies so she could observe her husband at work, and two windows would be sheer heaven. For the occasional rain she also wanted a covered porch so mud wouldn't be tracked inside from the rains sometimes coming up on the prairie. Then, in order to have a place for a rocking chair, rough-hewn boards made a floor for this convenience.

In the beginning it was lonely with few neighbors being anywhere close by. It was a treat, then, to have someone stop by, even if it was only for a drink of water or to ask directions. In time, however, Lillie had met her future husband, Samuel. He and his two brothers, Abraham and Jacob, had only recently moved to Indian Territory from Clay County, Tennessee. His older brother, Aloysius Ledbetter, Jr., lived just across the Red River in Texas.

After his father, Aloysius, Sr., remarried, Samuel and his brothers decided to strike out for the frontier to make their fortune. This decision to go west was made easier by the fact the four boys had a strained relationship with their new stepmother. Knowing Samuel as well as she did, though, Lillie guessed that his desire for adventure was the main reason for going west. He had too much respect for women to feel ill will toward his stepmother. Actually he just didn't want to talk about it. Memories of that chance meeting brought a slowly emerging smile to her parched lips.

"Who's outside, Ma?" the girl had asked, as she carefully pulled back the yellow-striped curtains decorating one of their two front windows. She really wanted to get a glimpse of who might be talking to Pa on the porch.

"Oh they're some young men showed up at our door a short while ago."

"Well, what're they a doin' here?" Lillie didn't intend to let the matter drop so quickly. Repositioning herself and stretching on tiptoes she was able to see beyond her father's broad back initially obstructing her view. There were two strangers; one didn't look too much older than she.

"How should I know," her mother answered. Little did she recognize the level of her daughter's curiosity in the discourse so low in volume as to make it impossible to make out more than an infrequent word. Mrs. Shaughnessy went on, "If you are so all-fired interested, why don't you just step outside for yourself. I don't reckon they'll bite ya."

Lillie straightened her apron and pushed back her hair. I wish I'd taken more time combing it this morning, she thought to herself. A pretty comb stuck in the back would surely lessen the stray hairs sticking out at odd angles as well. It was too late, though, for any major improvements on such short notice. With her eyes lowered, Lillie slowly opened the front door a crack. This, however, afforded no real view of the unfolding event. Impulsively she swung the door wide. Not knowing what to do next she tried to slow her heart beat as she carefully made her way to the opposite end of the porch, drying her hands on her apron as she made her way. She wanted to hear what they were talking about, but her motives for being there must not be so obvious. The squeaking boards of the floor followed her every step. This noise couldn't have sounded louder; the din eliminated any possibility of being quiet about the move across the short space from the door. Uncomfortably leaning against the corner column while gazing out over the countryside to the east, she considered her next course of action. As best she could while trying not to be obvious about her actions, she glanced over her right shoulder more than once in the process. She was successful. Her attention appeared to concentrate on an unknown creature moving in the woods off in the distance.

"Come on over here, Lillie. Meet our new neighbors from up the road a piece. This here's Samuel Ledbetter and his brother Abe. They're asking about a buyin' one of our heifers."

Tipping his hat, the older of the two said, "I'm Samuel. Seems like I'm the only one that goes by his full name. This here's my little brother, Abe."

"I am not little! I'm a grown man!"

"Time will tell, Brother. Time will tell," said Samuel.

Mr. Shaughnessy returned his smile.

"Well, I'm Lillie Shaughnessy, and I'm pleased to meet ya'll," the anxious young lady said. "You a goin' to sell them a calf, Pa?" Her eyes never left Samuel to even acknowledge the presence of his silent partner in this venture.

"I reckon we can spare one for the time bein'," her father answered.

"We'd be beholden to ya'll if ya could," the older of the two said.

Unable to hide her joy with the entire transaction, Lillie knew she couldn't remain on the porch and be reasonably composed. She next said, "If you'll excuse me, I better go give Ma a hand in the house. We're a makin' a peach cobbler, and I'm supposed to roll out the dough for the crust."

"I sure wish I had someone could make me a peach cobbler," Samuel had replied, as he watched the retreating figure make her less than graceful exit.

Again returning to the present with her thoughts, Lillie knew how she and Samuel Ledbetter looked forward to their first child. They had married when she was only 14 years old in 1891. After having lived in the Territory for almost four years now, she was beginning to feel more at home. It seemed that she and Samuel were close to fulfilling their deeply shared desire of having a child. They hoped it would be a boy. Every family in these parts wanted a boy as a first child. Not only did having a boy mean someone to carry on the family name, but it also meant there was someone to carry on the family trade as well. Maybe there would also be better crops if there were enough help to get all of the farm work done on time. Lillie secretly thought it would be nice to have a girl, too, so she could expect some help around the cabin.

She often had difficulty in getting all of her work done, and she had many fond memories of the special relationship between herself and her mother. Their many talks had been so enjoyable. To wish for a girl was just too much right now, however. Getting help for Samuel with the farm work was the first priority. This extra help was a key ingredient to their getting ahead in the future or to even surviving in this raw wilderness.

Lillie spent a considerable amount of time thinking about her soon-to-be-born child. Would it be healthy? So many children died before they were a year old. No matter whether the child was a boy or girl, the infant would be good company during the early years. It seemed like Samuel was never around. When he wasn't cutting down trees to be made into railroad ties for the "Katy" Railroad (The M.K.& T. Railroad ran through the area from Texas to points north including Indian Territory), he was outside doing farm work. This extra income was helping them save money for the day when they would own their own place. Right now they were just sharecropping with half of the income from the farm going to the landowner.

When you combined Samuel's pioneering spirit, born of Tennessee stock and English heritage, with Lillie's Kentucky spunk and Irish heritage, it left no doubt that the new child would have the right ingredients for success on the frontier. He or she would only need the right opportunities, and the rest they wouldn't worry about. If the child were a boy, perhaps he would some day help them to realize a lifelong dream, owning a farm. After all, it was almost 1895, and Samuel was already 31 years old. Men generally didn't live much beyond 40 years old in this country, so the luxury of time was running out. It was a hard life, and you didn't get too many chances to succeed. Furthermore, in these parts land ownership more than anything else was the principle sign of success.

There was talk of joining Oklahoma Territory further west with Indian Territory to form a new state. Maybe this new state would make life easier. Statehood always meant new settlers, and more settlers meant progress on the frontier. Statehood also meant there would be an increased chance for land grants, because this part of the territory had been left out of the original land rushes.

Homesteads of 160 acres of free land could well be the ticket to the future, if you could handle the responsibility. Then you were a landowner; you were somebody. Of course, in order to keep the land, you had to "prove up" on your claim by clearing and planting the land for five years, as well as building a house on the land in the process. That would be so much easier to do with a son to help out. Five years was a long time to survive the harsh conditions of a new land. It was worth it, however, they had told themselves many times. They were now in charge of their own destiny; that is if you didn't consider the weather and the many other conditions over which they had little or no control.

Right now, though, Lillie's mind was on the child she was carrying. Would life be easier for it than she had experienced? After all, in her seventeen years of life, there hadn't been too many changes that she could tell. Oh, there had been a few changes and improvements, she must confess. They had heard about some man up in Illinois named John Deere, who had continued to improve the plows used by farmers. He had once again redesigned the steel plow he developed in 1837. His first big improvement was in 1857 when he modified the walking plow by giving it three plowshares to cover more ground. Then in 1861 Deere added a seat to his invention, so the farmer wouldn't have to walk so much; however, in so doing it was necessary to return to a one-bottom plow, which meant only one plowshare would be turning the soil. The height of his genius was reached in 1890 when he was able to add a steel seat to a riding two-bottom plow.

But few settlers in this country could afford this timesaving device that was relatively comfortable as well. The common farmer of the territory was dependent upon what he could do with his own hands or what few pieces of horse-drawn equipment he could buy; that is, if he could afford to buy any implements at all. As a matter of fact, most farmers built some of their equipment out of wood or metal they could scavenge from the demise of something else.

Cost was not the only consideration in building one's own equipment, though. Sometimes what he needed couldn't be purchased anywhere. Actually, purchase might not be the correct word for these transactions. Bartering, or the trading of goods and services for needed goods and services, was the typical financial transaction for this day and age.

When all else failed, the local blacksmith could fashion the desired implement from crude drawings sometimes made with a stick in the dirt floor of his shop or made on paper by the person in need of doing things differently. Even spare paper was a luxury to some. After eight years of trying to farm, Pa Shaughnessy finally realized that his true calling was to be a blacksmith. Soon as his farm could be sold, he had moved his family to the outskirts of Durant and once again restricted his duties to the repair and manufacture of farm implements. This pleased many settlers from the surrounding countryside in need of prolonging the life of a needed tool.

The farmer's main concern, though, was whether or not he had enough hours in the day to complete his work, and this couldn't be done efficiently without tools. You only had six days in a week to do farm chores. You just did not work on Sunday, as that was a sign you weren't God-fearing enough. Besides that, it wasn't right to labor on Sunday. After all, as Pa Shaughnessy often said, "If a man can't git his work done in six days, what good use of gumption tells him he can git it done in seven days?"

On rare occasions Lillie would think back to that summer day in June, three years earlier on the twenty-first of the month in 1891, when she and Samuel had married. It was not an elaborate ceremony; Samuel had worn his best Sunday shirt along with a pair of denim work britches in good repair, while she had worn a new red gingham dress and a matching bonnet. She only had three days to make the dress after they picked up the material at the general mercantile store in town. Haste was absolutely necessary. They had heard that the missionary from Yarnabe, a small settlement southwest of Caddo, would be passing through on Sunday, so they went right in to Durant and got their wedding license. After all, you didn't get too many chances to be married by a "man of the cloth."

After Lillie and Samuel had picked up the marriage license, she and her mother had selected six yards of her favorite material at the general mercantile store. A new dress would be nice, she thought, even if she hadn't been getting married. Now she would own two nice dresses fit enough for Sunday wear. The four and one-half cents a yard they had paid extra over the eight cents a yard typically charged for calico was a luxury not soon to be repeated; the forty cents was no small amount, especially when you realized that it represented half a day's pay. The ten cents a yard charged for red ribbon was just asking too much at this time, though.

Thank goodness the storekeeper had a dress material that she liked. He only had two bolts of new cloth from which to choose. It would have been a plain dress indeed, if Mother Shaughnessy hadn't had rolls of white lace trimming to pretty the dress up some; she had brought the fabric all the way from Kentucky.

Samuel hadn't wanted any new clothes for getting married; he felt it was more important to spend his money on new farm equipment or to enlarge their livestock holdings. It was wasteful, he had said, to spend money in such foolish ways. Of course it did bother him some that the brogans gracing his feet showed the trials of carrying him through his many farm chores. At least he was able to scrub most of the remains of his treks through the corral from the scuffed and faded leather. Mother Shaughnessy had insisted, however, on her daughter getting married in a new dress. Samuel didn't have the heart to argue with her and wouldn't even try to change her mind. This wasn't true of his future bride, however.

"We're only gittin' married, Ma. Can't I just wear my `Sunday Go To Church' dress?" she initially argued. She knew that Samuel felt the money could have been better spent, but her parents were paying the bill.

"You hush now. I'll not have my daughter, my only daughter and child at that, gittin' married in something she's been a wearin' before. It ain't fittin'."

"Samuel would prefer any nice, clean dress. It doesn't have to be new."

"Your Pa and I won't hear of it."

"Did Pa say anything on this matter?"

"No, but he would if I insisted."

"I know he'd say somethin' if asked, but would it be 'no'?"

"This discussion is over. Now stand still while we see how much material we'll need."

Lillie and Samuel hadn't really known each other that long before getting married. Long courtships were rare on the frontier. No, they just knew they wanted to spend their lives together and raise a family. Sure, they loved each other, but love was not as important as surviving in the wilderness. Right now they could help take care of each other at a time when each new day brought many threats to one's survival.

Lillie and Samuel's attire was typical for most any frontier couple. Both were raw-boned and slender. Quite frankly, they looked out of place all "dressed up" for the wedding. Being tall, his trousers barely reached the tops of his work shoes, dusted for this special occasion. Maybe his suspenders, necessary because his slender build didn't lend itself to helping his trousers stay in the proper position, pulled everything too high. He didn't own a belt, and a three-foot length of cotton rope sometimes sufficed in its place. His one concession to Mrs. Shaughnessy's request for more formal wedding attire was to buy the twenty-five cent pair of suspenders. After all, sometimes a man has to let a woman think that she's in charge.

It was a simple wedding ceremony uniting Samuel Amos Ledbetter and Lillie Ann Shaughnessy. Her mother and father stood beside her during the ceremony. Abe and Jacob were there at his side. The brothers didn't have any quick way of notifying Aloysius over in Texas about the big event. No one was really designated in any role other than the bride, groom and preacher. The ceremony's main purpose was to give God's blessing to an earthly event necessary to survival in the wilderness. Their ruddy, leathery complexions, due to many hours spent working outside in the hot sun with little protection, made the two sharing vows look like they should be working in the fields instead of getting married. Still, they made a good-looking couple. At least they certainly looked happy. Reverend C.A. Desmond, an itinerant missionary to the Indians of the Choctaw Nation, solemnized the "bonns of matrimony" in this brief ceremony performed at Lillie's folk's house near Caddo. There was no honeymoon; there was too much work needing done on the home place.

Lillie and Samuel lived with her folks for almost six months after the wedding. They needed to build a new cabin before they could live on Samuel's place. Once they decided to get married, there was little time to build a cabin before the wedding. The dugout he had been using to live in before just was not acceptable as an abode for a woman, so Samuel had worked to cut trees down for logs for the cabin's walls every day after he finished working in the fields. Poplar trees were good for building cabins, as they were nice and straight, requiring minimal trimming. This meant he didn't have time to cut ties for the railroad, but that didn't bother him. The logs needed to be stockpiled for awhile, so they could cure out some before being used. Otherwise, there would be considerable shrinkage after they were in place, eventually leading to cracks between the logs. Cabins were hard enough to keep warm without deliberately giving the opportunity for cracks to form.

Samuel would still be building the cabin, Lillie reckoned, if a number of friends and neighbors hadn't come over to help put the logs in place. In one day the one-room cabin was ready for the young couple. Of course the ambitious workers had started at sunup and worked until after dark getting everything done. The walls were all up with mud "chinked" in the cracks between the logs to help keep the winter's cold air out. The inclusion of small stones to the chinking would help keep the mud from cracking so much in the future.

A roof of sorts had been made using the slabs of bark and wood left over from the times Samuel squared up trees for making railroad ties. A covering of straw and branches, along with a good pitch to the roof, would help keep water out. Eventually Samuel could split sections of cedar to make shingles for the roof. On that first day the windows were covered with cloth until glass could be purchased; glass wasn't easy to acquire and what little that could be bought was hard to see through due to the wavy lines it contained. The front and only door was taken off of the dugout Samuel had previously occupied as a bachelor, so they didn't have to expend the time to build another one. Also, the floor was dirt, and that represented a cost reduction as well. Of course after the dirt became pulverized from long usage, Lillie would have to get a tree branch and sweep it once in awhile.

Yes, little effort was required in putting the finishing touches on the cabin, not to mention the fact that initially nothing needed painting. The nicest thing about the cabin, Lillie had told Samuel, was that it was theirs alone. Granted, it was small, but they could do anything they wanted to it without getting someone else's approval. The slowest step in completing the cabin concerned the fireplace. Samuel had stockpiled stones in the process of clearing the fields for cultivation.

Actually, the fireplace building had commenced a few days earlier to allow the mortar to set. On this day, three men had begun immediately in continuing to put the stones together with mortar while others wrestled the heavy logs going up around them. It took three or four men on each end of the heavy logs to lift them into place. That only left three men to finish the fireplace, not counting those needed to prepare more logs for placement. Granted, the finished fireplace was not a work of art, but the function of the object was far more important than its beauty. From past experience they well knew the necessity of correctly positioning the "throat" of the chimney above the fireplace. Otherwise, the opening wouldn't ventilate correctly, and the cabin would continually be full of smoke. The hearth measuring six feet in width would certainly receive considerable use in the future. Also, the giant opening in the front could accommodate fairly large logs, thereby lessening the need to make extra cuts in preparing the firewood. As long as sufficient room was left on the left side to hang the large cast-iron pot for cooking venison chili or just plain pinto beans, enough wood could be inserted to burn for hours.

"Any special requests before we finish this fireplace altogether?" asked Ezekial.

"I don't want any smoke in the cabin," said Lillie. "What with the dirt floors, we don't want anything else movin' around in the air. Besides, it'll hurt your eyes."

"Then you'll want it to draw properly," said Cletus. "Of course we'll never get the cabin airtight, so there'll be plenty of air to feed the fire. In turn the heat will cause the air in the chimney to rise."

"I don't care what you call it. I just don't want a smoky cabin."

"If we built the throat of this contraption right, then, you're a going to have your wish," said Ezekial.

"Yes," said Cletus, "and it's a right pretty one with this red clay Samuel collected for the chinking. Why with this brown stone outlined in red, it looks like a fine tablecloth."

"Maybe someday Samuel will kill a brown bear for a rug to go on the floor in front of the hearth," said Lillie.

The day the cabin was built was a day never to be forgotten. It was a day when the air was filled with merriment and happiness. While some of the men strained to lift the logs higher and higher for the walls, others were trimming the logs yet to go into place so they had no bark or the sharp points of broken branches protruding from them. Then, while the older girls supervised the younger children, the women put together a feast rarely seen on the frontier. It was probably not so different from the first Thanksgiving holiday celebrated by the pilgrims. Wild deer and turkey were plentiful in the region, so more than one family shared the fruit of hunting ventures in the thick woods. Some people had brought fish caught only a day earlier and likely cleaned by firelight. Baked goods were in abundance. A few neighbors brought vegetables salvaged from a garden that had quit producing for the year.

Laughter was not in short supply. The cows would certainly be milked late tonight, as dancing was surely to occur before what little furniture the couple possessed was brought into the simple structure. Times like these helped one to forget, if only for a short while, all of the hardships of living in the wilderness. Better yet, such events served the important purpose of reminding everyone of their need to rely on each other when necessity arose. There were no government programs or services that took the place of individuals helping each other. The real benefit of self-sufficiency was the other side of this coin. There were no corresponding taxes to deplete one's meager earnings, either. Besides, use of the barter system meant that little money was in circulation, anyway.

"Have you about got things ready to eat, Lillie?" asked Samuel.

"I reckon we can take a few at a time to feed," she answered.

"That's what I had in mind," said Samuel. "That way work won't have to stop. If we get done in time tonight, we'll all sit down for a meal together. From the looks of that big meal you ladies have put together, though, we'll need a long time to eat."

"Well, you can't work that hard without plenty of victuals in your stomach. Otherwise you'll all be rundown before the work's done."

"I know, but I don't want the men thinkin' of a nap in the middle of the day."

"Hush up and begin callin' the men!" she had answered.

Lillie's thoughts were jarred back to the present by the crashing sound of something running through the tamaracks. A noise not easily recognized by an unseasoned settler. She was thankful for the sound, even though the noise soon disappeared. Perhaps it was a deer. Maybe Samuel could get them some fresh meat tonight. The last deer he had killed and hung in the shed out back was almost gone. As long as the cold weather lasted, and the deer's carcass was hung far enough off of the ground by a rope to keep small animals from eating on the carcass, there would be very little meat wasted. You couldn't keep meat like this in the summertime. It always spoiled before you could eat it. Worse yet, it would soon begin to smell. Wouldn't it be nice, she thought, if there were some way to keep meat cold for long periods of time in the summer, so it wouldn't spoil?

Supper was delayed that night. Actually, evening meal times rarely occurred at a consistent time. The settler worked until a task was completed, and completion times weren't always predictable. Samuel was later than expected getting in with Bossy, and milking seemed to take longer than usual. Lillie went out to talk with him while he did the milking.

"I heard something like a deer runnin' through the brush today. I thought you'd like to know that I cooked the last of the venison for supper tonight."

"Does that mean you want me to go a huntin'?"

"I was wonderin' about tonight. Maybe it's still close by."

"How long ago was it?"

"Just before I hung the last clothes on the line."

"Can't it wait for a day or two? I'm really too tired to go out tonight. Besides, the best time to hunt deer is about sunrise or sunset when they're a goin' to the river for a drink or to the fields to eat. I promise to git one as soon as I can."

"Okay, but you realize we don't have any fresh meat after tonight, don't you?"

"Couldn't you bake somethin'?" Samuel asked. "Cornbread and beans would be right tasty for one meal, especially with a strip of hog fat in it."

"Well, we sure don't have any pork right now. Besides, ain't you a gettin' tired of them beans, yet?" she asked.

Samuel never spoke. Actually he didn't seem to hear what his wife was saying. Surmising that her husband didn't really feel like talking, Lillie went back into the cabin to finish fixing supper.

It was a quiet meal. Samuel spent more time stirring the victuals on his plate than he did in eating. Once, though, he did ask if there was more coffee. His cup was soon filled with the steaming liquid carried in a blackened pot from the open fire with a folded rag used as a potholder. Lillie hated to see Samuel so exhausted from his work. She wished she could do more to help him, but being so close to having a child made it hard for her to get around. After eating, Samuel went on to bed, while she put their few dishes away. Before long she joined him.

Wash day had been long and tiring for Lillie. She couldn't drop off to sleep too easily, however. She lay awake, nestled in Samuel's arms, while he snored in a deep sleep caused by a long day's work of cutting trees and clearing more land for farming. Her mind was filled with so many happy thoughts. She was going to be a mother. This was the highest achievement she felt she could attain as a woman. Could there be anything better than this, she asked herself, as she dropped off to sleep. Even then, she dreamed about the future. It would be a happy life with her future child and her husband. She had grown to love both of them very much. In her dream she asked herself out loud, “Can there really be anything better than this?”

CHAPTER II

Watching the setting sun evoked emotions in Samuel like few other events in an existence with rare celebrations. The life of the settler, you see, centered upon events of nature ranging from the tilling of the soil to the welcoming of newborn creatures. He never tired of watching the sun go down in the evening. The retiring sphere could always be counted on to be a spectacular display of hues as it slowly slipped out of sight in the west. First, it would turn a shade of gold seen only on the finest brass. Then around the edges would appear tinges of pink, as though someone was adding the purest of blood as a coloring to the finest of white silk. The pink would start at the outside edge and slowly work its way to the center of the sunset in a reverse fashion, when compared to the ripples caused by the throwing of a rock into a tranquil pond.

Yes, looking west into the setting sun was such a beautiful sight; it held so much wonder and promise. The celestial sight often caused Samuel to think about his future. When everything about the setting sun was cheery, he generally had positive thoughts about what the future held. It was nice to have such an easy way to uplift his spirits. That is, if the weather was good.

There was no warmth in the clear air. Samuel hastened his steps not only to shake the penetrating chill from his bones but also to lessen the time of his exposure to one of the harsher elements of nature. He could now see his breath before his face. His sense of smell had long since abandoned him, but the accompanying congestion created by the cold air remained behind. The stuffy feeling was nature's way of saying winter was surely not far off. As he searched for Bossy, Samuel wished he had worn more clothing. The secret in combating the harsh weather of the countryside, he felt, was simply to add more layers of clothing. Of course the extra clothing made it more difficult to freely move one's arms or legs. The trade off for warmth, though, was a necessary evil. He wished that he had clothes warm enough to withstand the cold when worn alone. Tomorrow I'll wear my long-handled underwear, he thought to himself. Right now, though, he would like to find the cow in time to milk her before darkness overtook the pair.

It was not the weather or the cow that held his attention at this time, however. It wasn't even the beauty of the setting sun, which was rapidly dropping out of sight. No, Samuel's thoughts on this December 11th were on his seventeen-year old expectant wife, Lillie. Their baby was due any day now. The main concern preoccupying his fleeting thoughts was that the child be healthy and his wife safe. Many children and babies were dying in the area, not to mention new mothers lost during childbirth.

There really wasn't much medical care like they had had in Tennessee. Here, they had to rely more upon family or friends when someone was sick or having a baby. Lillie's parents, Clevon and Tess Shaughnessy, had only recently moved from Caddo to a few acres just outside Durant, which, at approximately 2000 population, was by far the largest town around. It was only about ten miles away. Maybe Lillie could stay with them until the baby was born. He would feel much better this way, in case there were complications. At least Durant had a doctor, which was more than Caddo had to offer. Besides that, he didn't want his baby born so far from town this time of year. He wanted the delivery to be where a body could get help if needed.

Samuel's mind drifted back to when he and his brothers had left their father's home to come out west. He was seventeen at the time. Aloysius Ledbetter, Jr., "Led," was the eldest at nineteen. The two younger boys, Abraham and Jacob, were fourteen and twelve respectively. There really wasn't much future for enterprising young men in that part of Tennessee. There was no land that they could afford, and most of the free land had been homesteaded. Besides that, there were exciting tales being told about Indian Territory and Texas. A man could get ahead, if he was willing to work. Well, entertain no questions on that; the Ledbetter boys were willing to work. The lure of the unknown was just too much to resist especially when you couldn't get along with your new stepmother.

He seldom stopped to think of his own mother, Carrie Ledbetter, anymore. Born in 1835 she had died when Jacob was born. Some said that the strain on her heart was too much for her during the birth. He remembered her being such a gentlewoman, always willing to hug you when you hurt or were troubled. Also, she could quote passages from the Bible about so many things that might be bothering you, and it often helped. Still, she was unused to the harsh wilderness of Tennessee.

Miss Lydia, his stepmother, was a different story. She was headstrong and accustomed to having her own way. Reared as an only girl in a family of five boys, she had to fight for her share of anything that came along. On the other hand, she did have a proper upbringing and she expected good manners to be the order of the day. As an adult she was not noted for good looks, just the ability to see a task to completion. By the time she married Aloysius Ledbetter, Sr., she was forty years old. Samuel suspected that she saw a chance, maybe her first and last chance, to get married. Also, he believed that there was a strong likelihood that she saw a chance to run a home without any interference. He further reckoned that Aloysius, Sr., needing someone to care for his four boys, wanted a nanny far more than he wanted a new mate.

Miss Lydia often expressed the fact that the Ledbetter boys were not her idea of well-mannered children. Furthermore, their fierce independence didn't set well with her. Perhaps it was an unwillingness to concede that someone else might be right. Anyway, he could remember the parting confrontation as though it was only yesterday.

"Who said you could take the horse over to the slough, Led?" she asked.

"Pa has always 'lowed me to do that," he answered.

"But, did he give you permission for this time?"

"No," answered Led, "we've just always understood that it was alright. Besides, I'm a grown man."

"Well, I run this household, and I say that it isn't proper unless I say so each and every time. As long as you live here, you'll do what I say. Do you understand that?"

"I guess, but I don't like it," answered the eldest boy.

"There's no place for guessing here. Either you know it or you don't. And my job is not to have you like it. Now you answer me proper like, and be quick about it!"

"Yes Madam," said Led.

"What did you say?" she asked. "Now get it right this time!"

"Yes Ma'am, I should have asked!" said Led as he abruptly turned and left.

Always wanting the last word, she addressed her final remarks to his back as he rounded the corner of their house. "Do it that way every time and don't you forget it!"

Turning to the remaining boys, she continued, "What are you waiting for?"

It didn't take long for the four boys to convene a meeting in the loft of the barn. There was no way the proper Miss Lydia could stumble in on them unbeknownst in that setting. She never went anywhere that her feet weren't planted on solid ground, and walking where the residue of an animal might be deposited certainly wasn't solid ground. The decision to leave was easily made. They had had enough of this continual reprimanding for the past eleven years. The only question was about Abe and Jake.

"I don't know about you two a goin', you're awful young," said Led.

"We can't go without them," stated Samuel. "It wouldn't be fair for them to have to continue with always worryin' about what she'd find wrong next."

"Well, you boys are fine strappin' workers for your age. It's a deal. We all go or no one goes. Of course you'll have to do your share of the work on the trip, and whatever Samuel or I says, goes."

"Fair enough, but where will we go?" asked Jake.

"Well, I hear tell that there's fine land for the takin' in Indian Territory," replied Led. "Isn't that what you hear tell, Samuel?"

"Yes, I heard two old boys down at the cotton gin just the other day a talkin' about it," Samuel replied. "Sure sounds like the place to be for four men itchin' to move on. First, though, I want to be sure where Abe is on this."

"I wouldn't miss a chance to get out of here for anything," said Abe. "I'll miss Pa, though."

"We'll all miss him," said the others.

To make a long story short, they all made the difficult journey. The Ledbetter boys arrived in the Territory during the summer of 1890 expecting to find wild, savage Indians wearing feathers in headbands and carrying tomahawks while hiding behind the trees. It sure would be exciting after all of the war stories generated by the Civil War. The brothers soon realized, though, that they had been misled by the tall tales they had heard of the west while still in Tennessee. The Indians here were peaceful with no outward signs of ever having been violent.

The Five Civilized Tribes of Indian Territory were organized into five Indian nations. These nations, named according to the major tribes, were the Cherokee, Chickasaw, Choctaw, Creek and Seminole. It was unbelievable how advanced these tribes had become. They had comprehensive school systems with academies for both boys and girls. They even had continuing education for their adults or sent tribal members elsewhere on scholarships for an advanced education. Also, they had judicial systems based on an elaborate constitution.

The Ledbetter brothers soon realized that the ideas they learned back east about Indians were only myths. These people were not heathen savages. They were human beings who wanted a better life just like the one desired by the Ledbetter brothers: a home, a family, land and the opportunity to get ahead. Yes, the education of the brothers about Indians had been and continued to be most enlightening.

If it had not been for crossing the Red River the second time, the Ledbetter boys would not even have known they were in the territory. Traveling west from Tennessee on the Southwest Trail, sometimes called the Chihuahua Trail after its distant termination point in Old Mexico, they had covered the width of Arkansas. Most immigrants went through Hope to Fulton, Arkansas, before getting their last outfitting of supplies for the remainder of the trip. Fulton's stores were kept supplied by riverboats and barges sailing up the difficult currents of the

Red River. This lengthy waterway journey through Natchitoches, Louisiana, to Fulton was sufficiently difficult that the merchants felt justified in charging quite high prices for their merchandise. Sugar at eleven cents a pound would be used most sparingly. Coffee rarely contained the desirable sweetener.

The Ledbetters saw no need in staying any longer than necessary in Fulton. While there were several bars and plenty of places for men to have a good time, they weren't the types of individuals to carouse around or "raise Cain," as it was called. Besides, their only experiences with women had been Mom and Miss Lydia, and that certainly didn't qualify them for the ladies of the evening of Fulton. Better yet, what little coinage they possessed was being saved for their new start in the territory. Instead, then, they used this opportunity to get a good bath in a protected cove just off of the Red River a couple of miles north of town.

Save an occasional hawk soaring high above their retreat or a rare fox coming down for a drink, this secluded bathhouse experienced no interruptions. The luxuries of a bath and clean clothes on the trail were rare, and they intended to take advantage of this chance to do something about it. Besides, the cost was appropriate for their financial condition. They even washed their hats, which were sweaty and discolored from long hours spent out in the sun. It was soon clear, though, that the sweatbands would never relinquish their dark discoloration. Actually, their efforts did little more than remove the dust from the limp headwear. Most importantly, the brims, necessary to protect their faces from the relentless midday sun, maintained their basic shapes. Any droop, however slight, served to make them more effective.

They had already washed their clothes and hung them on nearby branches to dry. It was late spring by now, so a fire was needed to take some of the chill from the air and help to dry their apparel. Wrinkles were of no concern to them at this time. More important was the relative freedom from the trail dust of their attire.

The bath was another story. If cleanliness was a virtue as the Bible taught, they had every desire to be virtuous in this respect. Knowing the temperature of the water led to delays in bathing.

"What you waitin' on, Led?" asked Samuel.

"Oh, the river seems awfully fast right now. Maybe if we wait, it'll git slower."

"Now you know the speed of this here river ain't a goin' to change any time soon. You don't reckon it has anything to do with the chill of the water, do you?" asked Samuel.

"Well I am right partial to warm water for bathin'," answered Led. "But if you're in such a all-fired hurry, don't wait on me."

So enter the swiftly flowing stream the reluctant travelers did. The cold, running water chilled to the bone. Their ankles soon felt numb, and the sensitivity was rapidly creeping up their extremities. A slow ache quickly set in. This was not to be a leisurely bath allowing the luxury of soaking foreign matter from the pores of their skin. Rather, it was more like a baptism substituting sprinkling for immersion. The boys exited the pool even quicker than their running entrance to the flowing baptismal. Even though it was coarse and scratchy, they each used the blanket from their bedroll to dry themselves. They could dry them afterwards by the fire. There just wasn't room to carry towels in their hurried departure from their father's home.

"What was your hurry there, Jake?" asked Led. "Little cold, were you?"

"No, it just doesn't take me long to bathe," was the boy's reply.

"If you're not cold, then why are you a standin' so close to the fire?" asked Abe.

"Just being sure there's plenty of light in order to do a right good job," the younger brother answered.

Immediately after leaving Fulton, the brothers had to cross the Red River for the first time. They used Thompson's Ferry. They could have had the horses swim across, but there was no need in taking such chances with the river being so high this time of year. The slow crossing also allowed them the opportunity to study the currents of the stream that had cooled their desire for a thorough cleansing. Not only did the water occasionally splash over the top of their unstable conveyance, but also on two occasions a partly submerged log collided with a thud on the upstream side. The horses were skittish as they spread their legs wide to withstand the rolling motion of this unfamiliar terrain.

These steeds weren't the only ones apprehensive about this crossing. Jacob was convinced it was only a matter of time until they all drowned. Still, the brothers found the ferry most interesting as well. The craft was built of logs lashed together with rope and roughhewn planking added across the top; this provided a somewhat flat surface on which to stand. A long, hemp rope, about one and one-half inches in diameter, was securely fastened to a large, spreading oak tree on the opposite shore. The other end in turn was wrapped several turns around an upright log sticking up about three feet on the front of the barge-like vehicle. As the crossing was made, a silent Mexican in Thompson's employ not only pulled on the rope, but he made occasional loops around the log to remove the slack.

"What's the rope for?" asked Abe. "Couldn't you make better time havin' two of us a pushin' them poles?"

"With water this high, and the currents so rapid, we can't take any chances on getting carried downstream," Josh Thompson answered. "During the winter months the current is slower and we don't always use the rope. Of course not too many travelers use the ferry then, so it doesn't matter much."

"Why do you even operate in those months, then?" asked Abe.

"Mainly for moving supply and pack trains," the proprietor answered. "For some reason people like to keep their matches and gunpowder dry. Besides, settlers like you coming at odd times of the year need a way across."

"Why do you say, `odd time of the year`?" asked Abe.

"Most of you folks are putting in your crops or at least working with what's already planted by now," answered Thompson.

"Makes sense to me," returned Abe.

"Suppose the land on the other side will change much?" asked Samuel, as he surveyed the countryside before them. He wanted more information about the journey awaiting the travelers now long on the trail.

"Actually the land itself won't change much," answered Thompson as he struggled with the long push-pole used to move the flatboat forward. "The big difference will be in the seeing of far fewer people. The Red River acts like a boundary line between the settled and the unsettled. You won't meet near as many folk on the trail on the other side."

"Is it more dangerous?" asked Jacob.

"Not really," answered the boatswain. "The Indians are generally hospitable. Of course you'll have to travel further to get help when you need it."

"Why's that?" asked Led.

"It's a big country," was the answer, "and not as many folks have seen fit to move over to the Texas side. Of course when you do find someone, they'll generally help you as best as they can. My advice to you is to become part of a settlement. Don't think you have to get clear away from other folks to find your place in this big world of ours."

Upon arriving on the westside, the Ledbetter brothers indeed found themselves in a sparsely populated area.

"Don't reckon we'll see you gents again," said Mr. Thompson.

"I reckon not," replied Abe. "This is a one-way journey. There's no lookin' back."

"You boys ain't a runnin' from the law are ya?"

"No, we're a runnin' from our pa's new bride that ain't got any idea about what us boys think is important. We'll teach her a thing or two. Now she'll have ta carry her own water."

"I hear ya'," said the rafter.

Immigrants heading for both Indian Territory and Texas continued to follow the Southwest Trail along the northern edge of Texas after crossing the Red River. They left a trail that was easy for Samuel and his brothers to follow. In places, the covered wagons left deep ruts, easily turned into slippery mud with a rain. While the countryside was green and beautiful, it was also becoming quite hot what with traveling in the early summertime. Still, the purple and green view of wild clover mingled with other wildflowers such as the colorful blue and white columbine was refreshing to the spirits of souls long in the saddle. It smelled like the flower garden Mother always maintained right up to her untimely death.

Sometimes, in order to rest their mounts, the brothers would let the horses walk for awhile, oblivious to their horses' brief pauses to sample the many varieties of grasses in the region. This helped the riders to rest as well, if they remained quiet and slumped in the saddle. If Samuel closed his eyes he became delightfully aware of a gentle breeze rustling through the treetops as well as the harmony of a large chorus of birds singing to an audience they would never know. The observant soul further noticed that the cutting off of one sense seemed to heighten the awareness of the remaining senses.

With his eyes closed Samuel was pleasantly aware of things he wouldn't normally have seen, such as the harmony of the birds occasionally being broken by the shrill screech of a distant bluejay in search of prey. Also, it was a joy to smell the freshness of the countryside after a summer rain. Of course there was the occasional buzzing of a fly in search of a landing site easily disrupting the pastoral scene. All in all, though, there appeared to be no need to rush to their final destination, unless they were running low on funds that is.

After some days of travel in Texas, Led decided he liked the looks of the country around Parker County near Forth Worth. Besides, he had an offer to work in a gristmill grinding flour. In the beginning the four brothers had always said they were going to Indian Territory together. But, Led decided he had traveled long enough. He had found his Promised Land in the northeast part of Texas. The lush green hills lacked the appearance of milk and honey, but they certainly looked beautiful to him. Samuel guessed that several weeks of horseback riding had taken Led about as far as he wanted to go. The part of a person that rides the closest to the saddle sometimes rebels at going any farther. Led did promise that he would come on to the territory and find his brothers if things didn't work out as he expected in Texas.

After resting up for a day and purchasing additional supplies for the final leg of their journey, the three remaining brothers struck out north heading for Colbert's Ferry, needed to cross into Indian Territory. Samuel was now the eldest of the weary travelers. The trio could hardly wait to reach the territory, because Texas looked so inviting, and it was tempting to remain there. But, when a Ledbetter had a goal for himself, it was hard to change his mind. All but Led, that was. Because they were traveling with what few personal belongings they could wear or carry on the saddle behind them, they were able to reach Colbert's Ferry in only two days.

The land on the north side of the Red River didn't look that much different than Texas, so Jake asked, "If the land is all the same, why ain't we a stayin' where Led's a stayin'?"

"Well," said Abe, "it's like this. Texas is older than the Territory. Seems like the Mexicans from Mexico have been settlin' this part of the country a lot longer than the Indians have been on the reservations of the Territory. Then a lot of land has been given to settlers here in Spanish land grants. Sometimes they git as much land as they can ride around in one day. That's a heap of land. The grants are all west of here, though, and then up into Colorado Territory. Actually, I guess Colorado is a state by now. Anyhows, none of this grant land is available in Indian Territory, and it means there's less land available in Texas. Our chances of gittin' free land to farm are better in the Territory. Why, we'll probably all be able to get our own land. It'll be just like crossin' the Jordan River into Canaan. We'll be just like the Israelites."

"How come Led's not goin' with us, then?"

"Well he's all tired out of travelin'."

"Then why don't we stay in Texas, too?" asked Jake.

"When you get your heart set on somethin', you have to stay after it," said Samuel. "You're welcome to stay with Led if you'd like."

"Will we ever see Led again?"

"Sure we will," answered Abe. "He'll be just across the river. Not more than a two or three day ride. If he doesn't come to see us, we'll go see him."

"Yes, but how'll he find us? He don't know where we're a goin'," said Jake.

"Oh, he'll know where we crossed the river. Everybody crosses at Colbert's Ferry. Then he'll just start askin' for us. People seem to know when strangers move in. Don't you worry none. He'll find us."

"I would certainly hope so. We've only got each other out here. No other kin folks to speak of."

Appearing satisfied that everything would be okay, Jake dropped the subject. They would travel only a few miles into the territory after crossing the river. The three travelers just wanted to make sure that they were really into their Promised Land before settling down. The Ledbetter brothers were soon to learn that they were in the Choctaw Nation with its southern seat of government at Mayhew. The Nation was further divided into districts. They were in the Pushamataha District, where the only settlement of any size was Durant. Pushamataha, a Choctaw chief, had served in the United States Army under Andrew Jackson. The town of Durant was named for a Choctaw Indian, Dixon Durant. Durant's farm and house were the closest to the relay station built for the Butterfield Overland Mail, a stagecoach line started in 1858 from St. Louis to California but now owned by Wells Fargo.

After spending some time in the general area around Durant working in a variety of settings, Samuel decided to settle near Caddo. Abe and Jake settled on a place together just a few miles away. It was impossible for settlers to homestead land at that time in the Choctaw Nation; they could only lease or rent land from a Choctaw Indian. The Indians had been receiving the land from the government in federal land grants of 160 acres each. Samuel made an agreement with a Choctaw to farm his land. The arrangement was that the owner would furnish the land and the seed, while Samuel did all of the work for half of the farm's earnings.

Samuel soon learned it was a continual job keeping the land cleared of trees and saplings, especially blackjack and scrub oak and mulberry trees. It seemed like if he didn't cut them down as soon as they broke through the earth's surface, he would regret it later. If caught soon enough, they could be pulled out roots and all, with a good, stout horse that is.

Bringing his thoughts back to the present, Samuel considered his current situation. This was a fertile land. It had sufficient rainfall, so vegetation, both wanted and unwanted, grew quite easily. When he had time left over from his farm chores, he would cut down the trees along the edges of the fields to clear more land for future farming. These trees could then be used for railroad ties when they were cut to the right size. The Katy Railroad was often in the market for more ties. Cutting trees down was hard work when you worked alone. The hardest part was cutting with the big bucksaw after notching the tree with a double bladed axe. Two people could saw right along when someone held onto each end of the saw. But when the sawyer had to work alone, it was extremely difficult for him both pushing and pulling the large saw while leaning over to one side.

Many a day Samuel could cut down only one tree after completing his farm work. While adding coal oil to the sides of the blade to lubricate the saw helped to make the work go faster, he was convinced that this was intended to be a two-man job. If he was lucky, he might even get the branches trimmed off and burned after cutting the tree down. On another day, after dragging the log in behind the cabin with a mule, he would find time to cut the ties. He looked forward to the day when his only work would be farm work.

While his father had been a logger for awhile, Samuel surely liked farming the best. Besides that, cotton was his main crop, so the fabric plant took most of his time. It sure would be nice, he thought, to have help on the farm.

It soon dawned on Samuel that he was running out of daylight. It wasn't often he got to daydreaming like this. But, then, it wasn't often that he would become a father. Well, anyway, he better get Bossy into the shed for milking. It would soon be dark, and he was tired. Maybe if he had hobbled the cow, she wouldn't have wandered so far from the cabin. It looked like he would have to milk in the dark again. That meant supper would be late as well. Would he ever get caught up on his work? He quickened his pace hopeful it might hurry the slow gait of the cow as well.

"Git a move on Bossy! We aim to be home before dark!"

While milking the cow, Samuel was reminded by Lillie that he would soon be eating the last of their deer meat. She mentioned hearing a possible deer close by in a thicket of tamarack earlier in the day. Maybe tomorrow he could find time to go hunting; fresh meat was always welcome. Tonight, however, his only wish after eating was to drag his weary body to the feather bed in the corner of the one-room cabin. He didn't even give Lillie her regular backrub, as he was much too tired. He felt bad that he couldn't give her something she dearly loved. Tomorrow night, he promised himself, he would give her an extra special backrub. The pleasure she derived from this simple act was always obvious. Being heavy with child gave her terrible backaches, especially on wash day, and the aches could best be relieved by the circular motion of his hands on her back.

Sleep came quickly for Samuel. Soon after dropping off to sleep, however, he found himself dreaming about Lillie and the soon to be born child. He smiled in his sleep as he remembered the first time he had seen his wife to be. It seemed like only yesterday when he and Abe had gone to the Shaughnessy's to ask about buying a calf for raising. Actually, the meeting had occurred a few months before he and Lillie were married in 1891. She had come out on the porch to see the strangers who were talking to her father. She had confided in Samuel later about the strange attraction she had felt for the older of the two brothers. Worse yet, she found herself unable to take her eyes off of him. Samuel in turn felt a special feeling of kinship for the slender, brown haired girl. Maybe it was because she appeared both shy and curious at the same time.

As he drifted off into a deeper sleep, Samuel hoped for a better future for both Lillie and the child he just knew would be a boy. He also knew that either a boy or a girl would make them both very happy; but it didn't hurt to wish for a boy. After all, he dreamed, hope helps to make things happen.

CHAPTER III

December 24th started as a cloudless day. The day should have been cold as well, but a warming trend had begun only the day before. Appreciative of the cooperative climate, Samuel got up early in order to finish his duties quickly. He began his chores in the dark by tossing hay to the calves and milking Bossy.

"Come on Bossy, let's git this over with. I'm a goin' to town to see Lillie. I'll even take in this milk. I'll tell her it's a present from you if you'll hurry."

Samuel knew that the speed of the milking process was in his hands. Of course a cow could become most uncooperative at times. Could she possibly have understood his eagerness to get on the road? Evidently so, the chore was accomplished in record time. Of course his wrists ached with the rapidity of the milking process.

"I'll bet it's a boy. Why in just a few years he'll be a milkin' you, too. Won't that be nice? His hands will be softer for a time, and you won't always be a waitin' on me to git in from the fields."

Lillie was in Durant with her folks. It wasn't hard to convince her to go there for the birth of their child. She, too, wanted a healthy child, and had been in town for almost a week. Samuel had many farm chores to complete in preparation for the approaching winter before joining his wife in Durant. Besides that, who knew exactly when the child would be born? He didn't have extra time to just wait around in Durant. Maybe the child would be born on Christmas Day. The thought of such a Christmas present appealed to him.

Most of the fieldwork was done for the year. Samuel generally spent his time tending livestock, cutting wood for the rapidly approaching winter and hunting deer for a fresh supply of meat. Maybe some day they could kill a beef to eat, but for now they would have to rely upon wild meat. Any livestock they now had would be used for expanding their holdings, not personal consumption. One just couldn't make enough preparations for winter; there was always more to be done. This year they'd need an extra supply of firewood just to keep the cabin warm for the baby.

Before leaving for Durant, Lillie had already gone around and stuffed rags into every hole and gap she could find. With the logs and lumber used in the construction continuing to shrink, gaps usually formed around the windows and doors. Kiln dried wood, necessary to prevent such shrinkage, was a rarity in these parts. Anyway, scraps of fabric below the standards required to make good quilting blocks were useful for closing holes. Lillie generally used a stick or small branch to poke the material as far back as possible into the hole. If the crack were between two of the logs, however, additional chinking with mud would be done before freezing occurred.

Samuel knew he'd better get into Durant soon. Lillie had told him when leaving with the neighbors the other day that she knew it wouldn't be too long before their baby was born. Maybe the child had already been born. Besides, he needed to take in another load of railroad ties to Durant. He didn't want to stockpile too many; one never knew when the railroad might quit buying them. Talk was that they wanted more uniformity than the settlers could provide.

It was a long ride of about twelve miles to Durant. With a mule pulling a loaded farm wagon, the trip would take all day on most occasions if Samuel planned to get home without staying overnight. He knew better than to start on such a long trip like this, unless he started early in the morning. That is, if he planned on going both ways before dark.

He had debated taking the ties on this trip, because riding the mule was so much faster. Riding on the wagon was such a rough trip; of course riding the mule alone without a saddle wasn't any better. Buying a nice saddle was high on his list for when he had extra money some day. A man ought to be comfortable while traveling, he reasoned. Well, at least he didn't have to go both ways on this trip, so he could start after the noon meal. Actually, some folks might not even call it a meal. The fare consisted of crumbling crackers in a bowl and covering them with milk. The process was quick and the product tasty.

Even though he was anxious to see Lillie, Samuel took the necessary time to carefully load the railroad ties today. No telling how long it might be before he would get in there again. Maybe transporting a few extra ties this time would help. Just the idea of making an extra trip to haul ties that could have been hauled this time helped him to make up his mind. Lifting the heavy ties was backbreaking work. It was easier if he stood them on one end, then toppled them into the wagon. In so doing he got a good whiff of the tie. He enjoyed the fresh odor of new sawn wood. Sometimes, though, he was straining so hard to lift the ties that he didn't notice the sweet smell brushing so close to his face. At least it wasn't his job to add the creosote; the pungent odor of creosote made from pine or coal tar was what made the wood smell so terrible when they were finished into railroad ties. Plus, creosote was the element capable of staining your clothes beyond the ability of any cleansing agent he or Lillie knew to restore the cleanliness of the original fabric.

In due time Samuel loaded the wagon. Since the railroad companies had adopted a uniform width of 4 feet 8 1/2 inches for the rails in 1866, it made the ties about six feet long. They stretched the full length of the wagon behind the seat. By placing five of the ties side by side and stacking them three high, he was hauling fifteen of them this trip. If he put too much weight on the wagon, he knew it would slow his travel down too much or possibly lead to a breakdown. He hoped this many ties wouldn't delay getting to Lillie's side.

Samuel had already made arrangements with the neighbors up the road to take care of Bossy while he was gone. It wasn't easy getting away overnight when you had a cow to be milked. Furthermore, it was cruel to skip milking a cow for even one time, so you had to make some kind of arrangement like this. The Wilsons had readily agreed to make the twice-daily trip to the Ledbetter place. After all, they knew about the Golden Rule. Besides, having a baby was quite an event in the area. People understood about the need for having help on the farm. They just hoped everything would be all right for both Lillie and the new baby.

Decent roads for wagons were a rarity in the backwoods of the territory. Occasionally the fortunate traveler might chance onto someone else's tracks until they reached more traveled thoroughfares. Granted, they weren't the turnpikes of Tennessee or Kentucky. Samuel just felt lucky that this wasn't the rainy season of the year. He had to cross both Caddo Creek and Blue River on the way. Neither should have much water in them at this time. Also, there were numerous gullies to be forded along the way. The chances of meeting other travelers were quite slim if you needed help or just wanted to see a friendly face.

There hadn't been too many settlers in the region up to this point, as homesteads were only for the Indians. Samuel looked forward to the day when homesteading would be opened up to everyone. In other parts of the state non-Indians could homestead; but only the Choctaws could own any land in this region. The United States Congress had decided in the 1880's, with the Dawes Allottment Act, to break up the tribal governments. This was accomplished by taking back the reservation land owned "severally" by the tribes and then giving each individual Indian an allotment of 160 acres. This way, each Indian was a landowner with title to a specific acreage of land. This approach would ultimately change the Indian culture, as it forced them to think more of their own needs instead of the tribe as a whole. Finally, this process would in turn open the way for homesteading to people other than Indians.

But, for right now, the process was not open to non-Indians in this region. Much as the Ledbetters desired property ownership, legal possession of land remained beyond their reach. This predicament was brought about due to the requirement of the national government that land ownership reside with Choctaw Indians with rare exceptions. Non-Indians could be endorsed for purposes of sharecropping by a Choctaw citizen. This, thereby, enabled the obtaining of a permit from the Choctaw Nation to conduct farming activities. This permit was necessarily renewed each year.

Needless to say, the Indians did not take too kindly to the earlier proposition contained in the Dawes Act. They thought that if they became civilized enough, the United States government might leave them alone. They did succeed in becoming more civilized, but this did not stop the gradual march toward breaking up the tribes. Samuel knew this reallocation of land rights was wrong on the part of the government. The action caused him great anguish when he realized that his hope for land ownership could be contingent upon someone else losing land they might have cherished very deeply. Still, all in all, Samuel strongly favored opening up the whole territory to white homesteaders. The stay was sometimes lonely in these parts, especially if you weren't an Indian.

Jenny strained hard as the wagon slowly began to move. She was a good mule, but the initial movement of the wagon was always the hardest. Samuel jumped off and pushed for a short distance, until the load could gain some momentum. The corner of the wagon gouged deeply into his shoulder. It felt like a knife at times, but there was really no choice in the matter. No need tiring Jenny out right at the start. If the takeoff had been an uphill start, there would have been no decision to make; he would have had to push most of the way up the grade. Another possibility would be to lighten the load, but Samuel wanted few ties remaining by the cabin.

Samuel considered Blue River to be the halfway point to Durant. It was always a relief to know you had gone most of the way. Thank goodness he didn't make this trip more often. He wasn't sure if his backsides could continue to take the pounding caused by these trips. One small bump wasn't bad, but the continual jerking motion of the wagon took its toll. A folded quilt on the wooden wagon seat helped in cushioning the pounding, but in due time Samuel determined that no amount of padding could give him the relief he desired. Many a teamster experienced hemorrhoids after spending excessive amounts of time bouncing on the boards that felt like concrete at times. Any relief to one's constitution was welcomed.

Upon reaching the river, Samuel took the opportunity to water Jenny while he walked around to stretch his legs. Jenny had been a faithful mule. After settling by Caddo, he had traded his horse and saddle for her and a plow. A saddle horse was nice for riding long distances, but a mule was made for pulling farm implements. Heaven knows what he would have done without his trusted animal. He decided that it wouldn't hurt to let her graze for awhile on some fresh grass as well. On the other hand, he didn't want to linger any longer than was necessary.

There was the pungent smell of a dead animal off to the north. Samuel tried not to breathe deeply. He didn't care to investigate the source of the stench, either. Still, he and his faithful beast of burden needed to recoup their strength. After a short while of the foul odor insulting his nostrils, he laid down on the grassy river bank and listened to the water gurgling over an obstruction caused by a fallen tree blocking the water's flow, Samuel was ready to be back on the road. Pausing to fill his hat with water, he placed it on his head. Granted it was cold, but it revitalized him for the journey yet to be made.

Once again he helped Jenny get the wagon moving. Of course he got his trouser legs wet in the process, and his shirt was already damp from the water still oozing from his hat, but Jenny definitely needed the added push this time. Worse yet, he was sure that this time there must be a cut in his shoulder from the force required to get the wagon rolling smoothly. The up and down motion of the wheels going over the rocks created the action of a saw.

Samuel was sure they could reach Durant before dark. It was a comforting feeling knowing he would complete the trip during the daylight hours; sometimes it was impossible to see the trail after dark, unless you had a full moon. Even then, the shadows could be deceptive. Until he made more trips, and the trails got better, Samuel knew he didn't want to travel much at night. It was too easy to slip a wheel off into a bog and get stuck. Of course Jenny could be counted on to pick her way as best as possible among the many obstacles they might encounter should the sun go down before they were ready. Her night vision far exceeded that of her masters, and she had proven herself reliable in the past.

Not too long after crossing Blue River, Samuel was getting comfortable with the creaking sound made by the movement of the wagon box where it was joined to the axle. I hope it has plenty of grease, he thought, because I'm not carrying my grease bucket on this trip.

While watching two scissortail magpies playing tag over his head, Samuel sighted a team and wagon approaching from the west. "Thank goodness," he sighed with relief, "the trail is dry." With his heavily loaded wagon, he could get stuck his wheels in the mud in wet weather if he had to pull off of the trail very far. Even when it was dry weather, it was almost impossible for two wagons to pass each other where there were heavy concentrations of trees and undergrowth.

When the other wagon drew near, he could see that it was Jackson Blue, a Choctaw Indian. Some of the Indians were highly educated and well-versed in politics. Jackson was one of those individuals. He even played lacrosse (or "istaboli" as the Choctaws had called it for over a hundred years).

Jackson was wearing typical Choctaw garb for attending tribal meetings. Seeing such attire in the wilderness was shocking for the settler unprepared for such extravagance. Samuel rarely saw an Indian dressed in such sartorial delight as Mr. Blue was now sporting. He had on what appeared to be a dark suit with extra wide lapels to match and a red sash. Samuel had heard that red signified his status as a warrior. Otherwise there was no outward sign to the finery that this was the case. Jackson's colorful headwear appeared to be an unknown material, but Samuel really couldn't determine the nature of the fabric. The construction of the unusual piece was like a farmer's cap with no bill. Triangular pieces of varying colors were sewn together to form an inverted bowl covering Jackson's scalp. If the Indian had a feather for his headpiece, the plumage was not readily visible during this chance encounter. Maybe Jackson was awaiting arrival at his destination before adding this symbol.

Samuel wondered where such fine clothing could even be purchased, maybe in one of the finer shops in Durant. Such elegance certainly wasn't bought in any place he frequented.

Likely someone within the tribe made it without intrusion by the white settlers. Samuel couldn't see Jackson's footwear, but he imagined it was comparable to his other clothing in style and cost. In contrast Samuel had on a pair of plain, blue denim trousers to go with a red cotton shirt, obviously in need of ironing for a town trip. His boots had been polished with axle grease, so they had a layering of road dust on them, much like the tattered hat he was wearing.

While his clothes showed evidence of wear, they were clean. Even in his finest Sunday wear, however, Samuel couldn't compare with what he now saw before him. At least his clothes were comfortable, he thought to himself. Someday, he also thought, I'll dress as well as that...someday.

"How are you doing Mr. Ledbetter?" the Indian asked. "Has your misses had her young one yet?"

"I hope so," said Samuel. "I'm on my way to Durant now to see."

"You people sure like these parts, don't you?"

"As a matter of fact, we like them real well. It's a place to grow and be on your own. It's a place to get away from crowded towns and not be all times bothered by town ruckuses."

"Then you're learning what we Choctaws have always known," said Jackson. "We wanted to see it stay thataways for just us. Now we see it can never be that way. At least if the white man had to come here, we hoped it was people like you and the misses. I hope there won't be a lot more, though."

"I agree," said Samuel. "But we found the same thing in Tennessee. Eventually there's people everywhere. Got to where there wasn't room to turn around. When a neighbor gets closer than half a mile, he's too close. Too many people. Just too many people. You Choctaws have a right to feel mad when that happens."

"Well, I hope I won't see it happen in my lifetime. There's nowhere else for us Choctaws to go. We've been moved every time we thought we had a home. I imagine you've heard about the Trail of Tears and what it did to the Cherokees?"

"Yes, everybody knows that story. It was a frightful thing happened to the Indians on that march. It wasn't fair at all. I'd hate to be moved off of my place like that, and it was totally unnecessary for so many of your people to die. I'd fight 'em."

"Fighting's not our way now. Do you really know why we're not in Mississippi anymore?" asked the Choctaw.

"Reckon I don't," answered Samuel.

"Well it goes back to about 1830. We were plainly tricked by the government agents. We signed the Treaty of Dancing Rabbit Creek. We lost our homes in Mississippi over that blasted treaty. Now it looks like we're slowly losing our land here as well. I'm not sure we want any more help from your government. It seems like every time they say, 'We're going to help you,' we lose something else. Does it ever end?"

"Prob'ly not. I still say that I'd fight 'em, with guns if necessary," stated Samuel.

"We have fought them, even up to your Supreme Court, but we always lose. And it seems like when we lose, we get hurt even more. We're through fighting. We're trying white man's ways now to see if that will help us protect our lands. Our ways didn't work. Maybe yours will. Sometimes I think they're punishing us Choctaws because we fought with the South during the War Between the States. We had a good record in our fighting for the Confederate Army. They always seem to forget that Choctaws fought under Washington and those other generals during the Revolutionary War. Maybe it's because we had slaves when we used to live in Mississippi."

"I didn't know your people fought in the war," said Samuel.

"Have you heard of John Drew's Regiment of Mounted Rifles?" asked the Indian.

"No, can't say as I have."

"Well, it was a military unit commissioned by the Cherokee Nation to protect its interests in the national conflict. My father was in a Choctaw unit fighting for the South during that war. It has cost us dearly for taking sides during that great battle. Yes, he was at the Battle of Pea Ridge. He lost his arm there, and it was all for nothing. Why, the Cherokees even had a general in the Confederate Army. He was Brigadier General Stand Watie. Yes we're all suffering for our role in that combat."

"Yes, and then maybe it's not because of your takin' sides in the Civil War. Maybe they just don't like all of the Indians. Seems like all times they're a pushin' y'all around."

"Well, whatever it is, we're definitely losing the battle. At this rate, we won't have any homeland at all before long."

"I can't agree with that. This is your land. We white folks only want land not wanted by the Indians." returned the farmer.

"There's very little land not wanted by my brothers," said Blue. "Say, I'm keeping you from getting to your misses' side. You better get on your way. I want nobody saying I kept you after dark."

"I wish I had more time to talk," said Samuel, "because you always make good sense to me. But you're right, I do want to reach Durant before dark."

"Give my regards to the misses," said the Choctaw, as he drove off with a wave.

Arriving at the Shaughnessy's just before sundown, Samuel immediately unhitched Jenny. He didn't have a pocket watch; it didn't look real late. The days were getting too short for a full day's work, so he knew it couldn't be terribly late with the sun recently resting for the day. Approaching the lights of the Shaughnessy house had eased the burden of traveling after dark. Finding some loose alfalfa hay and a barrel of oats, he gave Jenny plenty of both.

A farmer shouldn't hesitate to take good care of his mules. As a matter of fact, a good farmer always tended to his animals before seeing to his own needs. After checking the stock tank to be sure there was plenty of water, Samuel found a nail to hang the harness in the barn. You could tell how relieved Jenny was to shed the weight of the harness. She roamed freely around the corral for a full minute before getting a drink. Furthermore, she seemed to sense that she wouldn't be going right back to the farm. Assured that everything was all right with his mule, Samuel headed for the back porch of the house. He could dispense with the railroad ties tomorrow.

Before he could even knock on the door, Mrs. Shaughnessy opened it and exclaimed: "It's a boy!"

Samuel rushed to the bedroom where he knew Lillie and his son would be. It was hard to tell much about the new baby. Lillie had the newborn completely wrapped in a quilt she had made for just this occasion.

"Let me see the lad," he said, even before he had a chance to greet Lillie. Holding the tiny wrapped package up in an attempt to get better light from the lantern, he slowly turned the infant so he could see every angle possible.

"Wrap him up again," said his mother-in-law, "or he'll catch his death of cold. Pa, you stoke the fire!"

"Isn't he a good-lookin' boy?" Lillie asked, after her son was once again tightly swathed in his colorful quilt. "He's almost a week old. He'll be a real help for us on the farm one of these days."

"Yes, you can bet on that. I plan on us doin' lots of work together," Samuel said with pride in his voice.

For awhile Lillie and Samuel couldn't speak; their gaze only ventured from their son to occasionally lock onto each other from time to time. This infant with his eyes closed was a most welcome addition to the family. Soon thereafter the question came up "What shall we name him?" Usually names were chosen from one or the other's ancestors. Lillie and Samuel decided not to do this, however. This was a new land and a new family, so the boy should have a new name. Both remembered back to when they had been married. Neither could remember the first name of Reverend Desmond, who had married them. All either could remember were his initials, "C.A." The marriage had been the first major event in their lives. The birth of their son was now the second. Therefore, these two events would be tied together with the initials "C.A." Without knowing how the missionary used the initials, they decided on the names "Caleb Ashton," as neither Samuel nor Lillie could remember ancestors with these names. Caleb Ashton Ledbetter it was. The name had such a nice ring to it. The newborn's parents agreed they would call him Cal, as he just looked like he should be called Cal.

There were no problems when Cal was born, so a doctor was not needed. Mrs. Shaughnessy had taken charge of the delivery because she was quite experienced in such matters. She had even helped others out before who weren't relatives, so some considered her to be a midwife. As this was Lillie's first child, the delivery took longer. But, with Mrs. Shaughnessy's able assistance and constant attention, everything proceeded right on schedule. It really didn't matter that Samuel wasn't there; the women likely wouldn't have allowed him in the room anyway. Well, maybe he could have held Lillie's hand, as the delivery was painful and there were no medications for relief. Holding hands didn't stop the pain; it was just reassuring to know you were not alone in this momentous time.

Cal had a good set of lungs, so he easily made his wishes known. At least he expressed his discomfort well. The newborn was of a ruddy complexion like his parents. Maybe this coloration meant a good possibility for having red hair as well. Right now, he had little hair at all. Mostly he had a good appetite. Lillie found that she enjoyed nursing her son; it gave them such precious time together. He slept a lot during that first day. Lillie welcomed the opportunity to stay in the bed with Cal beside her. She thought it was a shame that Samuel couldn't share in all of the happiness she was experiencing right now. She had never before had any real idea of the joys of motherhood. The experience was like no other she'd ever had, and descriptions she'd heard didn't adequately impart the reality of the event.

Samuel had his feelings of pleasure, too. He was so proud of this small bundle of humanity; the baby had become a part of his and Lillie's life together. One of his greatest desires had now been achieved; there was someone to carry on the family name. Also, there was someone to help him in his quest to become a landholder, someone to grow up and work beside him on the farm. The achievement of Samuel's hope for land ownership was now closer than it had ever been. The roots of the Samuel Amos Ledbetter family were now firmly rooted in the red soil of what was to become Oklahoma; there they would stay, he hoped.

CHAPTER IV

What was it like in Durant (county seat of Blue County later to be Bryan County), Indian Territory, and the surrounding area on Tuesday, December 18, 1894, when Cal was introduced to the vastness of this world? News was often limited to the local scene in such rural areas because the smaller communities didn't have much contact beyond one's neighbors. There was a newspaper, *The Durant Democrat*, if you wanted to read the news. The paper could have been mailed, because smaller towns, like Bokchito, a few miles away, had been blessed with a post office since early in August. But, the smaller communities around Durant, like Caddo, Blue, Bokchito, and Wade, had residents whose first concerns were on a very local level. The price of cotton or a new pair of shoes was typical of news items they liked. It didn't interest most of the settlers that this year saw the beginning of a long rivalry in football between the University of Texas and Texas A&M.

News on a national level often seemed very far away to a territory that hadn't even achieved statehood. The important news on a local level, though, only contained the vital information for such a remote area. For example, a steak cost just over ten cents a pound, cheap compared to pork chops, which cost about eleven cents a pound. The penny difference could easily be prohibitive for the family on a tight budget.

"You seen the price of meat in the stores lately?" asked Samuel, as he looked up from the newspaper. "I could have a well dug for less than two dollars per foot, so I certainly won't be spendin' my hard-earned money on steak or pork chops. I'd much rather have someone build me a corncrib for a few dollars. A crib'll be around long after we've forgotten how a pork chop tasted."

"Oh, Samuel. You too often think more about the cost of somethin' instead of an occasional pleasure. Don't you reckon you're far too practical at times."

"Well, a family has to take care of its own basic needs first if it wants to survive. We'll have plenty of time later in life for pleasure. Right now, we're a helpin' insure our family's future."

"Can't you find somethin' more interesting in the paper?" asked his wife.

"Well, it does say that it's been just over one year since the biggest American land rush of all times was right here in the territory. It says that over one hundred thousand settlers were on the startin' line for the openin' of the Cherokee Outlet in 1893."

"There should'a been more people than that," said Lillie. "There was considerable interest for some time in openin' up Indian Territory for ownership by people like us. Why the `Boomers' have strongly supported the openin' of the reservations to white settlement for some time. It's a shame that they've sometimes resorted to crookedness to open these lands."

"Well, if they open up these parts to settlement, you can bet we'll be legal in our dealin's. A man can't call himself Christian otherwise."

"No doubt," responded Lillie. "We have too many friends among the Indians to consider otherwise. And I do want to do as the Good Book teaches us."

Actually, a considerable number of developments were happening during this era on the national scene, but they generally had little effect on the lives of the settlers in the territory. Alexander Graham Bell had invented the telephone in 1876, while Thomas Edison had invented the electric light in 1879. Then, in 1892, Charles Duryea converted a horsedrawn carriage to a horseless carriage by adding a small gasoline engine for propulsion along with a tiller-like device to steer the strange looking craft. He received the patent for the first automobile in 1895. This followed the development of the diesel engine in 1892 by Rudolph Diesel, but it would be some time before the diesel engine was installed in a vehicle. For the time being, this mechanical marvel was being used to power stationary type devices, such as water pumps in mines.

No, the common people were pretty much being by-passed by all of these new developments, even in the cities back east. As a matter of fact, the 1890's were actually considered years of depression by many in the United States. In 1894, Jacob Coxey led a band of individuals to Washington, D.C., in hopes of convincing Congress to establish a number of relief type programs to aid the unemployed. Coxey's Army served to no avail. They only managed to get arrested for trespassing at the nation's capitol.

One could never get away from the immediate needs of survival. They were always around, lurking to ambush the settler when they least expected them. The Indians were not the greatest threat to Samuel and Lillie's survival in the wilderness; their worst enemies were diseases, exposure to the winter elements and starvation. The very first thing a settler did upon arriving in a new land was to make provision for his family's food and shelter.

The easiest house to build was one dug into the side of a hill or embankment with a roof over it. Considerable caution had to be exercised with this approach, however. The settler certainly didn't want to dig where high water from creeks or rivers could wash away the house's walls or fill the home with water. It was usually necessary to use logs or timbers to build the front part of the dugout. Also, one had to use some material, such as branches, to make a roof.

While the dugout was considered a temporary dwelling, it had advantages the settlers could not match anywhere else, even when they built more elaborate homes. The main advantage was the ease with which it could be heated in the wintertime or cooled in the summer time. The temperature of the ground rarely changed. This helped to maintain a more even temperature so it was easier to heat the dugout on the coldest of days. It was difficult, though, to build a dugout of any substantial size or make it as attractive as a cabin or frame house. This was especially true when canvas was used to make the front or sidewalls of the dugout. Other advantages to dugouts included the speed with which they could be built or the lesser amount of building materials needed for their construction.

Samuel remembered his good fortune upon first arriving in the territory. His first domicile was a dugout. After searching for some time, he found the perfect place. He would have missed it, if he hadn't gone back into a stand of elm trees where he had seen a deer disappear. Here he found an embankment with the dirt rounded out about ten feet across. Immediately to each side of this natural indentation were trees with trunks generally 12 inches in diameter. He could visualize the removal of a few trees in the middle, except one used as the base for a table, while using the outer ring of trees as the basis for an outside wall for his home. Of course he had to dig the stumps down below the ground's surface. By using the forks of these remaining trees as "outside walls," the sturdy trunks would simplify adding a roof.

The work in modifying the surroundings was not as simple as Samuel had visualized, but the finished product was consistent with his expectations. He ended up with one room about sixty-five feet square for his living quarters. It was a strange looking affair. The walls were zigzagged, as the trees hadn't grown in a straight line. But this home was to live in, not show off to neighbors. Of course with time he would need to have more than canvas for the sides and a blanket for a door, but it was a home, his home, and the cost was reasonable. Certainly it was dark, as there were no windows. But it wasn't total darkness because the branches he had put up as a roof did let in some sunlight. The bad part was that these same openings allowed some rain to enter as well. He just made sure he didn't sleep nor have something he didn't want to get wet under these windows to the sky. He always, however, left a bucket under an opening to catch fresh rainwater, so he wouldn't have to carry so much from the creek about three hundred yards distant. Come wintertime he knew he'd have to make the structure provide more protection from the cold weather the new season would surely bring.

Eventually, most families wanted a log cabin, or better yet a frame house, as was generally seen in Durant. Attractive to dugout dwellers about a freestanding house was the ability to have windows on all sides of the house. Frequently the homes of the late eighteen hundred's frontier were quite small because they were hard to heat. Furniture was difficult to buy anywhere; most settlers were often content with what they could build for themselves. That is, unless they had brought furniture with them from back east, and it was a difficult chore hauling furniture long distances in covered wagons. Besides, the wagons didn't hold much furniture anyway.

Entering the home of a settler was to be greeted by a very bare dwelling. In addition to the bed and table, there were also one or two chairs, a woodburning stove or fireplace, and a freestanding cupboard or shelves on the wall for the few dishes they had accumulated. This sometimes included dried gourds, which were used to make bowl-type items.

The visitor to a cabin of this era was likely able to see everything the settler owned from a single vantage point, as the dwelling probably contained only one room with most of the furniture being homemade. What few clothes they owned would be hanging on a nail on the wall, if they weren't wearing them. Samuel and Lillie's cabin was no different. Their possessions were meager, just the bare necessities.

Samuel built their bed of pine branches by stretching rope across the opening at four to six-inch intervals. He also used the rope to interweave back and forth before adding a featherbed mattress. There were no springs. The bed looked more like a hammock in the middle than anything else did. As a matter of fact, it looked quite crude, but this sleeping platform cost very little. This was true of the table and chairs as well. Because of the difficulty in getting the legs even, both the table and the chairs often rocked instead of setting square on the floor. A spoon or stick under the correct leg generally solved this unevenness. Of course the floor wasn't exactly level, either. Two chairs were enough. Samuel could build more chairs if they were ever needed. Until then, the space could better be used for other things. Someday, Samuel and Lillie agreed, they would have a frame house with more room for a growing family.

The heat generated in the home by the cooking was appreciated in the wintertime. On hot days in the summertime, however, cooking was done outside on every occasion possible to escape the heat generated in the process. Of course cooking could be done early in the morning to help take the chill from the air; a pan of biscuits and some gravy certainly filled the bill. In the summertime, baked goods were rare indeed. The hot cabin was not the only problem with baking. Worse yet was cooking when the cook had no idea what the temperature might be in the oven.

"Could we git more light in here, Samuel?" asked Lillie. "When I'm not a cookin' inside, we don't have a fire to read by."

"We'll have to buy kerosene lanterns, then. Kerosene's a precious commodity, you know, so they can only be lit when absolutely necessary."

"I doubt we'll be a burnin' the lanterns that much. You are usually in bed by the time the sun goes down, anyway. Then in the summer you git up early enough to put on the coffee, and that requires a fire. No, I doubt that we'll need to buy that much kerosene. A soul would just like to have a few conveniences around to make life somewhat easier."

"We never moved out here to have life easier. We just live from one day to the next. I'll worry about tomorrow when it gits here. Our joy comes from knowin' that God approves of our efforts."

"Yes, but even God wants us to have some joy in life," said Lillie.

"Right now my joy comes from a seein' a good crop in the fields," was her husband's reply.

The preservation of food was most difficult, especially in summer. Leftovers from a meal were unheard of, as there were few ways to preserve food from one meal to the next. In the summer a family's meats on the table were often restricted to small animals or birds, such as chicken, rabbits, squirrels or possums. Frog legs were considered a delicacy. Also, when there was time to go fishing, catfish were especially desirable.

Larger animals, wild or domestic, were mostly eaten after the weather became sufficiently cold to store food in the fall or winter. Then, the animals could be butchered and hung in a shed or barn out of the sunlight. As long as other animals or birds of prey couldn't eat the carcass, and the temperature remained cool or cold, the meat could be counted on to be edible for long periods of time. If the settlers wanted to butcher a calf or hog in the summertime, they often had to share their meat with others, through selling or bartering, to insure its usage before spoilage could occur.

Working out arrangements with neighbors for the sharing of meat in the summer time contributed to feelings of kinship in isolated areas, such as where the Ledbetters lived. Lillie welcomed the chance to trade for some pork sausage, as Samuel dearly loved sausage for breakfast.

Some foods could not be prepared for each meal individually yet had to be available on the table for meals the year around. Dairy products were the main foods in this category. Cold water or the temperature of the earth below the surface could be used for refrigeration of such commodities.

"Are we always a goin' to haul water from the creek?" asked Lillie.

"Maybe it's time we dug a well or a cistern," said Samuel.

"What's the difference?" asked Lillie.

"If the hole's deep enough, the water will seep in on its own. In that case it's a well. Otherwise, we'll have to continue a haulin' water to put in the hole, and that makes it a cistern."

"Is it too much work to dig one?"

"We'll have to dig a deep hole ten to twenty feet into the ground. Depending on how easy the diggin' is, we could make it up to eight feet wide. Then it'll have to be covered with timbers and dirt. We'll leave an opening for a lid about two feet in diameter. Yes, it can be a lot of work, and I surely can't do it in the middle of all my farm work. We prob'ly will need to hire someone to dig it."

"You said there was a lid on top. Does that mean we'll have to crawl down inside for the water?" asked his wife.

"No, when the lid is opened there's room to lower a bucket for fresh water. You'll be pleased, there is another benefit to a well or cistern."

"What's that?"

"Well, after each meal we can place our butter and milk in a bucket, seal the top tightly, then lower the bucket down on a rope, so that all but the top is submerged. The cool temp'ature of the water will be adequate to store these items so they won't spoil before usage."

Cows were milked twice a day, so it wasn't necessary to keep milk in the home for extended periods of time. Butter, however, was another matter. If it didn't spoil, it melted.

The food preservation method currently used by Samuel and Lillie was to set a fruit crate or wooden box upright in a tub containing a few inches of water. After the milk was placed in the crate above the water level, a cloth was wrapped around the crate with part of the fabric reaching down into the water. The cloth would slowly pull the moisture out of the tub. Condensation from the moisture then kept the items inside cool, especially if there was a gentle breeze blowing. It was important to remember to keep adequate water in the tub, or this procedure failed to operate. Samuel preferred this method because he hated the thought of going into a cistern to clean it out when dairy products spilled there.

"What about bulky items like watermelons?" asked Lillie.

"We'll keep on a placin' them in cold, runnin' water down in the creek," answered Samuel.

"I was hopin' we'd no longer do it that way. That method has its drawbacks. It takes time to walk down to the creek. Worse yet, a critter can eat the melon."

"I know it's a cumbersome method, but it will rarely be used. Remember, we don't have the luxury of watermelon that often. I wish we could have it every day summer and winter."

"You'd get tired of it that often. Anyways, when can we start on the cistern?" asked Lillie.

"You womenfolk! You want everything done yesterday."

"Well, we shouldn't have to ask for ever'thing. You need to know we'd like things to be more convenient. It's for your benefit, too."

A vegetable garden or orchard helped to overcome some of the problems associated with food storage. If the settler couldn't have both of these food producers, at least they should have a garden. It took a few years to get fruit trees producing, while they reaped the benefits of a garden the first year it was planted. Because of the spacing in the time in which such items ripen in the garden or orchard, it became possible to have fresh food in your diet in the summer or fall.

Canning was popular, using a pressure cooker, or just boiling items in a kettle over an open fire, to preserve fruits and vegetables for winter use. This method was sometimes used for the preservation of meats as well, but not too often. As an additive for the often cooked biscuits, an especially good use of canning was in the preserving of jams and jellies for year round availability. Here, the canner would cut up the fresh fruit. Next, it was necessary to keep the pieces of not quite ripened fruit in a container of clear water until they had enough peeled and cut up for a batch. Then, they would transfer the pieces to yet another kettle of clear water brought to a boil. The fruit would now be cooked and steamed in a combined process until it turned to juice. With sugar added, beautiful jellies could be made from the liquid. It would then be poured into jars and left to stand in the sun for a few hours. The final step was to place an airtight seal over the container. Melted paraffin or wax was good for this sealing. Variations of this approach were also used for vegetables. Lillie especially loved to can corn and tomatoes. Both could be used alone or as part of a beef or venison stew on a cold winter day.

Another method for preserving meats in the summer time, besides canning, was to salt them down. The two main ingredients for this process, besides the meat, were salt and a wooden barrel. At the start, a thin layer, about one-fourth inch thick, of salt would be spread on the bottom of the barrel. Then a layer, about two inches, of pieces of the meat would be placed in the barrel. Next, another layer of salt would be put on top of the meat. This process would then be repeated until the barrel was full or the person doing the filling ran out of meat to be salted. The eating of salted meat required the exercise of some caution; adding more salt at mealtime sometimes resulted in meat too salty for eating. While some folks used sugar for curing hams, Lillie preferred the salt.

Caring for the family's dietary needs was an elaborate process on the frontier. Most foods were prepared from things raised, fished, or hunted right on the family place. Rarely did the family buy anything other than sugar, salt, coffee, or flour in the way of foodstuffs in town. Coffee cost about thirty cents per pound, so it wasn't always purchased.

As if Lillie didn't already have enough work to do, keeping the family properly clothed took a substantial amount of time, too. Clothes were worn as long as possible before laundering them, as getting them clean again took a considerable amount of time and effort. Not only did she wash the family's clothes, but she also made the soap with which to clean them.

Making soap was no easy task. The lye soap commonly used was made from lye obtained from running water through the cold ashes of a wood fire placed in a sieve-like device kept out in the yard, where she could catch the runoff water. This product was then mixed and cooked with lard, which was nothing more than the grease from cooking meats, such as bacon, or the fat derived from butchering a hog. After the lard and lye were cooked to the consistency of syrup, the mixture was ready for use as laundry soap. Sometimes the soap would be placed into containers and be allowed to set up in bars as hand soap.

If the makers of the soap were self-conscious about the smell of the soap on their hands or body, they would sometimes find a sweet smelling plant, such as ginger, and add the leaves to the cooking process to make the soap smell better. Lillie was a typical frontier woman. She told people that she wanted soap for cleaning, not smelling good. For some reason, she elaborated, it didn't smell like it was strong enough to clean clothes if it smelled nice.

Samuel noticed on one occasion, however, as they were leaving for town, that his wife smelled like flowers instead of lye. He commented, "Boy the smell of the flowers sure is a carryin' a long ways today. Doesn't it smell purty?" Lillie merely smiled and nodded her head in agreement.

It was difficult to keep from burning one's hands while doing the wash. If the heat of the water didn't hurt you, the lye soap would, because it was so caustic. Therefore, in order to keep one's hands out of the boiling water as much as possible, devices were made to stir the water. Mechanical aids, which could be purchased, were generally unavailable. The industrious woman, however, soon learned to make a paddle from a tree branch to stir her clothes in the wash pot. Lillie kept a forked stick for this purpose; it looked polished from so much use. The fork made it easier to pick clothes up and out of the boiling water.

Washing clothes was an all day job. Lillie had to keep track of so many things. There had to be a substantial bed of glowing coals for heat kept under the kettle while keeping the clothes stirred. Then the apparel had to be moved back and forth from the wash kettle to a rinse tub of clear water, and next be scrubbed on a wash board, with any of these steps being repeated as often as was necessary. It's a wonder anyone could keep up with everything needing to be done. It was an all day job. A body had to get up quite early to start the fire going under the kettle; if the kettle got too hot before the cold water was added, it would crack. Lillie always added a bucket of water before the fire was started; more would be added as required or she found time. These kettles were too essential to meeting the needs of these families to risk being cracked, thus depriving them of its use. If the family was large, the washing went on past suppertime, with time out only to cook a meal for the others. At least the Ledbetters didn't have large wash loads until Cal was born.

After the actual washing was done, it was necessary to hang the clothes out in the sun to dry. If the family didn't have a clothesline, the clothes could be hung on tree branches or a nearby fence. Then, if for some reason the clothes needed ironing, which was a rarity for men's work clothes, a whole new sequence of events was set into motion. Heavy metal irons were needed for the pressing of the clothes. A family generally owned at least two irons; while one was heating on the stove until it was hot enough to use, the other was in actual use. A very hot iron was needed for this process, along with an occasional sprinkling of water on the clothes being pressed, in order to do a good job. Often the woman only had one detachable handle for the two irons, which required changing it back and forth. A potholder or piece of padded cloth was needed to hold the handle, or the user might get burned. Sometimes she would wad up a portion of her apron for the task in order to save time.

Lillie never looked forward to the tedious task of doing ironing. Sometimes she felt like she might pass out as she performed a most difficult task. Wiping the continual appearance of sweat from her brow with the back of her empty hand, she managed to keep moving. Even in the wintertime in a relatively cold cabin, her forehead was damp from the heat of her labor. In addition to the heat, it was time consuming, as well as back breaking work.

She didn't own an ironing board, so she spread a quilt over the kitchen table for this task. Often her only opportunity to stand up straight was when she took a warm iron over to the fire to exchange for a hot one. Pausing briefly between irons, she would fill a dipper full of water from a nearby bucket in order to savor the sweet taste as the nectar of the gods slowly descended the caverns of her throat. Sometimes she would put some water into a wash basin and splash it over her face as well. The tingle of clear, cold water brought relief as nothing else could to a face flushed with heat.

No, Lillie did no more ironing than was absolutely necessary. Of course Sunday clothes were items meeting this requirement. "Isn't there somethin' you can build to make ironin' easier, Samuel?"

"I'm afraid you've asked me for the impossible," answered her husband. "I don't have the slightest notion of how to make that job easier. You already use two irons to speed up the process."

"Well can you make me feel cooler while I do the work."

"Well, I ain't got no time to stand here and fan you with a newspaper. I suppose I could add another window on the east-side of the cabin to get better airflow."

"I'll take any help you can offer me," she said.

A frontier woman was also responsible for the making of the clothes worn by her family. The buying of clothes in a store was virtually unheard of. Cloth was either purchased from a bolt of material in a general store, or it was obtained by cutting up sacks, such as large flour sacks, when the family bought their flour. Flour millers specifically designed these colorful materials for the aspiring seamstress. Patterns could be purchased for making dresses, shirts and the other few clothing items that they needed.

Sewing was done by hand, usually in a woman's spare time, sometimes with very poor lighting from the kerosene lamps. It was slow and tedious work making and mending clothes for the family. Therefore, clothes were worn until they were beyond repair. To give them up any sooner than this meant the arduous task of making another item, likely just like the first one.

Finally, the woman's day was rounded out with the assumption of the overall responsibility for the rearing of the children. This meant meeting their medical as well as their educational needs. Before schools for the children of the settlers were introduced into the area, the woman of the household also had to find time for the children's schooling. That is, she did if she and her husband wanted their offspring to possess the "Three R's of readin', 'riting and 'rithmetic."

Books in the home for instructional purposes were very limited. Of course everyone had a family Bible, and this could often be used to teach reading. Arithmetic was a different matter; one always had the opportunity to teach it in a practical, meaningful way. The family never lacked for livestock or jars of corn to be counted or profit to be figured. Too, items were in constant need of contruction or repaired, and this could involve materials lists or angles to be determined.

Every settlement was desirous of having a school to continue teaching the children beyond what could be taught at home. Samuel and Lillie certainly looked forward to a school being available when Cal was old enough to attend. Maybe he'd have to build one, Samuel told Lillie. While Cal was just starting to talk, they knew they would need some type of formal instruction in a few years. There were limits to what the settlers had the ability or time to accomplish. Furthermore, many were desirous of their children exceeding their parents in the acquisition of "formal learning."

The meeting of the family's medical needs was more difficult. Sometimes the attention paid to an illness or injury could mean the difference between life and death. Home remedies seemed to be the method of treatment in most cases. Kerosene might be used to kill an infection, or something tightly tied around the head might be used for relief from a headache.

The availability of medicine was a real problem, and the use of such remedies was not due to the lack of medicines from back east being available in the stores, either; there just was no cure or medicine developed for many common ailments in the first place. This led to many remedies being tried for which there was no medical proof that they would work. Kerosene, whiskey, honey and lemons were some of the milder potions kept around for emergencies.

Especially popular, but not always readily available, were treatments based on the use of plants, such as elm tree bark or the leaves of a chestnut tree, or wet tobacco juice to draw the pain out of a bee sting. Illness in the wilderness too often proved fatal. A way of life included burying the victims of an early death, be it caused by disease or just the harshness of the wilderness.

It should not be hard to see why Lillie would welcome help around the home. More than someone to talk to was found in the birth of a girl. A man's life on the farm was equally as hard as a woman's life. Samuel rose early enough in the morning to work all of the daylight hours possible. He started the day off by donning his bib overalls or denim trousers that likely hadn't seen laundry soap for awhile. While his wife was cooking a substantial breakfast that included bacon, eggs, biscuits, gravy, and coffee, he was probably milking the cow. The farmer was generally in the field by six a.m., though the height of the sun was far more important than the time of day when he started work. One couldn't be too early on matters like this. Besides that, Samuel didn't have a watch.

In a new land, such as Indian Territory, it was necessary to clear the land to be used for farming. This meant the total removal of trees and brush. Those farmers fortunate enough to sharecrop land owned by Indians sometimes found some or all of this clearing had already taken place. Trees were cut relatively short. If the stumps were to be removed by pulling, there had to be enough left, however, to secure ropes or chains for the mules to pull. Sometimes dynamite was used to blast the stumps from the ground. Another method finding favor was to dig down around the stump and cut it off far enough below the surface so that it wouldn't obstruct the plows turning the soil. There was nothing worse than catching a plow on a hidden stump. It was not only painful to the farmer, but it hurt the mule and the plow as well. It had only happened a few times to Samuel, but it happened often enough that he did all he could to prevent its reoccurrence.

Plowing virgin earth is a sight to behold. The slow but steady exposure of the rich soil, as it flows past the moldboard of the plow, can't help but lift one's spirits. Samuel couldn't be happier than when he was plowing new soil recently cleared for its first plowing. This meant his farm was expanding. The moldboard of the plow was curved to cause the sod being turned to fall upside down. The sod flowed past the moldboard like an endless ribbon slowly turning over to stare at the sun.

With the reins tied together and draped behind his neck, in order to free up his hands to try and control the writhing plow, Samuel walked in the furrow being created right in front of him. Sometimes stumbling over a clod, he seldom stopped, as time was too precious. The width of the furrow was never a constant distance, as the plow followed the path of least resistance.

Sometimes, Samuel said, he could hear the steel plow singing as the rich soil went over the moldboard. At the end of the field he would lay the plow on its side while Jenny was still moving, so it would come out of the ground. As soon as they made a wide arc, Jenny would once more be lined up to start through the field again. Samuel would then return the plow to the upright position to begin plowing a new furrow. The shape of the plow, along with Jenny's pull, would immediately take the plowshare beneath the surface like the submerging of a spoon in a bowl of hot oatmeal.

Following the plowing, it was necessary to harrow the fields. Harrows, made up of a frame with numerous "spikes" sticking down into the earth, were used to further break up the soil turned over by the plow. Clods or clumps of earth made it difficult for future trips through the field. Harrowing was essential to further prepare the ground for planting, which even further required different devices for different crops.

Corn was often planted with a simple hand tool, which required the farmer to plant each corn seed individually. The handheld contraption was first pushed into the ground. When a trigger was pulled, one seed was dropped into the soil beneath the surface. Lifting the planter allowed the dirt to fall back around the seed. This was a very slow and time consuming process for Samuel, but it was one that had to be done. More fortunate farmers had horsedrawn planters with a seat for their comfort, if you could call a metal seat comfortable. Such conveniences were called a "sulky," as a result of the iron seat on which the farmer would sit.

Once the corn was growing well, it had to be cultivated. Cultivation served two purposes. The shovel-like attachments of the cultivator cut off plants growing in-between the rows of corn; these were usually weeds. At the same time dirt was piled up around the corn stalk giving it additional strength and nourishment. Farmers lacking cultivators often used the time honored but distasteful method of hoeing the weeds by hand. Samuel used this method himself until he could finally afford a two-row, horsedrawn cultivator. The thought of acquiring many sulky type devices was most attractive to him.

In the event of a successful crop (such could be prevented by hail, the lack of rainfall, poor timing, etc.), the farmer's yield was still of no value unless it was harvested. Corn could be harvested in more than one way. It could be picked by hand while walking beside a horsedrawn wagon and throwing the individual ears in as they were picked. This slow process was made easier by having the sideboard of the wagon higher on the side opposite the picker. He could then bounce the ears off of the “bangboard” into the wagon. A good mule could keep the wagon slowly moving forward at a pace sufficiently fast to stay abreast of the farmer and yet not get ahead of him. Samuel used, as did other farmers, a special hook to help shuck the corn before throwing it into the wagon.

Another method of harvesting corn was to tie it into bundles of stalks up to 18 inches in diameter. These bundles would then be placed into “shocks” resembling teepee-like structures, whereby several bundles were stood upright by leaning them against each other with the bottoms of the bundles spread out for stability. This lessened the rotting of the corn until the grain could be removed from the fields.

All crops required varying methods of being harvested. None were easy. Some methods required large numbers of workers, such as the threshing of wheat. Part of the need for large numbers of laborers was due to the fact a community had very few threshing machines. Therefore, only one farmer’s wheat could be threshed at a time, so all of the farmers worked together at one farm until the threshing was done; then they’d move down the road to the next farm. Such times helped to make the settlers in a given area much more of a tight knit group. Also, thrashings became sort of a social event as well.

While the men toiled in the fields for such events, the women worked together to fill the laborers’ needs for large meals. This was helpful, as the typical long days of the farmer and his wife left little time or the inclination for socializing afterwards. Samuel and Lillie were quite willing to participate in these “threshing bees.” Actually, they looked forward to them. While it did require hard work, the task gave them a chance to enjoy the company of their friends and neighbors.

“Did you see all of the food they put away?” asked Lillie.

“Can’t rightly say,” answered her husband.

“Why, for one meal they ate ten chickens. Why it took three of us to pluck all of the feathers. And I’ll bet Margaret Moody and her crew mashed fifteen pounds of spuds to make tater salad. I don’t want to see any more chickens for awhile, unless they’re a layin’ eggs, that is.”

"Well, I don't reckon any man went away hungry," replied her husband. "As a matter a fact, every worker had a smile on his face as he walked back to the field."

"I know you sure didn't leave much for the womenfolk to eat. We were a scrapin' bowls all over for enough to make a meal for us."

"Couldn't you hide some for yourselves before we came in?"

"You know the men must be fed first. There's nothin' worse than a hungry man. Seems like a man never really gets the work done unless he's well fed. No, we'll not be a hidin' food. There's always the possibility we'll pluck another chicken later, if needed."

"I thought you were through with pluckin' chickens."

"We do what we have to do, Samuel. And today we had a full twenty men to feed."

"Well, you did a right good job, woman. I'm proud of you."

"Well, thank goodness they won't be back for awhile. Of course I do have to help out over at Moody's tomorrow."

The completion of harvest did not mark the end of the farmer's work for that year. No, it was then time to begin preparations for another year. Corn stalks had to be cut up, if they were still in the field, so they would be easier to plow, and the cycle started over again. Then, in the wintertime, many other tasks, such as gathering wood for heating and cooking or the slaughtering and butchering of animals, always needed attention. Just as it confronted the woman of the house, the man's work was always waiting to be done. Yes, Cal was a most welcome addition to the Ledbetter family. His work was already being cut out for him.

Life around the turn of the century was difficult. While most Americans had few luxuries, the settlers on the frontier had even fewer. Life was seen as that time in between birth and when one received his final reward in heaven. Many religions of the time taught that man worked hard in order to receive his or her just compensation after death, not before. Therefore, it was further preached from the pulpit, happiness here on earth might be due to living the wrong lifestyle. Many items of pleasure, such as alcohol, dancing, or seeing performances in a dance hall to name a few, were considered sure tickets to hell by some.

Preachers, such as Billy Sunday, traveled the country holding "revivals" with messages of "fire and brimstone." Fear of failing to heed their warnings, and not living a life of abstinence, kept many a soul wary of enjoying themselves from the fermented fruit of the corn. Sin was lurking everywhere to snare the unsuspecting soul.

Other individuals also came to the forefront during these times to help keep citizens on the "straight and narrow path," necessary for admittance to heaven, they said. Carry Nation of Kansas was just such an individual. When the U.S. Supreme Court weakened the prohibition laws of her home state, she, with the help of similar believing women, would march into a saloon and proceed to wreck the bar with axes while singing hymns. She was an overpowering force just by looks alone. With six feet of height and a weight to match, she also took on the evils of tobacco, corsets, and anything else she and her cohorts considered evil.

The world that Cal entered, then, was one of hard times and hard work, not pleasure. The only hope for survival was to adopt the protestant work ethic of a day's work for a day's pay. To do any less was sinful.

CHAPTER V

Samuel finally had his opportunity to homestead in Indian Territory. His good fortune came about in 1900. This land promising to hold their future wasn't so far from where he and Lillie had first lived after their marriage in 1891. The community nearby where they now found themselves had acquired the name of Hominy Corners over the years. It seems that two of the four corners surrounding the junction on the road between the towns of Wade and Albany, intersected by the road going due south out of Bokchito (Choctaw for Big Creek), always contained corn fields being grown for hominy.

Hominy, you see, is a delicacy to families like the Ledbetters. Hominy, though, is nothing more than a corn product that came to us from the Indians, especially the Algonquians, a tribe native to the northeast part of the United States. Once the corn is hulled with a lye process, it can be boiled and eaten as one course of the meal. While it is generally white in color, some varieties are yellow. As mentioned earlier, the fields opposite each other on the dirt road to Albany, Indian Territory, always seemed to have grain being grown for the benefit of producing this tasty morsel.

The other two parcels of land on opposite corners of the junction contained a general store and a school. The store, which at one time was called White's Mercantile, had slowly evolved into Hominy Corners General Store. The Whites never seemed to mind; business stayed about the same no matter what the sign out front proclaimed. They weren't getting rich, but they seemed to sustain a comfortable existence. Teams and wagons freighted in merchandise from Durant most every week. If you ever had free time on your hands, and that certainly was a precious commodity, it was a real joy to wander the aisles of the general store. A variety of odors ranging from the barrel of pickles by the counter to the fuel for the kerosene lamps displayed in the rear were always in evidence. It took superior olfactory discrimination to sort out the many odors when apples, oranges, onions and any other fruit or vegetable might be in season. Further complicating the identification of odors occurred when fresh bread might be available along with different types of pastries. Of course most families did their own baking, but sometimes the urge to purchase a delicacy already prepared could not be resisted.

Actually the kerosene supply was kept in the back storeroom. The customer desiring to replenish his supply brought his own container to be refilled from a large can possessing a potato for plugging the spout. The brown tuber could generally be twisted over and into the spout simultaneously, thereby minimizing the escape of odors that could permeate other commodities in the store. No one wanted to purchase merchandise reeking of kerosene.

Unlike some buildings in these parts, the store had a wooden floor. The boards were sometimes treated with oil, necessitating a layer of wood chips or sawdust to soak up the excess lubricant before it might soil into a fine pair of shoes. At least it helped to lessen dust deposits created by wagons passing by on the nearby road. Actually, it concealed more than lessening the presence of these airborne particles.

There was more to the store than the smells emanating from every direction, however. Just the sights to behold easily aroused a list of desires in the entrapped customer. The range of wares went from small farm implements (larger implements were frequently stored in the adjoining shed or barn) to all of the needed ingredients for the home baking that everyone did. Then, too, the seamstress could generally locate the essential supplies for any project she might attempt.

To the children, though, the most exciting part of the store was the counter containing jars of a wide variety of candies to be sold individually. Peppermint was a favorite, with licorice sticks (or a similar candy called horehound, which could also be made into a cough remedy), lemon drops and the list could go on and on. There was even peanut butter in wooden tubs that could be purchased in any amount.

“Our apples didn’t get a good do this year. How much are you a gittin’ for yours?” asked Lillie.

"Well apples are in short supply everywhere this year, Mrs. Ledbetter. Afraid I'm going to have to get thirty cents a bushel for them," replied Mr. White.

"If I git a full bushel, will you give me one of them crates they come in?" she asked.

"I reckon so. What do you aim to do with the crate?"

"They make the nicest places to put books that you ever saw. You just nail them to the wall facin' out," responded Lillie. "Now with two kids in school, we'll likely be a gittin' more books around the place. Why, just last week my folks gave us their old copy of the *Farmers' Almanac*. Soul needs places to be a puttin' everything. Someday we'll have a house that will hold all of our stuff."

"Yes," said Mr. White. "We're always needing more space ourselves. Why just yesterday the misses asked if I'd build her a new closet."

"I just wish we had one closet in our house," said Lillie.

"Where do you hang all of your stuff?" asked Mr. White.

"We have nails on the wall. Doesn't take a whole lot of nails just yet. Someday, though, we'll own lots of clothes and we'll need closets, too. That'll be the day."

"Yes, better times are a coming as sure as you're born."

"I do have one more favor to ask," said Lillie. "I brought in a dozen eggs from our hens that we don't need right now. Would you take them in trade for the apples?"

"Well, I'm only paying a penny apiece for eggs right now. Tell you what I'll do, though. You bring me another eighteen eggs by the end of this month and we'll call it square. Does that sound fair? You can take the apples home with you now that way. Chances are we won't have anymore by the end of the month."

"It sure does, Mr. White. It sure does. You write it down in the account book, though. I don't aim to short you none. Now you write it down, you hear?"

"Will there be anything else?" he asked.

"Now that you ask, Samuel has been askin' for some coffee. We've been out nigh onto a week now."

Leaving the store, Lillie observed the older men of the community congregating around the potbellied stove in an open area in the middle of the building. "What, pray tell, do you gents continue to find to talk about," she asked.

"Oh, Hominy Corners nevers lacks for good gossip," replied Jake Canfield. "Have you heard that Grandma Morrow is gettin' a new buggy?"

"How on earth can she afford such a luxury?" retorted Lillie.

"Well, it's actually not new," said Jake. "But, it's new to her."

"Really, being a widow, she needs good transportation. We certainly can't deny that. Of course if one of you fine gentlemen would marry her, she'd have fewer things to worry about."

"Whoa, don't mention marriage to us. Most of us have been there before. Right now most of us would just like a warm place to sleep and two or three hot meals a day."

"See there. You're givin' the best reasons there are for havin' a good woman around. Of course you've got to do it in a fashion that God would approve of."

"I'm sure God approves of us the way we are right now."

"Well you don't forget my words, you old rascals. Your time is a comin'."

Younger children were not expected to travel great distances to school, as the only way to get there was by walking. Large schools in the wilderness were a rarity. Instead, small schools could generally be found only a few miles apart. Cal attended Hominy Corners School, built by his Uncle Led, who now lived close by his three brothers. He built the small, whitewash structure for when his daughter, Ada, was old enough to start school, and there wasn't one close by. It was unusual for children here to attend school beyond the eighth grade, especially boys. If the family did want their child to continue on to high school, it was necessary for them to go to Bokchito, a few miles away. This also meant making boarding arrangements if there weren't family members in the town with a high school. Sending a girl to town for high school seemed the greatest waste of good money for rural folks, so it rarely occurred at all.

The school building actually occupied less space than the store on the opposite corner. Set back from the road about fifty feet, it measured a mere 25 X 25 feet on the outside. Each sidewall had six double-hung windows that were quite tall. This enabled additional lighting from the sun to assist the student in his/her studies. They already knew that good readers needed adequate lighting, and most families were desirous of producing good readers. Otherwise, how would they grow to be conversant in the Bible?

The rear of the wooden structure was actually the front of the room when you got inside either of the two classrooms. Each classroom contained four rows, one for each grade. Mrs. Allen's room had grades one through four, while Mrs. Greenlau's room had grades five through eight. Upon entering the building from the road a short hallway was encountered. Here, students found hooks to hang their coats and hats, with a shelf for lunch boxes. Each classroom had a potbellied stove to the rear of the room with a stovepipe attached to a common brick chimney in the middle wall.

For writing surfaces the students used a variety of tables acquired from civic-minded citizens of the area served by the school. Chairs were obtained the same way. The teacher's desk was on a platform elevated about ten inches above the remainder of the school floor. The full width of the wall behind the teacher's desk was used for the blackboards, with the alphabet in upper case letters neatly printed in a row at the top.

Outside the school building was a barren landscape where the children could run to their hearts' desire. A pole fence helped to delineate where the playground ended. To the rear was a stable where those riding some distance could leave their horse during the day. Most children, however, walked to school in whatever weather existed at the time. Just to the side of the school was a hand pump where water was drawn from a well. This served as the drinking fountain for the school. The water flowed into a large pipe about five feet long capped on the end. Holes, punched in with a nail and hammer, were spaced at one-foot intervals on each side. While one hardy soul pumped the water, others would stand by the holes where the water would exit. This permitted as many as ten children to get a drink at the same time.

The earth on the playground had long since been pulverized into dry powder, with an occasional sprig of grass being visible in spots. The rains that fell could quickly turn the area into a field of mud. Recess was sometimes held inside to prevent the inevitable tracking in of mud to the classroom. The only playground equipment was a swing set for four children and a simple teeter-totter made by one of the fathers. At least recess provided an opportunity to get outside for awhile. This gave the children an opportunity to "blow off the stink" observed Mrs. Greenlau.

Trained teachers were hard to find for the schools in the territory. Often an older teenager was recruited to fulfill these duties. In either case the teacher was the model of propriety. This almost always ruled out men or older boys for the task. No chances whatsoever were taken that the students would be exposed to anyone but a teacher of high moral standards. During the day these imparters of wisdom were the guardians of the soul of these youngsters and often resorted to the Bible in teaching lessons.

The pay for such servants varied because it usually consisted of one dollar per month per student. In addition, each family served by the school was expected to house the teacher for a proportion of the school year equivalent to the number of students they had attending the school. Teachers found that they spent more of their time housed by large families sometimes experiencing difficulty in meeting the nutritional needs of their charges. Of course the school year was not as long as they experienced in the eastern states or what the tribes provided for the Indians. Allowing time off for the significant farm functions during the year, such as planting and harvesting, often left only five months for schooling purposes. Schools at the turn of the century in the wilderness did not always receive the highest priority; survival, however, did.

It was December of 1903. Cal was almost halfway through the fourth grade. This was to be his last year of formal schooling. It wasn't that he was failing in school; as a matter of fact, he was a good student. Not only that, but he looked forward to going to school very much. It was just that he was needed at home to help his father on the farm. Samuel's long awaited desire of having Cal work beside him on the farm was soon to be realized. Sure, Cal had helped out before and after school, as well as during summers and cotton harvest, but now he was to become Samuel's full-time helper. It wasn't unusual for fathers to pull their sons out of school like this. Now, the Ledbetters could begin increasing the acreage of their farm even more. Cal looked forward to this new chapter in his life with great anticipation.

Still, Cal loved everything about school, especially arithmetic. The most fun was to be had by participating in the contests where they used their slates and chalk to work problems out at their desk or table. It was much too expensive to use writing paper for most school tasks, so each student had a piece of slate about eight inches wide by fourteen inches long. This piece of smooth black stone, made of the same material as the blackboards, was framed with fabric or wood, so it wouldn't break or chip on the edges. The teacher would usually read the arithmetic problem outloud as she walked around the room. Then, each student would do the problem as quickly as possible and raise his/her hand when done.

The students in that grade, usually numbering from two to six, would compete against each other. As they were called forward, each student would take their slate to the teacher, so she could check the correctness of their answers. Cal did well in these competitions. He enjoyed working arithmetic problems out in a race against time as well as against other students. He could even beat some of the kids in the upper grades. He already knew his multiplication tables through twelve and could both multiply and divide numbers with ease. Yes, he was going to miss the math contests. But, then, his dad was always challenging him to see who could count the rows in a cotton field the fastest or even more complicated equations, such as figuring out how much cotton they grew on an acre of land.

There were a number of Ledbetter families in the vicinity of Hominy Corners. By now Samuel had two children in school:

Cal in fourth grade and Myrtle in first grade. Samuel's other daughter, Jewell, was still too young to attend school this year. Abe also had two children in Hominy Corners School. His other two children were still too young to attend. Jake had married Jane Jones, a full-blooded Choctaw Indian, but they didn't have any children yet. Led and his wife, Mandy, had two children born in Texas. His other children were born in Indian Territory and now attended Hominy Corners School. Many descendants of the four Ledbetter brothers went to school there over the years. Cal thoroughly enjoyed going to school with all of his cousins. Every day of school seemed like a family reunion. Occasionally this created problems for the teacher. Sometimes the Ledbetters would rather talk about fishing than do school work.

It was often hard for Cal to keep his thoughts on his schoolwork. Of course he wasn't the only one having this problem. Children of this era did not like being cooped up inside school so much, especially if it was nice outside. Come to think of it, some didn't like being cooped up even when the weather was bad outside. On nice days, though, it was too easy to think of or dream about something exciting, instead of what the teacher wanted done. Why, just yesterday, he was thinking about earlier in the year when he and Myrtle had gone blackberry picking with Mom.

Blackberry picking was hard work, especially when you weren't tall enough to reach very high on the bushes. Those bushes seemed to have more thorns than berries, so it was difficult to move among them very well. Worse yet, the real tall vines drooped down and snagged your clothes like a fish hook if you weren't extremely careful. The thorns sure got in your way when you wanted to move fast, that's for sure.

While working his way around one side, so as to get in between the bushes, Cal was soon out of sight of both Mom and Myrtle. He didn't like working where his mother knew his every move. He did have a tendency to forget about picking blackberries from time to time, and she was quick to admonish him for his transgressions. He also couldn't resist eating a lot of what he picked. The taste of freshly picked blackberries was scrumptious, like nothing else they had to eat, that is with the exception of blackberry cobbler.

The sweet, and sometimes tart, taste of the berries was just too hard to resist. Occasionally he would put so many in his mouth that the juice would start running down his chin. He could explain the stains on his hands, but the purple around his mouth was a dead giveaway. When caught, he'd have to listen to his mother say, "You keep a eatin' all of them berries and we'll never have enough for anything else. Now you quit it!"

Pausing to pick thorns from his hand, Cal saw a black bullsnake slither among the bushes. He wanted to give chase, but he knew better than to follow it. The snake was harmless, but the thorns weren't. It wasn't much longer before he sighted a squirrel. Actually, he met it face to face in a small clearing among the bushes. The squirrel was just as surprised as he was at their chance encounter. Startled, Cal backed up, while the squirrel dashed up the nearest tree. Slowly, he worked his way around the oak tree trying to figure out how he might best capture this wily creature. He knew it would taste better than fried chicken, if Mom cooked it. She sure was a good cook. But his catching that squirrel was just not to be. No matter how hard he tried, he couldn't even get close to it. Oh well, he thought, there will be another time. He wasn't going to let this one failure take away his desire for fried squirrel.

Dad had been teaching him how to hunt both squirrels and possums. He was quick to learn the skills of survival in this backwoods country. He and Pa brought home fresh meat almost every time they went hunting. Getting a possum was less desirable than a squirrel, though; possum meat was so greasy.

The stillness of the air was shattered by his mother's piercing voice, "Cal Ledbetter, where are you?"

Now this worried Cal, as he only had a thin layer of blackberries on the bottom of his bucket.

"Over here!" he yelled back, while he frantically picked berries.

"Come on, it's time to git home!"

"In a minute!" he called back.

This allowed Cal time to pour what few berries he had out on the ground. Then, he quickly gathered up a small pile of leaves from below the tree containing "his squirrel." Even more quickly he placed what few berries he had picked on top of the leaves. Thank goodness, there were enough berries to cover the leaves. Upon rejoining Mom and Myrtle, it appeared that he had picked the most berries of all.

He felt a twinge of pride, simultaneous with a bit of guilt, in having outsmarted his mother, as she said, "Boy, we'll sure have a big blackberry cobbler with all of these berries."

Cal's feelings of having pulled a fast one over on his mother were short-lived, however. She didn't get mad at him too often. But when she did get mad, you knew you were "gonna git it" when she combined both your first and middle names. He was just outside the back door whittling a whistle from a short length of a green elm branch when he heard the yell.

"Caleb Ashton, git in here!"

Now that meant trouble, no question about it. The tone of her voice sent cold shivers running up and down his spine. Should he try to run for it, while he had a chance, or just go inside for judgement day? He had learned early in life, though, that running away from Mom wasn't using the gumption God gave man for such instances. Running would only make matters worse. Right now, if he went in, he'd likely only get a strapping with one of the leather straps used for sharpening Dad's razor. If Mom had to come looking for him, however, she'd probably cut a branch from some small, green willow sapling, to give him a switching.

Oh, how those switches hurt! There must have been something in that green bark that made them burn, because you couldn't bear to sit down for awhile after a switching. It was even worse if she made you bend over and grab your heels during the punishment, as this tightened the fabric in the seat of your britches and gave you less padding. He didn't know which hurt the most, a switching by Mom, or a paddling at school where the teacher swatted you extra hard with a board made special for inflicting pain as punishment. Sometimes, if he were around, Dad would protect you from Mom's harsh judgement.

Dad was nowhere in sight, so Cal decided to go inside. Mom's first words were, "Just what do you think this is all about?" as she held up the bucket of leaves.

It wasn't that he had picked fewer berries than Myrtle, just over two years younger than he was. It was the fact that he had tried to deceive his mother, and this deceit angered her so much.

The pain of the switching, not soon to be forgotten, didn't hurt Cal near as much as when he heard,

"Just for that, you don't git any cobbler tonight either. I'll teach you to try and make a fool out of me, young man!"

Now, that hurt. No one liked blackberry cobbler any better than Cal. Mom had a real special way of making them. There would be lots of blackberries and juice in them; but what made them so good were the chunks of biscuit dough cooked in with the berries and lots of sugar. Then, there would be a thin layer of biscuit dough with a lot of butter cooked to a golden brown as a crust over the top holding in the juices. Finally, Mom would sprinkle sugar over the whole thing. No punishment was as harsh as missing a serving of that cobbler, and he could already smell it cooking.

Cal was jolted back to reality when he heard the teacher tell him it was his turn to read. She knew he was daydreaming, and she wanted to teach him a lesson. Maybe he might just pay a little better attention in the future. It was unusual for Cal to be daydreaming this much, she thought to herself. She knew he dearly loved to read. He had told her about how much he liked the *McGuffey Reader*. All of the kids seemed to enjoy the stories in it. Most of the Ledbetter families seemed to have very few books at home, except for the Bible, so the books at school were extra special to most of them. Besides that, the Bible was just too hard to read if you were very young.

Sometimes Samuel would bring back a copy of *The Durant Democrat* from his trips to the city with railroad ties. Many were the times that the teacher knew Cal stayed up late to read by light of the kerosene lantern, when his chores were done, and he was through with supper. She was going to miss his academic ability, as well as his daydreaming and pranks.

Cal was embarrassed when the other kids laughed at his being caught unprepared to read out loud. It looked like it was his turn to be the object of the laughter. This was the reverse of what usually happened. He had a reputation for pulling pranks on others, especially when they least expected them. This was a trait, everyone said, that he had inherited from his father. At the same time, though, both also had a reputation of being counted on to help anyone in need of assistance. His father had always said, "Some day we'll be the ones needin' help, and you don't deserve help if you ain't willin' to give it." Besides that, Dad always told him, it was just carrying out the golden rule.

The end of that school day couldn't come quick enough for Cal. He didn't like being embarrassed in front of his cousins. The teacher, Mrs.Greenlau, sensed his need to escape the teasing he'd surely encounter outside the school building, so she asked him to stay after school. She wanted to talk to him anyway. Cal was real worried about being told to stay after school. Was he in that much trouble, he asked himself. Now I will get a switching from Mom when I get home. Maybe school is not that good after all.

The teacher tried to lead up to the subject she wanted to discuss in a roundabout way. "How does the cotton crop look this year, Cal?"

"Ya mean you want to talk about cotton? Does that mean I ain't in trouble?"

"No, you're not in trouble. I just needed to talk to you awhile. And don't say ain't. Say I'm not."

"In that case, we have a good cotton crop," said Cal.

"You like working in the fields, don't you?"

"Yes, ma'am, I sure do," he replied.

"Do you like school as well as doing farm work?"

"Yes I do, but Dad says I'm needed more at home to work than I'm needed at school. The only way we can grow enough cotton and wheat to support a growin' family, he says, is if I'm there to help him out in the fields every day."

"I understand," she said. "But that doesn't mean you have to quit learning. You know that you can learn anywhere you are, and that means places besides school buildings."

"What do you mean?" asked Cal.

"Well," she said, "when you're farming, you're always figuring out how to do things easier or better, aren't you?"

"Well, yes, I reckon so."

"Then you're learning. Schools aren't the only places to learn. They're one of the best, but they aren't the only place. Just like we learn in church, too."

"I really hadn't thought of it thataways," said Cal. "So I'll still be a goin' to school even though I ain't here."

"Not exactly," she said, while ignoring his use of the word ain't again, "but you can be learning all of the time, if you want to."

"I'm sure going to like this," he said, "because I like learnin', but I hate being cooped up inside a building all day. Course I won't get to see Bill and everyone as much."

"Well you just stop by and visit sometimes when you're not busy. Maybe you could be in one of our arithmetic contests. I know the other kids would like that, too. Or, if you are learning something from a book at home, and you can't figure it out, just stop by after school, and I'll try to help you."

"That'd be just great," said Cal. "Mom and Dad don't read too good. They try to help me when they can. But I know that when Dad sometimes tells me that he's too busy, I know it's because he can't read what I'm showin' him in the book. I sure would appreciate any help you can give me."

"There is one other thing, Cal."

"What's that, Mrs. Greenlau?"

"You know you've written some beautiful poetry for me at times. I'd like to see you continue."

"You mean like the time I wrote about the joys of climbin' a tree with no shoes."

"Exactly, but there are others as well. Just write what your heart tells you. The rest will come naturally."

Cal knew right then that he was going to miss school more than he had originally thought. After he went to bed that night,

Cal thought even more about this being his last year in school. He would really miss going to school because he enjoyed reading books and learning. Also, he would even more miss seeing his cousins and other friends at school every day. But, he also enjoyed doing the farm work with his father. He was too small for some farm jobs, such as plowing. It took a lot of strength keeping that plow in a straight line or at least following the furrow beside the one he had just plowed. Dad had said it wouldn't be too long, now, before he could do even that.

The job he was best at, Cal knew, was in planting grains. He could do as good a job as anyone, when he walked down the field broadcasting the seeds in a strip twelve to fifteen feet across. It didn't matter that the grain drill had been invented almost 60 years earlier in 1841. They couldn't afford one, anyway. It was easy, he thought, wearing that canvas bag with the straps over the shoulder, dipping in for seeds, and then gently throwing them in a circular motion with his right hand held palm up. You had to be careful not to plant too many seeds in a small area, though, as there might not be enough rainfall to give them adequate moisture. Not enough moisture could result in the grain withering and dying on the stalk if it germinated in the first place, or at least didn't put grains into the husk. If you planted the seeds too far apart, though, you were wasting a lot of hard labor put into the plowing or harrowing. Needless to say, it took a lot of skill to plant grains. Cal had acquired a real knack for broadcasting seeds at an early age, and he enjoyed it.

One job Cal could do well, however, he really didn't like. It was picking cotton. This work was hard on the hands because of the outer shell surrounding the cotton fiber; it was called the boll. It was quite brittle and tore at your hands. Wearing gloves helped, but it was still a most difficult task. As you were picking the cotton, you had to drag a large canvas or denim bag behind you to hold the picked cotton. Sometimes, children used burlap or "gunny" sacks from grain for picking cotton. This sack, dragging on the ground behind you, soon became quite heavy, even for adults. The worst part about the weight of the sack, however, was the way the strap cut into your shoulder. Even if you had padding for protection, it hurt.

Cal always knew there would be things about any job that he didn't like. This was indicative of his maturity level. Also, he knew because his father taught him about taking the good with the bad. It's the only way you'll ever get ahead, he was told. Learning such a lesson at an early age made Samuel proud of his son. Even though he was only nine years old, Cal was mature, as was often true for nine-year old boys on the frontier. Even though girls were allowed to continue in formal schooling much longer than boys did, generally up through the eighth grade, it didn't mean they lacked in maturity, however. They could help their mother do things such as wash dishes after school or after dark, while most of the man's work had to be done during daylight hours, while school was still in session.

Cal knew the reason why he liked working on the farm so much. It couldn't be said that he didn't like school or didn't like the teacher. He liked both very much. No, it was being out in the open fields all of the time, which he enjoyed. He guessed he could just stay outside forever, if he had the chance. Sometimes, he would sleep down on the creek while he had a fishing line in the water. The creeks and rivers weren't too big most of the year, so all he needed was a piece of string or cord with a hook tied on one end, and the other end tied to a willow branch to go fishing. If you ran the line between two of your toes just right while you slept, you would be awakened when a fish was on your line. Otherwise, during the day you needed a bobber made out of cork or dried wood, which the fish would pull under water when he bit on the juicy worm you had placed there.

As soon as you saw the bobber go under water, you would make a quick yank to imbed the hook in the fish's mouth, then swing it up on the bank of the creek. Samuel told Cal that if he didn't sit real still while fishing, the only ones he'd catch would be the blind ones that accidentally ran into his hook. Cal knew the secret about catfish; don't catch the real big ones. They didn't taste as good as the ones about twelve to fourteen inches long. If you caught them too small, however, Dad said you'd have to spit in the skillet to make them sizzle. Once you caught a good mess of fish, you'd get Mom to use her special recipe to fry them. Cal really didn't know how Mom cooked them. Maybe it had something to do with the way she rolled them in the corn meal before dropping them in the grease. Whatever recipe she used, they sure tasted good.

Anyway, whether it was fishing, farming or hunting, Cal knew that he loved to be outdoors. He could even be quite content just lying on the ground looking up at the sky when he wasn't doing anything. During the day, while taking a break from his work, he could lie back and envision the clouds being shaped like familiar objects such as a large billowing object resembling a castle. Or, at night, he could look up at the heavens and wonder if there might be life on another planet. Yes, Cal knew his niche in life was to be part of the great outdoors right here in Hominy Corners. He always vowed, though, that he would get more education in the future. He might not be able to go back to a school, but he would learn on his own if he had to. His taste for learning was as deeply imbedded in his mind as the red dirt sometimes was between his toes when he walked barefooted in the fields.

Forever emblazoned in everyone's memory is a place called home. It doesn't have to be the place where you were born. Hominy Corners was that place to Cal.

CHAPTER VI

Nineteen hundred and nine was off to a good start and well underway by anyone's standard. To say that this might possibly be the best year thus far of the Ledbetter's eighteen-year marriage would not be going too far. To commemorate, while documenting their obvious successes, the achievement of the family's financial independence meant having the family portrait taken outside of Lillie's new house on a beautiful July day. The photographer had even waited until late afternoon to avoid the direct rays of a bright, midsummer sun. Mr. Shanholtz felt, and Lillie concurred, that the lighting would be perfect at this time of day. Not a cloud dared dot the sky, and the sweet smell of crops in bloom in the nearby fields was a treat to be relished. If there was a breeze, it was blowing out of the east and away from the corral. The trees were motionless as if taking a nap. Even the squirrels must have been on vacation. Perhaps for a brief interlude the world stood still.

Samuel was willing to have the portrait taken anywhere if it had to be done, but Lillie wanted it right in every way. As far as the two in wedded harmony were concerned, the family was now complete; Cal was fourteen, Myrtle was eleven, Jewell was seven and Clevon was only a few months old. To say a boy was cute was permissible as long as he remained so young. Of course Clevon also looked husky in his white dress with all of the frills encircled in stair-step fashion. His legs were fat, but this would turn to muscle when he began to walk.

Samuel asked, "Why must little boys be put in dresses in the first place? I believe it makes him look like a girl, and my boys don't need to look like girls. Heavens, don't we have better things to do than mess with the divine order of nature?"

"Everyone does it," his wife replied.

"That's the last reason to do somethin'," said Samuel. "I honestly think you'd have Cal wearin' them, too, if everyone else was a doin' it."

"Whoa! Wait a minute," said Cal. "Leave me out of this talk. I won't even hear of it. It's bad enough that Clevon has no choice in the matter, but I do."

"You stay out of this Cal. This is between me and your father," said Lillie. Turning to face her husband with pointed finger, she continued, "And I certainly didn't want my family dressed any differently from anybody else's for their first family portrait. We've strived hard to get where we are today, and the world needs to know it. Why, I've a mind to submit this picture to *The Durant Democrat*. I do wish, though, that you could have worn a necktie for this special occasion. Why, we may never have another family picture taken."

"A tie would look real nice for this special occasion." said Mr. Shanholtz from behind the camera on a tripod, "and I'm sure the paper would love a copy when we're done."

"You keep out of this, too," said Samuel. "Farmers don't need no neckties. They don't look or feel right, anyway. People ought to see me the way I really am, with my workin' britches on. And the last place they need to see me is in a picture in the newspaper."

"People want to see you, not your line of work," Lillie came back.

"Well, what you see is me. And another thing. I still don't like my boy a wearin' a dress. Why don't you buy him some real clothes at Hominy Corners?"

"You know they don't sell clothes at the General Store for little boys," Lillie answered.

"Well, they better start sellin' them real soon like. A man doesn't like to see his son wearin' none of those girly things."

"Yes, I do intend to pursue that picture in the newspaper. That would be the right touch for all of those folks who never thought we'd make it. Who do I talk to at *The Democrat*, Mr. Shanholtz?"

"The editor, Mrs. Ledbetter, the editor."

Lillie did notice that Samuel attempted to straighten his coat and brush his hair out of his eyes at the last minute. He even licked his fingers to smooth the stray hairs in his moustache. Earlier he had trimmed his beard to a respectable length. It was showing a fair amount of gray to match his hair, which ended in a slight curl at the base of his neck. Maybe I should have cut his hair, she thought. Oh well, he was a handsome man; no one would notice his hair in the picture. At least Cal agreed to wear a blue necktie, having bought it special for the occasion. He even wore a right nice pair of brown suspenders that took him awhile to figure out how to put in place. Cal sure was agreeable, he might even be her favorite child, she reckoned. One's firstborn should be accorded that honor, she thought. They'd been through a lot together. Even with his impish ways, she loved him dearly. Of course his brogans did look out of place, but a man could only afford one pair of shoes at a time.

"Stand still, Myrtle. We'll never git this picture taken."

"There's a fly a botherin' me, Mama."

"You're just goin' to have to ignore it, child. I promise you can swat it in just a moment."

It took a number of poses to get everything just the way Lillie desired. Clevon kept squirming in her lap. By cuddling him tightly, though, she managed to contain his movements for brief periods of time. Mr. Shanholtz wasn't always able to snap the camera simultaneous with these momentary lapses in movement, but two good poses were captured for posterity. Also occupying her thoughts at brief intervals was the fact that she wanted to insure the picture exhibiting Jewel's new high top shoes and the summer dress she had recently made for this occasion. Not wanting to leave any task incomplete, she had repeatedly brushed the girl's auburn hair until it looked "real purty." Helping position her family, it was clear to the photographer that his patron wanted everyone to be sure and notice that the house was painted, so the picture was taken outside. Few people in these parts had painted houses with real paint. If they had any coating at all on their house, it was generally white wash. Lillie clearly wanted everything to be perfect in the portrait. With a nice frame gilded in gold, it would be most noticeable by the Seth Thomas Clock on the mantle. It's a shame the picture couldn't include the shiny, galvanized roof adorning the abode like a new Easter hat.

Samuel and Lillie felt blessed with all of their children being so healthy. The couple had lost two children, Ethel and Walter, during infancy, which wasn't so unusual. Having four healthy children like this was quite an accomplishment. It was right to feel proud. Lillie's only other wish was that the portrait show off the pretty colors in the attire worn here today. She had no choice, though. She'd have to be content with the brown and white tones in the finished product.

"Now this is one right good-lookin' picture," Cal said to himself, as he later looked at the finished portrait. He was especially proud of his being so tall and wearing a gold chain hanging out of his vest pocket. Just last year, when they were picking cotton in Myra, Texas, he had bought that chain and the pocket watch hooked to it with some of his earnings. Of course he gave most of his earnings to the folks for buying farm equipment. Oh, they didn't have too much equipment yet, but this cotton picking sure improved the chances of more being bought. They had even managed to put some earnings aside in a small savings account in the Bokchito Bank. He was glad to be able to help the family increase the amount of equipment they owned. Someday, it might belong to him, he reasoned.

It was hard to forget that trip to Myra last fall. Clevon had been born there. They named him Clevon after Lillie's father. They were tempted to name him after Uncle Led, who had died of consumption the year before in Elwood, Texas. Cal never knew why they didn't honor his father's brother. Anyway, the family was beginning to experience some prosperity, and they wanted to show it off. Cal was the proudest of all the children; he had been a significant part of the family's success. It was right for him to feel proud of his place as a wage earner.

Samuel and Lillie had finally been able to get 160 acres of prime Oklahoma bottomland of their own, and they remained in the vicinity of Hominy Corners. Their farm was on a branch of Blue River in Bryan County. Statehood for Oklahoma, accomplished with the joining of Oklahoma Territory and Indian Territory in 1907 to form one state, had helped to make it all possible. Homesteading was now legal for the Ledbetters. Dad, with Cal's help, was working right now to prove up on the land.

By the end of the second year after filing your claim, you had to have twenty acres cleared and ready for planting. Also, your house had to meet specifications. This was intended to prevent the speculator who might only want the land for resale at a profit to others. Still some profiteers circumvented the law by having houses built on sled-like runners that could be pulled from place to place, although this system didn't work well in the hills of eastern Oklahoma. Then, by the end of the third year, forty acres had to be cleared and planted. Settlers wanted to see it become free and clear; five years was a long time to have to prove up.

The house the Ledbetters had built was the one like they had always dreamed about. It was frame construction with the outside covered with shiplap siding. You know, like the lumber they used on the outside of some ships or barges. This provided a better seal against the elements of nature. There would be no more log cabins for them. They were landholders; now they could fix up their place any way they wanted. Actually they far exceeded any requirements set down under the homestead act which required a minimal structure measuring twelve by fourteen feet overall. Most homesteaders met the requirement with a frame shack covered with tarpaper. Rare were those taking time to expend efforts decorating the interior. Inside for many homesteaders was generally a dirt floor, much like Samuel and Lillie's original cabin built with the help of their friends and neighbors. Now, though, the Ledbetters were ready for far better than their earlier living arrangement. Their new home well reflected their improved status in this world.

The money they had been saving from cotton picking and selling railroad ties was not only used to help build this beautiful structure, but it was used to buy their first farm equipment. Of course their savings had to be supplemented with a bank loan. The bank had recognized the importance of Cal's contribution to the family income in granting the loan. Furthermore, the house and land were good collateral in these booming times. Then, too, the farm equipment purchased wasn't much. Mostly it included a three-bottom, horsedrawn gangplow, one of those John Deere models, and a two-row planter. This required, though, that they have a second mule to help pull their equipment. Also, they had a lumber wagon to haul corn or cotton into the barn or to town, when extra sideboards and a removable tailgate were added.

The mules were most important. They were named Jack and Jenny, even though the Jenny from their early years was already in mules' heaven, likely a peaceful place with lush grass and a cool stream nearby amidst the shade of towering oak trees and no harness anywhere to be found. Samuel was always partial to these names for mules. He wouldn't even consider any other. His father before him had used the same names. He was also very partial to mules. While they weren't as good-looking as a horse to most people, Samuel knew they were most dependable as a work animal. As a matter of fact, they were better at pulling equipment than horses, he had often said. Of course, they might not move as fast as a horse, but they certainly were better workers. Actually, a mule and an ox were very similar in their ability to work.

The main reason Samuel didn't have oxen was the difficulty encountered in getting them fitted with shoes to walk on hard surfaces. Hoists and heavy-duty, wide straps were required to raise oxen into the air for shoeing, as they refused to raise their legs for the job to be done. Also, a special stall was needed to help in this ungainly task as well. Of course the harness required for mules to pull implements was a large expense, when money was hard to come by. But you needed harness no matter what animal was used for pulling your equipment.

Cal had a difficult time understanding why mules couldn't be bred for more mules. It had something to do with a mule being the offspring of a male donkey and a female horse, so they couldn't reproduce. One of the nice things about mules, they were much easier to care for than horses. Cal looked forward to the day he would have his own mules. Maybe he'd have a horse to ride into town on Saturday nights. Enough daydreaming about what you don't have, he thought to himself. Well, Dad did say we'd buy a new reaper in time for the wheat harvest next year; that is if they had another year of good crops. McCormick-Deering did have good threshing machines and reapers.

A reaper would be an improvement over the scythe any day. Now, that would be a welcome addition to their meager lot of equipment. It was long, hard work cutting the wheat by hand with a cradle scythe. There was a real knack to making the wheat stalks lay down in neat rows, but the cradle attachment helped in that respect. It certainly was backbreaking work, however. Then, too, you had to do it right during the hottest part of the year. Well, anyway, you didn't need a lot of equipment for harvesting cotton besides a wagon and cotton sacks, just plenty of good, hard labor. At least you didn't pick cotton during the hot part of the year.

Yes, everything was going so well. Oh, there had been periods of sadness when the two babies had died. Dad had insisted that they be buried in a grove of oak trees up on the hill. This was their farm, too, he said, and he wanted them to enjoy the peace and quiet it afforded. After the different funerals, Cal could remember Mom closing her bedroom door to grieve at their passing. Sure, frontier women were tough; but you couldn't give up your own flesh and blood without feeling that a good part of yourself was being covered up in that grave as well. The crying spells happened every day for awhile, it seemed. They became less frequent with the passage of time.

Cal knew that Mama would never completely reconcile the passing of Ethel and Walter. He even shed an occasional tear for the departed infants. Of course it was only possible when he was alone. At least he could now look forward to Clevon going hunting or fishing with him. Of course he would have to put the worm on the hook. Dad didn't go hunting with him as much anymore. Work too often was the priority for him. It would be a long time, though, before Clevon would be old enough for them to get out together. Better yet, he looked forward to when his younger brother would be able to help with the farm work. He hoped it wouldn't be too long. After all, Cal reminded himself, he was already fourteen and not getting any younger. Why, he was already a grown man. Still, all in all, it was nice having Clevon around.

There were so many Ledbetters in the area that they were starting to joke about calling the community Ledbetter. Still, the name Hominy Corners had stuck even though the necessity of rotating crops sometimes found other than corn being planted on the corner plots. Actually, it wasn't a town; it didn't have a post office, which seemed to be the criteria for designation as a town. The school was the center of most of the area's social and recreational activity. They even held church services there when a preacher or missionary was in the area. Certainly weddings were held in the building for the locals. Not only did the three surviving Ledbetter brothers live in the vicinity, but other relatives as well were moving into the region. It seemed that the Ledbetter name was showing up more all of the time now. A review of the deed transfers for land recorded in the Bryan County Courthouse always found the name appearing from time to time. If it wasn't the name Ledbetter in the deed books, it was the name Shaughnessy, as the families had married back and forth now on a number of occasions. As a matter of fact, if you had counted the two names in the registry of deed transfers, you might have wanted to call the area Shaughnessy.

These were good years. Prosperity could be seen everywhere. All of the different crops, cotton, wheat, corn, tobacco and peanuts, seemed to do well in these parts. Still, a farmer wasn't expected to farm much more than 160 acres without some type of help with the farming. The labor required to plant, cultivate, and harvest the crops could be excessive at times. That is, unless you had sons to help with the labor or you could afford to hire farm workers. Samuel and Cal looked forward to Clevon joining them in the fields. Then they could easily increase their acreage under tillage.

Lillie was most pleased at her new frame house. It was the talk of the community, what with all of that fresh, white paint on the outside. That alone was a luxury. You know what Lillie liked best of all about her new house, though? The castle on the prairie had a small closet in each of the two bedrooms. She and Samuel's shared one, with the children sharing the other. The kids' bedroom had two beds. One bed was for the boys and one bed was for the girls. Someday she hoped Cal would get his own room. A man shouldn't have to sleep in the same room with girls, unless they were married, that is. Oh yes, the house had at least one window on each of the four sides with curtains in every one of them, no less. This meant Lillie could watch her children playing out front if she walked past the living room window, or see them enjoying themselves out back if she glanced out the kitchen window. It didn't matter if she was working at the stove or sitting at the worktable, she could see out the window. Not that she was worried, mind you; it was just such a joy watching the younger children play. If they weren't playing tag, they were playing hide and go seek, and if it snowed on one of those rare occasions, they played "goose-goose."

If you looked out the master bedroom window, you could see Blue River off in the distance. Well, at least you could see all of the foliage beside it. The trees and brush grew so close together that seeing through them was impossible. Samuel and Lillie didn't want to live too close to the river; one didn't want the younger kids yielding to the temptation of running water. Lillie felt so much joy in every aspect of "her" place. She even insisted that a special mantle be added to the wall of the living room, even though there was no fireplace. The single shelf was to display the Seth Thomas clock Samuel had purchased last year for their seventeenth wedding anniversary from a Sears Catalog for $4.95. Hearing the clock's cheery chime on the half-hour seemed to lift her spirits, as the clear note was a continual reminder that all was well.

Yes, the craftsmen brought out from Durant had built everything in this house to suit Lillie's tastes. This even included building the kitchen somewhat separate from the remainder of the house. As most months during the year were either hot or warm, there was no need in heating the rest of the house when cooking was taking place. First they had considered a totally separate structure about twenty feet behind the house with a wooden walkway to the backdoor for the cookstove. Lillie felt, though, that this arrangement would obstruct her view of the back yard. Thus, a portion of the back porch was partitioned off from the very beginning to contain the cooking equipment. This meant that the kitchen could be reached through an appropriately placed door without being exposed to rainfall. Yes, everything was just right. Contentment reigned as the supreme mistress in Lillie's mind. At 30 years of age, she was at peace with the world.

Not only was it the abode built to her specifications that Lillie liked, but everything surrounding the whitewashed castle had evidence of her touch as well. Samuel said little, but the improved housing had his blessing, too. His interests lay beyond the house, however. He especially liked the barn and pole corral off to the west that he and Cal had built even before the house was completed. Special care had been taken that it not be too close to the house, either.

"We don't want too many flies from the livestock comin' into the house! The smell we can get used to, but not the flies," said Samuel.

"Wouldn't it be easier to carry in the milk if the barn was closer?" asked Cal. "You know I spill a lot sometimes when it's cold, and I'm in a hurry."

"I'd rather we spilled a little milk now and then as have the smell of the manure so close by," answered his father. "Better yet, I'd rather the flies weren't so close to the house. We could learn to live with the smell, but you never get used to flies buzzin' around your head and settin' down when you least expect it. No, you can give me the spilled milk anytime. Now hear me, I'm not givin' you permission to spill milk, either."

"But we have a good screen door on both the front and the back of the house," said Cal.

"These doors won't keep them all out."

"Maybe we could buy better screen doors," said Cal.

"Show me a screen door that keeps all of the flies out. There isn't one made that's that good. Besides, they slip in before the door can close anyways. Even a stronger spring can't close it fast enough. No, this house is about done, and we'll have no more talk of changing any part of it. Furthermore, the corrals will be no closer than fifty paces from the house, and that's final."

The number of livestock owned by the Ledbetters was growing, so the sturdy corral was needed when the stock wasn't out to pasture. In addition they had built a barn with room for plenty of hay in the loft. The south side had a pulley rigged up special to raise the hay with hooks much larger than the hooks the icemen used to ply their trade. On the backside of the barn was a small tackroom to hold the harness for Jack and Jenny.

Attached, but off to one side of the barn so it was closest to the house, was a lean-to for a woodshed. No one liked to try and start a fire in the cook stove with wet wood. Worse yet would be to try and start a fire outside for the wash kettle when the wood wasn't dry. And no one liked to carry the wood any further than was necessary, either. At least the wood had a pleasant aroma, sometimes not unlike the cologne Cal splashed on his neck before going to a dance.

A real modern convenience, though, was the privy Cal and Samuel built out by the clothesline. Always before, the Ledbetters had been like everyone else and walked off into the woods to relieve themselves. A pole fence for squatting helped the process as well, but it could be hard on one's shoes. Neither way was civilized enough for Lillie; she needed her privacy. She always carried an item to hang on the clothesline when she went out. If anyone other than family happened to chance by, it looked like she was going to the clothesline. Otherwise, her journey to the privy saw no detours.

This was one nice privy, too. Some people called them outhouses or toilets. It was a two-holer. That way, if one of the boys happened to pee on the seat of one of the holes, the girls could use the one on the other side. There was just one thing missing in the privy, Lillie thought. They needed something besides a Sears and Roebuck Catalog for paper. Talk about modern conveniences, what will they think of next? she asked herself. It was a lot of work building a privy, so she knew she really shouldn't be asking for more than what they had already completed.

Samuel had told her about the art of building a privy. First you dig a hole about three feet by four feet wide and four to six feet deep, he said. Actually, you could dig it as deep as you wanted; the deeper the hole the longer it lasted. Then you built a little house about four feet by five feet wide and seven or eight feet tall beside the hole but a few feet away. Be sure the privy has a good roof on it, he said; no one likes rain dripping in the privy. Also, put a good catch on the door, so there is no doubt it will stay closed. Inside the little house you put a built-in bench two feet out from the back wall about twenty inches off of the floor with two oval shaped holes about sixteen inches long and twelve inches wide in it. The holes should be located so two people can sit side by side directly over them. Be sure the long sides of the holes are from the front to the back in the bench. Then you build a front on the bench that is watertight.

"Next," said Samuel, "you have to build in some kind of ventilation, or it will begin to smellin' pretty bad inside before too long. Two different kinds of ventilation should probably be used. One way is to drill holes, one half inch in diameter, in a pattern up close to the top on each side of the privy. That we'll do with a brace and bit. For the second type of ventilation, we'll git some stovepipe and put one end reaching down into the section under the seat. It'll be out of the line of fire. We'll have the other end reach up through and above the roofline at least two feet. Then we'll put screen wire over the top of the pipe, so birds won't fly down it. Finally, we'll get help and lift our new privy over the hole in the ground; needless to say, caution should be exercised here. Some people like to paint the outside as a finishing touch, but it isn't absolutely necessary."

Samuel and Cal didn't paint the small building with a regal throne inside. The exterior was built of slabs of wood with bark on them, so it wouldn't have painted well, anyway. The completion of the privy was cause for celebration. Another giant step had been taken in the Ledbetter's acquisition of worldly conveniences.

"Well, how do you like it, Mama?" asked Samuel. "Ain't it nice?"

"I'm sure proud of you menfolk," she replied. "Seems like you and Cal are always makin' my work easier or my day more enjoyable. What will you think of next?"

"I just heard the other day," said Cal, "about people in the big cities back east havin' toilets in their houses. Maybe that's what we should do next."

"How, pray tell, do they do that?" said Samuel. "Surely they don't cut holes in the floor of their house, do they? That doesn't make sense to me at all. Besides that, where would they put it and wouldn't it make the house smell somethin' awful?"

"You're not cuttin' any holes in the floor of my new house!" said Lillie. "I won't hear tell of it! Maybe you two have about given me all of these new-fangled contraptions I need for awhile."

"Don't fret none, Mama," said Cal. "Seems like these new-fangled inside toilets have pipes that take everything a long ways from the house and leave it underground. Of course you have to have water piped into the house to make it work."

"Well, you can get me water in the house any time. I'd like that. Maybe a nice pitcher pump from a cistern. You can just forget about a toilet in my house, though. I won't have any part of it!"

"Actually," said Samuel, "an outside toilet is more convenient, anyhow, when you're workin' around the barn. Let's just leave things be. God never intended for decent people to go to the toilet inside the house, anyhows. If he had, he wouldn't have made it smell so bad."

"Next thing you know," said Cal, "they'll be a washin' clothes in the house. I can see it now. There'll be water everywhere."

"It would be nice, though," said Lillie, "to be able to do the washin' without going outside all of the time."

Fruit trees grew in abundance behind the barn. Maybe they would bear fruit this year; at least the pear trees might. You had to plant more than one of every kind of fruit tree. There was something about the trees having to cross-pollinate each other, the Ledbetters had heard. Otherwise, the trees wouldn't bear fruit. So, even before they built the house, they planted apple, peach and pear trees. At least they might see fresh fruit before too many years. Of course there were mulberry trees growing everywhere. Then there were blackberries growing where the men had cleared a road to reach the river. As it took so long to pick enough blackberries when she wanted to make a cobbler real fast, Lillie would sometimes mix mulberries in with the blackberries to make a bigger cobbler. You had to be careful, though; if you got too many mulberries, it wouldn't taste near as delicious.

Down along the river were lots of pecan trees, which meant they could fix pecan pies whenever they wanted. Pecans didn't spoil if they weren't eaten right away. You just had to pick them up off of the ground and put them in gunnysacks for later use. A side benefit to all of the fruit trees was the beautiful aromas they gave off when in full blossom, especially the apple trees. The nose tickled by the delightful fragrance of an apple blossom was a happy nose. Maybe it was just the thought of the apple pies and cobblers she would someday enjoy, but Lillie knew she would love the smell of apple blossoms even if there weren't going to be any apples growing on the trees in the near future.

Lillie swelled up with pride at the world in and outside of her windows. When they were open in the springtime, she could smell the fresh air, which was so clear and clean smelling, especially after a summer rain. Maybe next year the air would also be filled with the smell of the blossoms from the fruit trees. Already she enjoyed the sounds of the bluebirds singing happily in the trees. Just watching the gentle sway of the curtains in the kitchen on a hot afternoon made her feel cooler. Can it possibly get any better than this? she asked herself.

The dream world of Samuel and Lillie started to shatter in 1913. Just five days before young Clevon's fifth birthday in October, Abe passed away in Bokchito. This was a most distressing time for the family. When Led had died six years earlier in Texas, it didn't hit home so hard. This was partly because Samuel and Lillie didn't even hear about the death until well after the funeral. But Abe was right here among them. Why, he and Samuel had worked together only last week, when Abe came over to see how the cotton was looking. The saddest part, though, was the fact that Abe was only thirty-one years old. Lillie was especially saddened, not only because Abe was her favorite brother-in-law, but also because he meant so much to Samuel. Also, he was married to her cousin, Jenny Shaughnessy. Abe's funeral was held in Hominy Corners School in commemoration of all his many fine contributions to the community and the school. No one would miss him more than Jenny and their children, the neighbors thought. What everyone didn't know was how much Abe had meant to Samuel who would grieve for a long time for his departed brother. Why, Abe had been with him when he first met Lillie. Only the four brothers would ever really understand the bond they had developed when leaving Tennessee; now only two of them remained.

By now, Abe's lone son, Carter, was only sixteen years old. He was able to do many of the jobs on the farm, but he just wasn't ready to assume responsibility for the total farm operation. All of the other Ledbetters and Shaughnessys helped out in every way they could to get the farm work done. Samuel and Cal spent all of their spare time in helping to get the harvesting done. Cal often stayed overnight, so as to be sure and get a full day's work done in the fields. Cotton picking time was when most of the help was needed.

Abe and Samuel had both been members of the Woodmen of the World, a fraternal organization expending efforts for people in need. Now it was time for Abe's family to receive help. The Woodmen had a number of members putting in long hours to help get the crops out of the field. Samuel, though, felt an obligation to do all he could for Abe's family in addition to being a member of the Woodmen. He took seriously the Biblical admonition that he was his brother's keeper.

Jenny was lost in her bereavement. She didn't know what to do or where to turn. Realizing Jenny's need for assistance, Lillie made a special trip over to talk with her.

"What will you do now, Jenny? Have you made any special plans?" asked Lillie.

"I don't know," replied Jenny. "Abe always took care of everything. I just did the cookin', sewin' and other things needin' done around the house. He made all of the decisions. I'm afraid I know nothin' about how this farm is run."

"What about the place? Can Carter keep it goin'?" asked Lillie.

"I really don't know. He's so young for so much responsibility. I wish I knew more what to do, but I don't. A woman just can't make it alone out here in the country. Without my Abe here, I just don't know what I'll do."

"Well, the Lord giveth and the Lord taketh away. I'm sure the Good Lord will provide now. We just don't know what form the providin' will take. Be assured, though, he will provide."

Jenny never ceased grieving Abe's death. At times, it seemed like more than she could bear. She tried to hang on, but she just was not able to keep the farm. It seemed like she lost even more of Abe's memory, when she had to let the farm go. What was the worse blow of all, however, was when she had to put all of the children in an orphanage in Pryor. How would she be able to survive knowing they were alive, but she couldn't address their daily care? She thought she could make it with Carter and Evie, who was now thirteen years old, helping her. But even this arrangement wasn't to be. They all had to go into the orphanage. Everyone went, including Ruthy, who had just turned five, and Wilma, born just two months before her father's untimely death.

"We can't let those young ones go into that orphanage," Lillie told Samuel.

"I don't know what we can do about it," her husband replied. "We don't have room for four more kids in this here house. It's bigger than we ever had, but it's not that big. That would mean eight kids in that bedroom. Besides that, Cal and I sure can't farm their farm as well, even with Carter helpin' us"

"Well, maybe we could take the two little ones," said Lillie.

"Now don't go talkin' about splittin' those kids up," her husband admonished her. "It ain't right."

"I suppose you're right," responded Lillie. "But lettin' them go into the orphanage isn't right, either. It isn't what the Bible requires."

"I'll make you a promise, then," said Samuel. "If all is well for us in five years, we'll get those kids back from Pryor. Even if we have to add room on to this here house, we'll do it."

"I'm not goin' to forget your promise," said Lillie.

Lillie was especially moved by the community's response to Abe's death and the events that followed. She could see how lost Jenny was without her beloved husband. Jenny's grieving was a slow and painful process; Lillie knew that the pain had to occur. All of the help in the world would not bring Abe back. Life was never to be the same for Jenny again. One generally becomes hardened to death on the frontier. It was a part of life you couldn't escape. But, when it occurred right in your own family, you realized that life was indeed short. Take Samuel, for example, he was approaching fifty years of age. This was longer than many of the men on the frontier lived. Were his days numbered, she wondered? He was the picture of health, and they were getting more prosperous all of the time. Maybe he should sit back and take it a little easier now. It was obvious that Cal would soon be able to take care of the place. Lillie put the thoughts of death out of her mind. She just could not dwell on the possibility that something might happen to Samuel, or to anyone else in the family for that matter. Granted, Ethel and Walter had died in infancy. But a mother knew better than to think all of her children would survive to be adults.

The next two years following Abe's death were good years on the farm. Samuel and Cal harvested bumper crops. Also, the prices for their wheat and cotton were high. This was a most unusual combination. Usually, if you had good crops, the prices were low, and vice-versa. But these were good times. The Ledbetters had money for an occasional luxury, and there was talk of adding onto the house. They even bought Mom a new Majestic wood-burning cook stove, more because they could afford it than that they really needed one; it cost less than $20, a tidy sum in these days. It had a nice, big firebox in it, so you could cook more things at one time. "So when we bring Abe's kids to live with us,' Samuel had said.

There were even six eyes on the stove. These were little round lids, right over the firebox, which you could remove with a detachable handle. That way, if the fire was already going, you could heat a pot of beans more quickly. You would just remove one of the eyes and put the pan directly over the fire. It thrilled

Lillie to have such a modern appliance right in her own kitchen. Why, it even had a compartment up on top where already-cooked foods could be kept warm, while other parts of the meal were still cooking. Some women called it a warming compartment. Better yet, the top of the stove was big enough to put a large griddle on it for pancakes.

If you wanted more heat for something being cooked, just move it to the back of the stove. If the stove wasn't hot enough in the first place, the solution was real simple, just put some more wood in the firebox. Lillie couldn't get over her new stove; with such a modern convenience, she and Myrtle would be cooking numerous mouth-watering pleasures like peach cobblers and mincemeat cakes. The menfolk would surely appreciate such efforts. Jewell helped out in the kitchen once in awhile, but she was quite content to let others do the cooking.

Maybe, now that they had a new stove, Lillie reasoned, Jewell would become more interested in cooking. She surely hoped so. With luxuries she couldn't even imagine as little as ten years earlier, the ultimate in lifestyles had now been achieved for Lillie. Well, if they just had a better way to clean clothes besides a scrub board and a kettle in the back yard, she decided, heaven on earth would have been achieved.

CHAPTER VII

The Ledbetter family's life was continually changing. Not only did they have more conveniences, but the opportunity was there for a wider range of recreational activities. That is they could if the activity didn't conflict with their beliefs of right and wrong. One event Cal would never forget happened in 1915. He went to his first circus. It was just across the river in Bonham, Texas. He had seen pictures of elephants in books at school, but it was hard to believe such a large animal truly existed. By now a new ferry had begun operating south of Yuba City, Oklahoma. This made Bonham less than 20 miles away. He could be there in a few hours. By staying overnight, he could enjoy himself with no limitation. Samuel didn't like his son missing so much time in the fields, but he could see Cal wanted to see those strange animals in the worst way. Therefore, no serious objection was raised to Cal missing out on working in the cotton fields for a couple of days.

"I don't want to see you makin' a habit of this, son," he had said. "A man's responsibility is to see that the work is done first."

"I've been workin' hard, Pa. I just need some time to have fun. Seems like the only thing we get done is work when I'm here on the place. The hoein' is caught up for now, and I need to get away for awhile."

"I know you do, Cal. Can't say as I blame you. Just don't forget your duties here on the farm."

"I won't, Pa."

"Could you pick me up some fresh chewin' tobacco while you're near a store? I seem to be runnin' low."

Arriving in Bonham, Cal proceeded to hunt for a place to get a drink. Something stronger than iced tea was what he had in mind. In his search for a suitable dispenser of strong beverage, he soon found the town was a frenzy of activity with so many festivities going on at the same time. The streets were crowded as pedestrians left the confines of the wooden sidewalks. Realizing that it might be hard to find a room, he paid early with the desk clerk at the Alexander Hotel. The price seemed especially high, but he paid the amount they asked with a silver dollar. No change was forthcoming, but he expected none. After all, his recreational trips were infrequent, so he might as well splurge. Also, this was considered by many to be the finest hotel in Bonham. He could have stayed for free a few miles away with one of his cousins in Ivanhoe. But Cal never wanted to be too far away from the center of activity. No, he would be right in the middle of all the festivities.

The parade was starting soon, so he found a spot to his liking in front of Clendenens Grocery Store. In no time there was little standing room left. He tried to stand so he wouldn't block anyone's line of vision. Off in the distance he could hear a band playing, especially the drums. It was time for the parade. Excitement was at a feverish pitch. While Cal enjoyed all of the hoopla, he didn't know how well he liked the hot sun beating down on his head. Good thing he was wearing a hat. He sunburned easily. Maybe he should have stood in front of a store with an awning. Well, it was too late now to change.

In no time the circus animals from the Ringling Brother's Circus came into view. Cal couldn't believe his eyes. There were the elephants, all in a row. Can you imagine it? They looked like they were tied together with the trunk of one holding the tail of the one in front of them. It was a good thing he'd seen pictures of elephants at school as a youngster. Otherwise, he'd think some strange kind of rope was tying them together. It could have been embarrassing; he'd have made a fool of himself.

Then the strangest thing began to happen. The heavy circus wagons, some being pulled by elephants, were breaking through the new pavement Bonham had just added to their streets. Not bothered, they just kept right on moving. This was also Cal's first experience with paved streets. He wasn't impressed. Dirt or gravel streets would never have had that problem! Still, he enjoyed seeing the lions and tigers in the cages on the colorful wagons parading before him on that noisy thoroughfare. Even more enjoyable were the organ grinder and his monkey, because they came up close for everyone to see.

Cal was a little apprehensive at first when the small animal with a brightly colored hat paused before him. Quickly dropping a penny into the tin cup, he stepped back to observe the continually moving bundle of arms and tail.

"I wonder if he'd be of any use on the farm?" he asked the man in bib overalls standing next to him.

The man answered, "Well, he is nimble, and he is quick, but he's awful scrawny. Besides, he'd probably just chase the chickens."

"Even that'd be better than some of our roosters," said Cal. "Do you reckon he could pick cotton?"

"Only if he had one of those big apes in that cage to pull the cotton sack," was the reply.

"I'd far rather have another brother," said Cal. "That bundle of fur acts too much like a girl for me."

Cal thoroughly enjoyed himself on that trip to Bonham. His world was greatly expanded from all he'd seen and done. He'd have to go to the circus again sometime, if he had a chance. He especially loved the high-wire acts. He couldn't imagine how the acrobats could be so peaceful, as they soared through the air. He knew that when he tried swinging upside down from a rope in the barn, he always felt faint and almost blacked out. No, it was much more fun to watch someone else do it. It was considerably safer to sit in the stands and munch popcorn, which he dearly loved, as to participate in such a dangerous vocation. When he wasn't eating popcorn, he was munching hot, fresh roasted peanuts. A sack lasted forever as he slowly cracked each pod to remove the delicious morsel.

Cal even enjoyed watching the elephants pushing the giant poles into place to hold up the huge tent before the circus started. Come to think of it, there wasn't anything he didn't like about the circus. It's a good thing he went to the circus when he did, though. A dispute arose between the city of Bonham and Ringling Brothers Circus over payment for the damage done to the streets by the heavy wagons and the elephants. Ringling Brothers never had another performance in that fair city south of the Red River.

Nineteen hundred and fifteen was the best year ever on the Ledbetter farm. The cotton fields approached solid white, as the yield was so bountiful. The other crops looked equally as productive. Fall foliage was evident throughout the bottomlands. Normally they would be picking cotton by now, but the fields were just too wet from all of the rain. The wheat crop, resembling a golden sea, had been harvested before the rains started. Now, though, it was just too muddy to pull the cotton sacks through the fields. This particular day the sun was shining, however. That didn't mean you could pick cotton. It almost always took longer than one day for the fields to be passable after a rain.

There was time to go dancing, however. Word was out that there was going to be a "Nigger picnic" by Hominy Corner School on Saturday night. Cal went by way of the Shaughnessys in the event one of his cousins might want to join the journey promising fun and fare for all attending. Upon arriving at the Shaughnessy home, he discovered that the older boys had left earlier than anticipated. Therein was a problem, after promising their folks that they would take their twelve-year old sister, Jimmie, with them, the brothers had slipped away. Now, Jimmie was most upset, to say the least. She was too young to dance very often, but if allowed to attend she would be an eager participant in all of the festivities.

Recognizing the look of desertion in her eyes, Cal asked, "Would you treat me with the pleasure of your company?"

Jimmie didn't need a second invitation; "I'm ready to go. I've got my bonnet, and my dancin' shoes are on my feet," she replied.

"Is it alright with your folks?" he asked.

"Just don't let her even get close to any alcohol or wild folks," answered Mrs. Shaughnessy.

"You got my promise on that."

"Time's a wastin'," said Jimmie. Sitting in front of Cal, she grasped the saddle-horn tightly. "Now don't let me get thrown off."

This was the typical Cal; it didn't bother him to take the younger set to outings. He was just like his father in this respect; he would do most anything for kids. Every place he went, he would always take time to spend with the children of the house. The opportunity for romping, wrestling, and rolling on the floor was rarely turned down by this gangly farmboy who was a child at heart.

Now, if you want to go someplace where people know how to have fun, just go to a Nigger picnic. Jimmie could tell you; merely ask her. The Niggers would build one or more elevated platforms up off of the ground. It was simple to do. They would simply cut off some trees that were in close proximity to each other. However tall you wanted the dance floor off of the ground dictated how high you left the tree stumps. Then, you'd build the dance floor on top of the stumps, with steps rising the required distance. Big dances utilized multiple stages, sometimes several yards apart.

Dancing completely captivated Jimmie's attention. She sat on a bucket of syrup with her elbows on her knees and her chin cupped in her hands. She was enthralled with the dancers spinning around the floor. Cal certainly didn't need to worry about her. She knew how to have fun, too! If she tired of watching one platform, she'd merely go to the adjoining one. You couldn't see anyone not having a thrilling time. Occasionally, a drunk would wander by, and you'd have to get out of the way. Otherwise, the pleasure seemed to go on forever.

There weren't too many drunks at these affairs. That's because they drank Choctaw beer, and everyone knew the alcoholic content of this beer was quite low. As a matter of fact, if they really wanted to get a "buzz on," they'd have to drink some hard liquor, which most of the picnic goers didn't have. Choctaw beer was homemade, so if you wanted any, you had to make your own. Oklahoma, you see, was a dry state. This meant the law forbade making or selling alcoholic beverages. This included beer, as well as corn liquor. You had to be real careful when you made your own home brew, though. Being caught by the authorities likely meant you were destined for big trouble. The officers of the county not only broke up your still, but they generally locked you up as well.

Choctaw beer had a different flavor with each batch. To expect otherwise was futile as the brewer put in whatever fruit was available at the moment to help in the fermenting process. While apples were considered the best ingredient, pears or peaches might also be used singly or in combination. You would peel the fruit, then let both the peelings and the fruit dry out in the sun. A porch railing was the ideal repository for this stage of preparation. Later, the shriveled products would be added to a mixture of barley, sugar and boiling water. Allowing adequate time for the fermentation to occur meant the beer was ready for consumption. Some people would just leave the beer in the barrel or tub and hang a tin cup where it would be easy to sample the finished product. Anyway, everyone developed a taste for Choctaw beer. Everyone, that is, except Jimmie. Otherwise, the beverage flowed freely at the Nigger picnics.

The dancing would go on for hours. There would be people playing guitars, mandolins, fiddles and banjos. Occasionally, one of these instruments would be homemade. If so, it was generally the banjo made out of a cigar box with fox hide stretched over it. What the musicians lacked in skill, they made up for in volume. Cal picked a guitar as well as anyone, so he was a welcome sight at these festivities. He picked his guitar for every dance, except one saved at mid-point for Jimmie. She held her flowing dress out with her left hand as he swung her around the uneven floor.

"Dance the next dance with me, too, Cal." she asked.

"They really want to hear me pluck those strings," he answered.

"Just one more, and I'll be happy for the rest of my life."

"Well, just one more, but after that you promise me that you'll just watch. Maybe you could dance with one of your brothers."

"I'd rather dance with you," she said. "You're more fun."

Lillie really didn't care for Cal going where there was so much alcohol flowing. However, he was over twenty-one, so she held her tongue. He could always be found in the midst of festivities, farm work permitting, especially if it included music.

Most of the Hominy Corner residents traveled to Bokchito or Wade to attend church. A small but devout group calling itself the Brethren of the Divine Holiness used the Hominy Corners Schoolhouse for Sunday services. During the services they referred to the building as their "Tabernacle." Considered the leader of this congregation, despite his young age, was Brother Ishmael "Fire and Brimstone" Thomas. He was called Brother Thomas to his face, though. No one liked to incur his wrath.

"Oh my, Cal, what have you been up to now?"

"Whadda ya' mean Mama?"

"Here comes Old Fire and Brimstone himself."

"Well tell him I'm not at home. He's the last guy I want to see right now!"

"I'm afraid you're too late, son. He's done seen you."

"Well, hi, Brother Ishmael. How're ya'll doin'?"

"I'm not here to pass the time of day, Ma'am. I need to talk to that rogue son of yours. Sure as all git out, he's a headin' fer hell with his sinful ways!"

"Pray tell. What are you talkin' about Brother Ishmael?"

"I have it on good authority that he up and took a young girl to that Nigger picnic the other night. Such carousin' is a certain ticket to hell!"

"Now Brother..."

"This is me he's rantin' and ravin' about Mama! I'll take care of this! First off, mister! This is none of your business. Secondly, I took my cousin to a perfectly legitimate affair. Thirdly, it was with her folks' blessin'. So you just git offa yer high horse while you can still see the ground. And I'll thank ya' kindly if ya'd leave my family alone. Now git!"

"You ain't heard the last of this, Sinner Cal!" he said, as he wheeled his horse around and rode away.

"Yes, and some day you and me's a gonna have us one fine go round. I look forward to the day!"

"I really wish you wouldn't make him so mad son," said Lillie, as she watched her son's tormentor exit the scene.

"He was mad before he got here," said Cal. "He'd be better off mindin' his own business."

"Still," she replied, "I'd rather he wasn't singlin' us out for his wrath."

It seemed like it would never quit raining that fall of 1915. It was the coming January before they could even get into the cotton fields to do the picking. Everyone in that part of Oklahoma worried about whether or not they'd ever get that fine crop harvested. It would be a shame to lose such a bumper crop with the prices so high. Samuel and Cal worked every possible minute available to them during the harvest. Hominy Corners School was closed so everyone could help in the harvest. You could always go to school. Right now, though, the important thing was to get the cotton in as quickly as possible. Clevon was only seven years old, but anything he could pick would be that much more. They were slow and methodical picking the cotton; you couldn't get the three to speed up if you tried.

"There's no need raisin' such a fine crop," Samuel said, "if you aren't goin' to harvest it right. Cotton only makes money when it's delivered to the cotton gin."

"Can't we pick even more," Cal asked, "if we do the easy part now and come back later for the rest?"

"No, we'll do it right the first time," his father responded.

Oh, it was cold for this time of year. It finally got so bad that the men started building fires at the ends of the fields, so they could get warmed up at the end of a round. A round was having picked one row to the other end of the field, then picking another row back. Sometimes Samuel would pick two rounds before taking a break.

The hours were long and tiring. Cal and Lillie noticed that Samuel just didn't seem to have his full strength anymore. Lillie tried to get him to leave the harvest up to the children. Samuel wouldn't hear of it. It wasn't right, he said; he had to do his part, too. Finally, Samuel could do no more. By February seventh he couldn't even get out of bed. There was no more fighting Lillie. He had pneumonia. There was no need going to a doctor, he insisted. Just let him rest in bed for awhile. It hurt Lillie deeply to see such a strong man in bed lacking the strength at times to even turn over. She kept insisting that Cal go for the doctor, but

Samuel always won out. After a few days it looked like Samuel was right; he was starting to look better, and his color was returning. Now he would occasionally sit in the front room in his rocking chair, where he liked to rock the children when they were small as he looked out the window. He was trying to see how the picking was going.

When Clevon and Cal came in at dark on Tuesday, he asked, "How's the harvest a goin'?"

"We picked close to a wagon load today," answered Cal. "Of course the mud does slow us down at times."

Samuel was pleased to hear that the work was progressing without him. "When do you think the harvest might be over?"

Cal didn't have the heart to tell him that it was going extremely slow without his father's help. "Well, it all depends on the weather. If the good Lord is willin', and we don't see anymore moisture in the fields, we might finish up by late March. Of course I could make better time with you, but I don't want you out of this house until you're well. Clevon and I will do just fine. We're just slower is all. He's goin' to make a fine cotton picker when the time comes. Right now the two of us will do just fine. I can't ask for any more than that."

"Well, you tell me if I need to be out there with you. A man has no business lookin' out the window with work needin' done. No, he has no business at all."

Just when it looked like Samuel was doing real well and would soon be back in the fields, he came down with diarrhea. There was no medicine Lillie could give her emaciated husband for relief, so it looked like he would just have to suffer through the terrible malady. Samuel's color returned to its previous pale tint. His cheekbones were more obvious with each passing day. The Ledbetters had heard that blackberry juice would help, but it only served to stain his clothing.

"It doesn't even taste good, and I like blackberries," said the beleaguered farmer.

"Maybe some of my hot biscuits might help," said his wife.

"Yes they would, but not right now, Lillie."

On February 14th of 1916 Lillie could see Samuel was deteriorating more rapidly. No treatment she tried was slowing the steady demise of her husband of twenty-four years. To continue with home remedies would be to ignore the seriousness of his condition. His resistance was feeble when she sent Myrtle to fetch her older brother.

Upon arriving in the field following her run across the rows of cotton, Myrtle's coat was torn; at first she lacked the wind to speak. Cal and Clevon were so busy that they didn't see her approaching. The earmuffs further restricted their hearing.

Cal looked up to see Myrtle at the last minute. "It's Dad, ain't it?" he said.

"Dad's a lot worse! Mama says you better ride for help!" she said.

Without pausing, Cal unhitched Jenny and headed for Bokchito. Lack of a saddle was the least of his worries. He'd just have to hope Doctor Winters had a horse ready to ride the return trip.

"Dad's awful sick! You have to come now, Doc!"

Pausing only long enough to discern acknowledgement from the physician, Cal dashed from the office. Kicking the mule in the flanks, he headed south as fast as the mule would run. This was the shortest time he'd ever needed to cover the four miles from Bokchito.

Cal knew by the looks on the faces of Myrtle and Clevon that he was too late. They didn't need to tell him what had happened, as he jumped from the mule. Daddy was gone. They said he was just sitting up in his rocking chair, when all of a sudden, he toppled onto the floor. When Doctor Winters arrived, he said that Samuel's heart could have withstood either condition separately but not combined. The dream of Samuel and Lillie was over, shattered on the linoleum of the front room floor. What had started over twenty-four years earlier, with so much promise, had come to an end. Samuel was dead at the age of fifty-six. There would be no more bear hugs or friendly smiles; there would be no more hard work from a man who thrilled at what his hands wrought; there would be no more teaching from someone who loved to show others how to do something. Finally, there was to be no further physical assurance that the gentle patriarch was by your side. Daddy was gone.

Some say that Lillie's world ended that cold February day. She had been through hard times before and had survived adversity. She had even managed to cope with the deaths of two of her children. But, she had survived all of these adversities because Samuel was by her side. Now, she asked herself, who will be at my side when I don't know what to do or where to turn? The memories of Jenny's plight following Abe's passing tormented her. Will it ever be worse than this, she thought. If so, her mind couldn't comprehend how she might cope with another tragedy.

It wasn't unusual for the weather to be cold in February, but this February day was colder than usual. Samuel was well loved by everyone. The school in Hominy Corners was crowded with mourners wanting to pay their last respects by attending his funeral. Many farmers stopped their cotton picking, even though a delay was ill advised at this time. All of the Ledbetters and Shaughnessys were in attendance, taking up over half of the seating space. Many little children attended the service. Samuel would have wanted it that way. He had loved children dearly and had wanted many grandchildren.

Funeral services are bad enough when the weather is nice. But they are especially depressing when the weather is bad. The preacher tried to say words that he felt Lillie and the family would find comforting. He talked about God's desire to help families experiencing the death of a loved one. Most of his words were to no avail. Lillie just wanted to see the service over. Nothing done or any words said would ever bring back her beloved Samuel. He was gone forever.

There were only two things Lillie remembered about the funeral service due to her bereavement. They were the singing of a new song, "In the Garden," and the reading of the Twenty-third Psalms. Everything else was a total blank for her. These words would always have a special place in her heart:

"1. The Lord is my shepherd;

I shall not want.

2. He maketh me to lie down in green

   pastures:

   He leadeth me beside the still waters.

3. He restoreth my soul:

   He leadeth me in the paths of

   righteousness

   for his name's sake.

4. Yea, though I walk through the valley

   of the shadow of death,

   I will fear no evil:

   for thou art with me;

   thy rod and thy staff they comfort me.

5. Thou preparest a table before me

   in the presence of mine enemies:

   Thou annointeth my head with oil;

   my cup runneth over.

6. Surely goodness and mercy shall follow me

   all the days of my life:

   and I will dwell in the house of the

   Lord forever.

The Woodmen of the World made a special tombstone for Samuel's grave. It was about six feet high with the stone shaped to resemble the trunk of a tree with knots in several places. The lines resembling bark were clearly visible. While the words sounded harsh, Lillie found some consolation in the wording the marker contained. "A Christian can not die before his time." To her this meant there was some divine purpose in his passing. Hopefully, she would someday know what that purpose might be.

With his father's passing, Cal felt he had lost the best friend he ever had. There would be a void never to be filled again. Because he didn't want others to see, he would sometimes go into the loft of the barn to spend some quiet time in his thoughts. Often he would feel a dampness in his eyes following these interludes of quietness in the still of the day. With the smell of hay ever around him, he would recall the happy times spent with his father. Samuel had taught him so much. For this he would be eternally grateful. As much as Cal knew about farming, he knew he couldn't continue alone. He needed the feeling that his father was still by his side.

On one excursion into the loft after a hard day in the fields, he lifted his eyes towards heaven and said ever so quietly, "Daddy, I can't do it without your help. I hope you'll be beside me when I'm workin'. Lord knows you taught me all about farmin', but we always done things together. You always told me how much you liked me workin' at your side. Well I never told you, but I felt the same way. Would you do something for me? Would you tell me when I'm doin' wrong? Just give me some sign. I'll know it's you. I'd be forever grateful for all of the help I can get. I'll be a talkin' to you again sometimes. Thanks Daddy. Oh, yes, and could you help Mama, too, Daddy. She's grievin' real bad with your passin' and all. She's not real sure what she's goin' to do. I'm not so sure myself. I know I can't take your place for Clevon, so would you watch over him as well? Seems like we all need your help, Daddy. We're never goin' to forget you, cause we love you so much. I guess I never told you that I loved you, did I? Well, I do and don't you forget it. I'll be talkin' to you more later on. Oh, by the way, could ya git old Fire and Brimstone Thomas offa my back?"

CHAPTER VIII

Cal had been a grownup for over ten years now. No living soul knew more about the running of the Ledbetter farm than he did. It seemed natural that he would assume responsibility for the operation of the farm. This extra accountability didn't always leave much time for going to dances, but the farm work was always done. Lillie was right proud of her Cal. Of course Clevon could always help with the farm work, and he did when he wasn't in school. Jewell helped out in the fields, when she wasn't in school or helping Mom in the kitchen. Myrtle had married by now and she didn't come around much anymore. She and her husband, Wilson Whatley, had their own lives to live.

Cal, just like his father, was a most friendly sort. He still found time to "socialize," just not the traditional form of socializing. One thing he found considerable joy in was visiting family members. Some times he would linger and end up staying overnight. He always found time to play with the kids. Everyone could tell Cal would someday want lots of children. He just wasn't content without several being around him. He and his brother-in-law sometimes discussed his future.

"When you gonna get married, so you can have young ones of your own?" Wilson would ask.

"Oh, one of these days," would be Cal's reply.

"What do you mean one of these days? You're not getting any younger, you know."

"Well, it scares me," said Cal.

"What scares you?" asked Wilson. "Women are okay, once you get to know them."

"It ain't that," said Cal.

"Well, pray tell, what is it, then?" asked Wilson.

"I just don't want to see a mother and children git left behind when the father passes away. Look at Aunt Jenny and now Mama. Things are tough for them. It isn't fair. I just don't want to see me cause that to happen to someone."

"Look," said Wilson, "you have to think about the good side, not the bad. My dad's gone, your dad's gone. So's your Uncle Abe and Uncle Led. None could help it. That's just the way things are. No one said it would be any different. You take life as it comes. Do all you can for your family while you're alive. No one can ask any more. That's the joy of life, taking care of your family. The other joys of life like having someone take care of you sometimes is just one of the extras that helps to make it all worthwhile."

"You mean I shouldn't worry none about my family's future?"

"No, that isn't what I'm a saying at all," said Wilson. "A man does worry about his family after he's gone. He sets aside so as they're taken care of, if he can. Abe wasn't able to do that like he wanted. But he tried. Lord knows he tried. That's all we can do."

Still, even with Wilson's encouragement, Cal did not see fit to get married. He was content to continue living with Lillie while taking care of the family farm. Of course he would date once in awhile. Cal always had time for pranks, too, no matter what he was doing. You had to have some pleasure in this world, he always told Lillie. If it wasn't tipping over someone's outhouse, it was something else. One time he pulled a trick on himself before he realized it.

It was on a dark Halloween night when he saw an opportunity for a real prank. There was a buggy with a silhouette just like his parked in front of the neighbor's house. Now the owner should have had better sense than to park it there, Cal thought. Besides that, he wasn't even at home. Furthermore, there wasn't even a lantern shining anywhere in the house, and it was sufficiency dark that he wouldn't be recognized. The neighbor must have walked somewhere. Good, that way he'd have plenty of warning when the owners came home. Cal rounded up some of his friends. Fred and Willie seemed anxious to participate in the deed. In short order the three proceeded to disassemble the buggy. Then the devious crew reassembled it on the peak of the roof. This was no easy task. It required numerous trips carrying the pieces to the edge of the house and handing them up to the willing recipient hanging over the edge. First went the four wheels; next went the pole for the harness to hook onto. The hardest part was getting the box of the buggy up there. It felt like it weighed a ton. At least there was no top frame and the accompanying canvas to weight it down. Ropes made the effort easier. It was completely dark by now, so the owner wouldn't even know about it until morning.

"Boy, there's goin' to be one surprised owner when he finds this," said Cal.

"I'll say," said Willie. "I reckon we'll teach him to leave his wagon out like this."

"We've outdone ourselves this time," said Fred. "It's getting' harder to come up with something new each year. What do you suppose we'll figure out to do next year? The ultimate trick is to get the person being tricked to help carry the prank out. Now that's my idea of a good prank."

"How about we turn a cow loose to wander around inside the school building," responded Willie.

"Nah," said Cal. "If they ever find out who did it, we'll be a scrubbin' that school from top to bottom. I'm not lookin' for a job scrubbin' the school building right now."

Satisfied at a job well done, Cal and the others walked home. Cal was tired due to all of this hard work; bed was a welcome relief. Can you imagine his surprise when the sun came up in the morning?

Lillie awakened him with a question, "Where's your buggy, Cal?"

"Out behind the barn where I always park it. Why do you ask?"

"You better go take a look. "I'm not real sure what's goin' on here, but I've got a feelin' that somethin' right unusual has taken place."

Hurrying out behind the barn, Cal could not find his buggy. It was gone without a trace. Someone had taken his four-wheeled conveyance without his knowledge. Possibly it was a Halloween trick. Cal didn't even need to look for it, though. There was no doubt in his mind as to where he might find his buggy. Parts of that buggy had certainly looked familiar to him last night. I wonder when they took the top off, he thought to himself.

Cal tried to get Fred and Willie to help him get the buggy down, but they refused. While he struggled with the monumental task of retrieving the buggy, they sat on the school grounds and drank beer while laughing at his predicament. Such misfortunes, he later told Clevon, should not deter such escapades. Once in awhile, he continued, the tables are turned on you as well.

By 1918 it looked like things were beginning to return to normal on the Ledbetter place. Lillie worried, though, because the United States had become heavily involved in the "Great War" in Europe (later to become known as World War I). So many lives were being lost; could Cal be kept out of the conflict? He was now twenty-three years old, and they were drafting everyone in this age range. He had done such a good job with the farm. He was so much like Samuel, she thought, a conscientious worker no doubt. By the beginning of summer, the crops were all doing well. It would be another good year, no doubt about it. Now if Cal just gets to stay here to harvest it, she hoped.

Staying out of the war was not to be for Cal. In early summer, he was notified that "Uncle Sam" required his presence. He reported for duty in the United States Army at Durant on the twenty-fifth of July to await further orders. They soon came; shortly thereafter, he was transferred to Fort Polk, Louisiana, for further training. Most every day contained some time spent in learning to march in formation.

"I wonder why they insist on us bein' in nice, neat rows?" he asked the recruit next to him. "Everyone knows you hide behind rocks and bushes to fight."

"Well I hear tell," the young man answered, "that marching is the easiest way to teach people to follow orders. When you learn how to follow orders, they'll teach you how to fight. I reckin I'm ready to learn how to fight."

"You mean you're tired of marchin'. Well I'm not at all sure about fightin', so I'll keep on marchin' awhile longer. I'm not afraid to fight, but I want to be real sure before things git hot and heavy." returned Cal. "My mama says the Good Book says not to fight."

"Well even the Good Book had fighting in it!" spoke up the sergeant overhearing their conversation. "Now you two keep your eyes open and your mouths shut. Why those Germans will hear you coming for a mile when you get into combat."

Sounds like what my dad used to say when we went fishing, thought Cal.

The training for all troops included instruction in the use of weapons. Cal, however, had additional instruction in carrying litters for wounded troops needing medical attention. He left the United States on a troopship bound for Europe on September the twenty-sixth of 1918. This crossing was the hardest part of the war for Cal. There was always the worry that a German torpedo might sink the ship. Many an American serviceman had lost his life just this way during the war, and almost twelve hundred people had perished on May 7, 1915, when a torpedo sunk the Lusitania.

The crossing took ten days out of New York Harbor. The fear of being sunk was not all that bothered Cal. This was his first time to be anywhere but on solid ground; unless you counted Nigger picnics. The continual motion of the ship was most unsettling, to say the least. As soon as the ship righted itself from a roll to the right, it made an equal move to the left. In the mess hall was a gauge with a pointer showing how far the ship listed to each side. Watching the gauge during meals, Cal was convinced that one of these times it would just keep going in a complete revolution. Also, the ship was extremely noisy, especially if you were so unlucky as Cal was to be bunked aft near the stern where you could hear the ship's steam-driven propellers speed up to a roar as they came out of the water on a high wave.

The ship was almost to Europe before his stomach finally settled down. The only way, he found, that he could keep from vomiting after eating was to make sure every meal contained plenty of soda crackers. He even ate crackers for breakfast. Thank goodness his bunk in the seven-tiered set of hammocks was on the bottom and near the head (the naval term for restrooms). Otherwise, he'd never have been able to make his mad dashes to the head when he felt like throwing up.

While the trip took only ten days, it seemed like an eternity to Cal. As quickly as possible his unit was moved to the vicinity of the fighting. Cal was a model soldier. He never saw any actual combat, but he was always aware of the fighting going on. That was because he worked in Base Hospital #216, just outside of Paris. He played a vital role in helping treat the wounded soldiers being brought back from the front lines. Some nights he could hear the sounds of war. If it wasn't the sound of the artillery batteries he heard, it was the sound of the bi-planes of the allied forces flying over to drop explosives from an open cockpit behind enemy lines. Cal's exposure to the fighting was short lived. Less than two months after his arrival in France, on November 11, 1918, an armistice was signed. While the war was technically over, his unit remained in France until a treaty could be worked out in 1919.

Cal never fully understood America's involvement in the war. Even when he was told about the murder in June of 1914 of the Archduke Ferdinand, heir to the throne of Austria-Hungary, it didn't make sense to him. He felt President Wilson was right in trying to keep the United States neutral in an issue involving two small nations. He could understand America taking the side of England in the conflict, but why did all of the bigger nations have to get mixed-up in the affairs of Serbia and Austria-Hungary, anyway? It was not Cal's place to ask questions, however. A private's job was to follow orders.

Being out of Oklahoma, other than picking cotton in Texas, was a new experience for Cal. Even a newer experience was dealing with people who didn't share the same language. Other new experiences awaited this soldier as well. Take bathing. There was no galvanized tub in the middle of the floor in the living room. Actually, there was no living room either, and fresh water was at a premium. The only option was to improvise. On one occasion he and some of his buddies were using a lake for taking a bath. Facing reality, the lake looked so inviting. The water was clear blue. Of course, the water was also cold, downright chilly to be exact. But, it felt good to know that you were getting to clean your whole body all at once. Actually, the water was as cold as the runoff from a mountain glacier, but you'd be all right if you didn't stay in too long.

Before the soldiers, better known as doughboys, realized it, a group of French women congregated around the shore of the lake. Try as best they could, Cal and the other soldiers could not convince the women to understand to leave. Evidently they didn't realize the American soldier's need for privacy. As the sun slowly set in the west, the men could see the women weren't going to leave any time soon, and the benefit of the sun's warmth was rapidly declining.

"What's the matter with those women? Can't they see we're taking a bath?"

"Beats me. Maybe they never saw Americans before. At least ones that weren't carryin' a gun and fightin'."

"Well I hope they see enough pretty soon. I'm freezin' to death."

"Can't anyone here speak French?"

"French? I never knew there was such a place as France before this fool war started."

"What shall we do? We can't stay in here. Maybe someone will come lookin' for us. They can ask them to leave."

"Now you know whoever comes lookin' for us ain't goin' to talk French, either."

After considerable discussion, the soldiers decided they had no choice; if they stayed in the water, they would surely freeze to death. It is doubtful that anyone could have dressed faster than these soldiers dressed, especially when you consider they didn't even take time to dry off. Disappointed that the show was over, the French ladies went on their way. Cal was firmly convinced that modesty was not necessary for valor.

Living in a war zone unsettles even the strongest of heart. Being in the midst of large numbers of people, one can still be overcome with feelings of loneliness. Sometimes, when off-duty in his tent, Cal would have time to lay aside the turmoil around him and let his mind wander back to simpler times. For once in his life he felt impelled to put his thoughts into writing, as Mrs. Greenlau encouraged him to do. The recording of these memories made the difference in his being able to handle the reality of the worldwide conflict in which he now found himself. His thoughts reminded him:

"Of rolling hills
    and cooling breezes
Of a neighbor's help
    and nature's teases

Of clear blue skies
    and a bluejay's call
Of winding roads
    and cotton tall

Of a fallen tree
    and waving wheat
Of fresh baked pies
    and cold milk sweet

Of sharpened plows
    and stubborn mules
Of straight corn rows
    and hand held tools

Of a baby's laugh
    and a mother's love
Of a father's grin
    and a gentle shove

Of a boyhood dream
    and speeches stirring
Of a panting dog
    and a cat's soft purring

Of a Negro spiritual
    and a hard day's labor
Of a willing soul
    and an unasked favor

Of a teacher's wave
    and tickled feet
Of help from above
    and words so sweet

Of times gone by
and chances taken
Of no more war
and a faith unshaken

Sooner or later all conflicts must end. They can not go on forever. This is true whether it's an individual's inner battle or a global war, as the Great War was. World War I officially ended on the morning of November 11, 1918. Ultimately, the Treaty of Versailles was signed on June 28, 1919. Cal's inner strength, gained from an upbringing of differentiating right and wrong, along with his memories of a better time, had given him the fortitude to withstand trials of the body and soul, when he never fully understood the cause of the war in the first place. This conflict could not end too soon to please him. His place was not here. It was behind a plow in Oklahoma, more specifically Hominy Corners.

Private first class Caleb Ledbetter returned to the United States arriving at Mitchell Field on Long Island, New York, on the 9th of May in 1919. Three days later, while still being processed for discharge from the army, he sent his mother the following brief note:

"Well mother I think I will be home in about two weeks. I am well and hoping you are the same.

Your son,
Caleb Ledbetter"

Seven days later Cal was mustered out of the service. He received separation pay of $168.93, which included travel pay to Durant and a bonus of $60.00, as authorized by the Revenue Act of 1918. It was a good feeling to be free again. Now, Cal knew, he could go back to farming, which he so dearly loved. He just couldn't wait to once again set his feet on the red soil of Oklahoma. Being at Hominy Corners, on the family farm, would be the ultimate experience compared to recent events in his life. He couldn't wait.

While Cal was in France, Lillie realized that she was unable to handle the farm alone. Clevon had only turned ten years old the previous October, so he was not old enough to assume any responsibility. The Woodmen of the World had done all they could in helping to harvest the crops Cal had planted. They were just too short-handed with all of the able-bodied men being called up to serve in the war effort. Lillie had done everything she could to keep things together. The farm was the last thing, besides the children, she and Samuel shared together. She had hoped, since Samuel's death, the land could be passed on to Cal some day. Without knowing when the war would be over, or even if Cal was alive or coming home, Lillie knew she could no longer keep the farm. As one last resort, she consulted with a fortuneteller.

"What do you suppose has happened to Cal?" she asked.

"He's alive. I can feel it in my fingertips," the fortuneteller told her as she caressed the ball on the small, round table separating her and Lillie. "I'm sure that Cal will be returning safely from the war. The newspapers say the war is already over, you know."

Lucy just knew she was being deceived, as the fortuneteller was likely afraid to give her the bad news. In gratitude she gave the fortune teller Cal's new saddle. Obviously he wouldn't need it anymore. The fortuneteller lodged no complaints over this turn of events.

The war was not only difficult for the fighting forces overseas, but it was a difficult time for those maintaining the families and farms back home. Americans united behind the war effort. Such unity had not been seen since America's involvement in the Spanish-American War in 1898 resulting in Spain moving out of Cuba and the United States buying the Philippines for twenty million dollars. Americans not only bought Victory War Bonds, but they rallied public opinion behind the troops sacrificing so much, even their lives at times during this great war in Europe.

But lives were being lost stateside as well. In Texas and Oklahoma there was a flu epidemic claiming the lives of those unable to withstand the attack on their bodies by such a dreadful disease. Hominy Corners suffered along with everyone else. While Cal's immediate family survived this hardship, they were unable to cope with the reality that they couldn't manage the farm without his able leadership.

Lillie now determined that everything must be sold. Clevon couldn't handle the responsibility of the farm. A farm sale was held. A strange thing happened during the auction, however. The same man kept kept buying up each item placed on the block by the auctioneer. Wallace Stepford, a traveling peddler making his living from goods sold from the back of his wagon, later approached Lillie and said, "I've bought everything you owned except the land. I might as well take you, too."

Shortly thereafter, Lillie and Wallace Stepford were married on the nineteenth of April. It was less than one week before Cal would set sail from France to return home. Stepford's son, Benjamin, and Lillie's daughter, Myrtle, were in attendance. Neither of the two getting married wanted any fanfare. There was to be no farm to which he could return. The shattering of Lillie and Samuel's dream was now final.

PART TWO

The setting now moves to Hempstead County, Arkansas.

CHAPTER IX

Sadie's thoughts were clearly somewhere else. Keeping her attention on the matter at hand was seldom easy now. She had to be careful, though, in daydreaming like this. Clayton, her two and one-half year old son, was playing somewhere, likely in the bedroom. No telling what he might get into. Last week he had tipped over a bucket full of drinking water in the kitchen and she didn't have the time to clean it up again. Then yesterday he had scattered dominoes all over the linoleum in the front room. For awhile she didn't think she'd ever find all of them, and she knew how Papa loved to play dominoes. She enjoyed having Clayton around the house. He was good company to her when no one else was around; believe it or not, he could carry on what resembled a conversation if you talked of subjects close to his interests. His vocabulary was growing by the day. He would bring up questions when she least expected them.

"Bebe, have a bebe?" he might ask.

"Yes, Mama's going to have a baby."

"Bebe dink?"

"Yes, the baby will drink," she would answer.

"Bebe dink?"

"Yes, baby will drink water. But first it will drink milk."

Sometimes the conversation might last for a minute or more; then the little boy would go back to his play. He never seemed to stay at any one thing for an extended period of time.

Sadie was thrilled at the thought of having another baby. She and Carson Leon Cantrell had been married on the 17th of December in the year 1902. Clayton had been born the following year on December 31st. One of the first words he had spoken when he started to talk was the word, "Papa". Already everyone was starting to call Carson by his new title, Papa. Even though he was only 24 years old, she could see he enjoyed his new title. Her husband loved children; it was written in his every move around Clayton. Usually men didn't marry until they were much older, but he had no desire to delay the big event.

Samantha Lucille Quigley had been born and raised right here in Arkansas. She had always lived within the confines of Hempstead County. The only times she had even desired to leave the county were those two occasions when she and Carson had gone to Nevada County, once to get a marriage license and later to register the certificate after they were married. It was so much easier to go into Prescott, the county seat of Nevada County, as it was closer to where they lived in northern Hempstead County. Traveling on the wooden seat of a bouncing wagon that threatened to collapse her spine brought no smile to her lips. If it weren't so much fun to go to town, she'd rather have stayed home.

Arkansas was really the only life Sadie knew. She had never talked much to her parents about her heritage. Of more concern to the Quigleys was the immediate state of affairs, such as, will it rain tomorrow? What was going on today or tomorrow was far more important than the past. At least that was the impression she had from her folks. Besides that, they had taught her all about the nation's history at school. What more was there in American history that she needed to know, anyway? Papa had been born about thirteen years after the Civil War, and the memories of that war were best forgotten. Everyone knew that Washington, only a few miles away, had been the state capitol for the first two years of Arkansas's statehood starting in 1836. Now it was the county seat; of course, the town of Hope was always calling for an election, so they could become the new county seat.

Residents of Hempstead County had every right to be proud; there was plenty of heritage right here at home. She and Papa had good reason to be equally proud. They were living in a promising land with a bright future. She hoped nothing would ever change that. Furthermore, she could dream about the future of her family all she wanted. A fine family was the most she could ever want to hope for, she thought to herself.

I better go and check on Clayton, she reminded herself. That boy could get into more trouble than a one-armed paperhanger. If he wasn't taking their few utensils out of the lone cupboard in the kitchen, he was pulling out the boxes from under the bed. She didn't like to keep things stored there, but the house lacked closets. When she walked into the tiny room she and Papa called their bedroom, Clayton was nowhere to be seen. Before she started looking for him, she knew she'd best see if he'd respond to his name first. Sure enough, as soon as she called his name, his curly head suddenly appeared from under the bed like a jack-in-the-box. His face evolved into a wide grin upon seeing his mother. Reassured that all was well, she returned to the front room. Sadie just didn't feel like doing much today. The days when she tired easily were more frequent now. It wasn't wash day, and she was all caught up on her sewing.

Papa had gone to his mother's, as she and her husband needed help with a new mule they were trying to break for pulling in harness. Papa would do anything for his mother. Sadie was proud that he was so devoted to the one that bore him. How a man treated his mother was a good sign, she had often heard, as to how he would someday treat his wife. The saying was right; she'd vouch for that.

Without realizing it, Sadie slipped off into a deep sleep in the rocking chair. The blissful state brought a smile to her face thinking about when she and Carson had first met. It had been several years earlier, after she had finished grammar school. She had heard her folks talking about the new family moving in just down the road. Widow Cantrell, it seems, had moved there after her husband passed away in Peoria, Mississippi. Her folks, knowing she had no other family in the vicinity, felt it would be best if she moved closer to where they lived. Their only delay in moving was the sale of the family farm. The move was quite an accomplishment; once they were on the road, it had taken three weeks with a team of mules and a wagon, to get her and her two boys moved. To make matters worse, Widow Cantrell's father had died on the trail during the move.

Sadie remembered her folks mentioning that Widow Cantrell had such fine looking boys. They were a welcome addition to the area. Both boys looked like they weren't afraid of a day's work, either. Tanned from long hours in the sun, they were rarely seen during the workdays of the week but what they were in the process of completing yet another task. Carson was the older of the two, with Charlie only a couple of years younger. Later she had overheard her folks say that there was a shortage of marriageable men around. She wondered why they had chosen that topic of conversation. She didn't know anyone wanting to get married.

Widow Cantrell later remarried. She had met Mr. Taylor (Sadie had never heard his first name used-even Papa called him Mr. Taylor) at a church social. It wasn't long before they were married and his new wife and her sons joined him on his quarter-section farm. Widows generally had the hardest time getting by without a husband to help take care of things. At least that is what everyone thought. Mr. Taylor was a widower with seven children, three boys and four girls. It sure made a houseful, what with Carson and Charlie there, too. Carson told her that he never forgot his life out where the Taylors lived. You see, after his mother and Mr. Taylor married, the combined family moved to the town of Hope. The journey to visit them was quite difficult, as it was over twelve miles away. By then Carson was a grown man of sixteen years. He had finished grammar school in Hope a couple years earlier, so now was his chance to get back out in the country, which he dearly loved. He found a job doing farm work just up the road from the Quigleys.

Sometimes, when Sadie would ride into town with her mother on Saturday evening for supplies, she might see Carson at the general mercantile spending some of his hard-earned wages. Will he ever ask me to go to a church picnic, she had wondered? Sadie smiled again, as she thought back to the time Carson first asked her if he might court her. He was so shy that he almost couldn't talk. As a matter of fact, he came close to turning and walking away, before he could get up enough courage to say much of anything. Knowing he wanted to talk, she found excuses to keep her mother from leaving for awhile. "Could we look at their stock of new thread?" she had asked. It wasn't a church social that he asked her to, either. There was a box supper coming up at the Washington School next week, he had reminded her.

How could she forget, she had gone to school there. Everyone kept track of what was going on at the school. After all, other than school and church activities, there weren't an awful lot of other things to do. It hadn't taken her long to make up her mind, either; yes, she'd go! Box suppers were special to the farm families. It was a good way to raise money for something extra, such as new blackboards for the school.

"You will have to meet my pa first, though," said Sadie. "A girl can't begin a courting unless her pa says it's alright, and he won't say it's alright unless he meets the man first."

"I reckon I can meet him," said Carson. "What time should I pick you up?"

"Well, it's a mile to the schoolhouse, so we'll need plenty of traveling time. Why don't you pick me up about five o'clock?"

"That'll be fine," he answered. "I reckon I can keep good enough track of the time to do that. Good thing this isn't my night to milk the cows."

"You better be on time. Pa doesn't like to be kept waiting."

All of the womenfolk or girls would put together a special supper for two people and then put it in a box, along with silverware and fine, cloth napkins, like they were going to a picnic. Then they would wrap it up in the prettiest of paper. The more colorful the better. The object was to get the box to the school without anyone seeing the wrapping, so the box would be anonymous. All of the boxes were then displayed with their pretty "disguises" on a table at the front of the room, to be auctioned off to the highest bidder, who then got to eat supper with the lady or girl preparing the meal. When the bidding got underway, the intended or boyfriend of the girl fixing this veritable banquet in a box was prepared to bid high, as he didn't want someone else eating with his girl.

Everyone knew that the boy or man would find out which box was his lady friend's beforehand, so she wouldn't get away from him. What generally happened, though, was that as soon as he started bidding, everyone knew whose box it was. Then, they'd deliberately run the bid up on him, so he'd have to pay extra for the privilege of eating with her. It could be a costly proposition for a young man unwilling to allow someone else the privilege of eating with his intended. Of course, if you were an old married couple, you might welcome the chance to eat with someone different. The worst of all possible fates befell the individual finding out that that special someone had given him false information about her wrapping, because she didn't want to eat with him.

Anyway, Carson had saved up his money to be sure no one cheated him out of his chance to eat with Sadie that night. She knew, too, that this man who caused her to tingle in his presence was prepared to bid quite high. The thrill of anticipation was almost more than she could bear.

As auctioneers are notorious for doing, he always set the initial asking bid quite high. Sometimes a jittery soul would take that bid without realizing what he was doing. While Carson was jittery, at least he didn't fall for that old ploy. After the bidding was over, he shared with Sadie what an ordeal it had been as he vied for the opportunity to eat with her.

"Would you look at this pretty box?" the auctioneer said. "Isn't it a sight to behold with all of the red and silver wrapping paper on it? I'll bet there's a right nice young lady just a waiting on someone special to share the meal inside this here box. What am I bid? Do I hear ten dollars? Ten, ten, do I hear ten dollars?"

Carson remained silent. He didn't want to tip his hand too early. Besides that, he only had six dollars with him. This was the total sum of his wages from the last week. He'd sure hate to see someone else eating with Sadie tonight. Maybe he could borrow some money from someone, if the bidding went too high for him. But who was there that he might ask for a loan? Perhaps Mr. Taylor would loan him some money. Looking around, he couldn't see his stepfather or mother anywhere, and where was Charlie when he needed him the most?

"One dollar," sounded from the audience.

Carson's heartbeat quickened as he anxiously strained to see where the bid was originating. He decided to wait and see before giving his first bid. Maybe someone else thought this was their girl's box. He remembered Sadie's words as they passed at the back of the room. She had said, "Aren't red and silver the prettiest colors you ever saw?" He sure hoped someone hadn't overheard her. Worse yet, was he bidding on the right box?

"A dollar and a quarter!" rang out from the back. The voice sounded like someone sure of himself.

Carson was shaking; he could contain himself no longer. "Two dollars!" he shouted.

As soon as he said it, he knew he'd made a mistake. People would immediately guess his intentions by his jumping the bid so much. He felt a knot beginning to form inside his stomach, as perspiration beaded up on his forehead. He'd have been wiser to only raise the bid by 25 cents at a time. Boy, he thought, I hope I haven't made a mess of this. The knot was growing; his face was soon wet.

"Two-fifty!" rang out.

"Two-seventy-five!" shouted Carson.

"Three!" was the immediate reply from the back of the room.

Now Carson was worried. Who was he bidding against? Suppose he had all kinds of money. Carson hadn't planned on spending so much. It hadn't crossed his mind that someone else might bid so high. Maybe if he upped the ante even more, he'd scare off whomever else was bidding. What if it didn't work? I wonder where Mr. Taylor is, he thought to himself. He had no choice; he'd have to take the risk.

"Three-fifty!" Carson called out with a pained expression on his face, as he wiped his forehead with a large, red handkerchief, already damp from the dilemma occurring before his very eyes.

The room became silent, as the crowd waited for a responding bid. They loved these bidding wars. Not only did they mean more money raised for school equipment, but it was exciting to watch those young fellows in love trying their darndest to make sure no one cut in on their intentions of dining out with their girl. Even more exciting was to witness someone paying a high price only to discover that they were eating supper with someone other than the person they intended. Love did cause some foolish mistakes to occur. Maybe this was another one of those times.

"Three-seventy-five!"

At this Carson really became worried. Now what do I do, he thought. At this rate I'll soon be out of money. Can I go any higher? He had no idea courting was going to be so expensive. Lord please bestow thy mercy upon me, he silently prayed.

"Four dollars! Do I hear four dollars?" cried the auctioneer.

"Four dollars!" called out Carson.

"I'm sorry, young man, but you really shouldn't raise your own bid," said the auctioneer. "We'd like to have your money, but it really isn't fair."

Chagrined at his foolish mistake, Carson realized that his bid had not been raised. The auctioneer was merely trying to get that one last bid, as they always do. Hoping against all odds that the bidding was over, Carson scanned the room to see if another bid was forthcoming. Almost as important, he was hoping to see that Sadie hadn't witnessed his near bungling of such an important event. Under his breath he whispered a prayer. "Please Lord, don't let there be any more bids."

"Four dollars... Four dollars going once.... Four dollars going twice. Sold to the young man with the black moustache for the tidy sum of three dollars and seventy-five cents! My good friend, you have made the bargain of the evening. Enjoy your meal and the company of a pretty young lady. The school appreciates your money. Just try not to outbid yourself next time. Of course some ladies are worth that extra bid."

Carson couldn't disagree with the conclusion of the auctioneer. It was a real bargain for the pleasure of eating with Sadie. "Thank you Lord," he had uttered softly, as he went to pay the cashier. He was amazed at how quickly the knot disappeared from his stomach.

Going outside to eat under the shade of a large magnolia tree, the tablecloth was spread over a thin stand of grass to try and avoid the fine dirt that stirred easily into the air. The young companions wanted as much privacy as the well-attended event might offer them. Over a meal of fried chicken and potato salad, along with several other items including apple pie, Carson had told Sadie of his thoughts and concerns while the bidding was taking place. Now that he had the pleasure of her company, he had said, eating was second priority.

Sadie shared her concerns as well. “Boy, I was sure scared with that other fellow a bidding. Who was he, anyway? Whoever he was, I reckon I didn’t want to spend my evening with him.”

Even though the words were never spoken, this was the time, then, that they knew of their true feelings for each other. Love was the only thing that could nudge eating out of first place for a Cantrell. Carson and Sadie courted for some time. They knew that there would never be anyone else for them. Her folks were right fond of Carson, which made it easier to go out once in awhile. Once the two made up their minds to get married, however, there was no stopping them. The courtship had gone on long enough. On the 16th of December they picked up their wedding license in Prescott. They were married the very next day by J.W. Harris, a Justice of the Peace.

Only the parents of the couple were present. Carson had stated more than once that he wished his father could have been present. He’d have liked Sadie, he had said, and she’d have liked him. Sadie was sure the feeling would have been mutual. It was a brief wedding ceremony; it solemnized what everyone present knew. Sadie smiled, when she thought about the significance of the legal ceremony. Theirs was a marriage no one could break asunder. Sadie had many happy memories about the wedding, even if it was such a simple ceremony. You can’t question the bonds, she thought, of such a union as this; it was made in heaven. Furthermore, she knew the child she was now carrying was also made in heaven. Could she ask for anything more than this, she asked herself as the dream culminated.

CHAPTER X

It had been a long time and a long way from Peoria, Mississippi. It seemed as though the world had completely changed since he was a boy fishing on the banks of the east fork of Amite Creek with his dad, thought Carson. People had told him that nothing ever remains the same. Now, he knew how right they were. His new life was a good life. He had a fine two-year old son and a loving, devoted wife. Soon she would have another baby. Oh, how his chest swelled with pride when everyone started calling him Papa. Best of all, though, was when Clayton first called him that. He never had any idea that he would ever be called anything but Carson for the rest of his life. Now Sadie called him Papa just like everyone else.

Papa recalled the long trip from Mississippi. Though ages ago, it was like only yesterday in his mind. He hadn't been aware that his father was so sick. His next recollection was his mother telling him that Dad had died in Alabama. When he left in the middle of the night, Momma said her husband had gone back to pick cotton to raise money for the family. According to Momma, Dad was buried there; no one from the family attended the funeral. They, in turn, had sent word about Daddy's death to Grandma and Grandpa. You know how mail was in those days, though. They never got word in time to do anything, either. It's a shame the Pony Express hadn't still been around. They had discontinued the service over thirty years earlier in the 1860's, when transcontinental telegraph service became available. Oh well, the Pony Express hadn't gone through Mississippi, anyway. Then, too, Momma hadn't thought of the telegraph, because of the state of shock she was in.

As soon as Momma's folks heard, though, they had come to Mississippi with a team and wagon. It didn't take Widow Cantrell long to decide to go to Arkansas with her folks. Actually, she didn't think too much about anything, she was grieving so much. Not much time was needed to load their possessions; they really didn't own much, especially furniture.

In addition to the farm, they had already sold Dad's team and wagon, so everything had to fit into Grandpa's wagon for this trip. They didn't have a covered wagon; they just piled up everything as best they could. Precious items, such as dishes, were wrapped in quilts to try and keep them from breaking.

The wagon box, made by Studebaker, was several feet in length, and about four feet wide. As it was originally two feet deep, they had made it deeper in places by the way they stood the bedsteads upright to form sideboards. Then they covered everything with canvas in case it rained. From a distance it looked like a covered wagon; it just wasn't weathertight. Thank goodness, there was rain only one time during the long trip, and that was almost their undoing. It sure was hot during the day, however.

They soon discovered it was easier to travel early in the morning and then late in the day. This allowed the mules and the milk cow they had brought along behind the wagon time to get a nice breather in the middle of the day. Also, it gave Carson's grandfather time to grease the axles, when it was needed. A wooden bucket swung from the rear of the wagon; it contained a mixture of tar and lard to lubricate the wagon's moving parts. While the job sounded easy, it was actually quite difficult. The wheels were kept from falling off with a pin through the axle after it protruded through the metal-lined hub made of hickory. The pin was easy to remove. As a matter of fact, if care wasn't taken to be sure it didn't come out, a wheel might fall off after bumping over a rock or a stump. The hardest part about greasing the axles was getting the grease off of one's hands after the job was done. It helped to get both hands full of sand or dirt off of the trail and to then vigorously rub them together, but sometimes even this method didn't work. In that case black hands were not unusual for the person performing the task.

While it was nice staying in the shade during the middle of the day, the traveler still had to contend with flies bothering him or her. Sometimes the sojourner was kept busy swatting the pesky creatures instead of doing chores needing completed. Even while the travelers were moving on the trail, the flies could continue to be a nuisance, as traveling was quite slow, and the winged nemesis seemed to love the smell of sweat. At least the animals had tails to continually swish back and forth for self-protection.

The days the weary travelers covered twenty miles warranted a celebration. Actually, ten miles should have been cause for celebration, as the journey was not easy on humans, beasts or their equipment. Usually, on these days they were too tired to celebrate, however. Often they just tried to find camping spots with soft dirt nearby so they didn't have to sleep on the hard ground. Carson soon found that pine needles or leaves from a magnolia tree spread out about six inches deep could also be used for a mattress. Most days, however, he was so tired he could have slept on a rock.

One time Carson slept by leaning back against a tree. In the morning he found himself curled up by the tree with no covers, his clasped hands serving as a pillow. At least he didn't have to put any covers away for the day. Even better was waking up to the gentle "whoo" of an owl and the smell of breakfast cooking. While the cooing of the bird didn't completely obliterate his backache, it somewhat lessened the strain on the taut muscles. Someone was always sure to be sleeping under the wagon. Carson's mother and grandmother were afforded some privacy in that Grandpa took the canvas from the wagon and fashioned it as best as he could to resemble a tent. The elder male preferred to sleep under the wagon.

"Boy, didn't it rain last night?" said Grandma. "The water ran right under the sides of the tent. Now all of our bedding is wet and who knows how well the stuff on the wagon fared."

"Well I can assure you that we didn't do much better," retorted her husband with a sneeze. "I'm all wet and don't know when I'll be a gettin' dried out."

"Don't you go and catch your death of cold now," said Grandma. "Do you hear me?"

"I hear you. But I'd like to know what I'm goin' to do about it."

"Well, for starters, let's get some dry clothes on you," said his wife.

"We really should be on the trail. We've got a lot of miles to cover today. We can't be a wastin' time for this," returned Mr. Seldon; by this time mild coughing fits had been added to his repertoire of noticeable behaviors.

Mrs. Seldon was not aware her husband was exhibiting so much difficulty as he walked to one side and behind the wagon until he stumbled from exhaustion.

"Grandma! Stop the wagon!" Charlie called out. "Grandpa's fallen!"

Camp was set up for a nighttime stay even though the sun was still high in the east.

"Now why are you stoppin' like this?" asked Grandpa. "We've got a lot of miles to cover yet today."

"We're going nowhere," his wife responded, "until you get to feeling better. No one said we had to travel every day on this trip. I wish we had more than this laudanum to soothe your pain."

But Grandpa didn't get better. The strength to raise his head was gone by nightfall. That man no more than fifty-five years of age went to meet his maker that night on the trail. How someone could be the picture of health and be gone the next minute was beyond Carson's ability to comprehend. Why, Grandpa had even been a veteran of the Civil War. He never complained about his lot in life. He merely expired while clutching the hand of his wife until the last ebb of life departed his presence. Uncurling his withered fingers was not easy. She had wanted to wait until they relaxed on their own. In the end the bony appendages were pried loose.

Grandma wanted to return the body to the homeplace for burial. The weather was too hot and humid, however, to even consider transporting the body on through Arkansas. Besides, there was no box available for this gruesome task. Carson and Charlie dug a shallow hole in a grove of jack oak about fifty yards off of the well-traveled ruts. The hole was dug in a clearing, as their simple tools likely would not penetrate tree roots without considerable effort. The corpse was placed in the newly dug hole with arms folded across his chest, and a piece of tattered fabric to shield his face from the dirt. Before continuing with the burial, the new widow asked to say a few final words.

Her words Carson could still remember. The simple words were, “Thomas Alvin Sheldon, I've known you for over forty years now, and I've never known you to shirk your duty. I don't consider this one of those times, either. You're always willing to help someone. I reckon this time your helping just ran out. We've traveled a long road together. Remember when we were kids growing up in this here state? We never knew it would end like this, did we? I'd hoped we'd spend our last years together in rocking chairs on the porch. Well, when I'm in a rocking chair, I figure you'll be there beside me somehow. Others won't know it, but I will.”

Turning to the others she asked for one last moment alone with her lifelong companion. The Cantrells never knew her final, departing words. Straightening her bonnet, she returned to the wagon. “I reckon you can cover him now. I don't want the wild animals bothering him none.”

The journey was so much quieter now. Carson and Charlie missed the words of encouragement so frequently received from their grandfather as they walked by the wagon. Grandma wasn't one to talk much now. Momma Cantrell did what little she could, but she didn't feel much like talking, either. By the end of the first day back on the trail, though, brief exchanges began to once again occur. Mostly, however, the talk was between the two widows in hushed tones that Carson and his brother could not hear.

By the end of the second day following the burial, the greatest worry seemed to be “How many miles can we make by nightfall?” It was a long day, almost seventeen miles were covered by Charlie's reckoning. Don't ask him where he got that number. It satisfied his traveling companions, however. While Carson and his family ate the evening meal, the cow and mules were given a ration of oats carried on the trip for that purpose. As space was limited, the barrel with the grain was lashed to the tailgate of the wagon with a rope. Because of the heavy work they were doing, the mules were given large amounts of the grain twice a day. The mules and the cow could generally graze on grass in the area during the noon break.

Hooking up the harness in the morning was no easy task. Handling the harness required considerable exertion in mastering the several connections. Carson, who had always helped his grandfather with the task, now found himself responsible for its completion. Actually the cowhide harness was somewhat heavy for a boy like Carson, but with the help of Charlie the job always got done by the time the women were ready to break camp. Campsites were usually selected because someone had been there before them and left rocks in a circle ready for a campfire. They did the same.

Carson would never forget that trek out west to Arkansas from Mississippi. It seemed like he had walked most of the way, which he may well have done. That is with the exception of the ferry ride across the Mississippi River at Natchez. Otherwise, somebody had to be walking all of the time, as there just wasn't enough room for the people and the few belongings and supplies in the wagon. Besides that, the roads were so bad that every once in awhile, someone had to help push the wagon. Also, nothing could ever be as hard as that wagon seat, he told himself. The road, actually it was just a trail of wagon ruts, had been well traveled for many years. However, the ruts just got worse with age, not better.

The setting sun was always a welcome sight, if you had made enough miles during the day. The first thing he liked to do when they stopped for the day was walk to a nearby creek or river and wash off the traildust. It would have been nice to put on clean clothes afterwards, but it just wasn't possible. Even if you walked away from the wagon, you always had to contend with dust and flies, so there was no need in wearing clean britches, anyway. At least he did rinse out his shirt in a stream most every chance he got. He was never quite sure how the women handled this problem. Sometimes he wished there had been some rain to settle the dust on the trail. Of course if it had rained, he and Charlie would have been pushing the wagon out of mudholes all of the time. There just was no easy way to make this trip.

Yes, it was a whole different world now, Papa thought to himself. He was already a father and another child would soon be here. He sure hoped everything would be all right with both the baby and Sadie. It was right to feel concerned; too many babies didn't make it coming into this world. Worse yet, too many women died during childbirth. It's a shame, he said to himself, that so many people have to die. And all because no one knows how to help them when they get sick. Well, anyway, he would do everything in his power to help anyone in his family needing help. Others also needing assistance could look to him for aid as well, he knew.

Break time was over; Papa knew it was time to get back to work. He had enjoyed working on a farm. By now he and his father would have been working together, if Dad just hadn't taken sick and died in Alabama. Oh well, if they worked hard and saved their money, someday he and Sadie would own their own place. It was too expensive to buy both a farm and all of the needed equipment, so they'd probably start off sharecropping just like everyone else. But he knew the time would come when they could say with pride, "This is our place." Right now he was content to work in a cotton gin until there was enough money saved up for he and Sadie striking out on their own. "Some day," he thought, "some day."

Papa was right partial to Sadie's folks. Her father, Joseph, was especially likable. He had no formal schooling whatsoever. He couldn't even read or write. His wife could, though, and that was plenty for the family. He had been born in Georgia in October of 1842; farm kids, or most kids for that matter, weren't expected to go to school then, and he didn't. Papa knew that his father-in-law had served as a private in the 10th Georgia Volunteer Infantry of the Army of Northern Virginia for the Confederacy. He knew little else other than that Joseph Quigley began his military service at age 17 and had been part of the surrender at Sayler's Creek, Virginia, on the 6th of April in 1865. The South had experienced many casualties on that date. Carson was thankful that his father-in-law hadn't been one of them.

"How come your daddy wears a patch over his right eye?" asked Papa.

"Well, he prob'ly won't tell you, but I will. It's the result of a bullet wound he got at Crampton's Gap in Maryland. They took him to Richmond, Virginia, for medical care. After about a month they let him return to Georgia for what you call convalescent leave. That's where he met my mother, in Fairburn, Georgia. Mama's kid brother in the army introduced the two to each other. There's been no other woman for him and no other man for her. They're in love as much today as when they married thirty some odd years ago."

Joseph Quigley did marry his wife, Martha, in 1866 after returning to Georgia following the war. She was only nineteen months younger in age. Her parents had moved to Georgia from North Carolina before she was born. After their eldest son, Ed, was born in 1869, Joseph and Martha moved on west to Arkansas hoping to prove up on some free land under the Homestead Act passed by Congress in 1862. It was disheartening for them to learn that Civil War veterans from the Confederacy were excluded from getting these homesteads under this act. Their chances to own a farm were set back for some time. By the time Papa and Sadie were married, Sadie had twelve brothers and sisters, of whom ten were still living. It was all Papa could do to keep their names straight.

Papa was glad his mother, Widow Cantrell, had brought him and Charlie to Arkansas. While he missed sitting under a magnolia tree with his fishing line in Amite River, Hempstead County was a fine place to live. Of course it didn't have sugar cane, either. Cutting off a piece of the sweet cane to chew was a delicacy that he truly missed. Of course the fertile county in western Arkansas was famous for so many other things, too.

Everyone knew that James Black had invented the bowie knife in Washington Township. People here didn't care about reports that a man named Pedro in New Orleans or someone named Noah Smithwick in Texas invented the knife. They even scoffed at reports that a real James Bowie in Philadelphia shaped the first knife. At least all reports agreed the knife was made of something akin to Damascus steel made only in

England. The "Arkansas toothpick" was one fine knife. Someday, Papa reckoned, he'd own one, too.

Other famous persons had lived in Hempstead County as well, including Sam Houston and Davy Crockett, before they had moved on to the Alamo. This had given the area quite a good reputation. The town of Hope, named after Miss Hope Loughborrough, a daughter of one of the directors of the Cairo and Fulton Railroad, was known everywhere for the fine watermelons raised in that region. Actually, Hope shouldn't have received so much of the credit, Papa thought, as the melons were raised all over the county. It wasn't unusual to see them weigh over one hundred pounds. They didn't taste too good when you ate the real big ones, though. They tended to be somewhat mushier. Just the thought of the watermelons caused Papa to lick his lips. He appreciated living in Arkansas. Besides that, this is where he had met Sadie.

There were so many fine points to Hempstead County. Not only was it a good land for growing melons and cotton, but it was the right climate for corn, oats, rye, wheat, tobacco, and all kinds of good vegetables. Only minimal tillage was required for fine crops. Then, if the agricultural production wasn't enough, there were mineral springs all over the county, which everyone said had medicinal properties. The economic base of the county was solid.

Certainly, Papa saw all of the advantages to living in Arkansas, especially Hempstead County, what with the fine land and weather they enjoyed. But, being the family man he was, he knew he really liked the reputation Arkansas had for its fine school systems. Free schools were available to everyone, paid with tax dollars mind you. That meant Clayton and any other children he and Sadie would have, would be able to get a fine education, likely better than their parents had received. In the beginning it was felt the citizens wouldn't tax themselves for schools, but the resistance to such a move was rapidly declining. Tax supported schools were appearing everywhere. The experiment for free public schools in Arkansas was working. Papa and Sadie were elated at being part of such a progressive state.

By now Papa and Sadie lived in De Ann, a small settlement in Garland Township seven miles east of Washington. It was really a small town; there couldn't have been more than one hundred and fifty inhabitants there, even if you counted the bums sleeping under the bridge on the creek. They were all good Godfearing people, too. There were two churches, two stores, a mill to grind flour, a cotton gin, a school, and a post office. Papa was proud to call these people neighbors. Yes, this was the place to raise children, no doubt about it.

That night as Papa and Sadie lay in bed, they talked for awhile before going to sleep.

"Did you feel the baby kick today?"

"Yes, the little rascal can kick quite hard."

"When do you think it'll be born?"

It was already the second week in August of 1906. She knew she couldn't go two more weeks before the child was born.

"Well, it will be this month. That's for sure!"

"I sure hope it's a boy," said Papa.

"You've already got a boy to help you," said Sadie. "I hope we have a girl this time. I sure could use some help, too, you know."

"Well, yes, a girl would be nice, too."

They agreed that there would always be time for more children, so they could have more boys later. After all, her parents had thirteen children of whom six were boys. Still, if it were a boy, you wouldn't hear any complaints from either of them. Boys were always needed for families planning on farming their own place. Just let Sadie and the new baby be healthy, Papa prayed.

CHAPTER XI

Nineteen hundred and six, Sadie questioned herself; could we be that far into the twentieth century? Nineteen hundred seemed only yesterday. And here it was already the twenty-second of August. She was thinking about the date. It was important to her; she knew her second child was going to be born today. If you asked her how she knew, she really couldn't tell you, other than that this was how it felt the day Clayton was born. She asked Papa to stay around the house in case she needed him. He really felt like it was a lot of foolishness, but he didn't want to upset her by being disagreeable. After all, she knew far more about having babies than he did. If you asked him about how he knew when a cow was ready to have her calf, he could tell you. It wasn't scientific, but he just knew, like Sadie knew when she was ready to deliver her baby.

Anyway, this was Wednesday, and Papa wasn't planning on going anywhere today. Things weren't too busy down at the Hope Cotton Gin, where he was now working.

The boss had said, "Sure, you can have the day off, but I don't want this happening too often."

The only work they were doing was going through all of the machinery to make sure it was ready for the upcoming cotton harvest. That meant replacing a pulley here or tightening up a belt there. You never could be too ready for the cotton harvest to start rolling in. Breakdowns later on certainly could make a mess of things.

No, now was the time to fix things, while they weren't busy. Papa was a good worker, so he didn't need to worry about losing his job. Papa knew it worried the boss, though, when it became known that he and Sadie were saving money to survive on while sharecropping a farm. The boss had told Papa that he hoped he would stay for a long time. Papa just had a knack for fixing things. Give him the essential tools of a forge, a vice, a heavy hammer and an anvil and he could fix most anything. You could find good dependable help these days, but you couldn't always find anyone that could always fix things like Papa Cantrell. As a matter of fact, they were talking about it just yesterday.

"You sure know how to fix things, Papa," said the foreman, suspicious that something might be taking place. "I hope you plan on being with us for a spell."

"Well, boss, it's like this. You know how much Sadie and I want our own place to farm. We've been saving our money nigh on two years now."

"I hope you all aren't planning on leaving real soon."

"No, it'll be awhile yet. We've only been able to set aside a dollar or two a month, sometimes more. At that rate it's taken us more than a year to even save enough to buy a decent set of harness, and it will most likely be used."

"How long do you think it'll be?"

"Oh, maybe in another couple of years or so. Can't rightly say yet. Don't worry none. I'll tell you well ahead of time when I'm going to leave."

"It's not that I'm worried about your leaving me sudden like. It's just that I'd wanted to have you training someone about using our equipment before you leave."

"I'd be more than happy to. There are't thatamany secrets to using a forge. A man will just have to learn what to do when the metal is at different colors after you heat it up. You dip it in the water before it gets the right color of hot, and it won't be tempered right."

"I wish it was that simple," said the boss. "Men who have worked around forges for years still can't do the work you can."

"Well, I'll teach him all I can. I know there'll be plenty of time when the day comes."

"In the meantime, I want you to know we like your work, and we'd like you to stay. You'll always have a job hereabouts. Long as I'm boss."

Papa and Sadie had moved into Hope a couple of months earlier. It wasn't that they didn't like living on the farm; they did. It was just that they knew they had to have a higher paying job for Papa in order to save money for striking out on their own. Papa knew he couldn't inherit any land, as he figured Mr.

Taylor was planning on letting his boys have his farm some day. Papa and Charlie had always known they were on their own, when it came to getting their own farm. Because of this, Charlie had already headed for Texas. He had told Papa about how much easier it was to homestead there. Why, he had said, the land was free for the taking. As a matter of fact, Charlie hoped that the free land wasn't gone already. Taking no more chances, he got on his horse and rode out of town.

Papa decided to fix the back screen door, seeing as he had to hang around the house today, anyway. The wire needed tightening with some new wood strips to hold the edges around the handle. He was still rounding up his tools, when Sadie called out,

"Papa, I need you!"

Papa dropped everything, thinking the baby was already on its way. "Is the baby coming?" he asked while brushing a chair aside as he entered the room.

"No", she said. "I was just thinking maybe you ought to go and get Mama. It's getting real close to time now."

"It'll take me three or four hours, at the soonest", he said.

"Well, get a move on it then!" she said.

Papa had kept the mule saddled, just in case this happened. He wished he had a horse, as they could run so much faster. In due time, though, he fetched Mrs. Quigley. He had had to hitch the wagon up at their place, as she made it clear in no uncertain terms that she wasn't about to ride on the back of a mule.

"Where's your wagon?" she asked as she stepped off the back porch.

"I brought the mule, instead," answered Papa.

"Do you honestly believe I'm going to ride that ugly critter with you? Besides, it isn't ladylike!"

"It would sure save us a heap a time. The mule is all ready to go," responded Papa.

"You get out in that barn and harness Old Nellie. Move! Time's a wasting!"

The mule trailed along behind the wagon as they returned to the Cantrell abode. Both Papa and Mrs. Quigley worried that they wouldn't get to Sadie in time. Papa made a clicking sound with his lips and snapped the reins up and down the whole time they were going. It did seem to make Nellie step up her pace a bit.

"Can't you make that horse move any faster?" asked Mrs. Quigley. "At this rate you'll be a papa before we get there. Don't you have a switch or something to tickle his rump? He'd get a move on then."

"If we go any faster, a wheel will fall off of this thing. Besides, you didn't give me time to cut a stick for a whip. Just brace your legs against that board there, hold on to your bonnet and pray we're in time."

"There was a buggywhip in the barn if you'd just looked!"

In due course, though, they reached their destination. Both rushed inside to see how Sadie was doing. You could see they were on time but not too early. Mrs. Quigley ordered Papa outside. This was women's business, she told him.

After unhitching and wiping the mule down good, Papa found a copy of the *Fort Smith Elevator*, a paper he had brought home from the cotton gin and sat down on the steps of the porch to read. Feeling the heat of a hot August sun beating down on him, he moved to the rocking chair in the shade. A man could get a headache reading outside like this. It was hard to keep his mind on the newspaper, but he did read the article on Julian Axlerod, from Drew County. It seems Julian was crossing a bridge over the creek, when a bolt of lightning and the accompanying thunderclap scared his horse. When the horse jumped off into the creek, Julian ended up with his leg broken in two places. "I'll bet that hurt a right bit," said Papa outloud.

Before he could finish reading the article, Papa heard a baby cry. It was a loud piercing cry that penetrated the walls of the house like a knife. Good, that means it's a healthy one, he thought. I wonder if they'll let me inside now? Risking the possibility he might be asked to leave, Papa went inside. Mrs. Quigley was holding the baby, just starting to clean it up. It was all red and not just from the blood.

"Look quick, and then get outside!" she told him.

Papa would have liked to hold the baby, but Mrs. Quigley was the boss in this setting. This was woman business. He did take time to give Sadie a kiss, as he was leaving the room. Risking getting in trouble, he hesitated and said, "She's sure a pretty one, Mama."

"I can see that," the new mother was able to form with her lips, but no audible words emerged.

"Thank you for such a healthy daughter," he said.

Though clearly in pain, Sadie smiled back with pride. The ordeal was worth the price; the joy would come later.

"I told you to scoot. Now that means park it outside mister," said his mother-in-law with a smile on her face.

Mrs. Quigley announced she would be staying for a few days to help out. Yes, she knew Sadie could probably manage just fine without her, but she didn't have too many granddaughters, and she wanted to enjoy this one all she could. The day after the delivery of the baby girl Papa and Sadie talked about what they should name her. After some discussion, they settled on Zelda Mae Cantrell. You couldn't have found a prouder set of parents than Papa and Sadie. Now, they had both a boy and a girl. Their family could be complete even if they never had another child. But, they knew there would be more children. If they were going to own their own farm, they'd need more children, especially boys, to help work in the fields. Farmers not only raised crops, but they raised the workers needed in the fields as well.

"Zelda Mae," Sadie kept saying over and over. Oh, how it pleased her to know she now had a daughter. She could already see herself and Zelda Mae working together in the kitchen someday. It couldn't be too soon to please her. Her daughter would be so much help, like she used to help her mother so much. It was a dream come true.

CHAPTER XII

It was the Christmas season because Mama said so. The year was 1910. Zelda Mae had turned four years old earlier in August. This was the first Christmas she especially looked forward to with anticipation. It wasn't just that she was really too young to fully understand and appreciate the event, but the last four Christmas seasons in her life had truly been meager. Oh, she had received clothes, which she dearly loved. Mama always made such pretty dresses. They weren't the frilly types; actually they were quite practical and made from a durable fabric like gingham, which could be most colorful. But toys, other than a doll made out of one of Papa's old work socks to look like a monkey, were never in her stocking. The family generally didn't put up a Christmas tree. They never had enough room in their tiny house for one. Besides, Papa rarely had the time to select and cut a tree, and Mama didn't have time to oversee the placement and decoration of the green conifer.

Anyway, the Cantrell home was crowded; making room for anything requiring additional space was generally not looked on too kindly. Of course the addition of children to the family was a different matter. They had no control over such happenings. Everyone knew that children were not planned; they were a gift from God, and gifts from God should always be accepted. Other than the Christmas stocking, little reference was made to Santa Claus in this residence. Christmas was a religious holiday and Momma made a point for it to be observed as such.

The evening before this special day always found Papa reading the Christmas story from the Bible after the evening meal was completed and the dishes were washed and put away in the cupboards. The story of Bethlehem and the manger was a story not only relished by the children, but a story they could identify with. One year Papa might read the Gospel of Matthew version, while the next year would be dedicated to the Gospel of Luke account. Papa put such feeling in his words, using intonation to distinguish between the principle characters in the story. This special Christmas Eve celebration ended with a brief prayer by Papa following a cup of hot chocolate, a drink only served for this one occasion during the year.

"Our Father, You have truly been bountiful to the Cantrells this year. We've had good crops and time for the harvest, so nothing was wasted. You've kept the family clothed, warm and fed. Surely no other family can be better off than the Cantrells. Oh, I know some have more money, but they can't possibly be more at peace than we are. We just want to thank You for the gift of Your Son and all the blessings You've seen fit to bestow upon us. It's so much more than we deserve."

Yes, Christmas always contained an element of tradition in the observance. This year, however, you could sense that Christmas was finally going to be different. It would remain for the children to find out just how different it would become. The Cantrell had moved to a bigger house when Papa started sharecropping a small farm over beyond the Washington Township a short distance. Down by Terra Rouge Creek he had found a pine tree about six feet tall to decorate for Christmas. Papa explained that to leave it uncut much longer would just lead to its growth being stunted. Too many other trees in close proximity were slowly beginning to crowd the smaller one out, and the curvature in the trunk caused by the seeking of the sun's rays necessitated removal of the lower two feet of the tree in order for it to stand erect. Zelda Mae believed that was the most beautiful tree she had ever seen. The plentiful water supply from the creek had kept its needles shiny and few were falling off.

"Can we put candles on the tree like the Magnusons do?" asked Zelda Mae. "It sure would look purty all lit up like that?"

Papa's answer was swift and unequivocal, "It's far too dangerous, child. We can't take the chance of the tree catching on fire."

"Oh, Papa. Just this one time?"

"Hush child! There will be no candles on the tree."

Allowing as how they sometimes used pine needles to start a fire in the cookstove on a cold morning added credence to his statement. Instead, then, they strung popcorn on strings obtained from feedsacks and made chains out of pieces of colored paper they had cut out of a catalog. Only Clayton was able to string the popcorn; he was almost seven years old. Clyde was two years younger than Zelda Mae was, so Mama was kept busy seeing that he didn't eat the popcorn after it was on the string. He could even swallow the string if given half a chance.

Zelda Mae and Clyde couldn't understand why there were no gifts under the tree. Tomorrow was Christmas Day, and it worried them for the tree to be so empty underneath. Before, when there were only stockings hung on the mantel, they usually didn't get separately wrapped gifts. The stocking held everything including apples and oranges along with their presents. Occasionally there might even be a piece of ribbon candy. This year with a tree, there surely would be "big" presents under the tree. Could they have been wrong? Christmas was more than just a tree, wasn't it? They had forgotten, at least Zelda Mae had forgotten, that the gifts were only brought out on Christmas morning. Clyde was too young to have ever known.

When they went to bed on Christmas Eve, Zelda Mae prayed that there would be gifts tomorrow, more gifts than they had had last Christmas.

Christmas morning started very early at the Cantrell home. Papa and Sadie were trying to get just a little more sleep. They had been up until after midnight finishing the presents for the children. Goodness, the sun had just started to come up, and all three of the kids were at their bedside clamoring for them to awaken. The three youngsters were all ecstatic; they wanted to open their presents now. It didn't matter that there weren't many presents under the tree. They wanted to open what was there. It wouldn't do to tell them, "Let's wait until after breakfast;" they wanted to open them now!

Clyde was the youngest, so he opened one of his three presents first. Guess what it was? Papa had taken a block of wood from a pine log and carved a small sailboat out of it. It even had a tiny little cloth sail the boy's mother had made. Clyde knew immediately that this was far superior to the plain blocks of wood he used to float in the washtub when Mama was through doing wash. He wanted her to do the wash right now! Better yet, we should all go down to the creek!

Zelda Mae was next. She could hardly wait. There were three presents under the tree for her. Which one should she open first? The smallest one won out, as it was closest. It didn't bother her that they hadn't used shiny store-bought paper to wrap it. She wanted what was inside. Still, she took the time to very carefully loosen the string tied around the package. Sometimes she demonstrated a willingness to be tidy about things. Suddenly she saw what appeared to be the bottoms of tiny shoes. She could hardly believe her eyes. No longer was there the desire to complete the unwrapping in an orderly fashion, as she shredded the wrapping. Could it be, please let it be, yes, it was a real doll, a China doll with a smile on its face and ruby-red cheeks. Oh how beautiful it was. She knew she'd never have a better doll than this. Already, she was trying to think of a name for her "baby." She didn't care that Mama had acquired an older doll and saved the head to make a new doll. It looked like new to Zelda Mae.

"Oh, Mama! This is the nicest gift I've ever had! But I didn't make anythang fer you."

"Oh, you'll give me many gifts in the future, Zelda Mae. For now you yourself are gift enough for me."

It was Clayton's turn now. His package was much bigger and oddly shaped as no box surrounded the object. Quite frankly, it was huge to the young boy. Who could guess what might be inside this package? It had to be nice if it was that big. It certainly was heavy, too. Wasting no time to heighten the anticipation, he ripped the covering from the object that had his mind wishing for all forms of wonderful things. It was a wooden wagon; just what he wanted. Papa had made everything on it, except for the axles he got from the cotton gin. Even the wheels were made out of slices off of an oak branch about eight inches in diameter. Papa had been able to make them almost perfectly round. Of course the hole was slightly off-center on the left-rear wheel which created a galloping motion when it was pulled. Forget the fact that no paint was in evidence, either, or there were more presents to be opened, Clayton didn't need to stay around to see what the rest of his family would find under the tree. He immediately pulled the wagon outside. Clyde went with him carrying his precious sailboat. He couldn't decide what to do first. Should he ride in Clayton's wagon or sail his sailboat first? He was perplexed to say the least. Maybe Clayton would pull him down to the creek in the wagon.

Zelda Mae decided she could take the time to open her second present, if she held her doll on her lap just right. She couldn't possibly think of anything else that she needed right now. Can you believe it? It was a doll bed. Papa had made a bedstead about fourteen inches long, and it was completely fabricated from metal. It had curlicues and everything on it cut out of a tin can for storing syrup. He had used tinsnips to accomplish the very delicate task of making narrow ribbons of tin into a work of art. The bed was painted a shiny black and Mama had made bedding for it. The last present contained a dress Mama had made for her. No doubt about it, this was the best Christmas ever. Zelda Mae doubted there would ever be another Christmas this nice. She was one happy girl.

Christmas vacations always end. It was time for Clayton to return to school. Zelda Mae wished that she were old enough to go to school, too. It would be two more years before she could start first grade like Clayton was attending this year. He went to a one-room school just half a mile down the road. If you asked him where he was going, he would merely answer "over yonder." When the neighbor kids would walk by, he just fell in line with them. That way, Mama didn't have to take time to be sure he got to school. You didn't have to tell him, either, he was always looking out of the window for the first sign that the other kids were coming. She did like to make sure he was properly bundled up, however. It could get pretty cold outside sometimes. Cold days meant he had to wear his shoes to school. During the cold months extra caution had to be exercised to prevent falling off the log spanning the creek.

The school Clayton attended only had thirty-two students in grades one through eight. They sat on benches. Boys sat on one side of the school and girls sat on the other side. Their benches, made out of a one-foot wide log split lengthwise, faced toward the front of the room. With the flat side of the split log facing up, the legs of the bench were made out of branches about four inches in diameter and eighteen inches long. These seats were most uncomfortable and had no backrests. Sometimes three or four children would share a bench, so they had to get along well with their seatmates. There were two buckets of drinking water in the room with metal dippers, so both boys and girls had separate buckets. In the middle of the room facing the teacher's desk and the blackboards were recitation benches. When the teacher was working with the first grade, she might have all of the first graders come up at once and sit on these benches. In the wintertime Clayton and his classmates looked forward to sitting on the recitation benches. They were situated the closest to the pot-bellied stove and everyone knows that the mind works better when it's warmed up.

The teachers in these schools were sometimes not much older than the eldest students were in age. It was possible to become a teacher upon completing the eighth grade. An aspiring teacher only had to pass a set of tests at the ninetieth percentile level on the various school subjects taught. That may not have been as easy as it sounds, however, because the curriculum contained not only reading, arithmetic and spelling, but it also included questions from studies in grammar, penmanship, geography and history to name a few. The schoolteacher could expect to earn the magnificent sum of twenty-five dollars a month, if they were in one of the more affluent schools.

The teacher at Terra Rouge School this year was a pretty, young woman. While her name was Eloise Tarpley, she preferred to be called Miss Eloise. The younger students found it difficult to pronounce her name; it often came out "Miss Lees," especially if the child was missing teeth. The older, eighth grade students had difficulty saying Miss Eloise because she was not much older than they were. Extra math work at the board after school and a talk with their parents seemed to rectify this latter predicament. She suspicioned that the parents played a greater role in the solution to this problem. Of course the only ones staying after school were the older boys, and they generally responded to physical therapy meted out by their father.

The school year was pretty short while the Cantrell children were attending. The dates of school attendance were built around when the various phases of farming occurred. That is, if you were needed on the farm, chances were that school was not even in session. You could generally count on going to school in the summertime after all of the planting was done. Then you would probably only go until it was the start of cotton-picking time late in September or early October. School started up again after cotton harvest, usually by the middle of December, if all of the crops were harvested. Frequently you could count on this school session lasting until some time in March. Then the kids would help at home with the plowing or planting. Some students ended up going to school a total of from three to six months out of the year. These time periods were deceptive, however, and varied according to the bounty of the crops. This meant that years of drought often resulted in a longer school year than usual.

The school day generally started out at eight o'clock in the morning and went until four o'clock in the afternoon. Usually forty-five minutes were allowed for lunch. The student didn't need a lot of time to eat the lunch carried in a small lard or syrup bucket. Recesses of fifteen minutes each were taken in the morning and afternoon. Otherwise, the students could be found hard at work in the classroom. Teachers were most intolerant of anything other than being studious. It was not unusual for them to walk among the students administering sharp raps with a ruler for the slightest of infractions of the many school rules. Also, it was not unusual to see students sitting in the corner with or without a dunce cap.

Recess was welcomed with glee. There were no restrooms in the building. As a matter of fact, the schools often lacked an outhouse as well. School buildings were almost always built close to a grove of trees for this reason. The brief recesses allowed time for some games, if you didn't have to go into the woods to relieve yourself. Zelda Mae's favorite games were ring-around-the-rosy and drop-the-handkerchief. However, she would not turn down a chance to jump rope with the other girls. The boys liked to play marbles or mumbledy peg, which required skill in flipping a knife. The boys and girls pretty much were not permitted to mix in their games. As a matter of fact, they were required to play on separate parts of the playground. Recess was fun anyway.

In time Zelda Mae was able to go to school as well. With pride she carried the small pail containing a sandwich, cookie and apple, as she tried to stay up with Clayton. He didn't want any little girl walking with him. As soon as they were out of sight of the house, he'd start running. Zelda Mae often found it hard even seeing him in the distance, as she literally flew down the wooded path leading to the small white building with a bell tower on top.

The school years passed quickly. Zelda Mae especially remembered the eighth grade, however. It was her favorite year. Being a member of the top grade in school meant you had special privileges. The older students not only had their own work to do, but they also helped the teacher. By now Miss Eloise had become Mrs. Hanna. Her new title carried even more authority and respect. The older boys would carry wood in for the heating stove and tend the fire. Also, they were expected to walk down to the creek every day and fill the two buckets with water. This was a welcome task, though, as the boys could always make the trip to the creek into a long adventure, especially if it occurred during a spelling bee. The older girls would help the teacher by having the younger students read to them. When it was time for the students to have a drink, one girl would carry a bucket of water, while another would let each younger child have a drink. It didn't take long with everybody drinking out of the same dipper.

School was more fun now. In the summer time Zelda Mae got to walk to school barefooted. If the road had been recently graded, she enjoyed seeing the indentations of her footprints in the fresh dirt. Then, too, she felt a strange sensation as she slowly worked her feet down deep into the fresh soil stirred up and then leveled by the horsedrawn grader. It was a pleasurable tickling as her toes slowly disappeared out of sight. She had to be extra careful not to step on goatheads or other stickers hidden underneath the surface, however, as they were just waiting to plant their teeth into the unsuspecting victim. Even with calluses on her feet the stickers could be painful. Then, on the way home from school, it was fun to wade in the cool, clear waters of the creek as well. If she waited until she was almost home to wade in the creek, and then let her feet dry first before continuing home, they weren't quite so dirty when she reached the front porch. Dirty feet were bad enough, but Mama sure hated muddy feet coming into her house.

Zelda Mae no longer studied reading in the upper grades; it was replaced by grammar classes. Fifth graders should have known pretty well how to read by that time, so their studies would be concentrated elsewhere. Being in this grade meant you were ready for more advanced studies. Zelda Mae really didn't care for diagramming sentences, but she did love geography. Many times she dreamed about faraway places and wondered if she'd ever get to see them. There was a lot of religious emphasis in the studies. Being required to memorize the Ten Commandments was not unusual. Maybe she could even go to the Holy Land some day. Mama said the rich folks did that. Zelda Mae loved reading the Bible. When she was twelve she further asked to be baptised. The DeAnn Church scheduled the baptismal ceremony in the pond up the road from the church. Zelda Mae wore her best gingham dress even though she knew it might get mud on it. In any case it would need washed no matter what happened.

"Who among you desires being baptised like our Savior was in the River Jordan?" asked the minister.

Looking around Zelda determined that she was not alone in this endeavor, as her shoes continued to sink in the soft mud on the bottom of the pond. Too, she questioned the rightness of her decision to participate. Still, she slowly raised her right hand into the air.

"All of you come forward and stand beside me here in the water," directed the minister.

"Do you accept Jesus Christ as your Lord and Savior?" asked Brother Greenwood.

"I do," answered Zelda Mae and her cohorts in unison.

"You go first young lady. You'll be perfectly safe. Just follow my lead," he told her.

Being first created a lot of apprehension for Zelda. She was hoping another might be chosen for the initial ceremony. Slowly she started a retreat.

Brother Greenwood, sensing her fear, immediately said, "Now step right up here. This isn't going to hurt, and you'll be safe."

"You'll help hold me up, won't you?"

"Why certainly."

Cupping a handkerchief in his hand over Zelda Mae's mouth and nostrils, the minister bowed the slender girl over backwards and pushed her head beneath the cold pond water. Holding her breath, she didn't inhale any of the brown liquid. Still, she came up gasping for air from the experience.

"I pronounce you a chosen daughter of the Almighty," said Brother Greenwood. "Go forth with the knowledge that our Heavenly Father is always on your side. Now, who's next?"

"I'm so proud of you," said Zelda Mae's mother. "That was a pretty grownup thing you just did. Being first wasn't easy, was it?"

"I was scared, but now I'm glad I did it."

The year was 1920. While Zelda Mae liked school, she really enjoyed helping Momma take care of the three younger kids. By the time she was finished with the eighth grade, Papa and Sadie's family included seven children. The older three in addition to herself, Clayton, Clyde and Claudine, could pretty much take care of themselves. Of the three younger ones, Sarah was almost six years old, Rebecca was almost three, and William wouldn't be one year old till November. Zelda Mae reckoned that she'd rather just stay home and help Mama take care of these smaller kids now. It was too far away to go on to high school in Washington, anyway. Maybe Mama would agree.

"Can I ask you somethin', Mama?"

"I suppose. What do you want?"

"Do you know I'm goin' to be fourteen pretty soon? And when I was baptised you said I was pretty grownup. Well that was two years ago."

"Lord have mercy on us. Are you really going to be fourteen?"

"You know I am, Mama!" said Zelda Mae with indignance. "Why, I'm almost a grown woman."

"Yes you are, honey. Don't pay no mind to me. I'm right proud of the way you've grown up. You've been a real big help to me, what with helping care for the young ones and the like. Yes, honey, you're right grownup. I declare. I'm going to have to keep better track of things."

"I really wanted to talk to you about somethin' else, Mama."

"I knew you did, honey. I figured you'd get around to what's troublin' you pretty soon."

"Clayton only went through the eighth grade, didn't he?"

"So, that's it. You don't want to go to school any more. Aren't you doin' well, honey?"

"Well I do know how to read and write. And I know my addition and my subtraction up to a hundred or maybe even a thousand or more. That's all that's important, isn't it?"

"Yes, they're important, but there are other things."

"Like what?" asked Zelda Mae.

"Like learnin' more about faraway places. That'd be nice to know, wouldn't it?"

"Yes, but it would just be seein' about them in books. I can read about them in books here at home."

"I don't reckon we have any books here."

"I know, but teacher said I could borrow one once in awhile from her."

"Well, it's alright by me. I'll talk to Papa when he comes in. I could use extra help around here, What with the three little ones. They're always under my feet. Besides that, you're mighty good company to have around. I'd always hoped one of my kids would get past grammar school, though. Maybe one of the young ones will."

"I'm not a sayin' I don't like to learn, Mama. I'm just a sayin' I'd like to spend the day with you even more," said Zelda.

"Sit down for a moment, Zelda. Maybe this is the time for us to talk about your future."

The two quickly poured themselves drinks from the waterbucket. Taking seats at the dinner table covered by a faded oilcloth, they both paused for a moment to look out of the window at the children playing tag in the back yard. William was asleep on his parent's bed.

"Would you smell those magnolias?" asked Sadie.

"You said my future? I'm not that old Mama. My future is still way off."

"It's never too early to be a talkin' about your future, Zelda. Like you said, you're a goin' to be fourteen pretty soon. Before you know it, you'll be a lookin' at the boys," Sadie commented as she brushed loose hair from in front of her eyes.

"Well, Adam Connors is one right goodlookin' boy."

"I know, honey. There comes a time when all boys are goodlookin'. Later, only some of the boys will be good-lookin'. Eventually, though, only one of them will be a good-looker like your pa is to me, and looks is more than what you see on the outside. It's what's in your heart that counts, Zelda Mae. It's what's in your heart that counts."

"I know Mama. I can see how Papa looks at you. You two are in love aren't you?"

"Yes, and we always will be," answered her mother. "I'd like to see you grow up and be married to a good man like your pa. Maybe you do need to spend more time with the young ones at home helpin' me. That'd give you a good idea of what the future's like. I'll talk to your pa, but I can't promise it'll be rightaways. It'll work better if I wait till the time's right."

And that's how it came about that Zelda Mae did not pursue her formal studies beyond the eighth grade.

CHAPTER XIII

Papa and Sadie had resided in relative quiet on a farm near De Ann, Arkansas, for some time now. This was their home, and it seemed like they had always lived here with a comfort achieved not unlike the joy resulting from an easy chair that knew every contour of your body. The couple had grown to love the plain clapboard house and surrounding quarter section like one of their children. While the farm wasn't paid off, and they didn't have a lot of money for luxuries, they were making their loan payments on schedule. The better the crops they had each year, the bigger the payments they were able to make to the Hope Bank. It was conceivable that the farm might be paid off ahead of time. Of course there had been a couple of bad years when the mortgage payments were quite small. This simple farm and family were everything they had hoped for, and they knew they would probably live out their lives here in western Arkansas. You would have to travel a long distance to find a couple more contented with their station in life than the Cantrells.

The love they shared, combined with the deep-down feeling that they belonged together here in the backwoods of a sparsely populated state, created a bond often unattainable by mere mortals. They may not have said, "I love you" too often, but such discourse was not a requirement to this relationship. The bond was shown in the way their lives harmonized together.

Not only was there love for their home and family, but Papa and Sadie loved Arkansas as well. It wasn't hard to do. The countryside was most beautiful. It was heavily timbered except for where enterprising individuals had cleared the vegetation for cultivation. Yellow pines dotted the rolling countryside. Other evergreens were quite predominant as well. But, then, so were hardwood trees of many varieties, especially oak and walnut. Should the landed gentry be so fortunate as to have these hardwood trees of sufficient size and quantity, furniture manufacturers would seek them out for the privilege of logging the beautiful trees for furniture and caskets sent all over the United States and beyond. Also, the terrain was heavy with underbrush of paw-paw, spicebush, buckeye, and sumac. Wildlife and birds of the air were to be seen in every direction.

If you got out of both the populated and the farming areas, back into the real hill country where there were no other souls, you might think you were in paradise. Arkansas did that to its inhabitants, no matter how brief their sojourn. The southern state had a way of taking hold of your mind that was hard to break. Anyone inclined to be a hermit could probably find his or her niche in the backcountry of Arkansas. Of course this paradise might have ticks, fleas and chiggers. Even Noah must have had them on the ark. You didn't expect the Garden of Eden in every respect, did you? But if you lived here, you would be highly likely to survive on the fruits of the area and your own hard labor.

Nineteen hundred twenty one was not unlike any of the previous few years, when it started off. The cotton harvest was over; it had been fair. Papa couldn't handle as many acres anymore. Clayton had married Bessie Witkins and moved away the year before, so Papa had cut back on the number of acres seeded to cotton. Eighty acres was as much cotton as they could reasonably handle right now. What with the cotton chopping in the summer time and the picking in the fall, Papa and Clyde had their hands full. Zelda Mae and Claudine helped out all they could, but the raising of cotton was heavily dependent upon hand labor. That was easy to see, when you watched someone slowly work his or her way down a row with a hoe chopping cotton. The blazing sun didn't make them move any faster. It just made them use additional energy to continually wipe the sweat from their brows.

In the process of chopping cotton, loose dirt and dust was forced into the air. An energetic chopper resembled a bull intent on flinging dirt over his shoulders with his front hooves; it cascaded in a circle around the perpetrator with a vengeance. This in turn left the cotton chopper covered with a coating of grime streaked by continual droplets of perspiration. As if that wasn't enough, flies were attracted to the sweaty laborer as well, buzzing relentlessly waiting for an opportunity to land. It was as if the tired serf was paying for his errant ways, though his labors and long hours offered little time for the commission of sins.

No one said chopping cotton was easy, but the work had to be done. Often the only relief found in the cotton fields was a drink of water. While cold water was the best at soothing parched lips, on the hottest of days any water tasted good. Then, too, if you felt there was plenty of water, it felt good to pour a dipper full over your head to help break the heat. Fall, with its cooling temperatures, was a welcome event to the Cantrells. Now it was cotton-picking time. The hoes had long since been put away to be awakened another year hence.

With free time on their hands, and it being a cool January, Papa and Clyde decided to butcher a hog. They hadn't tasted the juicy tang of fresh meat for some months, so now was as good a time as any to slay the fatted swine. Besides, there was a full moon, and everyone knew the meat was best if the hog was slaughtered during a full moon. It was common belief that the meat shrank if killed at any other time, resulting in more lard and less usable meat. Hogs were the best to butcher of all the farm animals. There was so little waste. You just didn't slaughter a hog without some preparation, though, as there was a considerable amount of preparation to be accomplished.

First thing in the morning Papa built a fire under a fifty-five gallon barrel, originally used as an oil drum, filled half-full of water. Any more water than that and the excess would be wasted when you lowered the hog into the bubbling cauldron. As a matter of fact, the water displaced by the hog might extinguish your fire. It was best to have the barrel and fire where the men could position a rope and pulley up above to raise the hog.

In time the water approached the boiling stage. At that point either shooting it or killing it with an axe abruptly ended the hog's life. Clyde killed this one by shooting it between the eyes with a 22 rifle and then cutting its throat with one of Mama's best butcher knives. As soon as the bleeding slowed, he and Papa drug it over by the barrel under the limb of a large oak tree where they already had a hoist hooked onto a substantial branch sticking almost straight out to the westside. Large metal hooks were placed in the tendons just above the foot on each rear leg. Now Papa and Clyde raised the hog up above the scalding water, exercising care to not tip the barrel, then quickly lowered the still beast into the boiling water. Steam cascaded into the air resembling the blowing of a whistle on a steam locomotive. After sufficient time had lapsed to loosen the hair, and it wasn't long with the boiling water, the two butchers raised the hog with the hoist and kept it suspended, while they proceeded to scrape the hair from its reddened skin. It was too much work to remove the skin from a hog, and little mistakes in cutting, referred to as button holes, made the skin unusable for most projects. No, this way was much easier. They repeated this process of dunking and scraping until the hair was completely removed. It was hard work done with rapidity; leisurely efforts were not possible, as the hot water cooled far too quickly. Time could not be wasted.

"Couldn't we have picked a better day to do this, Papa?" asked Clyde.

"No, you want it just above freezin' outside. That's the best time to butcher. Besides, the hot water and your fast work will keep you warmer than you want at times," answered his father.

"I reckon you're right. I really don't feel hot at all. Of course it might be more fun if we could work a little slower. A man needs time to think before he does something. Here we just keep a scrapin' or a cuttin' without a chance to think at all. Leastwise this is a good time to have a dull knife. I haven't made a buttonhole yet."

"You always did have a dull knife, Clyde. For once it paid off for you. Of course you rarely cut your thumb either. I suppose there are some benefits to havin' a dull blade."

"How heavy you think this critter is? Seemed awful heavy like, even with a block and tackle."

"It'd probably top out about five hundred and fifty pounds. A good thing we didn't put off butcherin' any longer. He'd a been too big. I don't like to butcher extra big hogs," said Papa.

"Notice how I shot him clean between the eyes? He was dead before he hit the ground," said Clyde.

"Yes, I have to admit you're a good shot, boy. You're a regular Annie Oakley. You were lucky, though."

What do you mean, lucky?"

"It'd be better if ya shot him in the ear. You were lucky the bullet didn't ricochet with that hard skull of his.

"Well, OK, but don't be a comparin' me to a girl, even if she was a good shot. How about I'm as good as Buffalo Bill?"

"Well, I'll admit you're one fine shot with a rifle. But watch what you're a doin' there. See those two buckets I brought? As you're cuttin' up meat, put the lean meat in one bucket for sausage and the fat in the other one for lard. Don't miss the fat around the intestines, either."

"Does that mean we're a goin' to have cracklin's?" asked Clyde.

"It sure does, son. We'll get Mama or Zelda Mae to render lard as soon as possible. They'll probably do it tomorrow."

"Should we save anything else?"

"By all means, boy. Every part off a hog is good for something. Why we can even cook the meat off of the feet."

"I'll bet we can't use the tail!" said Clyde.

"Now don't be too sure of yourself young one. A tail will do right nicely in a stew. We can even add the tongue for good measure."

"Somehow I suspect we're goin' to have stew one of these days, and I'll bet it's real soon," said Clyde.

"That's right, and that isn't all you're goin' to have either."

"What do you mean, Papa."

"We're going to have the intestines, too!"

"What for, pray tell?"

"You like chitlin's don't you, boy?"

"Is that where they come from?"

"I'm afraid so."

"I'll just bet you, Papa, that there's somethin' from the hog that you can't use."

"And just what might that be?"

"The squeal, Papa, the squeal."

Finally, Clyde placed a stout stick about twenty inches long between the two rear legs to hold them apart after the abdomen was split from the throat to the tail. This allowed for the removal of the hog's intestines, which dropped into a tub for later processing; Papa did it swiftly and surely. All that remained to be done was cut the meat up. Sadie, Zelda Mae and Claudine helped on this part. There would be mincemeat pies for sure now, once they got all the meat off of the head. One thing about butchering hogs, there was very little waste. Even the hair scraped from the body was saved to mix with plaster to help hold it together when house repairs had to be made.

There was always plenty of work to do in the wintertime, even if there weren't crops in the field. It was sometimes easier for the menfolk to come into the house earlier, however. It was cold enough during the day, but when the sun went down, you didn't want to be outside unless it was tending livestock or going to relieve yourself. Of course the older you were, the less attractive it was to go outside. By the same token, the younger you were, the less you wanted to stay inside the house, unless you had to do chores.

Tonight Papa and Sadie found time to just sit by the fire and talk while the older kids had gone to a dance at the schoolhouse. The younger children were already asleep in bed. Papa and Sadie didn't get too many chances like this to visit with each other. Their talk soon turned to their offspring. Seemed like they always found time to talk about the kids. After all, that was their reason for living, wasn't it? In their minds they knew their family was now complete with three boys and four girls.

"Do you know that our family is as big as Mom's became when she married Mr. Taylor?" asked Papa.

"Yes. Of course when Widow Cantrell married him, it was a combined family. Our family is all ours, and that doesn't count Mattie Fern buried in Holly Grove Cemetery, not less than a mile from here."

"You miss her, don't you?"

"A mother will always miss her child, even when the child has grown up and moved away."

"I miss her, too, Sadie. You don't have to be a momma to miss a child."

"I know, Papa. But there's a special bond between mother and child. You can cut the umbilical cord, but you can't cut that special bond. God won't allow it. It'll be there long after you're dead, too."

Oh, how it hurt to lose a child; neither Papa nor Sadie would soon get over the death of Mattie. Sadie reckoned she hurt the worse. She had carried Mattie inside of her for nine months, and the ache was worse than cutting off your arm to give her up. Sadie knew that getting over the death of a loved one was the hardest experience anyone would have to go through on this earth, especially when it was your husband or wife who had died. She saw how Widow Cantrell had grieved over the loss of Papa's dad. While she felt Widow Cantrell never ever fully recovered from the loss of her first husband, Sadie sensed that marrying Mr. Taylor had helped to ease the pain some for her.

"Promise me that you'll remarry if anything ever happened to me, Papa," said Sadie.

"I'd rather not even talk about the possibility. After all, I'm the oldest of us, and everyone knows that women outlive their husbands."

"Still, I want you to promise you'll do your best to remarry. I want the children to have a mama."

"You're their mama, and that's final."

"I know. But who'll look after them if I die?"

"Zelda Mae is good with the young ones."

"Humor me," his wife said.

"I'll agree, but only because I know I'll be the first to go someday, anyway. It works both ways, though. Promise me that you'll remarry, too, if anything ever happens to me," said Papa.

"Then we have an agreement." she responded.

"We have an agreement," her husband responded.

It was the fall of 1921. Cotton harvest would soon be getting underway. Cotton picking was not the main topic of discussion in these parts, though. There was an outbreak of typhoid fever in the county. The malady had everyone worried. It seemed that it happened more on the farms and in the smaller towns than it did in the larger cities. Talk was that it had something to do with how well the water was purified. Seems like water out in the country ought to be all right, everyone thought. It sure looked clean enough, and it tasted fine. They were hauling it from the creek in a wagon-mounted tank. Anyway, Papa heard that large numbers of citizens were dying from this dreaded fever. An uneasy feeling pervaded his every thought. The possibility that someone he knew might catch it kept him awake at night, and this was no easy feat for someone spending long hours in the field.

In late September Sadie came down with a severe case of diarrhea. As soon as she also developed a rash, everyone became extremely worried. Diarrhea was fairly common, but weren't these the symptoms of the dreaded typhoid fever? Sadie insisted that she would be better as soon as she could rest for awhile. Bring me plenty of chicken soup were her words. The small house was dark, the shades drawn to block out the light. Sadie said the brilliant rays hurt her eyes. The ever-vigilant mother wanted to get up and help Zelda Mae care for the children, but she was so weak that she could hardly raise her head.

Papa sent Clyde for Doctor Snyder. Clyde's only instructions were, "Hurry, she's failing fast!" The trip to Hope was in vain. There was no way the doctor could arrive in time. Sadie's light was snuffed out on the second of October in the year of our Lord, nineteen hundred twenty-one. Right in the prime of her life no less; she was only thirty-eight years old. She was leaving behind seven children and a loving husband. She even had one child, William, who wasn't quite two years old. Life didn't seem fair to the Cantrells. The person with primary responsibility for the nurturing of the family had so abruptly been taken away. Was there no justice in this world?

Typhoid fever can be highly contagious in certain stages. Because he really didn't fully understand such a disease as this, Doctor Snyder recommended that the burial be accomplished as soon as possible. One day after her death, Samantha Lucille Quigley Cantrell was laid to rest beside

Mattie Fern in Holly Grove Cemetery. Part of Papa went with Sadie into that dark hole in the ground. While his grieving was silent for his beloved Sadie, it was just as real as it would be for someone who cried out in anguish. If it wasn't for the children, he wasn't sure if he could have handled the mounting anguish. While death may be a part of life, there was no easy way for Papa to experience the loss of Sadie. As far as he was concerned, hope might spring eternal, but right now it was hiding its face from those needing consoling the most.

The internment was hard for the younger children. They attended the funeral, but the ceremony didn't make sense to them with Mama being in that box up at the front of the church. Strangers came around and hugged them at Holly Grove Cemetery. They even said things like, "God will take care of you." Zelda Mae and Claudine stayed right with the younger children. While the children's activity level was significantly curtailed, caring for them was no easy task. These teenaged girls were struggling to cope with their own grief.

"Is Mama comin' back?" asked Claudine.

"Mama's gone forever," replied Zelda Mae.

"How long is forever?" said Claudine.

"It'll be long after we're gone from this earth," was all Zelda could say.

"Then we're never goin' to see her again."

"Pastor Ross says that we'll see her up in heaven."

"Then I want to go to heaven," said the younger of the two.

As is so common to southern tradition, following the funeral service there was a big dinner put together for the Cantrells by family friends at the Holly Grove Church adjoining the cemetery. Tables were even set up under the trees by the side door. Every conceivable dish had been prepared from fried chicken and baked beans to blackberry cobblers and pumpkin pies. As plates were filled with varying amounts of life-sustaining food, the owner ventured inside the edifice to find a place to eat. That is unless they chose to kneel or sit on the grass now losing its lush greenness with the approaching cold season.

At first no participant felt like eating or talking. The silence was deafening. Occasionally the stillness was interrupted by uncontained sobs. After awhile a few could muster the courage to talk, but at best only in muted tones. In time, however, conversations sprang up among small groups seated around the church until the small structure was fairly buzzing. Food consumption generally marks the turning from grieving the past to looking at the future. Funerals provide the opportunity for this transition and the saying of good-byes.

"She was so young to have to go like this," said Grandma Taylor. "A woman younger than me shouldn't go so soon."

"Yes," said neighbor Thompkins, "and she's leaving so many young children behind. Sometimes life isn't fair. God must not have been watching out for her."

"Don't go a blaming this on God!" said Reverend Ross. "God represents life, not death. No, God's here to comfort us when things go wrong, not make them go wrong in the first place."

After the funeral the immediate family made the quiet journey to the homeplace. Knowing they might get their Sunday clothes dirty, Zelda Mae and Claudine helped the younger children back into everyday clothes. Awaiting the opportunity for uninterrupted discourse, Papa waited to talk to Zelda Mae about Sadie's death.

"I need your help more than ever now, Zelda Mae. I know you helped out a lot with the young ones before, while your mother did a lot of keepin' the house. Now I need you to do even more work. You'll have to keep house as well. Claudine will help all that she can."

"I sort of figured that would be the case, Papa. Don't worry none about me. I'll do all I can. There is one thing I'd like to ask, Papa."

"What's that, Zelda Mae?"

"Why did Mama have to die? It don't seem fair at all."

"I don't rightly know, child. It seemed like she was always healthy. I don't think she did anything wrong to deserve such an endin'."

"What will happen to us, Papa? A family has to have a mother? I'll do all I can, Lord knows how, but I can't take Mama's place. Oh, Papa, I'm scared."

"You've a right to be scared, Zelda. But the Lord will help see us through this. You heard Reverend Ross at the funeral."

"I heard him, Papa. But I'm still scared. You can count on me. I'll try and figure out what needs done."

"I know you will, child. I know you will. We all will. With the Lord's help, we'll make it. I don't rightly know how, either, but we'll make it. And, you won't have to take your mama's place. You're just takin' on more responsibility as a woman."

"What about William? He's just a baby. He'll never remember his mother. What can we do?"

"We'll keep her in our hearts. She'll be right beside Mattie Fern," said Papa. "That's where she ought to be. They're right beside each other in Holly Grove right now, and up in heaven, too. They can be besides each other in our hearts as well."

"But what about William?"

"Someday, when he can understand, we'll tell him all about his mother. Everyone ought to have good memories about their mother. It'll be our job to see that he knows about her. That he knows what a good mother she was. If she could have stopped from dyin', she would have. She'd a never left him. He'll understand. He has to. We'll help to see that he does. We'll help the other kids to understand, too. Mama wouldn't want it any other way."

CHAPTER XIV

Youth are seldom, if ever, equipped to deal with the loss of a parent. This is true whether they loved that parent or not. Zelda Mae and her brothers and sisters loved Mama more than can be put into words, and this made the loss even more difficult. Following Mama's death, this bond led to feelings they many times struggled to put aside. The hurting inside, however, often resulted in great physical pain that threatened to engulf their very being. The only relief, and then it was only temporary, was to slip away for time alone with Mama. This private time could generally be found only in one's mind, however. Sure, you could see evidence of Mama all around the house. For the longest time even the smell of her could be found in a clean pair of stockings. But you needed time alone to deal with your feelings on occasion. There was always a Cantrell, a Seldon or a Taylor around to lend moral support. As they say, "Time heals all wounds." But, it doesn't always take away the deep scars that can disfigure the soul if not treated properly. Only time alone with Mama could accomplish that.

Papa found some peace in going to Holly Grove Cemetery. It was hard at first going to Sadie's grave. He felt responsible for her death. If only they had had a different water supply, if only they had bought a farm somewhere else, if only he had called the doctor sooner.

All the ifs uttered in this world, though, lacked the divine gift of being able to restore the other half of the team that shared a common dream for so long. It was little relief when others told Papa that death could not always be avoided. He had done everything a loving husband and father could have done, they told him in truth. In this case, though, it was hard to accept that sometimes the prevention of death exceeds the powers and talents that God gives to mankind.

Many were the times Papa went to Holly Grove. He could have found Sadie's grave in the dark, and sometimes did. The site was just a couple of rows over on the west side of the pathway after going through the gate nearest the church. Papa had built plain wooden markers in the shape of a cross for both Sadie's and Mattie Fern's graves. He knew Sadie would have loved the simplicity of his efforts. Their love was private; the whole world didn't need to know about the affection transcending mortal man's ability to comprehend. Gaudiness with the grave markers would have brought attention in a way he knew Sadie wouldn't have liked. The kids approved, too, though they really didn't understand the significance of what he had done.

Zelda Mae grieved the loss of more than a mother. The two had shared many times alone during the course of the day, sometimes in silence as they went about their daily tasks. The bond was far more than mother-daughter or teacher-student. It was a bond that resisted letting go when one partner was called for duty in realms outside these earthly boundaries. Zelda Mae's greatest consolation was in knowing Mama was now at peace with the Lord. She likened it to the words of a poem she had once heard. She never could remember the exact words or the author, but she could remember the main idea. The poem revealed that death never ends one's life. It merely moves one's existence to a different realm in a more serene setting impossible to attain here on earth with all its imperfections. She especially loved the part about the vine growing through the crack in the wall. As we mortals are but flowers on the vine climbing the earthly side of the wall, we'll never get to see the beautiful blossoms blooming on the other side of the impregnable wall while we're alive. But we know they're there.

So it was with Sadie in Zelda Mae's mind. Mama still existed, as surely as the sun lifted its rosy face over the treetops and pushed aside the veil of darkness shrouding the eastern hills every morning. The problem was she wasn't visible to the mortal eye. Zelda Mae knew her mother must be a rare exotic blossom, too, as one in a vase found adorning the mantels of royalty. This was a gift of God. Someday though, we'll be granted passage to the other side of that wall. What a beautiful flower garden there must be waiting there, she thought. Even Mattie Fern would be present. I'll bet Mama is taking care of her right now. Being together surely made each of them bloom far more exquisitely than if they were alone. Now their existence was if they were part of a heavenly bouquet arrayed as a rainbow after a gentle summer shower, never to be seen by human eyes fogged over as only an earthly existence could allow.

You could occupy your time and it helped ease the pain, at least for awhile. It wasn't hard for Zelda Mae to keep busy. She now assumed much more responsibility for the three youngest children; this represented a tremendous workload for a fifteen-year old girl. Claudine had turned ten in April; as soon as she returned home from school, she would immediately busy herself with many tasks needing accomplished around the house. Clyde was always outside helping Papa in the fields all he could. Even though he had not finished school yet, he dropped out of the eighth grade to work beside Papa. Sadie would have been proud of her whole family. The motherless group had rallied by sharing the burden. Sometimes Zelda Mae knew that Mama was surely watching over her family though absent in body. Yes, every time she viewed a flower, Zelda Mae knew that Mama was beside her. For that reason, she was always hesitant in cutting flowers for display. "Let God decide when a flower is to be taken," she told others.

Years later Papa was to remember his vow to Sadie that he would remarry if anything ever happened to her. He didn't know why he made the vow, anyway. Sadie was the only love in his life; there could be no other. The words of his promise kept haunting him, however. Maybe he should remarry. It wasn't fair to Zelda Mae to have to be the woman around the house. At almost seventeen years of age, she had to be thinking of getting married herself. Of course she wasn't even courting, but that was probably because she didn't have time. What with taking care of all the little ones, she was going to bed bone-tired at night.

Soon thereafter, then, Papa saw an ad in the newspaper for mailorder brides. He hadn't courted since he and Sadie had gone together so many years before. Surely times must have changed by now. This might be a safer way to handle it; he'd just use the mails to do his courting. Following the advice of old Tom Keene, owner of Keene's Hardware, he purchased *Romance Magazine*. To say he felt foolish at this act would be an understatement. What will Sadie think of me now, he thought to himself. Surely in all of her wisdom she will understand, though. Spying the picture of a rather stout woman from Lexington, Virginia, he looked at her qualifications. She was well educated, possessing a high school diploma. She didn't indulge in liquor or any tobacco products as wanton women were inclined to do. Of course she'd never had any children or been married before, but one could learn to care for them. Zelda Mae would be a good teacher. Yes, Miss Edith Myrtle Culbertson was worth a one-cent postage stamp. He'd drop a card in the mail as soon as he got home.

"What you doin', Papa?" asked Zelda.

"Oh, just a writin' a card," he answered.

"Well, who you a writin' to?"

"You're sure a curious one, aren't you?" responded Papa.

"It's just that you don't write much. To tell the truth, I don't recall you ever writin' to someone before."

"Well, if you must know. I'm a writin' this gal in Virginia."

"Anyone I know?" asked Zelda Mae.

"No. As a matter of fact, I don't know her either."

"Then why are you writin' to her?"

"Oh, I thought I'd git you some help with the young ones."

"Haven't I been doin' the job right?" asked Zelda with a pained expression.

"You're a doin' fine, honey. It's just that you're goin' to think about gettin' married someday. I'd like to get you some help so that you're free to court and the like."

"Oh, Papa! I'm not thinkin' about courtin' right now."

"Well you will child. You will."

"Supposin' you do get this gal to come clear out west, Papa. There's no extra bedroom for her to sleep in. What'll we do then?"

"I was sort of thinkin' she'd sleep in my bed. Then we wouldn't need an extra room."

"Where do you get such ideas, Papa? Mama would never approve of such an arrangement."

"Everybody does it," her father answered. "Mr. Keene at the hardware store says someone always a askin' him about it."

"No what's an old man know about such things, anyhow?"

"Well, he does talk to lots of people durin' the day."

"You can't do it Papa. Mama would never say it's okay."

"Child, your mother and I talked about this before she passed on. She wanted me to remarry if anything happened."

"That may be, Papa. But I sure don't like the sound of things," responded his eldest daughter.

This romance, courtesy of the post office, was not to be, however. After a very few letters, Miss Culbertson asked for a picture of Papa. He obliged. Return mail brought back the message that he was too young for her. While this may have been true, it was often speculated that his being a widower with six children still at home was her main objection. The rejection brought a sigh of relief from Papa. Now he could truthfully tell Sadie on his visits to the cemetery that he had tried. Zelda Mae was relieved as well.

It seemed Sadie's watchful eye was over the family but not the farm. By 1923 it appeared as though one couldn't make it in farming in those parts. Good crops turned to bad. Not only was it a long, dry summer with little rain, but the bollweevils took most of what did grow. Furthermore, the price of cotton was down as well. An oilwell driller thought he could find oil on the Cantrell farm, but all he got were dry holes. Papa never really knew where to turn after that, he had tried everything he knew. Nothing worked. Then, he remembered when they had left Mississippi. Moving away had helped. They did get a fresh start in Arkansas. He also remembered the words of Henry David Thoreau once told him by a preacher over in Hope. "Eastward I go only by force; but westward I go free...." This made much more sense to him than Horace Greeley's admonition that the children had learned at school: "Go west young man, go west." He was now at peace with Sadie; he could move on, surely with her blessing. It would be hard leaving her and Mattie Fern behind, but Sadie would understand, he just knew she would. They had no choice; they had to leave Arkansas.

Because his love for Sadie had never faltered, he knew she had to be told first of the pending move. Wearing his best clothes, Papa went to the cemetery. Stopping at the gate he gazed over the small expanse of tombstones and markers. He didn't realize how barren the community cemetery really was. Now he wished he'd taken the time to plant something to cover the dirt over Sadie and Mattie Fern's graves.

Kneeling down with his hat in his hand, he stroked the stained sweatband while slowly turning the headwear in his calloused palms. With renewed courage he spoke in a voice broken by an occasional sob as he poured out his heart and soul to his beloved wife. "I wish I'd a brought you some flowers, Sadie. I know how much you loved them. This is a bad time of year for them, though. I didn't come here to talk about flowers anyhow. You know I can't keep a secret from you. I've got to talk to you about somethin' else, is why I come. Times are bad, Sadie. Did you notice how things aren't doing well this year? Cotton ain't doing well at all. We'll be lucky if there's any Christmas this year. We haven't got any money to speak of."

Standing in order to walk away for a moment, Papa looked off to the west before returning to his wife's grave. With his hat still in his hand, Papa resumed talking. "Sadie, if there was a better way to tell you, I would. There's so much more I'd like ta tell ya, but I just can't. Things happen that we have no control over. Ya just do the best ya can. The kids and I can't stay here. I'd drive into Hope if there was work to be found, or our problem could be solved, but there isn't any way. I can't think of a minute that you aren't on my mind, but there ain't any future here without you by my side. We could have made it with the two of us workin' together. I know we could have, bad crops and all. But you ain't here. Course that ain't your fault. No, it's more than that. Besides that, it's just things are all wrong fer us now in these parts."

"What I'm tryin' to tell you, Sadie, I'm thinkin' of movin' the family west. Startin' over. It won't be the same without you. But I have to do it. It's the only way left. You'll always be in my heart, Sadie. You'll always be with me and the kids. I know because you've been lookin' out for us. It's plain as the nose on my face. You've been lookin' out for the kids and me both. I appreciate it. Heaven knows I do. I wish you could have done something about the farm, though. But you couldn't. Anyhow, soon as we can sell the farm, we'll be movin' on. You'll be goin' with us. You know you will, Sadie. You'll always be in our hearts."

After briefly patting the mound over her grave and pulling some small fireweeds just beginning their growth, Papa stood. Looking every bit the beaten man with shoulders stooped, it was difficult to straighten to his full heighth. Glancing off to the setting sun in the west once again, he carefully pulled a handkerchief from his pocket, deliberately unfolded each section and wiped a tear from his eye. After refolding the handkerchief with care to be sure the corners aligned, he put on his hat. Pulling the brim tighter, he slowly walked away. More than once he tried to look over his shoulder. The strength for such a difficult task wasn't to be found, however. Sadie's grasp had been loosened, however slightly.

Clayton knew Papa was considering moving away for a fresh start, so he told him of a conversation he'd had with a friend returning from Laverne, Texas. Seems like they were finishing up a good year for cotton. They had greener grass, too, Art Morrow had said. The rains had come there and into parts of eastern Oklahoma, just across the state line. Papa reckoned he would rather go to Oklahoma; word was it was more like Arkansas. That way he wouldn't have to learn how to farm a different way.

The Cantrell farm totaled about 100 acres of tillable land. When sold, and all of the debts (including the remainder of Sadie's funeral expenses) were paid, there was enough money to buy a used 1920 Model T Ford pickup, valued at only a couple of hundred dollars. It was hard for Papa to believe that all he and Sadie had scrimped and saved for so long was represented by one used truck that resembled a covered wagon with an engine and no horses at the front. Papa and Clayton had considered a four-door touring car. Knowing the likelihood was great that they would once again be engaged in the pursuit of farming as a livelihood, they firmly believed that a vehicle more useful in hauling farm products would be most helpful in their future activities.

"Why, I bet it'll haul a bale of cotton with no problem," Clayton had remarked after seeing the vehicle for sale at the De Ann Cotton Gin.

Besides, you could haul more children in a truck, especially the one-ton truck with a seven foot and two inch pickup box like they now possessed.

"May both you and God forgive me," Papa uttered in a quiet breath to Sadie, "if I've done wrong. Only you, Zelda Mae and me need to know why we have to leave Arkansas. No one else needs to know. It's none a their bizness."

There was no looking back, however. In the latter part of 1923, following the completion of cotton harvest, the Model T rolled out of the yard for the last time. They weren't able to take many possessions; room was at a premium. Clayton was there to drive. This meant there were eight people in the truck counting Papa. He agreed for them to stop by Holly Grove Cemetery one last time. The kids wanted to say one last goodbye to Mama. He knew that he did, too.

CHAPTER XV

The Model T was erratic as a vehicle. Sometimes the "Tin Lizzy" might start on the first try, while on other occasions it might not start at all. Furthermore, the truck was designed purely as a utility vehicle, not a touring bus. You sure couldn't tell when the Cantrells drove by, however. Thank goodness they weren't all grown-ups. People figured if that had been the case, they'd have had to tie some of them on the back bumper, except the truck didn't have a back bumper. At least all of the Cantrells liked each other; no telling what might have happened otherwise with the crowding necessitated by this form of conveyance.

If everyone riding in the back sat down on the floor of the truck with one-by-eight inch sideboards on each side but not the rear, they weren't always visible from a distance. A canvas was at the ready to put over them should rain start to fall; no need to put it on sooner. Little chance of rain starting to fall, though, with the drought still exerting its power over the region. Besides, with a vehicle sometimes attaining speeds in excess of twenty miles an hour, the cover likely would have blown off when they reached cruising speed. Papa and Clyde joined Clayton in the front seat. Though by rights of age and position of authority in the family Zelda Mae could have ridden in the front of the vehicle, she chose to share the rear of the truck with her charges. You never knew what might happen without someone to provide the love and care her younger brother and sisters surely needed at this difficult time.

If onlookers were careful they could see a most subdued family in that big, black pickup leaving De Ann for the last time. The side trip to Holly Grove Cemetery had been difficult for everyone, especially Papa and Zelda Mae. The mourners didn't tarry long. Parting was brief. This was not to be their last trip to Holly Grove, they sincerely hoped. It was only, "Take care, I'll come again as soon as I can." Any more than that and they knew they wouldn't have been able to leave Arkansas. Papa remembered how hard it was leaving Mississippi and his father behind. That was easy compared to leaving Arkansas and Sadie behind.

Clayton said it would be better traveling if they went down Highway 67. There were no paved highways to speak of in late 1923. This was just the most traveled road, so chances were it might be easier traveling. At least the state and county were more likely to grade and maintain roads of this type. It was the old Southwest Trail. Beside the highway they saw open fields that would normally have produced good oats or cotton. The travelers could tell that the previous year must have been a bad year. They could further tell how much it hurt Papa to even look at the parched fields beside the dusty road. He spent considerable time looking at the floorboards of this black machine which rapidly lost speed with the encounter of each new incline of the thoroughfare taking the children away from the only home some of them had ever known.

After awhile Papa's countenance took on the appearance of a soul determined to meet the world head-on. As the slump slowly left his shoulders, his head began staying higher as well. Tired of looking at the holes strategically placed for a variety of pedals in the floorboards, he actually began to look outside the cab after awhile. Going through Fulton they went down the main street, which was Franklin Avenue. Realizing that the quiet pilgrims were looking to him for leadership, Papa's eyes took on a resolution they hadn't seen in years, as though they were saying, "We're goin' to make it. We can do it, I know we can."

Starting slowly he tried to point out points of interest, such as the Old Baptist Church built almost one hundred years before. This necessitated his leaning out the window of the right door, so he could be heard to the rear. He was doing his best to break the pall that hung over the family. Right now they just weren't too interested in information about local sights. Their minds were dwelling on other matters. Occasionally a muffled sob could not be contained.

After crossing the Red River they quickly passed through Texarkana on both sides of the state line. Here they also picked up Highway 82. They were no longer in Arkansas. Their lives had turned another page. It was the beginning of a new chapter in the history of the Cantrells. The countryside was already looking like it had been a greener year in these parts. Maybe, just maybe, that was a good omen. At least the sobs were occurring with much less frequency. Was Papa's example starting to carry over? An imaginary line couldn't be that important, could it? It must have been Papa and his increasing involvement in keeping the children informed as to their whereabouts.

The weather was frightfully warm. The Model T truck had two good sources of improved air conditioning while moving down the road. A vent above the cowling could be opened with a handle underneath the instrument panel possessing one gauge indicating whether or not the generator was doing its job. The cooling from the vent helped to provide airflow to the laps of the riders in the cab. Better yet, though, was the upper half of the windshield. By loosening knobs on each side, and pushing the glass forward, significant airflow to the face could be achieved. Of course travelers of short stature rarely benefited from the breeze generated. Actually, the open windshield also created the possibility for insects to enter the passenger compartment as well. Another opening lacked the desired effect for sure. The openings of the floorboards allowed air to enter the vehicle. The problem was that the air usually contained hot air and fumes from the engine as well, and this could become nauseating in due time.

In the summertime, on a long trip like this, they slept beside the road when it came sundown. The dim lights of the truck made it almost impossible to travel with any feeling of safety after dark. Actually it was more involved than this. The headlights on such an old vehicle worked best when running at full speed. As a result of the lack of batteries in most of these modern conveyances, the brightness of the headlights was directly related to the speed of the engine, due to the necessity for receiving power directly from the magneto, providing power to the sparkplugs. It was a no-win situation with headlights.

The driver found it important to drive at slow speeds on these rutted, dirt and gravel highways. A sudden swerve because of a rut or to miss a cow might peel a tire right off of the rim or cause the truck to overturn. This slow driving in turn, however, meant relying upon very weak headlamps, when bright ones were needed the most. The only other alternative was to drive in low gear with the engine revved up, but this would have been foolish at best, if continued for extended periods of time. Driving after dark, especially in unfamiliar country, was to be avoided if at all possible.

Anyway, it was too cold to get outside after the sun went down, so those that could slept in the truck. Parking in a grove of pine trees helped to break the wind. Also, it helped having so many bodies in the vehicle; they snuggled together to make it warmer. The quilts they carried for lap covers during the day were most helpful in combating the cold, night air. It was a long, uncomfortable night. Papa and the two older boys had trouble sitting up and sleeping. Long before daybreak, with a minimal amount of light, the still weary sojourners were back on the road. There was no need in sitting still in so much discomfort when they could have been travelling. Sunrise was a most welcome sight. They needed all the help they could get in keeping the inside of the vehicle warm. The vehicle had no sides above the doors, so it was extremely cold from the rushing air created by the movement. Some of these models had sidewindows, but they were worn out long before the Cantrells purchased it. Also, the truck had no heater; the only heat to conserve was body heat. Without the quilts they carried, everyone would have caught pneumonia at best. There was still no escaping runny noses and coughs.

You could tell spirits were continuing to improve the farther west they went. They were starting to sing songs like “Clementine,” “Oh Susanna,” and “She’ll Be Comin’ Round The Mountain.” Maybe they would even make 75 miles today. Singing helped. The harmony made the miles go faster. No one questioned that their travel was faster than a horse and wagon; at times, though, some doubt could creep in.

Meals on the trip came from what they could buy at grocery stores along with some canned goods they carried. Zelda Mae and Claudine had canned peaches, tomatoes, peas, greenbeans and corn in August. They bought light bread and some pieces of cured ham in De Kalb, Texas, for breakfast. All they had to drink was water from a gallon jug Papa had encased in burlap. If the burlap was saturated with water and exposed to moving air, it could keep the water somewhat cooler, but never cold this time of year. They made it all the way to Paris, Texas, before they had to eat again. Fresh fruit would have been good to carry on the trip, but it wasn't in season.

A real drawback to the Model T Ford was the placement of the fuel tank under the front seat. The only way to get the fuel from the tank to the engine was to rely upon gravity to do the job for you. When steep hills were encountered, it meant the front of the vehicle became elevated, eventually starving the engine of fuel until it died before reaching the top, if it was a long hill. This situation left two options to the driver. He could build up speed and get a run at the hill, often getting over the summit before the engine died, or he could back over the hill, as backing elevated the fuel tank above the engine.

Seeing a hill coming up often caused Clayton to have to make hasty decisions. Was the road so torn up with ruts that he wouldn't dare attempt to drive at speeds above 22 miles per hour, or could he get a run at it? Needless to say, there were times the Cantrell party found themselves in a vehicle slowly backing over a hill. Not only did this approach slow them down, but it was dangerous as well. Backing up a rutted hill with limited visibility for the driver was more than adequate cause for worry. At least Papa or Clyde would get out to help give Clayton directions or keep their eyes peeled for oncoming vehicles, so they could get the truck out of the way. At the same time Zelda Mae and Claudine would escort the children up the hill by walking in the barrowpit.

Getting down hills was also a chore, as the truck had such temperamental brakes. Mechanical brakes lacked many of the advantages of hydraulic brakes, so they were poor at best. This could easily give cause for concern when trying to navigate down a steep hill. In the event of a brake failure, which was known to happen on occasion, some drivers would gently push down on the reverse pedal, while others might push down on the left pedal slightly engaging low gear. In either case, it was hard on the transmission bands. Thinking the lever to the left of the driver's seat was an emergency brake could create problems for some drivers. This lever was often of no value if the brake pedal didn't work, because its sole purpose was to shift the vehicle from low to high range in the transmission.

It was early afternoon. Clayton reckoned Paris was as good of a place as any to head north into Oklahoma. Road signs were rare or non-existent. Often he had to stop in a town or at a farmhouse to ask for directions. Stopping at the infrequent service station for gasoline was also a good time to find out where they were. The problem was that they didn't stop often enough for fuel to suit the kids. These stops gave them a chance to run around for awhile or go off into the woods, and they were desirous of more opportunities to play.

Travel was very slow. More than once the sensitive vehicle had flat tires, as pneumatic tires were far from perfected. This lapse in inflation caused a lot of work, with getting the wheel off of the stranded vehicle being the hardest part. While Clyde went to find some large, flat rocks, Clayton would locate a tree branch. It had to be several inches thick and not so dry that it would easily break under pressure. Most of the rocks would be stacked up about one foot away from the axle closest to the flat tire, as the truck didn't have bumpers. The rocks could then be used as a fulcrum, while the branch was used as a lever to raise the handicapped vehicle. Both Papa and Clayton would push down on the outer portion of the limb to raise the truck, giving Clyde a chance to slide more rocks under the axle. Even more taxing labor was yet to come. Once the wheel was removed, the trio still had to get the tire off of the wheel and patch the tube.

This repair was done on the spot with a patching kit and two tire irons they carried under the seat by the gas tank. If the tire was in bad shape, the laborer would put a "boot" over the hole.

This boot was a heavy piece of rubber to line the inside and strengthen the tire while preventing the tube bulging out of the hole. If there weren't a boot to cover a hole in the tire, the tube would rupture once the tube under pressure worked its way through the created opening.

The final step before remounting the tire was to use a hand pump to reinflate the rejuvenated tube. The men took turns with the mechanical device, because it was hard work pumping up the tire. While Clayton and Clyde complained about the difficulty of fixing the truck, Papa secretly remembered the hardships of moving long distances with a team and wagon. This was an easy trip, he told himself.

The menfolk weren't especially amused by the prospect of changing a tire, but the younger kids welcomed these breaks for a chance to get out and run around. The stops did give everyone a chance to go and find relief for bladders and the like, so stops weren't all bad. Zelda Mae and Claudine watched over the younger children to keep them out of the way of the tire changing. It was too easy to get hurt if one wasn't careful. The truck could easily slip off of the pile of rocks and sometimes did. Once the tire was fixed, it took a little while to round up all of the children.

Zelda Mae soon got to where she knew the tire changing was almost done, so the kids were ready when the menfolk were finished. The piles of rocks were left beside the road, as someone was always fixing a flat tire and welcomed their ready availability.

Driving the Model T created a love-hate relationship. Drivers loved it because it so expanded their world and gave them access to places or things they might never get to see or otherwise experience. At the same time it gave them numerous headaches trying to solve the problems that kept cropping up with the car's maintenance. For example, it was widely noted that the owner needed to carry wire used in storing hay in order keep the vehicle running. Actually, the notion of baling wire originated from the fact that parts of the car body would sometimes break or fall off, and the best way to weld them back on or fix them was with the relatively slender wire being used as the welding rod. Until there was an opportunity for the welding to occur, however, nothing was better than this same baling wire to hold the errant pieces together in anticipation of a more complete repair being done at a later time.

Regardless of the problems associated with the Model T or other vehicles on the road, many people were desirous of owning their own automobile or at least being able to drive one. Henry Ford's innovation opened that opportunity to the masses of America.

Papa wished he could drive, so he could give Clayton a break with the driving. "Do you think I could learn to drive, Clayton?" he asked.

"It's pretty complicated, but I'll just bet you can do it," said Clayton. "See these here three pedals down here on the floor? No, not the tall levers, the pedals. When you push all the way down on the left one, you're in low gear. You have to hold it down as long as you want it in low gear, because there's a spring behind it. When you let up part way, it goes into neutral. Then you can't go anywhere. You just sit still. When you let all the way up, and it'll certainly end up there if you take your foot off of the pedal, you're in high gear, providing you've also moved this lever on the left here. Course you ain't a goin' fast in high gear unless you give it plenty of gas. That's what this lever is here on the right of the steering post. At the same time you give it the gas, you also have to advance the spark. You do that by pulling down on this lever on the left side of the steering column. And all of the time you're a steerin' the truck. When you really wanta go fast, you pull both ears down."

"What do you mean, pull both ears down?"

"Well you pull the spark advance down at the same time you pull the gas lever down on the other side here. You better be ready to fly down the road when you do that, because this here T's going to be a movin' right fast."

"Is that safe?'

"Only if you have good roads, and there ain't many of those in these here parts."

"What if you want to back up?" asked Papa.

"Then you push down on this here middle pedal on the floor," said Clayton.

"If that one pedal is to go frontwards, and the other one is for backin', pray tell what is the third one down there for?"

"It's the brake," explained Clayton. "You can't stop without it."

"Was it hard for you to learn all of this?" asked Papa.

"I must confess it wasn't easy. Course I did git off to a bad start."

"What do you mean?" asked Papa.

"Well, the first time I started it, it almost ran over me," said Clayton.

With a concerned look on his face, Papa asked, "How'd that happen?"

"Well, it's like this. You're supposed to retard the spark here before you get out and turn the crank for startin'. Also, if the emergency brake isn't on, the truck's automatically in high gear. Well, I forgot that. I just gave the crank one good turn. The next thing I know, the darn thing is about to run me over. First off, it almost broke my arm. I had to outrun it before it ran me down. Then I had to get in it and stop it. Shoot, I was tired, and I hadn't even been any place yet."

"Was that all of the trouble you had?" asked Papa.

"No, there's more. Once I got it going, I couldn't stop it at all. I yelled `whoa', and it just kept goin'. Then I stepped on this here other pedal. It slowed a bit, but she sure never stopped at all. Then I let up and she started to speed up again. I was a considerin' jumpin' for it, but I reckoned I'd better not give up just yet. I tried everything. I would have run into the straw stack if there hadn't been a fence around it."

"Well, what did you do?"

"Went until it ran out of gas. Thank goodness it was nigh empty of gas when I started out. I circled the dadburned barn four times or more, I reckon. Then I drove around the south pasture. It ran out of gas just before I got back home."

"Would it bother you any if you had to do all of the drivin' on this trip?" asked Papa.

"I reckon not," replied Clayton.

"Could I learn?" asked Clyde.

"Oh, I reckon you could," answered his older brother. "Right now, though, I need your help watchin' the road. Yell out if you see any cows approachin' the road. We sure don't need any more things to fix right now."

"You will teach me, though."

"Yes, brother. I'll teach you. Wait until we're settled in Oklahoma first, though."

At the end of the third day of travelling, Papa decided they had gone far enough. He knew the kids couldn't take much more of this hard, crowded travel. Besides that, was there really any need to go any further? They were in Bennington, Oklahoma, north of the Red River. Papa went into a Malouf's Grocery Store for some more supplies. He used this opportunity to inquire about farms he might sharecrop. Mr. Malouf informed the weary traveler of a place between the towns of Wade and Albany, about ten miles south and east. Papa decided to go first thing in the morning, so a third cold night was spent in the Model T by the side of the road.

CHAPTER XVI

Cal Ledbetter was courting May Tolliver. He supposed you might call it courting. He had gone to church with her once, and then later they had been seen at a dance together. He much preferred dancing to listening to preachers, and it involved more than having to sit still. If the time spent with May was courting, that was the extent of it.

Cal wasn't really interested in more than this right now. It wasn't that he didn't consider himself the marrying type; he just hadn't found the right girl yet, the one he wanted to spend the rest of his life with. There was nothing wrong with May. As a matter of fact, she was right nice to be with. Maybe he wasn't ready to settle down. He was only twenty-nine years old.

"Did you hear about the Cantrell girls up the road a piece?" asked Ben, Wallace Stepford's son and Cal's stepbrother.

"What are you talkin' about?" said Cal, "I don't know any Cantrells."

"Yah!" said Ben. "There's a new family up the road. The man's wife died back in Arkansas, and they just moved here about three months ago. He sure has some pretty girls. I think we ought to look into this."

"Well, I did know there's a new family over yonder. Course there are a bunch of kids. I reckon I've just been too busy to look in on them."

"I intend to know more about them girls," said Ben. "As a matter a fact, I'm a gonna stop by this afternoon."

"Aren't you supposed to be a plowin' over by the creek?" asked Cal.

"The fields over half done. Why, I can finish up anytime I've a mind to," retorted Ben.

"A man ought to look after his livestock first," said Cal. "Then, he ought to look after work in the fields. If there's any of his time left, he can practice being neighborly. Right now I'm still workin' in the fields. The Good Lord doesn't wait on fools and Englishmen, you know."

"Well, I don't reckon I'm a fool. I suppose you might say I'm an Englishman. At least Pa says we are. But I ain't got any time for worryin' about that. My work gets done. Like I said, I'm goin' to look in on them after dinner."

"Let me know how it turns out," said Cal. "Can't see as how I'm a goin' to change your mind about most things anyhow. Just keep your powder dry and your horse saddled."

Where the Cantrells lived wasn't on the road to town, so Cal really had no reason to go that way. On his way into Hominy Corners a few days later, however, the curious farmer thought he might just go out of his way this one time. After all, he thought, he should be more neighborly and look in on the new folks. Actually, the Cantrells had already lived there almost four months, and he hadn't even stopped over to meet them. Of course he worked from sunup to sundown on most days. His mother admonished him about the ungodliness of working on Sunday. He was going to have to do a better job of keeping track of things, he thought. Ben had warned him that the world was going to pass him by one day, and he wouldn't even see it happen. He couldn't afford to let Ben know that he had listened to him. By now, he and May Tolliver were no longer courting, so he would like to know more about those girls Ben mentioned.

Mr. Cantrell was out in the field. From a distance Cal could tell that the man was trying to do some plowing with a mule and a single bottom plow. The alert observer could also tell that the mule was working mighty hard and little ground was being covered. There were several possibilities for what might be causing the mule to struggle so hard in the harness. It might be that the mule was too young for such heavy work or it was untrained for pulling implements. Or, then again, it might be due to dull plowshares. The red earth did have a high clay content and might be packed like bricks. In that case only the best of plows would be up to the task.

Cal decided to approach the house first. No need interrupting a man at work. Zelda Mae answered the door. She was real polite to this stranger on their front porch. Besides that, visitors were rare in these parts, and he certainly looked harmless enough. No need scaring him off. Actually, she was quite taken with the man holding his weathered hat while wiping the sweat from his brow.

By now Zelda Mae had dated the Conover boy who lived in the direction of Wade a number of times, but she questioned his intentions. She thought she was real partial to him, until she discovered he was seeing someone else as well. Deciding that she could do better for herself, she wasn't going with him anymore. She was going to be eighteen years old this summer; Papa often expressed worry that she might be on her way to becoming an old maid. It was nice to know that there were other men in the area.

Before Zelda had a chance to speak, the caller had returned his sweaty hat to its rightful place and paused to scratch his elbow. It looked as though he was preparing to make a speech.

With eyes lowered, the stranger began his discourse, "Hi ya'll. My name is Caleb Ledbetter. People in these parts just call me Cal. I just wanted you to know I'm glad Mom and I have you as our new neighbors. If there is any way I can help you get better settled, I'd be right proud to help out."

Taken back for a moment by his quickness, Zelda responded, "High ya'll yerself. My name is Zelda Mae Cantrell, and you can help us. Papa's strugglin' in gettin' the ground ready for plantin'. Says he's havin' the hardest time tryin' to plow. Reckons it's a dull plowshare. Can't keep it sharp, he says. Is there anything you can do to help him out?"

She wanted to see more of this Cal. Maybe her request would help to keep him around.

"I reckon there is. The best blacksmith in these parts is in Wade. Someday we'll have one in Hominy Corners, so we won't have to travel so far. I'll go in with him when he has some free time, maybe later today. Actually, he should go in soon. A dull plowshare is right hard on a mule. It saps their strength without it bein' necessary. Yes, I'll help him. Maybe I should swing out into the field right now."

"Would you?" she asked. "We'd be right grateful, if you would."

Not wanting to immediately vacate the front porch, Cal next asked, "You wouldn't have a drink of water for a weary man, would you? Seems like I plumb forgot to carry my canteen today."

"I believe Clyde got a fresh bucket a water just this mornin'. I'll bet you it hasn't even warmed up yet. You wait right here now, and I'll fetch you the best water you've had all day," she said as she wheeled and re-entered the house.

Awaiting her return, Cal could see through the screen with ragged holes that the house had sparse furnishings. There was almost no furniture to speak of in the living room. In one corner were blankets and a quilt spread on the floor to make a pallet. Rolled up clothing, possibly a coat, was used to form a pillow. The bare room looked as neat as a pin, however.

"Now you just put your lips to this dipper of the nectar of the gods. Isn't that right good water?" she asked.

"Yes ma'am," said Cal. "I do believe that's the best drink I've had in a long time, ma'am. I appreciate your kindness, ma'am."

"You sure have good manners, mister. No one has said so many ma'ams to me in my whole life."

"My mother says we've got to treat women special," said Cal. "Otherwise, we'll spend our entire life alone. Now I don't reckon I want to spend my entire life alone. I've got a heap of livin' to do, and I don't figure I'll spend it alone, leastways if I can help it I won't."

"You mean you're not married?" asked Zelda Mae.

"No, I haven't found the right gal yet. The way I figure it, in time the right one'll come along. Well, I best get out and meet your pa before that mule gets plumb tuckered out. Right nice meeting you Zelda Mae. I'm sure we'll be seein' more of each other."

"Oh, you haven't seen the last of me, either, Cal Ledbetter. You just stop in any time now, you hear?"

Cal could see that this was one right nice girl. He'd like to see more of her. "Right now I better check on your pa."

It wasn't long before the neighborly soul had his chance to once again grace the front porch of the new family. He had stopped off on a Sunday afternoon to show the Cantrells his new harness on Jenny.

Before he had a chance to speak this time, Zelda Mae asked him, "I've got a right fresh pie just out of the oven; how about I put some of it along with a few things in a picnic basket?"

"Well don't your folks want none? They ain't goin' to like me too much if we take the pie with us."

"Silly! I made two pies. If they cut it small enough, they can all have a piece."

"Well, as long as we're not goin' to get in any trouble. I reckon we ought to be okay this time. But, I did come over here to show you my new harness. I'm right proud of that harness. I've saved a good share of my cotton earnin's for that leather."

"Well, you can show me how well that new harness of yours works, then. I'll just bet there's a nice place down by the creek, if we look hard enough."

Cal didn't need a second invitation. Over the next couple of months the young couple found time to get together once in awhile without a group of family members being in the general vicinity. Then, too, there were community dances to attend. Nigger picnics were no longer so frequent. Instead, there was more isolation between the two races. Dancing was still a most welcome activity. Without the Negroes present, it was called a hoedown.

It was not unusual on most any Saturday night to find a get-together at someone's place to dance, play cards or dominoes or generally swap tales over a bodacious potluck supper. The rules were not so different from the Nigger picnics. The liquor continued to flow, even though Oklahoma was now well established as a dry state. Zelda Mae enjoyed attending these events; she just did not appreciate the liquor. Her upbringing meant that she wasn't especially partial to dancing, either. She claimed that she had two left feet and they were always arguing over which one would lead.

Cal was kept busy playing his guitar, so it didn't bother him that she didn't dance. Leastwise, he told himself, no one else will be dancing with her, either. Zelda Mae much preferred to listen to the toetapping music. Maybe it's because I enjoy watching Cal so much, she thought to herself.

Along about early summertime Zelda Mae looked like she was putting on weight. She didn't appear to understand what was happening. She talked to Cal's mother, Lillie, about it. Lillie knew; Zelda Mae was expecting a child. Cal knew it wasn't his child. The Conover boy must be the guilty culprit, thought Lillie. Cal said that he and Zelda Mae had not been together, and she believed her son. Cal and Zelda Mae talked about her predicament.

"If Tom is the pa, then we have to get married, real soon like," she said.

"Does he know he's goin' to be the papa?" asked Cal.

"I don't rightly know," said Zelda Mae. "But how could he know? I haven't seen him for nigh onto...I don't know how long it's been. Before you and I started a courtin' I know for a fact."

"Well, if he doesn't know, I see no need to tell him," said Cal.

"Maybe we shouldn't be a courtin' until I can decide what's right in my heart. I don't want to hurt no man, Cal, but I have to do what's right."

"Yes, you've got to do what's right," said Cal. But, what am I goin' to do?"

"I hear you and that May Tolliver were right friendly before I came along. What about May?"

"I was a hopin' the Mae in my life would be you, not May Tolliver," answered the beleaguered farmer.

"Are you upset with me, Cal?"

"I'm upset with us, Zelda. Just when things begin to look good, our life starts to tumble."

"It'll work out for the best," answered Zelda. "Just wait and see. Things will work out."

"I don't know about that," reasoned the despondent Cal, as he turned to leave.

Zelda Mae did indeed resume courting with Tom Conover. She was seen at a church social on a Saturday night. Cal was right partial to social events that didn't disrupt his getting work done in the fields. As he prepared to enter the Hominy Corners Schoolhouse where church functions were held, he saw Zelda

Mae and Tom across the room. Immediately turning, he boarded his horse for a wild ride into Wade.

Josiah Culpepper could be counted on to have some right good corn liquor that the authorities did not know about. It was a long night as Cal drank far more than he would have ever dreamed possible. Josiah awoke Cal at sunup. With a splitting headache, the visitor had no idea where he was or why he was there.

"You and that little lady have got to get some things straight," said Josiah.

"What are you a talkin' about?" asked Cal.

"You put away a lot of my best corn squeezin's last night," said Josiah.

"What's that have to do with a lady?" responded Cal.

"Well, in between every drink of my juice, you mentioned her name," said Josiah. "Something May I reckon you said. I didn't know you were still courting May Tolliver."

"It wasn't May Tolliver," said Cal. "Don't you pay no mind to my babblin'. When I'm a drinkin' who knows what I might be a talkin' about, and I'd appreciate you keepin' quiet about tonight."

Cal's timing in leaving Culpeppers could not have been worse. Who should he immediately encounter but Fire and Brimstone Thomas. With his head feeling oversized, Cal was not desirous of any argument at this time.

"And how are you, Brother Thomas?"

"Don't Brother Thomas me you scalawag! You're drunk aren't ya'? The worst kind of sinner you are! Sinner Cal, you're a goin' ta hell as sure as you're born."

"I won't deny I've sampled a little of the Lord's vineyard. But I certainly ain't drunk, and only God knows where I'll be a goin' when I leave this here world. It's fer damned sure you ain't deciding my future fer me! Besides, can't a man even have a headache without someone jumpin' to conclusions?"

"You're right on one thing, the Lord will decide where everyone's a goin' when the leave the face of this here earth. And, I have a good idea 'cause he talks to me."

"I don't doubt that ya hear voices. Folks like you hear lots of strange things. I'll bet the Lord Almighty isn't the one doin' the talkin', though."

"Take my word for it. The Father in heaven and I are on speaking terms. Oh, and one more thing. He certainly doesn't want drinkin' referred to as samplin' the Lord's vineyard."

"What I do is between me and the Lord, and I'll be a sayin' whichever I feels like."

"Yes and I'm the messenger of the Lord! You'd do well to listen to the messenger!"

"I've got places to be," said Cal as he spun and hurried away.

Lost and unable to understand his own feelings, Cal did go back to talk with Zelda Mae. He informed her that her expecting another man's child did not bother him. In his mind there was no doubt she had really lacked the experience to deal with her own feelings in a courtship. Maybe it wouldn't have happened if she'd had a mother to advise her before it occurred. By now, though, Lillie had sort of become a mother to her. His anguish centered on his role in what would happen next.

Zelda Mae heard out the confused man, then she began her explanation of the previous evening's events, "Caleb Ledbetter, I reckon I did wrong by you. There's so much I've been afraid to tell ya. Actually very few around here besides Papa, Claudine and me knows the real story about what's happenin' ta me. Tom Conover is not the daddy of my unborn child. I reckon I was with child when we left Arkansas."

"Where does Tom fit inta everythang, then?"

"Nowhere. I just needed time ta sort things out. He asked me for a date, and I wanted ta git outta the house."

"What is it ya want ta tell me Zelda Mae? Know this, though, ya really don't owe me no explanation."

"You've been so good ta me, though, Cal. I really want ta tell ya'."

"If it'll make ya feel better, then okay."

"Well I was only seventeen. I was over ta Grandma's house helping cut up some pork. When we finished, I started ta walk home. There was no one ta give me a ride, but that didn't bother me none. I've always loved ta walk, and it was less than a mile. I took a shortcut through Bilyew's pasture. Next thing I knew...it hurts ta talk about it. No, I need ta tell someone."

"Does it need ta be me?" asked Cal. "Maybe you'd rather talk ta my ma. I could fetch her in no time."

"No, you really need to know, and I need ta git it out. It hurts carryin' it around."

"Well, go ahead then. I'm real partial to ya no matter what happened."

"It helps ta hear that. It really does."

"Please continue, then, if that's what ya want ta do."

"Well, anyway, I'm a walkin' beside a haystack as I crossed the pasture. I've walked that way before with nary a problem. Next thing I know someone grabbed me and pulled me up against the haystack. He wasn't nice ta me. He tore my dress takin' it off. I fought back, but it did no good. He wouldn't stop! He was on toppa me."

"Who was it, Zelda Mae?"

"It was the Bilyew boy. I knew him when we went ta school tagether. He was four years older than me I think. Anyways, now I'm a carryin' his child."

"Why, I oughta go back ta Arkansas and whup him good," said Cal.

"It won't do no good," said Zelda. "He's in prison now fer killin' someone. He said he'd kill any of us that said he did this. It weren't one of the family he killed, though. He just had a mean streak about him."

"Is that why ya left Arkansas, then?"

"Yes. We've been a tellin' folks it was cause of poor crops. We did have poor crops, but that's not why we left. Papa just wanted ta git us away from any chance of harm. He didn't even want Mama ta know about this, and she's dead. Most people we knew in Arkansas didn't know I was with child when we left. I didn't know I was with child. That's a fact. The less people know, the better. We'd like things ta stay that way. Other than Claudine, no one otherwise knows about the real father of this here child."

"Well, I hate ta see ya havin' ta leave Arkansas under those circumstances, but now that ya did, I'm glad you're here. You sure put me through a whole heap of misery, though, Zelda."

"I know," said Zelda Mae. "Can you ever forgive me?"

"You know I can, Zelda. You know I can. And I want to be a papa to your child, too."

The baby was born on September 7, 1924. It was a boy. Zelda Mae couldn't think of a name for him. For the first few days he was referred to as "Just Him." After awhile this was shortened to "J.H." Later Zelda Mae was to name him Joseph Henry to use the initials he already possessed. The initials J.H. stuck, however, as everyone seemed satisfied to call him by the now familiar initials. Zelda Mae didn't mind, either. J.H. it was then. He certainly was a likable little rascal. Cal certainly enjoyed coming over to hold and play with him. He even liked taking J.H. along occasionally when he and Zelda Mae went courting.

It was clear that Cal accepted J.H. as his own. The family on both sides knew and understood what was taking place, so they weren't bothered, either. Anyone else's opinion didn't matter. There was no problem with the boy's parentage to the people where it mattered.

You could tell 1924 was their year. All of the time now Cal and Zelda Mae referred to we and us on everything they did. You'd have thought they were already married, except Cal went home at bedtime every night.

"I declare," Lillie told him one evening, "I believe you eat more meals with the Cantrells than you eat with me. Is Zelda Mae a better cook than I am?"

Not wanting to find himself in a no-win situation, Cal would answer, "Now you know Momma that you've been the best cook there is for most of my life. Can't you be a satisfied with that?"

"Don't go and get upset over your momma, son. Can't I poke a little fun at you now and then?"

Cal usually walked over to the Cantrell place, so Zelda Mae always admonished him to bundle up good. Catching cold from the winter air on his way home would not be on her head. She was most protective of the man in her life, and it went beyond the attire he wore. His stocky figure reflected more and more the fullness of the meals served by the woman in his life. She already had visions of the time they would be husband and wife.

The week after Christmas of 1924 Cal asked Papa Cantrell for Zelda Mae's hand. He looked so funny before he actually asked. He was like a horse tied up too long at the hitching post in front of Hominy Corners General Store. After supper with the Cantrells, he had just walked back and forth on the porch without saying anything. Zelda Mae suspected what was going on, but she didn't say anything. No sense scaring him more than he already is. She wished she could ask Papa for him. But that was the job of the man to ask the father for his daughter's hand in marriage. Pretty soon Cal threw caution to the wind.

He blurted out with a twisted tongue, "Can married and I get Zelda Mae?"

Papa had a hard time keeping from laughing as he replied, "What took you so long?"

On the fifth day of January in the year 1925, Cal and Zelda Mae went into Durant to pick up a marriage license. It didn't bother them that both of their names were misspelled when the license was recorded. They were in love. They didn't even notice how bumpy the ride home was in the lumber wagon Cal had bought for $45 the year before. They could hardly wait to get married. Zelda Mae insisted, however, that she have time to make herself a new dress for the ceremony.

Zelda Mae and Lillie worked together. It didn't take long when the two of them teamed up. In no time they had a right nice violet colored dress. It was a pretty dress with long sleeves to help stay warm. Her bonnet didn't match, but it was such a pretty white, who cared?

January seventh was a quiet day in Bennington, Oklahoma. Of course it was Wednesday, which should have been a quiet day. Farmers generally didn't have a reason to be in town during the middle of the week, and most of the people in the area were farmers. *The Durant Democrat* might have given the reader the impression that not a lot was going on out of the normal course of events. The headlines included notice that the Golden Gate Girls from Vaudeville would be at the Liberty Theater. Also, next week, it said, there would be a two reel silent movie, "Sandra," shown at the theater. It was a comedy.

The paper even had advice on how to darken your hair. Just mix sage tea with sulfur and people won't even know if it's naturally dark or not.

There really wasn't much going on nationally. Cal and Zelda Mae could have cared less. They knew what was important on the seventh of January. Today they would become Mr. and Mrs. Caleb Ashton Ledbetter. Oh, how Zelda Mae loved the sound of that name. She knew how much they loved each other. They were going to spend their lives together. The world would just have to take care of itself for now. Their priorities were clear. Today was Cal and Zelda Mae's day.

The trip into Bennington seemed like it took forever. They left bright and early in the morning. Cal had harnessed Jenny in the dark. He could do it by feel. It's likely he didn't have a clear head about him, anyway. Frost was still on the ground, and it glistened on the trees as the sun hit it, sometimes sparkling like diamonds. Word had it that the justice of the peace in Wade was gone on a trip, so they'd just have to go where there was one. It was a long trip just to get married, so they went alone. The January air was cold and crisp. It had a bite to it, but they shared a quilt for warmth as they sat atop the narrow wagon seat.

Friction from the continual jostling went unnoticed. The long trip gave them plenty of time to talk. As though they had never had a chance to broach the subjects before, they shared their hopes and dreams in great detail. They both wanted more children, lots more. J.H. would love it, too. There would be a farm they owned someday.

Sharecropping would be all right, but it would only be an in-between step until they could actually own their own place. They would raise plenty of cotton, a small plot of tobacco, a few acres of peanuts and some wheat, too.

"Just where is all of this a goin' to take place, Cal?" she asked.

"Why, right in Hominy Corners. There's no other place I'd rather be in this world. I've been overseas. I've even seen Paris, and there's no place like Hominy Corners."

"Well, there is one place," said his bride to be.

"And just where might that place be?" asked Cal. "We're not in heaven yet, and I don't reckon on goin' there any time soon."

"Hope and De Ann, Arkansas."

"I'm sorry. I keep fergettin' about yer ma being buried there. Yes, I'll bet they're nice places, too. We can visit there sometimes, but our families are here now. Is there any chance that Bilyew boy will cause a problem for ya'?"

"No, he's been put away fer a long time. Otherwise, Mama and I were always close. I feel so far away bein' in another state from where she's buried. Promise me, we'll go there sometimes to visit. I always feel so close when I'm by her and Mattie Fern's graves."

"I feel the same way when I'm by my pa's gravesite, too. No question about it. Both of our folks were special people. They deserve our visitin' them from time to time. But I hope you'll agree to live in Hominy Corners with me Zelda Mae."

"Oh, I'll live wherever you live, Cal. But I'm goin' to hold you to your promise to visit Holly Grove Cemetery with me."

"We'll go there one of these days. I can't promise when, but we'll go there."

Yes, they had hopes and dreams aplenty. Things were going to be different. Things were going to be better. They just knew they were. They had already had enough heartache for a lifetime, what with Cal's father, Samuel, and Zelda Mae's mother, Sadie, having already gone on to their just reward.

They talked so much that they weren't even aware of how hard that old wagon seat truly was. It could have had splinters and they wouldn't have noticed. They probably didn't even need the quilt to stay warm. Love was wonderful, but it could also be strange. While it almost always heightened emotions, it sometimes dulled physical feelings.

"Do you know a preacher in Bennington?" asked Zelda.

"Afraid I don't," answered Cal. "Thank goodness Brother Thomas is not there. But we'll find someone to tie the knot for us."

"Who is this Brother Thomas, anyways?"

"Ishmael Thomas. He reckins he's a minister. I guess he is, but he's mainly a thorn in my side, if you want to know the truth of the matter."

"I thought all ministers were nice."

"Well, this one ain't."

Wanting to change the subject, Zelda Mae blurted out, "I wish my mother could be here with us!"

"And my pa, too," answered the soon to be husband.

"She'd a helped me make a new dress just for this occasion."

"My mother helped you," responded Cal.

"I know, but it's not the same as your own mother helpin' with the sewin'," returned Zelda. Anyway, I needed a new dress right now, anyhow."

"There'll be plenty of new dresses in the future, too," said Cal.

"You're right. You know, though, Cal, your momma does remind me of someone else now that we're talkin' about it," said Zelda.

"And just who might this fortunate person be?" he asked.

"Well there's a story in the Bible about Ruth and Naomi. Have you heard of them?"

"Can't rightly say that I have," answered Cal.

"I'll tell you more about the story some day. Basically it's a story about two widows living with each other because they've both been left alone in this world. It seems that Naomi is Ruth's mother-in-law. Instead of returning to her own people after her husband's death, Ruth chooses to remain with her mother-in-law. The words she used tell how I feel. 'Your people are my people'."

"Yes, but you haven't been widowed yet."

"I know, but your momma has been so good to me. Of course my family will always be there, but I miss having a momma to talk to. Your momma fits the bill right nicely."

"Does the story have a happy ending?"

"Yes, it sure does."

"Then I'd like to hear the full story some time."

In no time the trip was over. They had talked so much that the outskirts of Bennington had slipped right up on them. They weren't worried about eating. They were here for something else. After asking for directions, they found the Justice of the Peace, I.W. Washington, at home. They were dismayed to learn that they would have to have witnesses to stand up with them at the wedding. They had come ten miles all alone. It was too late and too far to go back home to get family members as witnesses.

Mr. Washington figured such a nice looking couple shouldn't have to make such an important trip a second time. He suggested two ladies that might be witnesses for the ceremony. His wife, Rachel, and Margaret McQuithey stood beside Cal and Zelda Mae for that most momentous occasion. You'd have thought they had known the bride and groom forever, the way they carried on. Rachel played the piano, so they would have some music. Neither Cal nor Zelda Mae could later remember what she played. It was an unfamiliar tune by someone they had never heard of named Mendelssohn.

The newlyweds spent that first night at a hotel in downtown Bennington. After getting a late start the next day, they traveled all day to reach Durant. Cal wanted to go to the Liberty Theater to see the Golden Girls live on stage that night. After all, he had told Zelda Mae, they wouldn't be in a town with a theater too often. Zelda Mae didn't take too kindly to dancing girls. Her church upbringing told her that was wrong. Instead, after a nice meal in the hotel dining room, they returned to their room. After all, she had never stayed in a hotel before. Furthermore, anything costing 35 cents a night was expensive, and she wanted to make the most of it.

The time this couple spent on their honeymoon was a time to forget the cares of this world and just enjoy each other's company. It was a short time away from the farm, however. On Friday morning, January ninth, they registered their wedding certificate with the Clerk of Court, Frank Buford, in Durant. The official honeymoon was over. They had to get back to Wade. There was work to be done. Perhaps they could feel an occasional bump in the road as the heavy wagon slowly made its way home behind the steady pull of the mule central to their making progress on the farm.

The real love story for this man of 30 and woman of 18 started on a summer day at a farmhouse between Albany and Wade, Oklahoma, in 1924. This heaven on earth was located near the community of Hominy Corners, a place to be forever etched in their collective memories, never to be removed. That simple ceremony in Bennington on January seventh of 1925 merely solemnized and consummated what God forever intended to be. Cal and Zelda Mae were now husband and wife. A deeper love could not be found. Let no man put it asunder.

CHAPTER XVII

Happiness is more than a state of mind. It grows out of a feeling all is right with the world, especially your own immediate world. When you can get up each morning and see that all is well around you, it is possible to experience a state of mind, which ignores many of life's problems. This is sometimes referred to as the honeymoon period of a marriage.

Cal and Zelda Mae had just such a time in their marriage. If there were problems, they didn't know about them. For some time they didn't even seem to notice the frequent bumps encountered in the road while riding in the jolting lumber wagon on Saturday afternoon shopping trips to town.

Happiness was easy to achieve for this couple in love. Sometimes it only took a gentle breeze at their backs while going about their work. At other times a kind word would suffice. The price was within their range.

The beginning of married life was indeed blissful for this happy couple. An observer could tell all was well. Cal and Zelda Mae didn't seem to have a care in the world. Zelda Mae sang as she worked in the kitchen, even though it might be on a hot summer day. She just wiped her brow with her apron and continued about her business. Cal hitched up the mules with a smile. Everyone commented on what a happy life they must have together. Sure, it wasn't easy for them with the almost total lack of modern day conveniences, even for 1925. But they were happy, as only two individuals in love could be. Their love was built on a commitment to each other, not on having their material needs met.

It didn't even matter that they shared common living quarters with Papa Cantrell and his family. It was crowded, but the house just seemed to be naturally designed for multiple family units. It was designed and constructed like two small houses close together with a common roof made of corrugated tin going over both, while covering an open area between the two units. This open area in the middle was called a “dogtrot.” It could also be used as a porch and often was.

This type of house was not unusual in those times. It certainly made it easier for two families living together like the Ledbetters and Cantrells now found themselves doing. They especially enjoyed time together on the porch to just sit and relax. The open area between the two units was especially good for permitting breezes, and shade was always present during daylight hours.

The rocking chair found there rarely rested during the evening hours after a hard day’s work until about sundown or a little later. The men found it to be a good time to roll a cigarette, as a few minutes were necessary for the process. When heavily involved in a busy project during the day, it was sometimes hard to find the time for this endeavor they considered essential to take their mind off of the task at hand.

Many men took up chewing tobacco to get around the restraints created by the simple task of rolling their own cigarette. Papa Cantrell was one of those individuals. In the evening, though, Cal took the time to take out a pack of cigarette papers and carefully separate one away; they sometimes stuck together. Using his index finger as a guide, the paper was turned with the edges up in order to hold the loose tobacco without spilling. It formed a “U” with the thumb supporting one side, while the middle finger supported the other side. After placing the tobacco in the resulting groove, Cal licked the length of one edge so the paper would bond together when it was then rolled on around the crushed leaves of the plant originally used by the American Indians to concoct a drink.

The finished product of Cal’s efforts was an ugly, flattened white object with strands of tobacco hanging out of each end. The cylinder could be expected to flare up when first lit because the end was mostly the paper. During the course of smoking the cigarette, Cal would occasionally find it necessary to spit out pieces of loose tobacco ending up in his mouth. Sometimes he wondered if the act really was that relaxing. As a matter of fact, it could be a downright nuisance at times.

The women were more content to sit and visit while enjoying a cooling breeze, should they be so fortunate as to have one at this time of day. Actually, their main goal was to get out of the hot kitchen whether there was a breeze or not. A woman couldn't sit peacefully for long periods of time however. Zelda Mae's hands had to be doing something, be it crocheting, churning butter, or anything else permitting conversation while completing the task at hand.

A second important ingredient in these evening get togethers for the ladies was time to sit down. Often they had spent most of the day on their feet, and their constitutions were weary. A porch step or any chair would fill the bill, but a rocking chair was heaven on earth; just get that weight off of their aching feet. These settlers of the porch could sometimes be seen fanning themselves and "shooing" away pesky flies. The oft made remark calling Oklahoma natives "sooners" was thought by some to mean they'd sooner sit on the porch, rock, and swat flies as anything else. The porch and the rocking chair were essential to the way of life for these times. They were social institutions.

"Did you all hear about what President Coolidge said?" asked Claudine.

"We're not goin' to talk politics, are we?" replied Zelda Mae.

"Well, what are we a goin' to talk about, then?"

"Just a minute now. What did the president say?"

"Well, I heard that he said the country was better off now than it had ever been. I believe he used the word prosperous."

"How can that be? We barely have enough money to buy sugar and flour. And, pray tell we could all use new clothes. And where do we get the money for material to make them?"

"I'm just a tellin' ya'll that's what he said." replied Claudine.

"Well, I declare! I wish them fool politicians would have come out here in the country and find out what it's like without any money to buy a new pair of shoes. Then they wouldn't be a usin' such high priced words like prosperous."

Porch conversations ran the full gamut from who's courting whom to how straight the rows of cotton were over on the Beames place. Everyone had an opinion on everything, even if he or she had never heard of the subject before. Nothing was sacred, except the word of God. Everything was fair game on the front porch, especially if Mrs. Wilson's pickles didn't turn out right.

Living like this seemed the perfect arrangement. After breakfast Cal would often walk down the narrow, dirt road to town to go to work. During the day, then, Zelda Mae would have the company of her sisters, should she feel lonesome when not taking care of housework. Claudine was now the woman of the house for the Cantrells at the age of fourteen. Sarah was almost eleven, while Rebecca was going on eight. They helped take care of young William, age four, and J.H., less than one-year old, when they were not in school. It seemed like the way to live. As a matter of fact, the two families couldn't envision living any other way. Wasn't everyone supposed to live like this?

Occasionally Ben Stepford, Cal's stepbrother, would stop by. He might bring over a mess of catfish to be fried or just drop in for a free meal. You could see he was taking a real liking to Claudine. Right now, though, he seemed to be content to work on the farm with his dad and do a little fishing and hunting. Also, Cal's brother, Clevon, would come over as well. He was sixteen years old and already quite a good worker in the fields with the Stepfords. He and Ben were the best of friends.

There were so many people living in this double house, with so much activity going on, that it was just the right place for having a good time. People were always coming and going like the train depot in Durant. Maybe the people at the depot had a better idea of where they were going, but they probably weren't having near as much fun as this household seemed to be experiencing.

By the time fall arrived Zelda Mae began to experience some changes in her body. She suspected what was happening this time, however. While it was really too early to tell, she had a hunch she was expecting a child. No one could have been more pleased at this prospect than Cal and Zelda Mae.

Cal loved J.H. like his own child; the two couldn't have been any closer. But, this new baby would be of his own flesh and blood. Somehow it felt different to him. He had always dreamed of having a big family. Now it seemed like they were on their way to achieving this goal. You would have thought Zelda Mae was an invalid when Cal was around. He wanted to do everything for his loving wife. Zelda Mae had a hard time getting him to understand that she was quite capable of working and felt uneasy being waited on so much. Her duty was to serve, not be served. Cal persisted in his efforts, anyway.

Before there was an opportunity to confirm a new baby was on the way, tragedy struck. J.H. came down with a severe case of diarrhea. In those days it was called "summer complaint." Every mother worried about this malady. There wasn't any cure for the problem, and it was sometimes fatal. He was only fourteen months old. Zelda Mae prayed that he would regain his lively ways.

Her memories of the losses of Mattie Fern and Mama pushed her to do everything for the young child to help ease his suffering. She even refused to sleep at night so she could hold and rock him, often dozing off in the rocking chair after succumbing to utter exhaustion.

Cal got up quite early that morning on October 30, 1925, to catch a ride into town to go to work. He was leaving the wagon at home, should it be needed. He had no idea of the events about to unfold on that quiet autumn day, or he surely would have stayed with his family. There is no doubt, however, that he could not have helped his stepson, anyhow.

About mid-morning Zelda Mae dozed off from the length of her vigil and the accompanying exhaustion. During the course of her brief nap she awakened troubled by what crossed the threshold of her weary mind. Initially she thought J.H. was sleeping due to his being so weak and ill. A careful investigation, however, revealed that his was a labored breathing as though each breath might be the last. Zelda called out in anguish as she viewed the pathetic little boy on her lap. Claudine heard the troubled cry and soon ran to get Papa

Cantrell. He was not to be found; she was unaware that he was out in the field milking the cow.

In a panic Claudine then ran to one of the neighbors, but it was too late. When she returned, all was quiet except for the muffled sobbing of Zelda Mae slowly stroking his hair while rocking her son on her lap. J.H. had already taken his last gasp of breath in his young mother's arms. Already his soul was winging its way to another world. Once again, Zelda Mae had to cope with the realities of death in her immediate family. Probably the only thing worse than losing a parent or spouse is losing one's own child. She didn't know how much more of these calamities she could take. Was death never to quit haunting this family?

Cal made a simple cross out of old barn boards with only the boy's initials on the cross member. In the briefest of ceremonies J.H. was laid to rest there on the farm, where he had lived his short but happy existence. Papa Cantrell said a few words after reading the 23rd Psalms out loud from the Bible.

"Our father. You saw fit to bless us with this here little boy. We know he was a gift from you to us. It seems like ya wanted him back ta join his grandma up in heaven. We hate to see him go, God, but he's yours. We'll miss him somethin' terrible, but we now return him unto you."

Bowing his head in reverence, while simultaneously stooping to grasp a small handful of dirt from the pile beside the grave, Papa said, "Ashes to ashes, dust to dust." Then, he slowly turned his cupped hand over to release the dirt over the small casket constructed with pine boards taken from the side of the barn where the little boy so often loved to play.

At the conclusion of this highly emotional service, Zelda Mae would leave with Papa at her side after gently dropping a small handful of dirt into the gapping hole in the ground, while asking that no flowers be placed on the grave. This most unusual request was hard to understand, but the young mother's wish was carried out. Cal remained behind to cover the small wooden box holding the lifeless body of a cherished soul destined for even more happiness had he lived.

When others volunteered to assist in this difficult task, Cal politely said, “No, this is somethin’ I have ta do alone.”

Covering the grave was to be the last visible act he could perform for a boy that had become so close to him. Even more, he had become part of the hopes and dreams of a man in need of something to clutch as he looked into the future.

The world outside the few Ledbetters, Cantrells and Stepfords living around Hominy Corners, and their descendents, would never know of a little boy who had brought so much happiness to those around him in his brief life of just over one year. Neither his birth nor his death was ever recorded with the public officials of Bryan County.

The fact he even existed was rarely to be known outside the hearts and minds of the descendents of those few family members present at that simplest of funeral ceremonies on a gentle hill. A hill where cattle now quietly search for sustenance, unaware of a young mother’s love for her child and the tears shed on that soil which continues to bring forth new life sustaining forms of wild grasses and prairie flowers.

Removing his sweat-stained hat, Cal simply said, “No one will ever know how much I loved you boy. You’re like a piece of me. Look my daddy up there in heaven. Maybe you two could work together there. Heaven knows I’d a liked for it to a happened here, but some things just ain’t meant to be. God bless you boy. I’m truly sorry that things didn’t work out different for us.”

When death revisits a family, experience does not necessarily make it any easier. Zelda Mae was most grievous over J.H. Now she knew there were three blossoms she’d someday see on the other side of that wall with a vine growing through the crack: Momma, Mattie Fern and J.H. Maybe someday she’d even meet Cal’s father when she herself crossed that wall dividing mortals from the immortal.

At nineteen Zelda Mae had already known the pains of life as few people will ever know them at that age. The only thing besides the love of Cal and her family that kept her going was the belief she had in God and the hereafter. Also, she received immense support from the fact she would soon have another child. She was determined that this new baby would have all of the love she could give it. After all, God was blessing her and Cal with a new child conceived by both of them.

While Cal did not appear to take the boy's death as hard as Zelda Mae did, you'd still have thought he had lost his own son. No longer was J.H. to be the boy to someday grow to manhood and work beside him on their farm. While Cal's dream was not taken away, it was sorely shaken. He and Zelda Mae were never to discuss J.H.'s death other than between themselves, and that was most rare. The hurt was just too great. It has been said that the sharing of a common adversity brings two people much closer together.

This was especially true for Cal and Zelda Mae. The grief was not to go away any too soon, either. The failure of parents to discuss the death of their child can sometimes lead to more problems, not less. Cal and Zelda Mae's ability to survive such a difficult period was a tribute to the depth of their love, not their knowledge of how to cope with grief. Furthermore, the love multiplied with time. It would take more than death to separate these two.

Cal remembered the peace he felt in France just from being able to put his thoughts into writing. While he never read the poetry of others, he did from time to time use this medium to deal with his own internal turmoil. Words he couldn't speak could be printed on a piece of paper, sometimes to never be seen by anyone else. Zelda Mae was not to know of Cal's expressions through the written word. Following the death of J.H., and prior to the birth of Pearl, he once again put his pen to paper with the following results:

OH MY SOUL

What waits o'er yon' distant peak,
    for the weary in search of rest?
What waits o'er yon' distant peak,
    to a soul longing unpained breast?

What tarries 'cross the fertile valley,
    beyond productive fields sufficient?
What tarries 'cross the fertile valley,
    to the soul aspiring gifts efficient?

What lingers 'hind tomorrow's door,
    remote from vision, oh so blind?
What lingers 'hind tomorrow's door,
    to one's soul a peace remind?

What lies 'round the river's bend,
    midst cloaks of darkened haze?
What lies 'round the river's bend,
    to my soul near end of earthly days?

Rest waits o'er yon' distant peak;
Gifts tarry 'cross the fertile valley;
Peace lingers 'hind tomorrow's door;
Unclouded vision lies 'round the river's bend.
OH MY SOUL-A NEW LIFE BEGINS.

Pearl Louise Ledbetter was born on July 16, 1926, the summer after J.H. was laid to rest. Maybe it was best that Cal and Zelda Mae's first child was a girl, as she was less likely to be seen as a replacement for the deceased J.H. Instead, the infant girl symbolized the new beginning for this young couple with so many hopes and dreams for the future. Her being born in a strawberry patch further symbolized a family with its roots in the soil. Actually the house where she was born was in the strawberry patch, but the symbolism didn't change. They could only have been happier if J.H. had been there to welcome this tiny bundle that kicked and screamed until she learned to smile and laugh.

"J.H. would'a loved a little sister," Zelda Mae reasoned.

"It isn't of any value to base your life on what mighta been," said Cal. "We only have one child now. The lives of the three of us has to go on. I wish J.H. could be here, too, but he isn't. We have to get on with our lives."

Cal's desire to be silent about J.H. hurt Zelda Mae. She carried so many feelings of grief inside of her that she wanted to share with her devoted husband. It's a troubled soul that carries such a heavy load. What she didn't know was that he carried so much sorrow inside of himself as well. But he honestly believed that time would heal all wounds. Little did he know that wounds of this type sometimes healed more quickly when out in the open air.

Pearl was named after one of Lillie Stepford's cousins, Pearl Shaughnessy. Cal had always been quite partial to the Shaughnessys, as his mother was born a Shaughnessy. With this abiding affection in mind, he wanted his eldest named after one of them. Zelda Mae was thrilled at the name as well. She had grown even closer to Cal's mother, Lillie, as well as the other Shaughnessys. With all of the adversity they had already shared together, this was a fitting decision. The crown jewell of the Ledbetter family, then, would be a pearl.

Grandma Lillie, as she was to be called hereafter, now had several grandchildren presented her by Myrtle and Jewel and now Cal. Grandma Lillie could tell she certainly liked the beginnings of these families. They were a living legacy to the life she and Samuel had started together in 1891. Samuel would have been proud of his growing family and their achievements in the ten years since his passing.

Zelda Mae and Cal saw the birth of Pearl as the first important bond to be added to their wedding vows. The birth not only strengthened their relationship, but it added a powerful new dimension. They knew they could now survive any hardship together. They just needed time to overcome the setback in their lives caused by the unexpected passing of J.H.

The dreams and hopes shared in that lumbering wagon on the way to the justice of the peace in Bennington, Oklahoma, were not to be forgotten. They might have to wait awhile, though.

"Maybe we shouldn't have no more children just yet," was the way Cal put it.

Zelda Mae agreed. There were happy times during these years. If Cal and Zelda Mae weren't actually involved themselves, it was still fun to just sit around and talk about what someone else was doing. A source of humor for all of them was trying to stay up with the antics of Ben and Clevon as they went through the courtship stage. As stepbrothers living in the same home, they were inseparable.

It was amusing, to say the least, to hear Ben talking about holding the horses in a nearby grove of mulberry trees, while Clevon slipped up to Olive Bell's window to get her to come out so they could go courting. Her father was a county commissioner, and he really didn't want his daughter dating the likes of Clevon Ledbetter. It was costing the county money rectifying the damage created by Clevon and his cohorts.

Yes, it always seemed that Ben and Clevon were involved in some prank. Cal missed being involved with the two. He vowed that he'd start going out with them again someday, just for good clean fun, mind you. Zelda Mae wasn't sure she liked the sound of this. It further seemed like Ben and Clevon were always involved in the rumors going around those parts. Without this form of entertainment, life might have been dull for the Cantrells and Ledbetters, however. It was too far to go into Durant to see a silent movie or watch a stage show. Besides that, Zelda Mae really didn't approve of such "fun."

The only entertainment left, then, were the increasingly rare Nigger picnics, along with the antics of Ben and Clevon. Well, there were a few other things like church activities and an occasional dance held in someone's home to name a few, but they weren't always lively enough for Cal.

When weather didn't permit sitting on the porch or their attendance at area social functions, the family still had plenty to occupy their time. Playing dominoes was just one of their favorite pastimes. Zelda Mae preferred "regular" dominoes, which consisted of forming skeletal like chains with the black objects, while trying to make the numbers at the extreme ends add up to units of five. Myrtle referred to it as playing "chicken tracks."

Cal preferred playing "moon" with the dominoes, whereby the game had trumps, such as sixes, and the purpose was to catch as many "tricks" or go-rounds as possible. The player who found him or herself far behind, and the game almost over, had one final salvation. They could "shoot the moon." If the bidder then captured all of the tricks, they won the game. Considerable skill was required to win at either Cal's or Zelda

Mae's preferred game. No small amount of time was spent playing dominoes.

"Git inside quick, Zelda Mae!" said Cal.

"Pray tell why?" responded his wife.

"Here comes Fire and Brimstone Thomas. You don't want'a know him. He is bad news."

"Well, okay. But I'm a listenin' in."

"Good mornin', Brother Thomas. What can we do fer ya?"

"You never learn, do you Ledbetter?"

"What are ya talkin' about, Brother Thomas?"

"I've been a hearin' about all a those wild parties you and those Cantrells have been a havin'. Such cavorting will surely guarantee the Lord's wrath upon yor household."

"What on earth are ya talkin' about Fire and Brimstone? This here's a God-fearin' law-abidin' family!"

"I'm talkin' about playin' dominoes and cards. They're games of the devil. You're a headin' straight fer hell, Caleb Ledbetter. I'll bet y'er all a swiggin' that corn liquor, too. The Lord has no need for yer kind!"

"I believe I've told ya before. This family doesn't need yer kind a 'terpretin' the Lord fer us. We do fine on our own!"

"You'll see, young man! You'll see!" said the visitor as he rode away.

"What was that all about?" asked Zelda Mae as she returned to the porch.

"Pay him no mind," said Cal. "He's the worst kind of Bible thumper, a self-appointed messenger of God. I'll bet if he is a messenger, God has no idea what he's about. He'd fire him fer sure if he knew!"

"Well, I don't like him a comin' around here."

"Now ya' know why I asked ya' to git inside."

The family continued in their "evil" practices. Even Zelda Mae saw no wrong in what they were doing.

One other pastime was rare, but when it occurred, it was enjoyed by all, well almost by all. That was the rural custom of shivareeing. This old custom had many variations, but the end result was always the same. The new husband and wife could count on being placed in an embarrassing situation and would not have participated had they known it was coming.

Central to the custom as the Ledbetters knew it was a wheelbarrow. Within a week to one month after the wedding, "friends" of the couple would arrive unannounced and proceed to carry out the ritual. First the new groom would push his new bride, sitting awkwardly in the bouncing, weaving wheelbarrow, down the lane or street by their home amid the clanging of pots and pans or anything else equally capable of making such a loud noise. Then, it was time to reverse the roles, with the new bride pushing the awkward contraption with a single iron wheel in front, often making it list to one side like a ship about to go to the bottom of the sea.

While the new wife generally did not push it as far as her husband did, this was symbolic of the need for both of them to do their share in the newly created family. Then, while the newlywed's attention was being diverted by this "moving" experience, other friends were rearranging their house by moving utensils to different cabinets, etc. They might even remove all of the lanterns from the house, leaving the couple in total darkness until replacements could be procured.

A shivaree wasn't complete, however, until something was done to the couple's bed. It might be as simple as putting rice in it to the more complex task of rearranging the slats, so it would collapse at the most inopportune time.

"Do you remember our weddin'?" asked Cal.

"I sure do," answered Zelda Mae. "Now what brings such a thing to your mind? You thinkin' about getting' married again?"

"Nah, it's not that. I was just recallin' our getting' shivareed. It's funny now that I think back on it."

"It wasn't funny then!" said Zelda Mae. "Of course all of the people had fun but us. I wonder whose idea it was to put those chocolate covered beans in the young one's potty pan?"

"Leastways it was a new potty," said Cal. "The worst part was fixin' our bed like they did. We no more than straightened our legs out to sleep and that bed hit the floor. I'm surprised it even lasted till we got in. We could have been hurt in that ruckus. Had to sleep on the floor that night. Must have taken us nigh onto two hours to find those slats come mornin'. They was in the barn. I reckon they intended for us to have to sleep on the floor that night. We didn't even have any light to look for them with."

"Yes, we had to spend the night on the floor. But we weren't hurt. Anyhows, why you bringin' it up now?" asked Zelda Mae.

"Oh, I'm a thinkin' a those two boys, Ben and Clevon. Seems like they's always a pullin' pranks on someone," said Cal.

"I'll bet they're the guilty parties that tied our bed up!" said Zelda Mae.

"I wouldn't be a bit surprised," returned Cal. "I'm thinkin' those two will be a gittin' hitched themselves one of these days. I do believe it's their turn to reap what they sowed."

"Oh, Cal. I love it when ya quote the Bible."

While there were many opportunities for the sharing of good times, heartaches were still to be a part of their lives. Tragedy does not wait to come around until you're ready. On October 4th of 1928, death once again showed its face to Cal's family. His younger sister, Jewel, now twenty-six years old, died of complications in carrying the child she was expecting.

The whole family was bothered that a mother so young could be taken so quickly. Her three children were ages seven, four and three. The children's father, George Reeves, was well up in years. There was doubt he would be able to care for such young children on his own. Cal and Zelda Mae were to take these three children in as their own for quite awhile, until George's older daughter by a previous marriage, Bonnie, could take them to live with her family. Now the young couple had four children to feed and clothe. Cal felt that there was no choice, nor would he have wanted it any other way.

Memories of his cousins, the children of Abe and Jenny Ledbetter, going into that orphanage in Pryor, Oklahoma, haunted him, and he could do something about it. Waiting for the right time to do something, as his father waited sixteen years earlier, allows too many opportunities to go by. Worse yet, it permits responsibilities to go by as well, and we aren't always revisited with a second chance.

"You know the passage in the Bible about bein' our brother's keeper?" asked Cal.

"Yes, I rightfully believe everyone knows they're supposed to do that," answered Zelda Mae."

And you believe it means sisters as well?"

"I swear, you can read my mind can't you? Yes, I'm talkin' about Jewel's young ones."

"I know you are," said Zelda Mae. "We can pick them up today, if you've a mind to go for a ride in the wagon. I suppose we ought to be sure George isn't up ta the job first, though. Anyway, they're his kids and it's his choice, I reckon."

George was relieved at the new turn of developments. He was at a total loss on how to care for his young children. In his grief over Jewel he couldn't clearly think about his options.

It seemed natural that Cal and Zelda Mae would care for Jewel's children. Clevon and Olive were married in December of 1927. They weren't ready for a family yet. Besides, Olive was only thirteen years old. Also, her father still wasn't sure how well he liked Clevon being part of the family, and to have additional Ledbetters be part of the bargain could very well eliminate any approval that might be forthcoming. Ben Stepford and Claudine Cantrell were also married in 1927, but neither were blood kin to Jewel

Actually, it seemed that Cal and Zelda Mae were the only choice left, as they would permit the children to remain in familiar surroundings. No one truly realized that it was not a difficult decision for the couple to make, however. Cal and Zelda Mae knew they liked having children around, and no one had more experience at raising children than Zelda Mae.

The Ledbetters never really knew, though, if the three children would always be able to live with them. There was always the chance Mr. Reeves might remarry and want them to once again live with him. Also, Zelda Mae was again expecting a child. Therefore, in their minds Cal and Zelda Mae knew the first part of their dreams and hopes was surely going to come to pass. They would have a large family. Now if they could only own their own farm as well.

Belle Anne Ledbetter entered this world with a cry and a kick on January 30, 1929. The Cantrells said they could see a resemblance to Sadie in her face, even at such an early age. Let there be no doubt, the Cantrell side of the family was going to be represented. That made it even, because they had also said Pearl favored the Ledbetter side of the family.

Belle, as she was called, might have picked a better time to enter this world. Black clouds were already hovering over the United States. Don't get the idea, now, that she was to be one of those dark clouds. No, the clouds were forming because there were feelings of unrest building up on the horizon of the nation's economy. When Belle was almost nine months old, the stock market crashed on Wall Street.

Not that Cal and Zelda Mae had any money invested there, mind you, but the thunder of the crash was to be heard throughout the land, and evidence of the lightning could be seen on all sides. Panic followed. Businesses failed and unemployment skyrocketed as America had never known. Some men of means were reduced to selling apples on the street, if they hadn't jumped out of a tenth story window first.

When renting a hotel room, potential occupants in New York City were sometimes asked, "For sleeping or jumping?"

Cal and Zelda Mae were spared the losses of large sums of money in the stock market. They didn't have any money to invest in the first place. But, they were not to escape the aftershocks of the crash.

CHAPTER XVIII

The "Great Depression" was to be unequalled as to its negative impact on the United States' economy. Unemployment reached thirty per cent at times when twelve was considered quite high. Businesses and farms were failing throughout the land. The United States was a nation in despair.

This was not just an American problem, however; it was a global problem. Europe and the remainder of the world suffered equally as harsh a fate. If ever there was a time for America to be concerned about the survival of its system of economics and way of life, it was now.

Wall Street and rural America saw the depression from differing vantage points, even though the interests of both groups were primarily financial. The rural states, especially Oklahoma, Texas, Montana, Wyoming, Colorado, New Mexico, Kansas, Nebraska, North Dakota and South Dakota, had an additional problem compounding the failure of Wall Street. It was the "Dust Bowl." It is hard to describe an event rarely seen since the dust bowl era. Even the dust bowl, though, had its roots in the economy just like the speculation that devastated Wall Street. During the 1920's, the price of wheat expanded to double what it had been prior to the end of World War I. Farmers, seeing a chance for large profits just like those the Wall Street speculators saw, immediately more than doubled the amount of land they had in cultivation.

This plowing of the prairie grasslands was due to the farmer and rancher's failure to heed the warnings of those who knew the likely consequences of such plowing. The price of this failure was high. The roots of the grass, necessary to keep the dirt from blowing, were no longer in place. The wind was in command.

Coupled with the increased number of acres in cultivation was a drought of immense magnitude lasting for seven years. It reminded biblical scholars of the drought and famine in Egypt when Joseph came to the Pharaoh's rescue. Beginning in the early 1930's the rains stopped, or at least decreased significantly in the dust bowl states. With underground moisture, which is nature's way of storing water for future use, in short supply, the future truly looked bleak. Then, without the roots of the grass to hold the dirt in place, the wind began to rearrange the earth's surface to its liking in the dust bowl states.

Experts estimated that hundreds of millions of tons of earth blew to neighboring states. The eastern seaboard states were even to feel the fallout of this catastrophe. Dirt fell from the skies on such cities as Philadelphia, Washington, D.C., and New York City. One time it was recorded that clouds of dirt reached hundreds of miles out over the Atlantic Ocean.

A drought by its very name also implies heat. Temperatures well in excess of one hundred degrees sometimes accompanied these storms. Maybe this was that period of time on earth preceding the millennium. Was this the beginning of Armageddon?

"Do you think God is mad at us?" asked Papa Cantrell.

"I've never seen anythang like it," answered Cal. "The wind comes up every afternoon and blocks out the sun with the dirt it's a carryin'."

"What can we do to stop it?" asked Papa.

"I'm sure well-rooted grasses would help, but how can we git them ta grow? The wind will just keep a blowin' the coverin' away from the seeds. Maybe if we planted deeper next time it would help."

"But there's no moisture in the soil to speak of now," said his father-in-law. "Seed can't germinate without moisture."

"A good rain would be a mighty blessin'."

"We haven't seen rain in these parts in over two months. As a matter of fact, it could well be three months. A man loses track of time when everything is a goin' wrong," was Papa's response. "And everything is certainly goin' wrong now."

"Maybe we've angered God," said Cal. "Heaven knows we could'a done a better job of carin' for what he gave us."

Whatever it was, the lifeblood of the Oklahoma farmer, along with other dust bowl farmers, was being drained away as surely as the sun came up every day. It was hard for Cal to go out after a dirt storm and find his equipment completely buried under a pile of sand or dirt. Worse yet was to find the blowing dirt piled high and covering the fence, allowing his livestock to walk over and away. That is, if they hadn't choked to death on the dirt first. Cattle had actually been seen heaving and vomiting dirt.

Consider, too, the unfortunate soul driving down a country road with no way to escape the cloud of dirt often reaching over fifty miles per hour. It was not unusual for the particle laden wind to sandblast a car, removing the paint or pitting the windshield unmercifully.

On rare occasions parties with cars in need of paint were known to take advantage of these storms to get new paint jobs courtesy of the insurance companies covering their vehicles. Many individuals needing and unable to afford a new paint job, however, were often unable to afford car insurance as well. Worse yet, like the Ledbetters, they likely couldn't afford a garage to protect their uninsured vehicle, either.

"Why is your pickup truck outside, Clevon?" asked Olive.

"Oh, I'm just havin' it sanded," her husband answered.

"Is that right?" questioned his wife.

"I pay insurance. I'm entitled to some return on my investment."

"I still don't think it's right," said Olive.

"How does a red pickup strike you?"

"And some black fenders for contrast," answered Olive.

Zelda Mae also found her busy schedule now contained a new activity. When a storm cloud was sighted, she had limited time to wet cloths and put them over all of the cracks surrounding doors and windows. A failure to take this precaution sometimes meant a home with an inch or more of dirt or sand on everything in sight. Often her home was still the recipient of these deposits, even though she took the prescribed steps.

Zelda Mae certainly didn't want to cook during a dirt storm, either. Her food would have tasted gritty or worse unless she at least covered her cooking utensils. Furthermore, she knew a complete housecleaning was in order after every one of these storms. It was totally impossible to keep out most of the dirt deposited by the wind. Of course much of this problem was due to the failure of the Ledbetters and similar families to live in airtight structures.

Asking Cal about how bad the dirt storms were would sometimes get the reply, "The dirt in the air was so thick that a pilot in an airplane got out and walked to the ground from five-thousand feet up in the air because he couldn't fly into the wind." This may not have been an exaggeration. The dirt blew so high that it was difficult for the planes of the 1930's to fly above the storms.

Cal was often unable to come in from the blowing soil. He had to stay outside and try to get his livestock into a sheltered setting. A barn provided the most protection. To get the stock to shelter, though, meant leaving the confines of the home and venturing out into the gale wearing a cloth, preferably wet, over his face to stop the dirt from being inhaled. It was easy to gag with the taste of the gritty powder in his mouth and nostrils. But a good farmer like Cal, or any caring soul for that matter, knew the necessity of protecting his animals from the awful malady descending upon them from the skies. These storms brought death to man and beast alike.

Correcting the problem caused by plowing up the grasslands took a long period of time. Some of the first shelter belts in the United States, rows of trees planted to help abate the winds, were put into use in the dust bowl states. Simultaneous with the planting of shelterbelts was the reseeding of the prairies back to grass to help hold the soil in place. It would take decades to repair the damage caused by those hoping to increase their wealth.

Cal would never forget a time that he and Zelda Mae couldn't escape a dirt storm. They were returning home in a truck. Off in the distance they could see a brown cloud beginning to form. The wind was already buffeting the vehicle as though it was a mere leaf caught in the flow of a rapid creek.

As the foreboding cloud grew nearer and nearer, Cal accelerated the truck even more. Not only did they want to avoid being caught in the swirling mass of dirt and debry; they wanted to be sure everything was secure at home. Even more they wanted to be sure their children still at home were protected from the destructive power of this unbridled air pressure.

"Can't you go any faster?" asked Zelda Mae.

"I'm afraid to," said Cal. "One of these ruts could turn us too much, and then the wind would blow us over, and this ain't even our truck. Papa Cantrell would be mighty unhappy should we turn this here truck of his'n over."

"But we gotta git home to those kids of ours," said his wife while wringing her hands. "Maybe one of them's outside where they don't belong."

"You know Pearl will look after them. That girl has right good gumption for her age. I'll bet she's already stuffin' rags in the cracks around the windows by now."

"Well, I'll feel a heap better if we get there right soon. Maybe she's out right now roundin' up the stock. Maybe the little ones are all alone."

"Now, Zelda," said Cal, "she knows the kids come first. She isn't about to desert those kids when she's in charge."

"Well, I got my faith in that girl, too. Still, it's askin' an awful lot of someone that ain't ten years old yet."

"If we could get there any quicker," said Cal, "we'd do it. Just sit back and hang on. We'll be there soon as the Lord permits."

Breathing was getting harder and harder. It seemed like the dust located every opening in the truck in making its presence known. That wasn't hard. The truck was far from airtight, and the dust was so fine that it needed only the slightest opening to gain admittance. The windows didn't fit tight, either, and the floorboards were like sieves.

The two passengers in this lifeboat on the prairie held handkerchiefs over their faces to keep from breathing the dust. These filters helped lessen the amount of the choking reddish-brown substance they breathed, but they still found themselves gagging from time to time. It wasn't long before the chocolate colored substance began to taste like mud in their mouths, and they soon wouldn't be able to breathe through their noses at all.

Cal slowed the truck to a crawl as the fury surrounding them increased. At times he couldn't see the hood of this ark making its way through a sea of blowing dirt. Part of the time the only way he knew he was on the road was by the feel of the ruts transmitted through the steering wheel.

Tumbleweeds blowing over the hood of the truck occasionally interrupted the monotony of the blowing dirt. As the dirt thinned out periodically, they discovered that they could see the sun trying to break through, much like during a severe rainstorm.

"Could you keep your eyes open for our road?" he asked. "It'd be right easy to miss it in this storm."

"It's all I can do to see the radiator cap," she responded. "Wait! Isn't that it over there?" as she pointed to the right side of the road now visible for a brief moment.

After what seemed hours of driving, Cal thought he recognized the mailbox. Was it theirs? Being on the leeward side of the truck, he got out to make sure this was the right gate. It was. In finding this fact to be true, however, it seemed like the truck's door would be ripped from its hinges by the raging storm. Also, the heavy coat of dirt already covering the interior of the vehicle increased in depth in the process. It might as well have been a dump truck from the amount of dirt it was carrying.

Turning right onto the farm lane meant heading directly into the full fury of the maniacal storm. There was no other way, if they wanted to get home. Cal slowly inched the truck forward until it actually touched the side of the house. No need in running any farther than they had to. Besides that, they almost ran into the house before they saw it.

Even though the children had put seals around the door, it was easy to open with the full force of the wind pushing on it. As a matter of fact, Cal almost felt the knob torn from his hand as he turned it.

What he and Zelda Mae found greeting them was not a welcome sight. There was a covering of dust about one-fourth inch deep on everything in view. As bad as it appeared, Zelda Mae wondered how the dust could be spread so uniformly. It seemed as though some gigantic force had lifted the roof of the house long enough to sprinkle dust everywhere, much like a mother might put talcum powder on a baby's bottom. As a first step following a storm, shovels were necessary to remove the dirt from the house. It was no easy task.

"We did just like you said," reported Pearl. "We wet some of your quiltin' squares and put them at the bottom of the windows and doors. Why the wind was blowin' so hard we had to prop a kitchen chair up against the back door. We figured it would never stay closed without help."

"That was right good thinkin'," said Zelda Mae. "I'm very proud of you kids. Dad and I feel bad that we weren't here to help you any."

"Oh, we knew what to do," said Belle. "We watched you do it before."

"Have you seen Old Bossy and her calves?" asked Cal.

"Last I saw them they were hightailin' it to that grove of trees by the creek," said Pearl.

"I reckon they could have found shelter there," said Cal. "Wait'll this here storm lets up some and I can go and check on them. The wind should die down pretty soon."

If there was ever any good that came out of these storms, only the children could find it. The rearranged landscaping included dunes the consistency of fine silt; it looked like sand, though. That is with the possible exception of coloration.

These deposits of dirt often obscured large objects, which was why the snowdrift appearing mounds often came to be in the first place. With a few tumbleweeds in the appropriate places, the plow or other implement was soon buried with only an occasional handle protruding like a sentinel on a hillside.

These dunes were ideal for running and jumping, if done with care. An abrupt halt due to running into a metal object was no one's idea of fun, but the playing and burying of each other in the dirt as finely textured as sugar was the poor child's version of playing on a beach where water didn't exist.

"Can't you kids find a better place to play?" asked Zelda Mae.

"But it's fun, Momma," replied Pearl. "It's soft and you can slide down the hill on it. It's really fun if you have something to ride down on."

"I didn't say it wasn't fun. But do you have to git so dirty?"

Some "Okies" felt it was necessary to leave their homesteads behind and move away. If the wind didn't take their farm, they thought, the banker surely would. Others saw the storms as warnings from God that he was quite displeased with the use of his land.

Whatever the reason, Oklahoma was not the most desirable place to be right at that time for many citizens, farmer and city dweller alike. Cal and Zelda Mae were not to be in the group migrating to California looking for an opportunity for a new beginning.

"Mama. You think we ought'a head out west and pick some cherries in the San Joaquin Valley?" asked Cal. "The poster says there's lots of money to be made. Why we could buy a farm in no time, we'd be awful rich."

"I've never heard of no San Joaquin Valley. Pray tell, though, how do you reckon we'll get to this here valley? Why we haven't even got any vehicle with a motor up front, and I sure am not makin' that ride with a mule and a wagon," Zelda Mae answered.

"You do have a point there, woman. I reckon we don't have any way to get there. That does create a problem or two, I'll have to admit. Let me think on this here proposition for a minute."

"I don't really figure a minute of my thinkin' is going to solve our problem," said Zelda Mae. "What's going to solve our problem is when we hunker down right here in Hominy Corners and take care of business."

California was seen as the Promised Land for many Oklahoma natives. The chances for renewal in this land had to be true. There were newspaper ads, as well as posters on telephone poles, pointing out the multitude of jobs awaiting those who would make the journey to the "Golden State."

What many of these soon to be migrant workers didn't realize was that they were being enticed there to multiply the number of available laborers, thereby forcing down the pay of all field workers. Many of these new arrivals with their hopes and dreams renewed found jobs of less than survival wages, or some found no job at all.

Soon there were unemployed living in tent cities, hoping for enough to survive from one day to the next. California didn't want many of these Okies, however, as they were often destitute with no real means of support. The promised land took steps to get rid of large numbers of these poor migrant workers, even going so far as to sometimes give them gas money to return to their home state.

While almost all of the Okies traveling to California were quite poor, a few were better off than the others. Folks said that the better off ones were easy to spot. They had two mattresses on top of their car, while the poor only had one mattress tied above. Even two mattresses, though, were not enough to realize a dream built on false hopes. Cars with these and other objects adorning their tops filled the highways back to Oklahoma as well. It was not a pretty sight. Defeat never is.

Resisting becoming part of this exodus from Oklahoma was extremely hard for Cal and Zelda Mae. Their roots and destiny were buried deep in the red soil around Hominy Corners. Many were the times Cal was confronted with friends and neighbors moving away, and for the longest time he was called upon to resist the lure of the promised land by the Pacific Ocean. After all, he would tell himself, all I want is to sharecrop a few acres to try and hold my family together.

It was soon obvious, however, that for right now he would have to be content with working for others. Whatever the future would be, he kept telling himself, it would be in Oklahoma. It might not be Hominy Corners, but it would be Oklahoma.

"What are we goin' to do, Zelda Mae? We can't make a livin' here, and we've already decided that California is out of the question."

"The Lord will provide."

"The Lord expects us to do our share of the work, though," her husband answered.

"You've heard, I know, about bein' between a rock and a hard place, Cal. Well, I reckon that's where we find ourselves right now."

"But nobody said we had to stay there," returned Cal. "We have to at least try to help ourselves out of this mess we're in."

"I can't question your tryin', Cal. Maybe, though, there's some kind of compromise in the choices we have to make," said Zelda Mae.

Cal finally determined that the only way he could hope to provide for his family was to get away from them and look for work. As he would need to travel great distances, his family would stay with Papa Cantrell while he went away to seek work. Zelda Mae agreed to this venture. At least their roots would remain planted in Oklahoma, a state she had grown to dearly love.

Not wanting to deprive his family of their transportation, Cal elected to walk to towns in the general vicinity of Hominy Corners as he sought work. It was not unusual for him to walk ten miles in the course of one day. As this search proved increasingly fruitless, he slowly expanded the lengths to which he would travel in the pursuit of gainful employment.

While he was not exactly hitchhiking, he would sometimes gain a ride. Many drivers during the depression era were quite willing to give a lift, always cognizant of the admonition of John Donne, "There but for the grace of God go I."

Cal's travels did sometimes take him far from his family but never from their hearts. His first letter home said:

"Oklahoma City,
Oklahoma
August 24, 1930

Dear Wife and Babies,

How are you all by now? Fine I hope. I am well and hope you are all the same. I ran into Myrtle yesterday. Granny and all are doing well. Things sure look bad here. Hundreds of people are out of work. Mr. Reeves thinks he can get me a job. I will stay 3 or 4 days and see if I can get a job. If I don't, I will be at home this week some time. I want to work awhile if I can. They have good cotton from Choctaw on to the City. Of course it won't stay good if we don't get more rain.

I'd do anything for a day's wage. Heaven knows I can do most anything. I've tried getting up at four in the morning to get in lines by the mills, and there's always someone ahead of me. I'll bet they're sleeping in line in order to be first. Well, if it works for them, I'll be trying it, too. I reckon I smell pretty bad. I've been sleeping in my clothes. I suppose I could take a bath in the creek, but it's dirty water if there is any water at all. Can't see how it'll help me be any cleaner, but I'll try.

Well I don't know much to write, so I will close.

Kiss the babies for me.

C.A. Ledbetter
231 W. Choctaw Street
Oklahoma City, Oklahoma"

Zelda Mae was always to treasure this correspondence with Cal. One day later she replied:

"Wade, Oklahoma
August 25, 1930

Dearest Daddy,

Will try and write you a few lines in answer to your letter I received today. Sure glad to hear from you. How are you by this time? For us all up, but I am so lonesome that I can hardly stand it. Have you got you a job yet?

We got a good shower Saturday night and it has been cloudy yesterday and today. I think we will get plenty of rain now. It sure looked like last night it would rain the bottom out but it didn't.

Pearl said last night at the supper table, "I wish Daddy was here. Don't you Momma?"

Belle had her bloomers off yesterday, and William asked where they were. Pearl said Momma strained the milk with them.

Claudine and Ben stopped by. They said they had a big fire in Wade last week. Jim Tiebolt's house burned and the barbershop, blacksmith and another building or two were lost as well. Jim said if the wind had been blowing, the whole town would have burned. The fire started about 1 o'clock in the night. It started in the drug store.

That beef peddler was here again Saturday, and Ben was out in the yard. He hollered and said Zelda, you want any meat? I told him I didn't, and the man that pulled the little wagon even said, Zelda, we got some fine meat. We just can't afford such luxuries right now.

Well, I will close. Answer soon.

With lots of love,
Zelda Mae

Mail delivery was good in those days. Cal answered by return mail the same day he received his wife's letter. He missed his family.

"Oklahoma City, Oklahoma
August 27, 1930

Dear Wife and Babies,

How are you all? Fine I hope. I am all right, but I haven't found any work yet. I have walked 100 miles since I have been here. There are 40 men to every job. I will try another day or two, and if I don't find something I will be at home soon. I sure would like to see you and the boys. There are sure lots of people here.

I've tried bathing in the creek. You know it doesn't work too bad. It at least takes the sweat out of the collars and from under the sleeves. I wish I'd brought some extra clothes with me, but, then, I'd have had trouble carrying anything. I sure do miss your hot coffee in the morning. It wakes a man up real fine.

I couldn't get my papers fixed here. They will have to be filed at Hobart. I have been out to the State Capitol. It sure is some place. Mr. Dollarsworth has taken me to U.S. Veterans Bureau. He tried to get me examined, but they said I would have to wait until they called me. I'd even work for the government to tide us over. Course I don't hanker to be inside if I can help it.

Tell Belle and Pearl that Daddy is coming home before long. Tell them Daddy said to be good boys and he would bring them some candy. I'll bet they would like some licorice right nice. Well I don't have so much to write, so I will close. Kiss the babies for me and answer soon.

Does Mr. Cantrell think the rain will help the cotton? People everywhere would be much happier if it did. I know it would make it easier for me to find work. A man can't care for his family if he can't have an honest paying job.

Love,
C.A. Ledbetter
231 West Choctaw Street"

Cal called Pearl and Belle "the boys". His desire for a son was quite evident. It was equally as obvious how much he loved his family, as his fourth grade education did not lend itself to the laborious task of expressing himself in letters. On one hand he had to go away to try and earn money to support his family. On the other hand, he and Zelda Mae could hardly stand to be separated. Frustrated at his failure in finding gainful employment, Cal was to return to Hominy Corners to a house shared by Ledbetters, Cantrells and Stepfords. The severity of the families' economic plight dictated that they share living quarters on Papa Cantrell's farm to survive.

The small house was beginning to look like the refugee camps seen on the newsreels at the Durant Theater. The Stepfords had three children to go with the two Ledbetter kids, and Zelda Mae was expecting again. By now the three Reeves' children were with their older stepsister.

Alvina Jane Ledbetter was born on June 27, 1931. Surely, Cal thought, there has to be a boy born in this family someday. He had his heart set so much on a boy that he already had a name picked out for him. It was to be Alvin, so he could call him Al. Yes, it would be confused with his own name on occasion, but that was a small price to pay for having a son.

Refusing to give up their dream, then, Cal and Zelda Mae named the new infant Alvina. She was called Jane, though, not Alvina or Alvie. Possibly they didn't want to waste the name Alvin in the event a boy might be born someday.

"Do you think we'll ever have a son?" asked Cal.

"The Lord willin', we'll have lots of sons," said his wife. "We're still young yet. There are children yet to be for us. We just have to be patient."

"Well I certainly hope the Lord sees fit to give me a son real soon like."

"Right now we best be a thinkin' about how we'll feed the ones we have," his wife stated.

"They're always on my mind," said Cal. "Seems like everywhere I go I'm reminded that I have a family to support. I'll go to the grave knowin' I have a family to support."

"Yes, but that won't be anytime soon. Right now we'll take care of today. If there's a tomorrow, we'll worry about it when the time comes."

"You know good and well, Zelda Mae, that you worry about the future just like I do."

"Yes, and right now it's gettin' us nowhere. I get so tired of worryin' about tomorrow. It's always there like a black cloud hangin' over our lives, and the cloud never goes away. Will things ever be alright, Cal?" she asked.

"If we don't have hope," he answered, "we don't have anythang. We have to have hope, at least that the young ones will grow up in a better world than we did."

The only jobs Cal could find were rare and of short duration. One day he might be cutting up blocks of ice at the ice house, while the next day might find him helping to unload boxcars for the railroad. He considered himself most fortunate if he could find work two days in a row.

Eventually, through the efforts of President Franklin D. Roosevelt and his programs called the "New Deal," Cal found some relief in his economic plight; at the same time he was able to become a better provider for his family.

He joined one-half million other young men of the nation in working on projects designed to conserve the country's resources. For awhile he lived in CCC Camps (Civilian Conservation Corps) while helping in flood control and related projects. Cal, as did many other CCC workers, eventually left that program with a lasting impression about the workings of camps with all male inhabitants. For example, the cooks were selected according to which one did the most complaining about the meals provided. Griping, therefore, became an art, if it was to be done without penalty.

"This is the saltiest meat I ever tasted," said the man next to Cal.

"What did you say?" asked the cook.

"I said this roast is right salty, but that's just the way I like my meat."

"And what about my collard greens?" asked the cook.

"Oh, they're the best I've had the pleasure of eatin' this week," was the reply.

"Good, because you're gittin' more tomorrow. I like to keep you boys happy."

"Oh, I'm a happy one alright. I'm so happy I could just die right here."

"Good!" said the cook. "Because they ain't a goin' to git any better than this," as he turned to stir a pot of boiling water for beans, "unless you think you can do a better job."

Tiring of a daily diet of pinto beans, the men began dumping the seeds from the legume family into the creeks or burying them. The supply officer for the group, thinking the men must surely love the beans, as the supply was always depleted, increased their ration of this commodity. The vicious cycle would then be repeated. Overall, though, the CCC Camps were the salvation of the Ledbetter family. At least this innovative program helped put beans back on the table at the home place.

There were so many ways to prepare the delicate lentils that some variety in their menus could be achieved for a time. Adding sliced or diced onions was helpful, though it did cause people to draw back from you. Cornbread crumbled into the bowl of steaming morsels was friendlier to the neighbors, if you could be friendly after eating beans.

"I'm sure glad we have beans to eat," said Pearl. "I believe they're one of my favoritest foods."

"Well they're certainly cheap," said Zelda. "We can buy them in one-hundred pound bags."

"I wonder if Daddy is gittin' any beans to eat?" asked Pearl. "I feel sorry for him if he isn't."

"Oh, I'll bet he's well fed," answered her mother. "If he ain't, it ain't his fault."

It was to be 1933 before the question of "Will we ever have a boy?" was answered affirmatively. Abraham Taylor Ledbetter was born on July the 12th. Cal now saw his hope renewed for someday farming side-by-side with a son. Not only that, but he saw the continuance of the family name, Ledbetter, in that small, reddish, newborn infant. Both sides of the family were honored with the name. There was cause for celebration. Cal and Zelda Mae had discussions about what it meant to now have a son. New possibilities existed with the birth of Abe.

"Maybe we ought to start lookin' for a farm next year," said Cal. "You know you can't do things like that any too early."

"Why he's just been born," his wife answered.

"Yes, but in just a few short years he'll be a doin' chores and helpin' in the fields. I reckon we ought to keep our eyes open. Besides, with Pearl, Belle and Jane we can do a heap of work right now. Why them two older ones can pick cotton beside most men right now."

"Do all of our children have to work so young?" asked Zelda Mae.

"They do if we're a goin' to make a livin'," answered Cal.

"I reckon you're right about the young ones a workin'," said Zelda Mae, "but are we ready for a farm now? We don't have any machinery. We do have one mule, but folks are startin' to farm more with tractors and stuff now."

"We don't need tractors. My daddy did just fine without them. Besides that, hay is cheaper than gasoline," said Cal.

"I hear you can't farm near as many acres without a tractor, though. We've already got four kids to feed. It'll take a good sized farm to feed six of us."

"We'll just raise a bigger garden, then. We've always been good with gardens," said her husband. "We'll get by. Don't you worry yourself any. We'll be alright by and by. Then by the time Abe is nine or ten, he'll be a big help. We can farm even more acres. He and the girls will help chop and pick cotton for us. Why, we won't even have to pay anyone to do any of them jobs. Shoot! Woman, we've never been closer than we are right now to havin' our own farm."

Cal was indeed so close to that part of his dream of once again having his own farm that he could just feel it in his bones. Abe was the key. Now managing his own destiny was possible. He'd have rented a farm that day, but they generally weren't available in the middle of a growing season. Someone else already had them and would until after harvest. As long as he could see the possibility of the fruition of his dream, Cal could continue to get by for awhile, but it was never out of his thoughts. Best of all, it would be right here in Hominy Corners.

As time went by, Cal was not to see any immediate benefit from having a son, other than the pleasure of his company. Times continued to be hard. Land ownership was still to be "next year," so he and the kids had to be content to travel and pick cotton for other farmers.

When all of the children were old enough to pick or pull cotton, the family could do quite well financially. Picking cotton was slower. One had to take the time to pick the cotton from the individual bolls, stiff hard shells surrounding the cotton fiber, by hand. Pulling cotton, where you pulled the entire boll off all at once, went faster but paid less. Eli Whitney had invented the cotton gin over one hundred years earlier, but some gins did not have all of the capability of this timesaving convenience. That is, they could only process picked cotton, not pulled cotton.

During the days spent in the fields picking cotton, the Ledbetters sometimes lived out of tin cans for their noon meal. Zelda Mae would pack a lunch, which might consist of Campbell's Pork n' Beans, Vienna sausages, deviled ham or sardines when they were lucky. Otherwise, it would be cold cornbread and beans or baloney sandwiches.

Water was kept in a five-gallon cream can. Cal would buy a block of ice from the local ice and coal house on the way to the fields to keep the water cold. It was necessary to split the block in half or smaller pieces in order for it to fit through the neck of the can, and a dipper for drinking would be hung on one of the handles on the side.

The brief amount of time taken for eating was often the only break of any length they received. When you're paid by the hour you can afford to take breaks, Cal said. Otherwise, breaks were a luxury that few could afford. Anyone wanting a drink during the course of the day would need only a minute, two at the most, to get water. Leisurely breaks were not even allowed for the noon meal. Time was of the essence. Picking cotton was for the strong, not the weak or faint of heart.

The travels of the Ledbetters took them further and further from Hominy Corners as they practiced their chosen trade of the moment. On some jobs, especially after the family acquired a car, they worked by the hour, such as when they were chopping cotton. Then, an old alarm clock was kept on the front seat of the car for telling time, as no one wore or carried a watch.

On one particular day it seemed as though Pearl, Jane and Belle each advanced the time on the clock some as they went by in order to get off work early that day. Each child did not realize the other was doing it as well. When Cal went by the car to check the time, he discovered it was much later than it appeared. The kids were quickly loaded into the car for the trip home. In Hobart, outside Gish's Funeral Home, was a large clock. As soon as Cal saw that clock, he knew what was going on. He immediately turned the crew around and returned them to the fields for more work before sundown. "Who's been messin' with that clock?" he asked.

Each of the two older girls pointed at the younger sister and said, "She did!"

"Well, let me tell you rascals somethin'. We had a job to do in that field, and we needed all day to do it. I won't be cheatin' any man out of the time he has rightfully comin'. If any of you pull that stunt again, I'll heat your britches like they were on top of a cookstove! Do you hear me?"

"Yes, Daddy!" they all chimed together.

Zelda Mae did not accompany the family into the fields. Her place was in the home caring for the needs of her family on that front. In time all of the children would work in the fields, but such couldn't even be considered before they turned five. Besides, she and Cal had a very special kind of love, and it was not uncommon in that time and place.

Cal was head of the household with responsibility for providing for his family's material and security needs. This also meant he made the major decisions. Zelda Mae was subservient to him. The role of a woman was to stay in the background and support her husband's desires. This certainly was a biblical directive, and Zelda Mae was very biblical. Thus, both members of this relationship accepted their roles with only a rare question. The strength of their love left no room for doubt about this arrangement.

"You know, I worked in the fields when I was a girl."

"That may be, but I'll not have my wife a workin' outside the home," answered Cal. "Your number one job is makin' sure the children are cared for."

"We could use the extra money."

"We don't need the extra money that bad," replied Cal.

"Yes, but we could own our farm that much quicker."

"You can't compromise your principles for any reason. Much as I'd like that farm right now, nothin' has changed. Patience is what we have goin' for us. The farm will happen. Take my word for that. It was good enough for my father, and it's good enough for me."

"Maybe I could watch the young ones while they played in the field. They'd enjoy watchin' you work."

"Well, I suppose that might be possible. But only if the weather is good. I don't want my children freezin' in the fields. If it even looks like it might turn cold, they're goin' home."

"Whatever you say," his wife answered.

As the weeks and months of the depression continued to go by, the fortunes of Cal and his family did not greatly improve.

They still found themselves as vagabonds in search of a home. Their base of operations always seemed to be around Hominy Corners, close to where Cal was born and Grandma Lillie now lived, although they could venture far afield at times.

Grandma Lillie's second husband, Wallace Stepford, had passed away in 1929. Stopping by her house was done with care, as she was such a lonely woman living all alone. Always wanting to be prepared for any situation, she kept a suitcase packed in order to leave with whatever relative stopped by. On those occasions when Cal knew it was not possible for his mother to come along, he found it necessary to slip in and tie her suitcase to her bed so they could have time to make their getaway. As much as he loved his mother, there was no way he could take on extra responsibility at this time.

"I wish you'd treat your mother better," said Zelda Mae.

"What do you mean?" asked Cal. "I'm doin' right by her."

"I know you think you are, but she's just lonely. She'd be no harm with us."

"She's too old to work in the fields," said her son. "And, we'd have difficulty puttin' her up when we find housin' at some of our work sites."

"She could watch the kids while I worked in the fields beside you."

"This discussion is over, Zelda. You're not workin' in the fields, and that's final!"

When your dream is big enough, and your patience is tested long enough, your turn will come, though. In 1934 Cal seized an opportunity to return to farming on his own. The Bell place was available for sharecropping near Bokchito. Mr. Bell was Clevon Ledbetter's father-in-law. The original farm was one hundred and sixty acres of which forty acres were farmable. An agreeable arrangement for the Ledbetters to sharecrop the Bell place was soon reached. Nothing was put into writing. The deal was consummated with a handshake.

Cal, with the help of the girls, managed to clear an additional forty acres of brush and trees for farming. This was accomplished by cutting down and removing the stumps of scrub oak, locust trees, and blackjack, to name a few. Some of these trees were large enough to use in making fence posts.

About ten acres of this expanded farm were planted to cotton. Then, a small plot was planted into tobacco for Cal's own use. The remaining acres were put into peanuts, corn, and sugar cane. One portion of the land was left untouched, as it contained a goodly number of pecan trees. Cal and Zelda Mae figured that the nuts they didn't eat could later be sold in Durant.

On April 7, 1934, Cal borrowed fifty dollars from the Farm Credit Administration, an agency of the United States Department of Agriculture, at five and one-half per cent interest to purchase equipment. Using borrowed money, along with the approximately three hundred dollars received as a payment for his military services in World War I, enabled the process to get underway.

Being a first-year farmer in those days was an expensive undertaking for Cal even though the equipment he used was all horsedrawn, handling either one or two rows at a time. His government money, plus the family's savings from picking cotton, was barely adequate to purchase the needed implements.

While far more sophisticated equipment, such as gasoline driven tractors by John Deere or McCormick Deering, was available, and he could have borrowed more money from the bank in Wade, Cal still wanted to use the old ways on his farm. This was similar to the way he and his father had farmed, and he saw no reason to change now.

Even if he wanted to modernize, Cal couldn't have afforded it. The end result, though, was that much of the work on the Ledbetter farm was also done by hand, when more modern farmers were covering many more acres at the same time with more efficient mechanized equipment and fewer hired hands.

"Ain't we a gettin' awful deep into debt, Cal?" asked Zelda Mae.

"You can't begin farmin' without plenty of cash," answered her husband. "Why I reckon most people need upwards of a thousand dollars to get started. We're able to get by with less because we're not a buyin' any tractors or the like."

"Well, it still scares me that we're so deep into debt. I've never heard of so much money in my born days."

"Like they say, you have ta spend money to make money," said Cal.

The Ledbetter family still found it necessary to live off of the land to sustain themselves during these years on the Bell place. Times were still quite hard, though. One of Cal's first purchases was a team of horses. Misfortune couldn't wait to strike these new entrepreneurs. Within one week after the team's acquisition, a bolt of lightning killed one horse.

Then, before too much more time had elapsed, the family was notified that their milk cow had brucellosis, a condition requiring the destruction and burial of the cow. As there was no government reimbursement for destroying the cow, it was some time before they were once again to have their own milk on the table. Without the assistance of Papa Cantrell in furnishing dairy products, no one really knows what their fate might have been.

In order to feed a growing family Cal and Zelda Mae cut corners on every turn. On occasions Cal would walk into Hominy Corners with a seventy-pound sack of corn slung over his shoulder. He could get this corn ground into cornmeal at the mill attached to the general store. The transaction merely required that he give Mr. White one-eighth of the finished product. It looked like a losing proposition. One-half of the corn had already been given to Mr. Bell as payment for the farm. Now, an additional portion went to the mill owner, leaving Cal and Zelda Mae with less than one-half of the original amount raised. This couple struggling for survival had no choice, however. They did what they had to do.

"We're not gettin' ahead Cal. We never have enough money for supplies, and the children no longer have a decent pair of shoes," said Zelda Mae.

"But we have each other," replied her husband.

"That doesn't put food on the table, though."

"Well, we'll just have to work that much harder," said Cal. "We knew this wasn't goin' to be easy. The worst part of the depression is over. When everyone's doin' their part, times will get better."

"I'd still like to work in the fields. I'm strong and I'm not afraid to work."

"A woman's place is in the home, Zelda. I appreciate your offer, but nothin' has changed."

"I was just tryin' to help, and the good Lord knows that we need help."

A community press was also maintained in Hominy Corners on some of the school property. This mechanical device powered by a mule was used to press the syrup out of sugar cane and sorghum to make molasses. Once again, it was done on a share basis but in a different way. Many families would put their cane or sorghum stalks together into a bin after having stripped them of their leaves. Then the mule would slowly walk around in a circle turning metal wheels that gradually squeezed the sweet juice from the compressed stalks. This juice could then be cooked into molasses. Each family was trusted to take out their correct share of the molasses. The honor system served everyone well.

More than once Cal was heard to say, "There is only one thing I like better than lasses, and that is mo-lasses!" He loved it on biscuits or cereal equally as well. Molasses was the primary source of sugar for this hungry family. The sticky substance could even be added to coffee as a sweetener, but it always found its best usage on homemade biscuits.

While Cal had more than an adequate supply of farm workers living right in his own home, he often stated his two rules for the employing of hired help. First, they could not roll their own cigarettes, as was common in those times. Instead, he figured a worker ought to buy those already rolled and in a package. Secondly, they could not wear straw hats. Any worker violating both of these simple rules was a lost cause, he said. When he was asked why he used the rules, he replied, "If they ain't a standin' around a rollin' a cigarette, they're a chasin' their hat when the wind blows it away."

Interestingly enough, Cal personally violated both of these rules. He not only wore a hat at all times to protect his rapidly thinning hair, but he rolled his own cigarettes using Country Gentlemen Tobacco.

"Cal, we're almost out of groceries. What are we goin' to do? We have so little money available," said Zelda. "We have canned tomatoes and berries, but you need meat once in awhile that sticks to your ribs."

"How about lard?" asked Cal.

"Yes, we do have plenty of lard from butcherin' our last hog. But you can't eat lard, and if you could it wouldn't stick to your ribs."

"No, but you can cook meat in it. It's my job to get meat for the family. I'll go huntin' today as soon as the chores are all done. It shouldn't take me more than an hour or two."

Snow during the 1930's in Oklahoma was a rarity. When the family was having a hard time financially, it provided an opportunity to restock the family's larder. It only had to snow a few inches. Cal would wrap his feet in burlap from gunnysacks to help withstand the cold temperatures and go rabbit hunting. No firearms were used. The rabbits were tracked in the snow until they burrowed underneath the surface of the snow. At this point a noticeable hump marked the spot. Cal would then step on the rabbit's head and pull until it was decapitated.

On one hunting trip he brought back almost thirty rabbits. Some were packed in salt in a wooden barrel for later use. While this method of hunting seemed grotesque to some, it was a source of meat for the family living on a tight budget. Others considered it a delicacy and relished the taste even when funds were plentiful.

Zelda Mae did her share in this partnership as well. Through her efforts the family was able to live on a very tight budget. The two big savings she made were in making the family's clothes and in being able to preserve so much food for later use. Hominy Corners now had a large community pressure cooker holding up to forty-eight quart jars for canning. Zelda Mae never missed an opportunity to set aside provisions for the coming winter months.

Another big money saver of Zelda Mae's was in the making of quilts. Most of the family's bedding consisted of quilts, and she was able to handmake all of them. Sometimes she would make them alone, while at other times she participated in quilting bees. She enjoyed the quilting bees more because she could work with several other women and join in the friendly chatter about the community's happenings.

"Have you heard there's a new way to make coffee?" neighbor Hickam asked.

"What do you mean there's a new way to make coffee?" asked Zelda Mae. "I reckon you have to boil the water no matter which way you fix it."

"Well, you still boil water. But the ingredients are different."

"Pray tell. What are you talkin' about?" asked Zelda Mae. "I'm hopin' you're a goin' to make sense pretty soon. Right now I reckon I don't know what you're talkin' about. Either you make it with coffee or you don't. Now which is it?"

"The way I hear it, if you find you're running out of store-bought coffee, you can substitute carrots," said Mrs. Hickam.

"Carrots!" everyone hooted.

"Yes, carrots!" retorted Mrs. Hickam.

"Are you a pullin' my leg?" asked Zelda Mae. "That's it. You're a pullin' my leg. I can't wait to tell Cal about this. He'll get a good laugh, sure enough."

"If you all will give a soul a chance to explain. You'll know I'm making sense."

"We'll be the judge of that," said Mrs. Perkins. "Now you go on and tell us all how this here miracle is done, makin' coffee from carrots."

"I've been a tryin' to tell you," said Mrs. Hickam. "Now you all hush up and listen for a spell. The way I hear it you slice thin slices longways on a carrot. Then, you put the pieces out in the sun to dry. After they're all sort of like dried up, you grind them up like coffee. Now I will admit, it's probaby weak coffee, but it's coffee, never the less. If it's too strong, though, you can add a portion of water to it until it gets downright tasty."

"Well, Lordy be," said Mrs. Perkins. "I reckon I'm goin' to try that. We're all the time runnin' out of coffee, and nothin' makes my man madder than runnin' out of coffee."

"Sounds like the Choctaw beer that Cal used to make," said Zelda. "But if it's cheap, and your man likes it, I say let's try some of this coffee. Seems like it should have a different name, though."

"How about Cherokee coffee?" said Mrs. Hickam.

"Sounds good to me," returned Mrs. Perkins. "Next time she'll tell us how to make gold out of feathers. I do worry about you Hickams at times."

"I'd be more worried about Fire and Brimstone Thomas hearing about making a drink out of dried carrots. I'm sure it'll be listed as a sin somewhere. Iffen not, he'll say so anyhow."

Yes, quilting always held an attraction for Zelda Mae. She would not deny that she thoroughly enjoyed the stimulating conversation sometimes produced at these sessions. When a quilt was needed in a hurry, however, she was known to make one out of denim during the course of one night by working alone until it was completely done at about sunup. Granted, it was not one of her beautiful designs in this case, but it felt just as warm on top of you.

When the family could not afford the cost of her sewing supplies, she would make quilts for others and let them pay her with the fabric she needed to make her own. For the cotton lining in the quilt she often would pick her own cotton from the fields and remove the seeds by hand.

Zelda Mae's contributions to the family's wellbeing were significant. Cal did not object to these rare instances of cotton picking. After all, they were part of the clothing construction process.

Another way the family had for raising money, separate from the sale of their crops, was in the sale of eggs. On those occasions when eggs were taken into town, Zelda Mae first packed them in a water bucket with layers of cotton separating them. The cotton packing was to try and minimize the jolting movements of the old farm wagon used for trips into Bokchito.

These extra eggs the family did not need for their own were traded for flour, coffee, tea, sugar and salt.

"What you a goin' to get with your egg money this week, Zelda Mae?" asked her husband.

"I guess we need some salt and pepper," she answered.

"And what else?" he asked.

"Okay, let's hear it. You need somethin', don't you?"

"Do you suppose there would be money for a new pair of shoelaces for my brogans? I've been usin' wire, but it doesn't bend well. Sometimes it downright hurts."

"I'll see if we can stretch our funds that far. Mind you, it may not be possible, and if it isn't I'll make you a pair from some material I have."

"Maybe you should make me a pair, anyway. Just don't use red material like you did on Pearl's."

"You have to admit, though, Pearl thought they were right pretty."

Not only were the Ledbetters diversified in the raising of money, they were frugal in how they spent it. Anything that could be made by the family was not purchased. In addition to Zelda Mae's efforts in making clothes and bedding for the family were Cal's efforts in other areas. For example, he kept a steel last necessary for making most shoe repairs. In addition, he did haircuts for everyone needing them, with length of hair being more important than looks. Money was in too short a supply to be spent needlessly.

Every effort was expended to make the farming a successful enterprise. If long hours and perseverance were the essential ingredients for a project to work, the Ledbetters could not be found lacking. Cal and Zelda Mae's venture into sharecropping was not a success, however. It was only a matter of time before the percentages would work against them, such as having such a small portion of the corn left when cornmeal was ground for Zelda Mae's baking needs. The drought didn't help matters, either. The family was not able to keep the sharecropping agreement. They left the farm with heavy hearts.

It was to be a long time before they could pay off the government loan, but it was paid off, and the very nature of the sharecropping agreement insured that Mr. Bell received his share of the farm's production. They used their equity in the few remaining pieces of farm equipment to cover their debt at the Hominy Corners General Store. At least they still had a team and wagon for transportation, however.

"We didn't make it, Cal."

"It wasn't for lack of tryin', Zelda Mae."

"I know that, Cal. What do you suppose went wrong?" asked his wife.

"Oh, the whole country's in trouble. I suppose our timin' was bad. Everyone is a goin' broke."

"Mr. Bell's not goin' broke," stated his wife.

"That's true. But his land and equipment had been paid for long ago. We tried to start from nothin'. That's where you get hurt today. You can't start from nothin'."

"Do you think we'll git another chance?"

"Oh, we'll get another chance. But it can't be until we're better off. We won't be borrowin' money next time, either. We'll have the money in hand before we attempt such an undertakin' again. That could take years."

"We've got time," were Zelda's words.

Children continued to be added to Cal and Zelda Mae's family on a fairly regular basis. Any more regularity and you'd have been able to set your calendar by them. Mattie Jean Ledbetter was born in Bokchito, Oklahoma, on November 17, 1935, and on the night of August 26th, 1937, Martha Sue would join the family. The family size was not to stabilize at six children, however.

Trips to Hominy Corners were not so difficult as it appeared. This was true at least in terms of transportation. The family still relied upon their team and wagon for the weekly or less trip. You would have thought it was a safe way to travel. They all fit in the wagon quite nicely; this was much better than they would have fit in a car.

This travel arrangement was not without hazards, however. On one of these trips Jane had the misfortune of playing under the two by twelve-inch plank placed across the wagon box. The board, which was not fastened down, was used as a seat while enroute to town on a wagon designed to haul farm products. Cal and Zelda Mae were on the seat while Jane played under it. Whether it was due to rough road conditions or being improperly positioned, the plank slipped to one side and Zelda Mae's end fell on Jane's head. Needless to say, the weight of both Cal and Zelda Mae did great bodily harm to the hapless girl. For awhile they didn't know if Jane was dead or alive in her limp, unconscious state. Cal carried her to a nearby farm pond. Zelda Mae trailed close after her husband and splashed cold water in the girl's face.

Eventually the injured girl was revived, but not without some anxious moments. The typical response of the Ledbetter family in cases of this type would be to care for things as best they could without a doctor. The possibility she might have a concussion would not be considered. Ledbetters were not taken to doctors except in life or death situations.

"I can't stand the thought of losin' another child, Cal."

"You won't, if I can help it."

"Nobody should have to experience the loss of their own child."

"You reckon we ought to take her to a doctor?" asked Cal.

"I would feel better if we did," answered Zelda Mae.

"It won't be free," responded Cal. "But if that's your wish, it will be done. Really, though, she looks fine now."

Even though the depression was not to end for some time, the Ledbetters were beginning to have renewed hopes for a brighter future. With everyone old enough for the task picking cotton, the family now found it possible to accumulate enough money to buy the family's first car in 1938. Granted, it was only an old 1926 Model T Ford, but it was paid for in full.

The Ledbetters were never to return to mule-drawn conveyance as a form of transportation. It still was not advisable to be out on the road after dark, however, because the cars continued to have such poor lighting from the headlights. Nighttime trips called for Pearl, the eldest child at age twelve, to sit on one of the front fenders astraddle of the headlight holding a lantern up high for maximum lighting. Only then could Cal see well enough to stay on the rutted roads they traveled. Still, the car was a great improvement over the horsedrawn wagon.

Not only did the Ledbetters buy a car, but other conveniences were forthcoming as well. In 1938 they also bought their first radio, made by Motorola for just under ten dollars, to replace the hand cranked Victrola used to play records. Cal strung a copper wire up to the roof of the house, then across to the tops of outbuildings to give this luxury an antenna. This type of radio known as a crystal set took the country by storm, as common people could now afford one of their very own. Previous radios had cost hundreds of dollars. Also, this new radio was battery operated, so you didn't need a house with electricity to enjoy the thrill of radio signals.

Cal's favorite programs were the world heavyweight championship boxing matches. When they were on the air, he would require the kids to play outside, so as not to disturb his listening. As a matter of fact, the kids weren't even allowed to play close to the house in order to insure the quietness necessary to overcome the radio's poor reception. Hide and seek played in trees far from the house was ideal. The kids thought they were getting the best end of the bargain. Besides, who wanted to listen to a fight when they had the freedom to run and play outside?

The radio operated off of wires run from the car's battery parked close to a window in the living room. Sometimes Cal would have his less fortunate neighbors with no radio over to listen to the fights with him. It was real hard, though, determining whom the less fortunate than the Ledbetters were.

During the early years after Cal and Zelda Mae acquired a radio, boxing was in a new era. Joe Louis became the heavyweight boxing champion of the world. The fact that a colored man could defeat a white in a boxing match was unheard of. Oklahoma was a southern state, when it came to race relations. Coloreds had to know their place, and defeating a white in a boxing match was not one of them.

Cal reveled in the victories of the "Brown Bomber," however. While he appeared to be segregation minded on the surface, in his heart he was not. On one hand he denied colored people the right to eat at his table; on the other hand he was very much concerned for their welfare. You might say he was paternalistic by nature. At least some folks called his attitude paternalistic, but Cal's feelings were much deeper than that. He considered colored folks to have far more rights than the government gave them. He was their friend.

While the main purpose served by the radio was entertainment, it sometimes struck fear in the heart of the listener. Nineteen thirty-eight, the first year the Ledbetters owned their radio, was one of those times.

One evening there was a radio broadcast announcing the landing of Martians in New Jersey; pandemonium followed. It was unbelievable that such a thing could happen, but right there it was on the radio, a running account of the hysteria created by these foreign visitors. All ears were glued to the radio for over an hour as the announcer described the happening. In the background could be heard the sounds of screams and people in panic.

A frightened nation was relieved to later learn the truth. They had fallen prey to the antics of Orson Welles. He had delivered one of the most realistic dramas ever heard over the air. No longer were the Ledbetters sure they could believe what they were hearing over the airwaves. Up until now, anything emerging from the small speaker was considered gospel.

Another modern appliance now owned by the Ledbetters. This marvel was a used washing machine made by Maytag. Built in 1914, it had a small, one-half horsepower, gasoline engine for the agitator and a wooden tub. The family did not have electricity yet, even though great strides had been made since the 1920's when efforts were begun by the REA (Rural Electrification Administration) to get electricity into the rural areas. It was necessary, though, to attach a ten-foot hose to the exhaust of the washer's engine to get the fumes out of the house via a window. Also, the family did not have running water in the house, so the kids were required to carry the water in buckets or tubs for long distances on wash days.

The main feature of the washing machine was the agitator, which didn't work so differently from the stick Grandma Lillie used to stir the clothes in the pot over the fire in the yard many years earlier. After washing the clothes, Zelda Mae still needed to run the clothes through the wringers by hand, however, to get the water out. Occasionally someone would allow their hand, or worse, to get caught in the wringer.

The only way they had to dry the clothes after the washing was completed was to hang them out on the clothesline. While wash day was greatly improved, it was still just as big an event for Zelda Mae, even with more modern appliances, as it had been forty years earlier for her mother-in-law. Of course she had many more children to wash clothes for than when Cal was a baby.

Finally, the family acquired a refrigerator to replace the iceboxes they had always used. No longer would they have to rely upon the iceman to make his rounds delivering ice to his customers. Besides that, iceboxes were getting few and far between, so ice was also hard to get delivered. Zelda Mae was most proud of her Frigidaire, even though it was a used model. Having leftovers was not a big problem, but the family did need a better way of preventing food spoilage.

"Can you imagine one family experiencin' so much of what the world has to offer?" asked Cal.

"Well, I imagine Henry Ford has conveniences we never heard of," answered Zelda Mae.

"Yes, but we expect the Henry Fords and the John D. Rockefellers to live that way. Now us folks are a different story. I never thought I'd ride in anything without seein' a horse's tail in front of me. Of course that doesn't include a train or a ship. Anyway, poor folks rarely have much, and we have more than many I know."

"You've tried real hard to provide for our family, Cal. No one can ask for any more."

"Well, we're not through, either. Why someday, we'll still be able to go to the toilet without goin' outside or messin' up the floor."

"Oh, Cal. You have the funniest sense of humor sometimes."

"That may be. But mark my words, we're on our way up. Yes, and we'll own a better 'frigerator someday, too."

The 1930's were almost complete with one minor exception. War was on the horizon. On September 1, 1939, Germany invaded Poland. Once again families began to fear the possibility that one of their sons might be called to fight in a world war. Granted, the United States was able to stay out of the initial conflict for awhile. Hadn't World War I or "The Great War" been fought to end all wars? But, it was to be just a matter of time?

Cal was too old and had too many children to worry about being called to once again wear the uniform of his country. But what about Zelda Mae's younger brother? Would William's recent marriage to Cal's niece keep him out of the conflict?

While living on the Ramsey place near Bokchito, the family took another significant jump in numbers on January 23, 1940. Zelda Mae knew it was time to deliver her baby. Furthermore, she and Cal knew it was going to be a large baby, as she had gained so much weight during the pregnancy.

When it became quite obvious the time was near, Cal went to fetch a Negro mammy mid-wife to assist in the delivery. Tish, who had helped deliver Mattie Jean, was not available, so he had to find a new one to help this time. Upon his return to the home, it was quite obvious he had taken too long. He was shocked to see Zelda Mae in bed holding twins, one boy and one girl. She had delivered the babies on her own, while Pearl, aged twelve, had been in the next room.

When Zelda Mae was asked why she hadn't called on Pearl to assist, she replied, "She's too young to deal with matters such as this."

"She has to learn sometime," said Cal. "What's wrong with right now?"

"When she's a little older she'll git plenty of chances to learn what it's all about. Let her be a girl for awhile longer."

"Well, alright. What shall we name these little rascals, anyhow?" asked Cal. "If we're not real careful like, we're going to run out of names one of these days."

"Well I've always been sort of partial to namin' one of my kids after your mama," said Zelda Mae.

"You mean you want to name the girl Lillie Ann?"

"No, just the Ann part. We could name her Colette Ann, and that would get both sides of the family. You know my cousin, Colette Sue, back in Arkansas?"

"I've heard you speak some about her, but I can't say as I know her. That would be a right fine name, though, I reckon. What about the boy, though? Got any ideas there?"

"How about Cole Almon. That's a right good name. Besides, I once knew a preacher man with that name. He'd be a good one to name our boy after. What do you think about that?" asked Zelda Mae.

"Colette Ann and Cole Almon it is, then. I sure hope folks don't go a confusin' those two names. They sure sound a lot alike to me."

The family was less than equipped to deal with these new additions, especially in sleeping arrangements. For awhile Cal found himself evicted from his own bed, now full with Zelda Mae and the twins occupying it. He found it necessary to improvise in solving this new problem. He finally resorted to a makeshift arrangement requiring ingenuity. He used two kitchen chairs propped upside down on the kitchen floor whereby the tops of the upside down furniture came together to form a "V". This allowed him to elevate and thereby rest his head. Simultaneously, he elevated his feet from the floor in making a most unusual bed. Only a weary soul would resort to such a unique sleeping arrangement. It was appropriate, though, as Cal was a unique individual.

Acquiring enough diapers was also a problem for the twins, as so many of the garments were now needed. Usually it meant the recycling of large enough pieces of cotton or flannel fabric for this purpose.

Other substitutions were also used to solve additional problems. Providing a pacifier for the cranky child, "sugar titties" were made by placing a scoop of sugar onto a dishtowel. Then the sugar was tied off with a knot to prevent it from falling out. Colette or Cole could suck on one of these for hours and be quite satisfied.

Cal tried to get into Durant, the county seat, at least twice a year. These trips were also used to register new members of the family, should any have been added since the last trip. He didn't always succeed, so some children did not receive birth certificates. With six girls already, and only two sons, he was beginning to think God didn't intend for him to be a farmer, anyway. Things in that department just had not gone well at all.

CHAPTER XIX

Various reasons have been given for the United States coming out of the Great Depression. One of the most offered explanations was the "New Deal," a comprehensive attach on the nation's economic ills established by President Roosevelt to deal with high unemployment and the failure of businesses, especially the banking industry.

The other most frequently given reason for America's economic recovery was the beginning of World War II. The Americans became the major suppliers of armaments to the Allied Nations. This in turn helped return American factories to full production with a commensurate lowering in the unemployment rate. Simultaneous with this development, American farms stepped up their production as well to help supply our allies with foodstuffs.

When Hitler of Germany and Mussolini of Italy were waging war against the nations of Europe, England and France carried the brunt of the battle for the major allied powers. Also, while Russia was initially siding with the axis powers, it was later to come over to the side of the allies. It would be wrong to overlook the courageous efforts of smaller countries, such as Hungary, Poland, Norway, and Czechoslovakia as well in resisting the aggression of the axis powers; their resistance to being overrun was most admirable. Furthermore, they helped keep the flame of freedom held high until the U.S. could join the war effort.

The Rome-Berlin Axis Agreement of 1939 was expanded to include Tokyo in 1940. The important thing to remember is that the United States managed to stay out of "active" involvement in the fighting for some time. That is until Japan bombed Pearl Harbor on December 7, 1941. Then the Americans had no choice; the fight for the freedom of the world was now their fight as well. Their involvement was long overdue.

When word of the bombing of Pearl Harbor first came over the radio on that Sunday morning in December of 1941, the Ledbetters initially met it with some skepticism.

"Is this here another one of those fool Orson Welles' putups?" asked Cal. "I don't want to be taken for a fool a second time in just three years. Besides, ain't this a Sunday morning? The radio ought to have good preachin' and good footstompin' music, not another one of his fool jokes on us poor people that don't know any different."

"Besides that," retorted Zelda Mae, "with the movement of those troops in Europe, I reckon it would represent poor judgement to be a broadcastin' such a message over the air if it wasn't true. There ought to be a law!"

"These fool radios," said Cal. "You don't know when to trust them and when to turn away."

"Can't you git any other station, Cal?" asked Zelda Mae.

"Can't we go ahead and listen to this?" asked Pearl. "This might be better than Fibber McGee and Mollie."

Turning the knob slowly, Cal was able to tune in another station. Again the Ledbetters kept their ears glued to the radio. This time the horror revealed among the static and screeches over the small wooden box was for real. The United States was at war!

"I can't believe it," said Cal. "In just over twenty years, we're in the middle of another big fracas in the world. We'll be in Europe before you know it. Us Americans can't seem to stay out of wars."

"Yes, but the people bein' hurt are our friends, Daddy," replied Zelda Mae. "We can't let them down now right when they need us the most."

"I know. I guess what bothers me the most is that we always have to be involved in somebody else's fight."

"I don't like that at all myself. But we can't let Japan do that to us!" said Zelda Mae.

"What about William? He'll have to go, you know."

"I know, and I wish he didn't have to go. Lord knows it's bad enough when you don't know anyone in the fightin'. But the good Lord will keep care of him if it's supposed to be thataway," said Zelda Mae.

"Yes, He will. Actually we've been in the war awhile now, and people just wouldn't say so," said Cal.

"What do you mean, we've been in the war awhile now? We haven't got any boys fightin' over there."

"No, we haven't got any boys fightin' over there, but we've been a givin' them all of the stuff we can like ships for a long time now. I believe Roosevelt calls it lend-lease. He don't lend-lease me nothin'. Why's he so all-fired anxious to lend it to people he don't know?" said Cal.

"Oh, it's probably that old argument, keep the battle off of our shores," retorted Zelda Mae. "Besides, is that legal like to lend them all of that stuff? Isn't Congress supposed to declare war or somethin'?" she asked.

"Maybe it's legal like, and maybe it isn't. But no one's makin' him quit. No, we've been in the war awhile now. Maybe this Pearl Harbor thing will make us stand up like we ought to and do our share."

"I thought you didn't want us Americans in other people's wars," stated Zelda Mae

"When we're attacked, the rules are different I reckon. Just like a man, a country has to defend itself. Why I'd fight myself if I was younger!"

"Oh, Cal. You're needed at home. You have a big family ta provide for."

The American people rallied behind their leaders to support the war effort in any way possible. Even with American soldiers dying all over the world, morale was high. The people had a common cause they could unite behind. Even simple things could make them feel a little better as they went about their work, such as seeing a hastily drawn picture of a nose, forehead and fingers on the top of a fence with the inscription "Kilroy was here" beside it. James J. Kilroy, a shipyard inspector, found his name could bring a smile to the face of the dourest of individuals, when scribbled on a wall or fence. Yes, the simple things made the war effort more bearable.

While the Ledbetters were now able to afford more material items, neither of the foregoing reasons of the implementation of the New Deal and the beginning of WWII ended the low-income status of the family. They were to continue living as they had for some years during the 1930's. Economically, the depression was still very much a part of their lives. Even after the war, they found it necessary to continue to use tin cans for drinking glasses; so as to not break Zelda Mae's prized goblets saved for Sunday use only.

Also, very large vegetable gardens were still highly necessary to feed a growing family. Not only did they help meet the family's dietary needs during the summer, but homecanned food was an absolute essential to see the family through the winter as well. Zelda Mae was to be seen quite often in her homemade bonnet working in the garden. Also, there were several kids helping out there at one time or another.

It's interesting that America adopted the principle of "Victory Gardens" to help free up fresh fruits and vegetables for our fighting forces. The practice of such gardening was already going on among many families of the nation like the Ledbetters. It was a principle with which they were well familiar. There was no doubt as to whether or not it would work. Yes, the putting of all available spaces into the growing of corn, tomatoes, and other vegetables made sense, even if it might be limited to a window flower box.

"Zelda Mae. I swear you could grow tomatoes on the sidewalk," said her husband.

"Oh, Cal. You can be so funny sometimes. You know I can't grow things on a sidewalk."

"Well, nearly you can. Why you've been growin' turnips in tincans."

"I'm just tryin' to feed the family."

"If we'd stay in one place long enough, we'd have a fine garden."

"What do you want me to grow most?"

"Some corn would be right nice."

"You're not thinkin' of makin' corn liquor, are you, Cal?"

"No, I'd just like some good roastin' ears. The only other things that good is tomaters and watermelon."

In the fall of 1940 the Ledbetters were to move to Ft. Cobb, some distance west of Bokchito and Durant. Earlier Cal had gone on ahead with the car and found a job for his family in the cotton fields pulling bolls. Clevon and Olive Ledbetter assisted in the move.

The army could have learned a lesson from this movement, due to the numbers moved with so little equipment. Riding in the front of the small 1938 Chevrolet pickup were Clevon, Olive and Grandma Lillie. In the back, sitting on mattresses, were Zelda Mae, Pearl, Belle, Jane, Mattie Fern and Abe, not to mention the twins. Everyone in the back would take their turns holding or caring for the twins.

The pickup had sideboards with canvas stretched over the top for a cover. This made it hard for the smaller kids to see out. Sometimes someone would lift Martha Sue or the twins so they could see over the sideboards and out from under the canvas covering the top.

The similarity for Zelda Mae and the earlier exodus from Arkansas was undeniable. Each move of this type compounded the feelings of failure in their current situation. Otherwise, this trip was like being in a submarine for the smaller kids. They had no idea where they were going, and the trip seemed to last forever. Just looking out seemed to make the trip more exciting, though. Zelda Mae soon noticed they were less cranky when a game was made of the activity. Still, the little truck was sufficiently loaded to make it hard to move around with any degree of ease.

As the back of this small pickup contained eight passengers and their basic necessities, such as diapers for the twins, it was necessary to pull a small trailer as well to hold the family's meager personal possessions, such as bedsteads, bedding, canned goods and a few items of furniture. The housing provided for migrant workers usually contained a wood cookstove, so it was not necessary to own or move one.

Due to a limitation of space in the trailer, however, they had to leave one of the family's treasured sources of entertainment, their RCA Victrola, behind in the house they vacated. While no prearrangements were made, Clevon and Olive retrieved it for them at a later date.

The Chevrolet pickup with its small six-cylinder engine was unable to endure the long, all day trip of about two hundred miles to Ft. Cobb. A few miles short of the original destination the clutch on the little pickup could no longer perform its required duties.

The Ledbetters managed to contact Zelda Mae's sister, Rebecca, now living near Gotebo, Oklahoma, with Luke Gardner, her husband of four years. The Gardners towed the tired pickup the remainder of the way into Ft. Cobb and got the family to its destination.

This willingness of both Clevon and Luke to help out, sometimes at great expense to themselves, was typical of the family relationships that existed. Cal and Zelda Mae would have done the same thing for them. It was not unusual for any of them to even help non-family members in the same way. This helping was part of an unwritten code closely adhered to by rural inhabitants, which grew out of the Golden Rule. You were not only your brother's keeper; you were your neighbor's keeper as well.

"Can't I pay you for your help, Luke?" asked Cal.

"You don't take money for helpin' someone," said his brother-in-law.

"A man can't just walk away without givin' something," said Cal.

"Oh, you can give somethin'," said Luke. "But not to me."

"What do you mean?" asked Cal.

"Well, you give to the next person in trouble by helpin' them," said Luke. "By doin' that, you'll have paid me. That's all the pay I ask."

"The cost is reasonable," returned Cal.

This sojourn to Ft. Cobb was a temporary move. It was not to be their permanent home. When you chop or pull cotton for someone else, you're destined to keep moving on if you want to survive. This was the life of an itinerant laborer. Also, when there was work to be done for hire, if you were old enough to work you seldom attended school.

Cal and Zelda Mae next took their family on west to Hobart, where Ben and Claudine Stepford now resided. For a brief while the two families shared a farmhouse. Eventually, the Ledbetters were to live in a number of places in and around the

Hobart area. At one time they were even to live above the sale barn where livestock auctions were held, as there was room for two families there. Clyde Cantrell, Zelda Mae's brother, and his family lived in the other unit. Neither "apartment" was of any substantial size. Sharing among the children of the two families was the order of the day. No other choice was possible.

With each move made by the Ledbetters, there was always the hope that the next move would be back to Hominy Corners. A dream of this magnitude never dies. It may get put on hold, but the essence lingers like a fine perfume.

"I wonder what it would be like to have a room of our own?" asked Clyde.

"You're askin' a right difficult question," returned his wife. "We've always shared a room with someone. If it hasn't been one of my family, it's been one of yours."

"I know. But wouldn't it be nice to be able to close the door and hear nobody else breathin' but the two of us?"

"Oh, Clyde. You're such a dreamer."

Cal and Zelda Mae continued to want more children. They would have had nine children, except Zelda Mae had a miscarriage. Recognizing the loss of this unborn infant, along with the death of J.H., they realized that with Zelda Mae's advancing age and their economic status, their ambition of a large family was likely fulfilled. Would there be any more children. Neither Cal nor Zelda Mae was getting any younger. They thought that they would have to be content with what they had in the number of children.

Surprises do happen, though. Growth in the Ledbetter family was far from over. Jimmy was born on October 22, 1941, while Franklin was born on March 31, 1943. After a lapse of three years, Joyce would join the ranks of this family on July 19, 1946. If J. H. had lived, this couple would have had twelve children. This time for sure, the ranks would close and allow no further admittance.

The other half of that dream shared in the farm wagon on the way to Bennington to get married was yet to be realized, but was not to be forgotten. It was merely put on hold. Actually there was plenty of help with farmwork should the option of returning to farming once again become a reality. He didn't know how, but someday Cal knew that he and Zelda Mae would own property on which they would once again raise crops of some kind. Lord, just let it be Hominy Corners, he prayed.

Entering the vacant auction ring for livestock in the salebarn, Cal removed his straw hat, looked toward heaven and said, "Daddy, I'm doin' my best to git back to Hominy Corners. Right now, though, it just doesn't seem to be possible. Times are bad. Of course they're better than they were durin' the depression. But they've got a long ways to go until they're as good as they were before you died."

Slowly moving his hat around in circles while grasping the brim, he continued, "It ain't as easy now to git a farm. Land isn't free anymore. You got to buy everything. I always said I'd never get one of those newfangled tractors, either. You know they got rubber tires on them now? I wanted to farm like we did together, Daddy. I don't reckon that's possible, anymore, though. You can't make a livin' on a quartersection of land like we generally did. You're goin' to have to learn how to drive a tractor for me, Daddy. You reckon you can do it. The price you get for your crops ain't hardly enough to raise a family, so you got to have more acres. I could teach you how to drive a tractor, Daddy. That's if you've got a mind to learn how. I guess it's better than walkin' behind a mule all day. You even got room to carry a drinkin' jug on the fool thing with you. Now you take young Abe. He's like your brother, Daddy. He can learn real quick, and I'll bet Cole makes quite the hand when he gits older."

Wiping a tear as it ran to the tip of his nose, he looked to insure that he was still alone. Seeing no one he spied a bale of straw to one side. Wanting to rest while he collected his thoughts, he sat to one end so he could place his hat beside him.

Once again, looking at a stream of light entering the large cavern through a hole in the roof, his words continued in a slow and solemn fashion. "I'll git another chance, Daddy. I know I will. It's just a matter of time. I'm a good man, Daddy, and you know what they say about not keepin' us down. I reckon it's takin' me so long to git started again 'cause you aren't here to help me out. But I got me one right goodlookin' family, ain't I? Don't they remind you of 1909 when we were all together at Hominy Corners? Well, I best be a goin' before someone comes a lookin' for me. I'll be a talkin' to you again one of these days."

In Hobart, Cal found employment with the city in the street department. Often he worked side by side with Clyde Cantrell. Sometimes the children would come down to see what Daddy was doing. On one occasion one of the kids had the audacity to refer to Cal's boss as James. A strong rebuke soon clarified that the man's name was Mr. Dunavin. Cal did not want his children showing disrespect for their elders. The family may have been on hard times financially, but they were still to exhibit the qualities of a respectable family, as passed down on both sides from the Ledbetters and the Cantrells.

"Now you tell Mr. Dunavin that you're sorry. I won't have one of my children a showin' disrespect to one of their elders."

"We're sorry, Mr. Dunavin," said Abe.

"Yes!" chimed in the others. "We're sorry."

"This won't happen again?" asked Cal.

"No sir!" responded the children in chorus.

A family such as Cal and Zelda Mae's didn't need money for much of their entertainment. There were so many relatives around who were willing to share in good, clean recreation that one didn't need to look elsewhere for fun. It was not unusual to see the menfolk involved in a game of throwing horseshoes. Or they would all get together to go rabbit hunting.

Cal had a Stevens single-shot 22 rifle that he treasured highly. With the capability of firing only one round before reloading, he felt it improved his accuracy immensely. This was different than the Colt 22 rifle Samuel had used to teach him, but it was equally effective in the hands of a skilled marksman, which Cal clearly was. These hunting trips were almost always successful for bringing home game. Using that same Stevens rifle, Cal imparted the skills necessary for the frontiersman providing for his family to his sons. All were taught the correct usage of a weapon before reaching their teenage years.

While all of the adults were engrossed in their talking or hunting trips, the younger children could always find plenty to do, not necessarily with their parent's permission. They loved to go swimming in the creek or in the new swimming pool built by the city in Hobart. Even games so simple as running along the top of the stone wall surrounding the salebarn property and the swimming pool, or even just chasing each other, were highly prized.

On other occasions, trips to the Gardner's farm were a special enjoyment to the Ledbetter kids, as they especially treasured the different pace and activities of the farm. In this way they were no different than their father.

These were happy times, at least for the children. They didn't know how poor their parents really were. Enjoyment was not measured by how much money was spent to obtain the fun, either, and the amount was often nothing. No, success was measured by the amount of pleasure derived from participation in the activity.

Another great source of pleasure was the infrequent visit of Uncle Clevon and Aunt Olive from Bokchito. Clevon Ledbetter was always quite prone to pranks even as an adult. On one occasion he even convinced Abe and the younger boys that the only proper way to eat food was with Louisiana Hot Sauce as a topping. The brothers were seen more than once putting this hot sauce on cookies they were eating. On other occasions they were content to listen to Uncle Clevon talk of his escapades.

One especially funny episode the family loved to hear was about when Clevon donned an old, black, hairy coat. Wearing the coat, he slipped up on his unsuspecting co-workers out in the woods in eastern Oklahoma. They worked in a gravel pit during the times when he could get away from work on the home farm. Seeing such a hairy creature from a distance, as he made his way among the trees and the shadows, set off a series of rumors about a bear taking up residence in the woods. Other rumors, such as hunters saying they were going to shoot that bear, caused Clevon to consider dropping this source of self-amusement.

"You're a goin' to get shot one of these days, Clevon Ledbetter," Olive kept telling her husband. "You know how jumpy those fellers are a gettin', and some of them are right good shots with a gun, too. Don't tell me it ain't a goin' to happen, either. Last thing I need to be is a widow woman like your mother. And if you come home full of buckshot, I reckon I'll let you stew a little before I help pick those steel balls out of your backside. You never heard of anyone being shot in the front unless they were robbin' the bank. You hear me, Clevon Ledbetter?"

The price was becoming too high, and Clevon knew it. But his sense of humor didn't prevent him from convincing Abe that he would hold up a blanket while the boy changed into a swimming suit by the creek. Abe only needed the blanket dropped once while he was naked and the family was all nearby to learn that Clevon got his enjoyment in a wide variety of ways.

"Come back here with that blanket, Uncle Clevon. The girls will see me."

"A little sunshine never hurt anyone," his uncle answered.

"Yes, but there are parts of me that have never seen the light of day, much less a girl."

Zelda Mae and the womenfolk were generally content to sit around and talk while the menfolk and children were elsewhere. That is after they got the dishes done from the meal just completed. Most often their idea of fun or a good time was not to go out and run around. Rather, they preferred the more sedate activity.

"You know, I think old Truman's makin' a right good president. He isn't afraid to say what he thinks. Besides, he has a stubborn Missouri streak in him a mile wide. He ain't afraid of them Japanese and he ain't afraid at all of those bigshots in Washington, D.C.," said Zelda Mae.

"Yes, but what are they goin' to do about all of those soldier boys a comin' back from the war?" asked Claudine.

"And the sailors, too," said Sarah. "Don't go a leavin' the sailors out. After all, little brother William has seen his share of the war, too."

"Well," said Zelda Mae, "the way I see it. They're goin' to have to have jobs. You can't have that many menfolks runnin' around without jobs. It isn't American like."

"I hear tell," said Rebecca, "there's goin' to be a G.I. bill for the veterans to be trained for jobs. They're goin' to help them go to college. Isn't that something?"

"What's G.I. stand for?" asked Zelda Mae. "When the doctor says it, it means part of your stomach. That don't hardly make sense to me. They a goin' to train them all to be doctors. Lordy, won't that be good? Look at all of the times our family could have used a doctor. Why, maybe Momma would be alive today if we'd a had a doctor close by."

With tears flowing down her cheeks, she wiped her face with her apron. "Why, J.H. and Cal's daddy would be alive as well, not to mention Mattie Fern."

"William can go to college, too," said Claudine. "Can you see little brother as a doctor? Course he never went to high school. I reckon it would be kind of hard for him to go on and be a doctor. Course he's smart enough. People like us just never get the chance for good schoolin', do we?"

"Wouldn't it be great to have educated kids?" said Zelda Mae. I reckon you can't ask for much more than your kids goin' to high school. The important thing, though, is that they get a good job."

"I reckon William can get a good job," said Sarah. "Why, he's been trained one a them woodworkin' fellers. What do you call them? Carpenters? Yes, he trained as a carpenter for the navy. There'll be lots of work for the carpenters with all of the boys a comin' home from the war."

"Maybe he'd build us a good house," said Rebecca. "Seems like every house we have ever lived in was cold in the winter time and blowed plumb full of dirt in the summer time. Yes, I reckon I'd like William to build a house for us someday. We'd pay him of course. Soon as the farmin' starts a payin' better.

Why I reckon I ought to go talk to Luke about it now. Can't be a thinkin' about a big job like that any too soon."

"I'm just glad to see the boy come home," said Zelda Mae.

The children really did not know the significance of the term "Bombs over Tokyo" used in their play, as they spread their arms like the wings of a bird in flight and acted like airplane pilots simulating an attack on Japan. They had heard the term over the radio, and it sounded exciting. Hobart was to see physical evidence of the war effort right there in their midst. During the war the defense department maintained a prisoner-of-war camp. The facility was located on the eastside adjacent to the salebarn.

The Ledbetter children spent hours watching the German prisoners playing basketball on the outside courts, while they were confined to a fenced-in enclosure. Sometimes large searchlights would draw lines across the sky in nighttime drills designed to locate enemy aircraft in the event of an invasion.

At the end of the war the camp was closed and everything sold. Cal bought a stool, later to be lengthened into a bench by putting longer boards on the top and sides, to allow four or five children to sit on one side of the table during meals. Not only was there a lack of space for enough chairs for everyone to sit at the table, but the Ledbetters didn't own that many chairs in the first place. The most immediate good news about the end of the war, however, was the safe return of William Cantrell, Zelda Mae's baby brother, from his duties as a SeaBee in the U.S. Navy.

The children were not always aware of the nationwide efforts to insure that the country's fighting forces were properly equipped, fed and clothed. This is because what some people saw as a reduction in the availability of goods in the stores was just more of the same for the Ledbetters. They already found far more in the stores than they could afford to buy.

Rationing, with the use of tokens and coupons, was a method used by the government to restrict purchases by the civilian population to the barest of essentials, thereby freeing up the nation's manufacturing capability for supplying the military effort. Citizens couldn't buy key items, such as tires or meat, without a coupon, and new cars were totally unavailable for anything but military use from 1942 through 1945.

Leave it to American ingenuity, however, to deal with such problems. The Cantrells and Gardners traded their meat coupons to the Ledbetters, who desperately needed them. In exchange they received coupons for tires, which Papa very much needed to keep his farm operation going.

As far as new cars went, Cal and Zelda Mae were never ever to own one. In 1944, though, an unusual opportunity presented itself. Pearl, when she was only sixteen years old, had married William "Wild Bill" James in 1942. They now lived in Las Animas, Colorado. Pearl happened upon an individual in Las Animas with a large, four-door 1928 Buick inherited in an estate. It was a one-owner car with very few miles on it. She called her folks; did they want to purchase this fine automobile?

Receiving an affirmative response, she delivered the car to Hobart. This car was to be Cal's pride and joy because it was so dependable. The kids loved it, too, because it was so roomy inside. Now they wouldn't be so crowded when they traveled. Not only that, but the car had a spare tire mounted on each front fender, next to the running boards! Also, it had a big trunk attached on the back to hold their belongings.

Many events were to become part of the Ledbetter family history while they lived in Hobart. Some were sad, while others were funny. Some were even both. Take the time, for example, when Momma told young Jimmy to burn the trash. He did as he was told; he went into the room containing the trashbox and lit the refuse on fire. If it hadn't been for the prompt action of the Hobart Fire Department, the house surely would have burned to the ground. The scary part was that Zelda Mae was confined to the bed when it happened.

Every person has an "Achilles Heel." That is, they have a weakness that could lead to their destruction, or at least have very negative consequences for them if not handled properly. Cal was no different.

A problem becoming more noticable was his attraction to alcohol, sometimes coupled with playing the card game of pitch. Over the years he had always managed to make his own home brew or get his hands on the devil's brew in some way. While it never cost him his job, it did create lots of heartache for Zelda Mae. For some reason she had always been most intolerant of alcoholic beverages. She never loved Cal any less for his drinking, however. Still, she seriously considered finding Brother Fire and Brimstone Thomas' counterpart in Hobart. Maybe he could put the fear of God in her spouse.

Zelda Mae always made it clear how she felt about liquids from the devil. For whatever reason, Cal always enjoyed his beer. Some say that when you have eleven children and little income, you have to drink. Anyway, it was a part of his life, excessively so sometimes.

The children were awakened on rare occasions by the sound of the caps popping off of freshly brewed bottles of beer he and his nephew, Billy Reeves, had made in the basement. Zelda Mae didn't find the noise funny, but the thumps of the caps hitting the underside of the floor under their beds did amuse the kids. Listening to an occasional pop and then a staccato of sounds brought up visions of an enemy machine gun firing on their position as they slept in the trenches of an army in a foreign land. Yes, it was funny listening to the fermenting beer as it erupted. Well, it was funny after you finally realized what was happening.

"Lord have mercy, what's that noise?" asked Zelda Mae, as she and Cal were awakened in the middle of the night.

"What noise?" was Cal's sleepy reply.

"That poppin' noise. Reckon someone's tryin' ta break in?"

"Don't you fret none. Everthing's alright!"

"Wait a minute," said Zelda Mae. "That's the fool beer you and Billy have been a makin', ain't it?"

"Don't worry none about it. It ain't goin' to hurt anything."

As laughing could be heard from the back rooms, Zelda Mae was even more serious in her indignation. "Now you've gone and awakened the kids up. I wish you'd quit makin' that fool brew you're always cookin' up. I don't like the kids seein' you drinkin' it. It ain't good fer them."

"Long as they don't drink any, it won't hurt them none."

"I do wish you'd quit your drinkin'."

"Now you know I just want a friendly drink now and then. That's alright, ain't it?"

"At least find a better place to let that devil-inspired liquid age. This wakin' the kids with such a ruckus in the middle of the night ain't any good at all. The kids'll be a havin' nightmares. I don't know what's the worst. You drinkin' that fool liquor, or the kids havin' nightmares."

"Maybe I could find a better place to brew the stuff."

"Where is Brother Fire and Brimstone Thomas when I need him?"

"I don't want to hear his name again!" said her husband.

"If you don't want ta hear his name again, I'd be a stoppin' this liquor business."

Cal did occasionally find better places to make his homebrew, but even though he sometimes cut back on its consumption, it was always to be a part of his life.

Nineteen forty-seven was to be a big year for the Ledbetters. In May, the second girl was to get married. Jane, fifteen years old, wed Walt Billings in Hobart. During that same summer Cole and Collette, accompanied by Belle, traveled to Colorado to visit Pearl and Wild Bill. The older sister so longed for the company of family and was willing to settle for even the younger ones.

After Pearl brought them back, there was discussion about the benefits of the family living in Colorado. Cal knew he'd like to care for his family better. Maybe a move would result in a higher paying job. The decision was made to move to Colorado that fall. Thinking the old Buick would not make the trip, as the wooden spokes in the wheels were badly worn and replacements weren't readily available, Cal purchased a Hudson Terraplane.

CHAPTER XX

Perhaps symbolic of the Ledbetter's state of affairs were their possessions. The furniture was meager. The couple didn't have much in material goods to show for twenty plus years of marriage. The rundown condition of the table and chairs was typical of all their limited possessions. A coat of varnish or paint would be a temporary solution to a long-term problem. This was not a condition to be readily solved.

"Do you think we're a makin' the right decision, Zelda?" Cal asked of his wife. "I reckon we could stay somewhere in Oklahoma. Anywhere, as a matter of fact."

"It's your choice, Honey," she replied.

"I know. But we're in this together. You've always been by my side. You don't complain about our movin' around the country. But this move is different. We're a movin' to a different state. I've never done that to you before."

"I'm not used to makin' choices like that, Cal. Papa never asked me before we moved from Arkansas. Everyone knew it was his choice to make. Well, I figure this is your choice to make this time as well. After all, the Bible tells us to follow our man wherever he goes. It's not for me to question. Just like Sarah followed her man Abraham, I'll be by your side wherever we may end up. You'll git no argument from me, either. Just lead the way."

"I know, Zelda. But we've always been each other's main support. No question about it. I can't go anywhere if you're not happy. I'd rather stay here if it means you'll be happy."

"I can't be happy, Cal, if we can't get new shoes for the kids or you can't even have a decent cup of coffee. I know you say it's all right, but that concoction I make still tastes more like dried carrots than it does coffee. Besides, I don't want to always have to see the kids workin' every wakin' hour in the fields while they're little. I want to see them get a decent education, more than you and I had."

"It's pretty risky movin' to Colorado like this," said Cal.

"I know. But Pearl says they're hirin' lots of new workers. The war is over, she says, and everyone wants to get the country movin' again. Yes, it's risky. But we've always takin' risks. What makes this so different is that we'll be a ways off from the family members who've always helped us. Of course Pearl and Bill are there. I'm hopin' that we won't need help, but if we do, they'll help."

"I'm a failure for sure," said Cal. "I don't seem to be able to care for my family like a man should. I shouldn't always be a lookin' to others for help."

"Now, Cal. You know you're tryin' hard. You've never been one to shirk your responsibilities. No one works harder than you do. It's just that things don't always seem to go our way. I don't want to hear any more about your bein' a poor provider. You're doin' the best you can. Just promise me one thing when we move to Colorado."

"What's that, Zelda Mae?"

"That we'll return to Hominy Corners to live out the rest of our lives, when the time comes, and we'll surely know when the time comes. I'll always be by your side Cal. Just make me that one promise."

"You know that's my dream as much as anyone's, Zelda. No promise could be easier to make. I hope it's as easy to accomplish."

Leaving southeastern Oklahoma and the country around Hominy Corners was by far one of the hardest things Cal and Zelda Mae ever had to do. It wasn't just the leaving of many relatives behind on both sides of the family, either. It went much deeper than that.

The transplanting of anything, animal, human, or vegetation, is not done without some cost being assessed. Plants and animals have been known to not survive in their new environment. While human beings are more flexible in this respect, a toll is always taken in some way for them as well.

Granted, there are rewards to sometimes be acquired by moving, but some entity is always left behind. Once the decision was made to leave Hominy Corners, though, it made little difference whether or not they went ahead and left the entire state as well. To break an addiction sometimes requires total abstinence not merely cutting back on the object of one's desire.

The Ledbetter's roots were well established in the red soil of Oklahoma. This anchorage was not subject to question, so they could have lived in so many towns, such as Durant, Bokchito, Benninton, Wade or Hobart, while maintaining a semblance of their roots. They could well have moved to a town they had never seen before somewhere else in the state. Oklahoma even grows on people living there that aren't native. But when you're born there, you're endowed with a heritage never to be forsaken.

The unseen element is hard to explain; it must be an ingredient in the blood of native borns that doesn't function right when they cross that mystical boundary of a state line to move away. Even going into Texas, which has a close kinship to Oklahoma, doesn't make the crossing any easier. When you're born an Okie, you'll die an Okie, no matter where you live. Therefore, Cal and Zelda Mae's decision to move out of state was born of necessity, not a desire to forsake their roots.

Times were difficult for the Ledbetters in 1947. It should have been a time to feel positive about the future. The nation had entered a new era. World War II was over. Men home from the great conflict were reunited with their families. The nation was well on the road to recovery. There were feelings of optimism, the likes of which citizens of the United States had not known in many years. To Cal and Zelda Mae, however, it was a time of continued struggle for survival. They worried about how and where they could meet the needs of a large family.

Oklahoma, it appeared, was not to be that place at this time. Pearl, Cal and Zelda Mae's eldest child, and her husband, Bill, had found success in Colorado. They had stayed there after Bill was discharged from the army. Maybe, just maybe, there would be a brighter future for the Ledbetters in this mountainous state as well. Of course where Pearl and Bill lived was in the prairie part of the state.

Zelda Mae would have gone to the ends of the earth with her man; he meant that much to her. After twenty-two years of marriage she would never question his intentions. While this decision to move was Cal's alone, if he wanted it that way, he would not have done something to which she really objected. This was most typical of marriages for those days and times. These many years of working with and beside her had taught him so much about the depths to which human relationships can soar.

No, these two people deeply in love wanted to make the move. It was a joint decision with no votes taken. They just understood each other. Colorado would be their new home. The car was loaded in preparation for a permanent move. Well, permanent until they could move back to Hominy Corners.

On a cold November day they left Hobart, Oklahoma, for Las Animas, Colorado. It troubled the soul to leave family members behind. At least it wasn't like leaving Mom or Mattie Fern in Holly Grove Cemetery in Arkansas or J.H. buried on the farm in Wade, Zelda Mae thought. Instead, the relatives being left behind were other than immediate family members. Even Jane, their third eldest, and her husband, Walt Billings, made the trip with them. Due to the fact that Jane was five months pregnant, the trip was especially difficult for her.

Still the various Cantrells and Ledbetters and their families were being left behind. Most difficult to accept was the issue of leaving Zelda Mae's father, Papa Cantrell, and Cal's mother, Grandma Lillie, behind in Oklahoma. Cal and Zelda Mae each had a most special relationship with their lone surviving parent. Surely Lillie and Papa understood that this relocation must happen. Without the move, the Ledbetter's future might be much diminished from what it might have been. But the move held out hopes for a brighter tomorrow.

Moving in a westerly direction always seemed to be the key to another chance. The Rocky Mountains beckoned for the Ledbetters to come. How could they refuse the lure of greener grass on the other side of the fence? The move was not to be denied. The time had come to acknowledge the restless spirit in

Cal's breast, begging to be set free like a butterfly desirous of escaping the confines of a caterpillar.

The trip was difficult. The car was quite crowded and uncomfortable. Buying the Hudson Terraplane might have been a mistake. This advancement in technology lacked many of the better qualities of the older Buick Cal had traded. To make matters worse, it was not as roomy inside. Right now, however, the only choice was to keep forging ahead. Rest breaks were a rarity.

After awhile the kids were wishing for flat tires in order to get out of the car for a chance to move around. The trip reminded Zelda Mae of the Cantrell trip from Arkansas to Oklahoma twenty-five years earlier. At least the current car was warmer, not like the "air-conditioned" Model T of days gone by.

There were all ages of "kids" in the car ranging from Jane, who was sixteen, down to Franklin and Joyce. At least Belle had gone on ahead, so some space was freed up. Cal and Walt shared the driving duties. Still, with nine travelers in this automobile, which had already seen its better days, memories came back to Cal about the troop ship on which he had sailed to France during WWI. Hammocks seven deep for the doughboys left little room for unfettered movement. Cal recalled that he couldn't even turn over on that earlier trip, once he crawled into his bunk for a night's rest. Worst yet was the fear that the rusty chain links holding the canvas tenements aloft might decide to separate company, and on a very few occasions they did.

But Cal was the captain of this ship rushing across the rolling sea of prairie grasses on a ribbon of concrete, so his destiny was now in his hands, not someone on the distant bridge of the ship that he could not see. "We're well on our way, Zelda," he said.

"Yes, to worlds unknown. I wonder what Colorado is like?" answered Zelda Mae.

"I know that there are mountains. I've never really seen a mountain. Suppose we'll find time to climb one?"

"Sounds like too much work to me," answered her husband. "We're a gettin' too old for mountain climbin', Zelda Mae."

"We're not old dogs. We can learn new tricks."

"I'm fifty-two and will soon be fifty-three years old, Zelda. I'm satisfied with the tricks I already know."

"Well, it is goin' to be a new experience."

"You won't get any disagreement from me," Cal told his wife.

One of the few luxuries permitted on this voyage was a most infrequent sharing of a bottle of Royal Crown Cola while Cal, Walt or Abe filled the car with fuel and checked the oil and tires. This servicing was not quickly done, as the gas pumps in the stations required no electricity. Looking like sentinels standing tall, they were pumped by hand. First, the customer or service station attendant would pump the desired amount of fuel up into a glass bowl on the top of the pump by hand using a lever on the side. There were lines painted on the glass cylinder indicating how much fuel was in the bowl. Then the gas would be allowed to flow by gravity down into the vehicle's tank. The price usually ranged between twenty and thirty cents per gallon. Sometimes it cost as much as four dollars to fill the fuel tank with the precious liquid needed to keep this army on the move.

"Don't spill a drop," said Walt. "At twenty-three cents a gallon we can't have it evaporatin' on the ground."

"I'm careful," said Abe. "You just watch and see."

This migration was over four hundred long, weary miles. Going through familiar countryside in the beginning wasn't too bad, but the view soon changed to places they had never seen before. Well, except for Cole and Collette, who had been this way before in the summer of 1946, the countryside was new. Of course they didn't remember too much of that earlier adventure, so they and the first time viewers were equally intrigued at the new sights until boredom and fatigue took over. Breaks for any reason were to be avoided if possible. Time was in short supply. Taking any longer than necessary to get to Colorado meant being cooped up in a car with eight other souls whose patience may have worn a little thin at times.

"Momma," said Cole.

"Hush, child. I'm tryin' to talk to your father."

"But, Momma!"

"Don't raise your voice to me young one."

"But what about Collette," answered the frustrated boy.

"Alright. What about Collette?" asked Zelda Mae.

"We left her at the service station," said Cole.

"Didn't you count the kids?" Zelda said as she turned to her husband.

"No. I thought you did."

"Well, nobody did. Do I have to do everything?"

"Turn it around Walt," said Cal. "We're never goin' to get to Colorado at this rate."

The journey north and west went through Sayre and Boise City, Oklahoma. After that it was a long, relatively uneventful drive across the prairie with no landmarks that interested the youngsters, except for Two Buttes on Highway 287, to Campo and Springfield, Colorado, and the three state lines they crossed.

After leaving Oklahoma for awhile to enter a corner of Texas, they re-entered their home state in order to cross the panhandle, a vast expanse of land whose main inhabitants were jackrabbits looking for shade and sagebrush looking for rain. Without these state borders as demarcation lines, the younger kids were thoroughly convinced they would never reach their destination. "We must be goin' to the end of the earth" was often uttered out of desperation. Even the older kids and Cal and Zelda Mae from time to time questioned their ability to survive such a long trek.

The resemblance to the behaviors of the crew of Christopher Columbus in 1492 must have been quite striking. At some point that Hudson was surely going to drop off the edge of the earth or be eaten by a dragon. Unquestionably, the anxiety level of the "crew" reached epic proportions on occasion. In time, however, the scared feeling would subside, only to be replaced by boredom. "Burma Shave" signs, however, occasionally interrupted the monotony of the trip.

Burma Shave, a manufacturer of shaving cream, would place humorous or philosophical signs along the roadway out away from the cities, as a way of capturing the traveler's attention. These red signs with white lettering were about 12 inches high by 48 inches wide on a post holding them about four feet above the ground. The signs were in a series about one-eighth mile apart inside the fence lines along the side of the road, so you had to wait a short while to read the next part of the saying. This added some suspense to the witty or insightful expressions. A typical set of signs would generally start off with something like “WANT TO”, then a short time later you might see, “BE WEALTHY”. On down the road might be “TRY WORK”, and a little later would be such as “NOT LETHARGY”. The series of signs would then close with “BURMA SHAVE”.

The Ledbetter children old enough to read looked forward to these signs. Each time the sayings occurred, they contained a new proverb or humorous admonition. The real value in these signs, however, was in the breaking up of the monotony of a long trip. In so doing they likely served as a safety feature as well. That is, they helped keep the driver alert and awake.

In Lamar, Colorado, they turned west on US 50, the highway that would go through Las Animas. It followed the old Santa Fe Trail part of the time. This historic trail played a vital role in the opening up of the lands later to become Kansas, Colorado and New Mexico for early day trappers and traders. Driving upstream of the Arkansas Valley by the many farms visible from the road raised this family’s hopes to new heights. The excitement of the car’s occupants steadily increased as they began to see the name of their destination listed on billboards. When the sign by the side of the road finally said, “Las Animas-7 Miles,” it was a relief for Cal to honestly say, “It won’t be long now,” when asked, “Are we there yet?” for the thousandth time.

This was a switch from his usual joking answer to such questions. Earlier when they asked such a question, it wasn’t unusual to get a reply like “You know what the monkey said when the train ran over its tail?”

In unison the kids would reply “No!” with considerable exuberance.

“It won’t be long now,” Cal would reply.

The kids picked up the sincerity now present in his voice, though, as they approached Las Animas from the east. By this time everyone was looking out of the windows hoping to be the first to catch a glimpse of this town they would call home. And there it was! Off in the distance to the left, silhouetted against a setting sun as only Colorado can produce, could be seen this town that would soon be the new home of the Ledbetters.

Even though from afar the image resembled a large animal settling down to hibernate for the winter, the excitement continued to reach even new heights as the heavily laden car crossed the narrow Arkansas River Bridge coming in from the north. The first houses they encountered were different than they had left in Oklahoma. On the right were monotonous looking adobe labor shacks for migrant workers brought in from Mexico to work in the melon or onion fields. This long row of gray dwellings with no grass, just dirt and weeds for yards, certainly didn't look appealing. There was no sign of life in this continuous row of tiny hovels; they were depressingly empty this time of year.

But as they proceeded on down Bent Avenue, the houses took on a charm all their own. It was exciting to see so many businesses and places to go. Yes, this town was going to be acceptable.

In no time they arrived at the house built by Pearl and Bill James on Vine Street in that part of Las Animas across the tracks known as "Hollywood." As everyone was so curious about this town soon to become their new home, Pearl tried to give some of the local history as well as to explain the meaning of the name Las Animas to the multitude of guests in her not too large home. The name had something to do with being Spanish for "the city of lost souls." The words had a foreboding sound. At the same time, however, they had a sound of promise for the weary travelers. Herein was another chance from which new beginnings often emerge.

Las Animas, the county seat of Bent County, was built at the confluence of two rivers, the Arkansas and the Purgatoire, better known as the "Picketwire" by the early cowboys due to their difficulty in pronouncing the word Purgatoire. The early history of Bent County (named after William Bent, one of the original builders of the early day Bent's Fort) revealed many exciting tales about explorers, trappers, traders, cowboys and Indians. The region had become a strong agricultural center noted more for the fine crops raised instead of the reckless life associated with a new frontier.

"What kind of town is this here, anyway?" Cal wanted to know.

"It's a farmin' community," said Pearl.

"Well what about those tales you just told about Indians and cowboys and the like?"

"Oh, they're still around these parts. But they ain't like they used to be."

"Yes, and just what do you mean by that?" asked Cal.

"There did use to be Cheyennes and Arapahoes round. But they were all put on reservations a long time ago," explained Pearl.

"You mean this country did the same things to the Indians around here?" asked Cal.

"Well this wasn't exactly like they treated the Oklahoma Indians at all. It was different up here."

"In what way?" Cal wanted to know.

"They gave them land up north and east of here. On the other side of the Arkansas River."

"Are they still on that reservation? That's like lockin' a man up in his own home. That's what it is you know. That way doesn't work. It never worked!"

While Cal wasn't too sure about the role of the Indian in the early history of the area, he certainly liked the looks of the land in the fertile valley along the river bottom they had just traveled. Las Animas, then, was to be the city of the future for the Ledbetters, until they could return to Hominy Corners, on a permanent basis that is. Time would tell, but it didn't hurt to be optimistic. Hope springs from a positive attitude, not past failures.

Cal's first real job in Colorado was working on the Fort Lyon Canal, an irrigation system used to bring the precious mountain water necessary for the success of the many farms of the

Arkansas Valley. This was a totally new experience for the transplanted farmer, as the hills of Oklahoma often precluded the movement of water in this fashion. His first assignment included helping clear this waterway of obstructions, such as deposits of sand or tumbleweeds.

This menial labor was temporary employment. The tasks generally could only be done during the winter months when farmers were not running irrigation water for their crops. Cal really wasn't too impressed by this type of work. Besides, Colorado was a lot colder than Oklahoma, and it wasn't fun working in extremely cold temperatures, especially when you sometimes got wet in the process. Still, it was work, and that put beans on the table for his family.

Cal was later to be employed by Robert Crisafulli. The Crisafulli farm was located a few miles west of town. Situated in the middle of productive fields, the view contained a variety of crops in every direction. An inquisitive lad, such as Cole, not yet ten years old could only sit in the shade and dream of the mysterious world beckoning from just beyond the golden horizon rising above the gently swaying rows of corn. The green stalks always seemed to be waving with the message, "Goodbye, we'll have to go on without you." On a still day the friendly green giants kept their tasseled heads bowed with paper-thin arms held close and motionless.

The rough, rutted, gravel road not more than a stone's throw in front of the rundown, old farmhouse called home disappeared beside the grassy crest of a rock-covered hill rising like a pyramid from beside the meandering Arkansas River. Peaceful scenes quite similar to this were often seen on calendars from the Texaco Service Station or interlocking, jigsaw puzzles bought at Woolworth's "Five and Dime" Store.

Of course such pictorial scenes rarely showed the disruptive aftermath of a passing vehicle. To be caught in the swirling, brown clouds following the vehicle meant being momentarily blinded with a burning sensation in one's watering eyes. At the same time the unfortunate soul gasped for breath as the fine, dry mist penetrated heaving lungs. Spitting mud afterwards was sometimes necessary to clear clogged air passages.

Zelda Mae never liked the swirling, rooster-tails of choking dust trailing the infrequent motorcar or roaring truck loaded with Hereford cattle headed for the sale at Winters Livestock Auction in La Junta. She had long ago given up the daily efforts of trying to remove the rapidly accumulating layers of grime with the consistency of fine flour from the window sills with chipped paint or the well-worn, pine furniture she and Cal so much treasured. Besides, her children made far more demands on her time with greater urgency than that required for housecleaning. Yes, it did bother her when an errant child used the dust as a tablet to write their names in a manuscript consisting of large swirls and curlicues. Worse yet was when she found someone had added spittle to his or her artistic efforts with the fine residue of wind to complete a crude yet unique form of finger-painting.

Actually there was little furniture requiring dusting in this sparsely equipped home. This family large enough to field a softball team possessed not even most of the bare necessities in household goods. The meager living room furniture, some made with hand tools by Cal, consisted of unpadded benches and a “flowerdy” couch which made into a makeshift bed at best.

Dining-room chairs were a luxury still in the dreaming stage. Only the food-stained table made of course, pine slabs was needed to complete the limited inventory of traditional pieces. The store-bought oilcloth purchased by the square yard resembled a checkerboard when used on Sunday’s table. When clean it added a certain elegance to a meal otherwise noted more for nutrition than atmosphere.

With Zelda Mae’s prized cut-crystal glasses used only on the Sabbath to replace used peach cans for drinking, however, these well-attended meals did represent a joyous time in this crowded household. Still, the benches, hard as granite on your bottom, provided little comfort for the tired back. Well, they could be used for the partaking of meals or listening to Fibber McGee and Molly on the little Motorola Radio needing antenna wires strung to the weathered, red barn located in the middle of a nearby corral.

Actually most of the well-padded family preferred to sit on the bare floor made of fir, softwood much like pine. They used the plastered wall with sandpaper texture as a much-needed backrest. Soft cushions or pillows stuffed with goosefeathers were deemed a luxury at times like this.

Hidden by a linoleum that was once brightly colored in geometric patterns of pink and gray, the large, open expanse of floor was easy to clean when needed. Brooms made of corn tassel could remove simple dirt easily tracked in from the yard. A rag mop was used for more enduring deposits that might originate in the corral. Actually the chocolate-colored dirt was not readily visible as the dim, single lightbulb in the porcelain fixture with a dangling pullchain revealed few blemishes after the sun went down.

Dustpans were not needed as the daily accumulations could be swept out a beckoning door, once the sagging screendoor was propped open with a ten-gallon cream can to override the tightly coiled spring.

Yes, the abundant soil of the fertile fields was a necessary part of everyday life to the farm family, but so was the ever-present dirt brought in from the graded road leading to that mysterious world beyond the horizon called town. Life would never be the same after the rain-caused ruts were removed and the road was paved to look like a licorice stick from the air.

The boys liked the gravel road, because it contained so many rocks an ideal size for throwing. They held contests throwing stones across the road to see who could get the most projectiles in the open mailbox. Passersby must have wondered aloud about what an ugly mailbox located beside the road and what made it look so strange. It was almost as if some powerful creature had been inside trying to escape.

"Do you boys have to keep that mailbox bent up?" asked their father.

"We're only playin', Daddy," answered Jimmy.

"I don't mind you playin'. But I'm afraid you'll get rocks out in the field where they don't belong. Worse yet, I'm afraid you'll hit a passin' car. We haven't got money to replace a windshield."

"We'll be careful, Daddy," said Cole.

"Couldn't you do something different?" asked Cal.

"Maybe we could nail a bucket to the barn," responded Jimmy.

"Better yet," said his father, "just paint a bullseye on the side. I believe Mr. Crisafulli will let us have some leftover paint. You boys make more than one circle, then you can see who comes the closest to the middle. I just don't want any rocks in the field or any people or livestock gettin' hit. Do you hear me? And be sure and let Franklin play, too."

"Yes, Daddy," the two boys answered together.

The small house provided by Mr. Crisafulli for his hired help was totally inadequate for such a large family as the Ledbetters. It only had one bedroom. The first order of business was to immediately enlarge this house. Consequently, two bedrooms were added on the westside of the house. One of the new rooms was for the girls, while the other room was for the boys. Other than location, no identifying decoration revealed the gender of the inhabitants. It was impossible to find a place in the house to be alone.

Privacy, a most precious gift for members of a large family, was almost a non-existent commodity inside this home. Anyone desirous of getting away from all of the activity would have to leave the house. Going out into a neighboring field or the garage was best for this. Even then, the privacy might be short lived.

There was no indoor plumbing in this humblest of abodes. A simple pitcher pump mounted on the countertop on the north wall in the kitchen supplied the family with cold water; hot water could only be obtained by heating it on the stove. This hand pump had to be primed by pouring a cup of water down a recession surrounding the pump rod on the top. This water also served to keep the leathers soaked. The leathers, washers named after the material used in their construction, provided a seal around the pump rod down in the well to minimize leakage as the water was drawn up the pipe. If too much delay occurred between uses, the pump would need reprimed.

Collette thought they were now partaking of the pleasures of the ultimate home; they had "runnin' water." Still, a bucket of water with a dipper hanging on the side was kept on the counter for those needing a drink.

The Ledbetters were truly blessed. That's because they were spared the difficult chore of going outside to carry in water with a bucket, though other opportunities were provided for them to experience something on occasion that few people in warmer climates ever learn up close. One thing about getting water from an outside pump can only be learned for one's self. Vicarious living does not pay adequate homage to sticking one's tongue to a frozen pump handle, only to realize it won't come loose without the agony of literally tearing it away. In the process of this maneuver the tongue has no choice but to give up at least one layer of the delicate tissue encasing it.

No, the experience derived from the bonding of wet skin to frozen metal would last a lifetime. Everyone needed to do it at least once. Any less and a lasting memory would not be achieved. Franklin had more than one indelible impression of this phenomenon. He just wanted to be sure that he wasn't imagining things the first time.

"Maybe if we poured hot water on his tongue," said Cal, "it would turn loose."

"No, the metal must be warmed to equalize the temperature of the two objects," replied Mr. Crisafulli.

"That handle is in inch thick and two inches wide. I'm afraid it can't be done in any short time," said Cal.

"Then we'll have to pull it off very gently," returned his boss.

Removal of the tongue from its metallic captor exceeded any pain imagined by Franklin. Drops of blood formed on his lips.

"I can't even put medicine on it," said Zelda Mae.

"I reckon it'll quit bleedin' after awhile."

"Maybe some ice cream would make it feel better," said Collette.

"Right now," her mother responded, "nothin' is goin' to make it feel better."

There was an outhouse behind the house. It wasn't too far from the fence encircling the yard. Immediately across the fence from the outhouse was a huge pile of corncobs. This placement of the corncob pile was no accident. Mr. Crisafulli had to have the ears of corn shelled somewhere in order to market only the kernels of corn. Why not shell the corn in a place to achieve maximum benefit?

Therefore, the corncribs holding the newly harvested corn were placed close to where the hired help lived. As soon as the corn was sufficiently dried, it could be shelled. Ultimately, a huge mound of corncobs was formed, much like the formation of a mountain growing out of a volcano, as the corn shelling was slowly brought to a close.

The uses of the cobs were multiple. They could be used to start a fire before adding coal in a cookstove or potbellied wood heater, or they could be used in place of toilet paper in the outhouse. While there were additional uses for the cobs, the Ledbetters pretty much restricted their use to fuel for heating. Sometimes, in order to save money, heating fires consisted only of corncobs. However, they tended to burn quite rapidly when used alone, and this necessitated frequent trips to the cob pile.

The heating of the small house was minimal. The fire was allowed to die out during the night to conserve fuel. Without thick layers of Zelda Mae's quilts, the night, wintry air might have been unbearable. In the morning Cal would get up and light the fire in the potbellied stove. This meant it would take awhile to warm the house, and then only the living room was heated.

The cookstove in turn would raise the comfort level of the kitchen and dining area. Waiting for the house to warm was often punishment, however, so it was not unusual to see the shivering Ledbetter kids standing outside but close to the house on the east side in the early morning. The heat of the sun was warmer than being in the house.

By standing close to the white, stucco exterior, the kids also received the welcome sun's rays reflected behind them, helping to elevate the temperatures of both sides of their chilled bodies at the same time. It was still better to be in the house once the stove started to warm things up. On an early morning, though, the sun provided a welcome respite from the cold night air that the heating fires needed time to overcome.

It would be hard for anyone to forget just how hot their clothes could get from standing too close to the hot stove, especially if they soon thereafter sat down and in the process stretched the hot fabric of their clothing tightly over their buttocks. It was funny to see Abe sit on a hot rivet used to hold his overalls together. Funnier yet was to see Jane sit on the hot metal snap her garter belt needed to hold her stockings up.

Unscheduled dances of unknown origin could be seen at most anytime in the Ledbetter's house. History will always be denied the choreography of these movements, as the careless originator failed to record them for posterity.

"I'll bet you can't dance like that again, Jane," said her father.

"Who would want to duplicate that feat?" she answered.

"Oh," said Cal, "I've been to many a dance, and nobody moved as fast as you did. Give me a little time and I'll figure out a tune to go with it."

"And just what will you call this tune?" she asked.

"How about, `There'll be a hot time on the old stove tonight?'" he answered.

"I was thinkin' more of `Snap it up'," said Zelda Mae.

"Real funny," said Jane.

Heating a house with a woodburning stove was not easy. An ideal fire was one that allowed the recipient to be lightly toasted on both sides. Often, though, the toast was burned on one side, while the other side remained uncooked.

There was always the problem, however, with the temperature being too hot up close to the stove, while it was cold several feet away. Then, too, you had to continually bring wood, corncobs or coal into the house when it was needed, not to mention always carrying out the remaining ashes after a fire.

Keeping a fire going in the home twenty-four hours a day was just not done. To do so would not only have been a luxury, but it would have been a monumental task. Who wanted to get up every two or three hours during the night to stoke the fire?

The lack of a bathroom posed additional problems for the family other than having to go outside to relieve one's self. The taking of weekly baths was not a simple task; it required foresight and planning. A large galvanized tub about thirty inches in diameter was placed in the center of the floor of the kitchen or the front room. It was filled just over one-half full with water heated on the cook stove. One at a time each child would bathe, sometimes with the assistance of Zelda Mae or one of the older girls.

The boys would often complain about the severity with which their ears were scrubbed. "If your ears ain't red," Zelda Mae would say, "then they ain't clean!" The same bath water was used for scrubbing by everyone. As some water was lost due to splashing, or just getting carried out of the tub by wet individuals, it was replaced by more from the container on the stove.

It should be immediately evident that bathing every Saturday night was a major undertaking. Furthermore, there were other complicating issues as well. While privacy was desirable, it was hard to achieve. Generally the boys would bathe first, then be relegated to the boys' room while the girls bathed. Also, needless to say, clean bath water was a luxury. Finally, the floor was almost always left standing in water from exuberant bathers. At least the linoleum was impervious to water. Someone had to mop the floor immediately afterwards, though.

Bathing was not an activity to anticipate, especially by the four boys. It was seen by them as something to get out of when possible. It certainly was not considered a form of relaxation by Martha Sue or Collette, either. Tales they had heard of ladies lying back and enjoying a warm bath didn't make sense. How could anyone relax with their knees touching their chin while bathing? At least it wasn't difficult for them to wash their toes in the small, round galvanized tub used by the Ledbetters.

"Why do we have to go to bed so early tonight?" asked Abe.

"So your sisters can take a bath. I want you out of here for awhile," answered his mother.

"But we took baths first last week, too," said Cole.

"Hush! And do what you're told," said Zelda Mae. "Now get a move on it!"

Evenings at the Ledbetter's house were fairly typical for farm dwellers. After supper was over and the dishes were done, many evenings were spent up close listening to the radio. Getting too far away meant the missing of key lines due to ever-present static.

Laughter was a frequent occurrence when everything could be heard falling out of the closet in episodes of "Fibber McGee and Molly." Also, it was not unusual to see everyone paying close attention as the Lone Ranger was heard to say "Hi ho Silver away!" One of their favorite programs, though, was "Amos 'n' Andy," containing episodes of colored folks caught in many a humorous situation. It was a shock to later learn that the authentic sounding black characters were actually white folks playing a role. Worse yet, their antics did not portray colored folks in a positive light.

The Ledbetter's most liked American program at night was "The Grand Old Opry" out of Nashville, Tennessee. They heard it only at night when some stations were allowed to boost their wattage during broadcasting, while the remaining stations went off of the air.

Trips to town were few and far between; they were a rare treat. When the trips were made, though, they generally occurred on Saturday afternoons. While Cal and Zelda Mae would shop, the kids would see a movie at the Saturday matinee of the Ritz Theater. The cost per child was 11 cents, of which one-cent was tax. It didn't make any difference what was on the silver screen; that was their favorite. Almost always the fare was westerns such as Gene Autry or Lash LaRue. Occasionally they would see the Bowery Boys, a group of bumblers always in a predicament in the big city.

On the rarest of occasions a shopping trip might have been made on Saturday evening because Cal didn't get the afternoon off. When the shopping was completed, the family would not immediately leave for home. Instead, they would do as many other families did.

While Zelda Mae would remain inside the car, the others would sit or lean on the hood of the car and greet passers-by walking down the sidewalk. This was not only a form of recreation, it was a way of learning the happenings in the area. Cheaper entertainment could not be found anywhere.

"How're you doin', Mrs. Pawling?" asked Zelda Mae.

"Oh, fair I suppose," she answered. "Nice night isn't it?"

"Yes, and the bugs aren't too bad either. Maybe it's too early in the year for them to git bad."

"Oh, they'll get bad soon enough. Before long we'll be carrying a flyswatter everywhere we go."

"Tom got his crops in yet?" asked Zelda Mae.

"He's working at it. I reckon he'll finish plowing next week. How have you been?"

"I bought my flour last week in the nicest sack. Cole will be sportin' the prettiest shirt you ever saw one of these days. I hope they keep that fabric for awhile. I sure would like to make Abe one just like it."

When extensive shopping was required, the family generally went to La Junta. The store there most liked by Cal and Zelda Mae was Montgomery Wards, or "Monkey Warts," as Cal called it. Wards carried more equipment like Cal wanted, such as new chicken waterers or tires for the car. If they wanted bib overalls for the boys to wear to school, they could buy those at Penney's in Las Animas.

Most of the clothing worn by the children was handsewn by Zelda Mae. She never made overalls, however. She patched many a pair, though. While shopping or movie going was fun, the kids all looked forward to the return ride upon the completion of their shopping trip to La Junta. This meant a stop at Wisswells for delicious homemade ice cream. This delicacy was needed to fortify them for the long trip of twenty miles back home. The frozen delight was not only a fitting climax on which to end the shopping trip, but it could well have been the only reason for going to La Junta if the truth were known. Of course you would get no argument from Cal, either.

The years spent on the Crisafulli's place were happy years for the Ledbetters. Cal and Mr. Crisafulli were always on the best of terms. The children enjoyed playing with the Crisafulli's children.

Separating the two houses was a horse pasture about the size of an extra large football field. While it might sometimes be bumpy from hoof marks made in the mud there by Blacky, the horse living there, it was an ideal place to play softball. "Work-up," where there were three batters, while the remaining participants played a base or a field position, was a favorite pastime.

The Crisafulli children often joined these major league ballgames. If the horse pasture wasn't available, however, the large dairy barn or other buildings and haystacks, along with the surrounding fields, provided settings for many an hour of play. The dairy barn with two tall silos resembling gigantic chimneys serving as sentinels at the front of the structure was best remembered for the Halloween parties hosted for the area by Mrs. Crisafulli.

If these sites were off limits, the kids would generally build a pair of stilts or something equally as exciting to entertain themselves. Even then, the days weren't long enough to schedule all of the activities they wanted to do. Of course if they had still been living in Oklahoma, they would have been chopping or picking cotton instead of playing so much. Well, they did help in some of the local hoeing or harvesting of crops when Cal heard someone needed help, but they never missed an opportunity to play with or on whatever was available.

Toys for them to use were almost non-existent, so they either had to make their own toys or play wherever they found the most amusement. Both were done. The girls made their own dolls, while the boys made sleds or used small blocks of wood for tractors or trucks on the closest pile of dirt. Dirt piles were easy to find because the yard contained no grass.

Something both the boys and the girls enjoyed doing was fastening a Prince Albert tobacco tin on the end of a stick and shaping it in such a way that it could be used to push the metal hoop from a wagon wheel around the yard. Not knowing they were poor, and thinking everyone else was equally as destitute, made it easier for the Ledbetter kids to accept their lot in life.

Christmas couldn't be counted on as a source of toys. This was the time of year to be sure the children had plenty of school clothes. Cal and Zelda Mae had three times during the year to outfit their children with new clothes, and Zelda Mae made most of those clothes. These few times for buying or making new clothes were just before school started, as gifts for Christmas, or at Easter time. Otherwise the children received shirts or dresses made from the flour sacks, as a large amount of flour was used for baking by Zelda Mae.

"What do you want for Christmas, Daddy?" asked Mattie Jean.

"I really don't need anything," answered her father.

"Well, if you'd give me some money, I'd like to buy you somethin'," responded the girl.

"First of all, I don't think we have money to spare on gifts. But if you want to get me somethin', how about makin' it for me?"

"But I don't know what you want."

"You could make me an ashtray," he answered.

"How could I do that?" she asked.

"Oh, you'll think of a way. Just use your imagination. You'll be surprised at what you'll think of sometimes. Surprise me. I'd like it better that way," he responded.

The Ledbetter children attended Cornelia School, a two-room country school about two miles away, serving grades one through eight. The only times the children did not walk to school were on days with extremely bad weather. The school was not so different from what Cal and Zelda Mae had attended, except it had two outhouses, one for the boys and one for the girls.

The kids were surprised to learn that the Big Chief writing tablets they used were no different than the ones their mother had used as a girl in Arkansas. Also, Cornelia School had a stable in the rear to house horses during the day for children using four-legged forms of conveyance to get to school.

The school was the center of most of the social activity for the area. Box suppers and school plays were just two of the many activities enjoyed there. A favorite happening, though, was the end of the year picnic held on the school grounds.

Parents and everyone for miles around would come to participate in the meal fit for a king and the festivities designed for all ages. George Desmond, whose daughter Caroline attended there, could always be counted on to provide the ice cream. Following the demolition of a large meal, there would be sack races and a multitude of other equally as entertaining events.

This was a close knit community. Cal and Zelda Mae enjoyed being a part of it. They especially liked the school. The Ledbetter children did very well there under the tutelage of Mrs. Roswell. Also, they fit in with everyone else, as most of the boys wore bib overalls with gallouses for suspenders.

Cal still experienced somewhat of a problem with alcoholic beverage during his years of working for Mr. Crisafulli. While it was not as great of a problem as he had experienced in Oklahoma, it still created difficulties for him. On one return trip from town late at night, where he had enjoyed the fruits of John Barleycorn, Cal had the misfortune of having a telephone pole jump right out in the middle of the road before him. It was unbelievable; the pole landed upright and it was square in the middle of the roadway.

Realizing the only safe and logical thing to do was avert a collision, he drove off into the barrow pit beside the road. By this time the reality of what had happened occurred to him. Besides that, the cold night air combined with the sharp blow administered by the steering wheel when the telephone pole was hit helped erase the last remnants of a foggy brain. Being frugal by nature he placed the not quite dead bottle of liquor up the road a short distance. The location was by the second telephone pole, to later be retrieved by Pearl and Belle one day hence.

The car, a 1941 Chevrolet purchased from Mr. Crisafulli, required a new paint job once the fender was straightened. Cal's ability to joke at his problem bothered Zelda Mae. She didn't find it amusing when he would comment about being a magician. "I can just be walking down the street," he would say, "and turn into a bar."

"I still believe that I need to talk to Brother Fire and Brimstone Thomas before you up and kill yerself, Cal."

"I said I didn't want to hear his name again!"

"Yes, and I want my husband safe. If need be, I will call Brother Thomas!"

"I'm a tryin' ta do better."

"That's not good enough. At the very least don't do things the kids'll hear about."

"Give me another chance?"

"Okay, but y'er a runnin' outta chances."

The late 1940's and early 1950's were never to be forgotten by Cal and Zelda Mae. A new generation was added to the family. Jane gave them their first grandchild in 1948. Samuel Amos Billings was born on March 22 in Weatherford, Oklahoma. This birth set the wheels in motion. Grandchildren would be added to the family on a regular basis. In 1949 Jane and Walt would name their second baby, Caleb Ashton Billings, after his grandfather.

Cal and Zelda Mae couldn't have been more thrilled at the many additions that began to occur to their family. The first one to be named Ledbetter was not born until 1953. Abe and his wife had Carson Leon Ledbetter named after Papa Cantrell. Now, after his father before him, a Ledbetter would insure the continuation of the family name.

Abe was not to be formally educated beyond the seventh grade. His help was needed in meeting the financial needs of the family, so Mr. Crisafulli hired him to help complete the many farm chores needing done around his place.

The tall boy worked beside Cal in the fields. They both greatly appreciated working with such a knowledgeable individual as Mr. Crisafulli. He was one of the few college educated, or "book farmers" as they were frequently known and often ridiculed in the area, individuals to be respected for his knowledge of farming.

Standing amidst the windrows of new mown alfalfa hay, Cal watched two scissortail magpies sitting on a fence. If they were communicating, it was impossible for him to hear in the still quietness of the early morning when the dew had yet to recede in order to escape the warm rays of sunlight. Treatment of the curing hay fascinated him. With the modern equipment owned by Mr. Crisafulli, it was simple to turn the hay over so it would cure on both sides. The old method of using the large, springtooth, sulky rake had been greatly improved upon. For a moment Cal almost felt guilty at being a party to the use of this advanced technology.

Realizing a conversation he had had with his departed father many years earlier, Cal removed his hat and looked above the tamaracks in the distance as he gazed towards the heavens. Thinking of an earlier request he had made, he took a few moments to pause and say, "Daddy, I know I asked you to be with me as I learned to be a better farmer. You did just that. I know you did. I always wanted to farm just like you did. But times are different now. They just ain't farmin' like they use to do. Now they've got equipment like you never seen before. I hope you don't mind how I'm a changin'? If I'm a goin' to make it in this here farmin', I'm a goin' to have to change. I know Mr. Crisafulli is the one a teachin' me. You'd like him Daddy, I know you would."

Seeing Abe approaching from the house with a burlap-wrapped jug of water, Cal said, "I'll be talkin' to you again one of these days," as he returned his hat to a head with a meager portion of hair.

In 1950 Mr. Crisafulli introduced concrete irrigation ditches to the area. With Cal's perseverance and knowledge of building, along with Mr. Crisafulli's ingenuity, a model farm was in the making. Numerous projects of this nature were attempted on a regular basis, with many of the efforts achieving success. Therein was a problem, however. Individuals of the caliber of Mr. Crisafulli can best serve humanity by working on a much larger scale than is provided by the family farm. He answered the call to serve his fellow man. After public service at both the local and state level, he was elected to serve in the Colorado Legislature. The operation of the Crisafulli farm was to no longer be managed by him, it would be rented to someone else. Cal was unable to take advantage of this opportunity, so he would seek employment elsewhere.

With a sense of deep loss over no longer being able to work for Mr. Crisafulli, Cal and Zelda Mae moved into town. They rented a large two-story house on the southern perimeter of Las Animas from Joe Bishop, the high school janitor. Once again they had a house lacking in modern amenities. They would continue to walk to the end of a path to relieve full bowels or kidneys.

People were all around on every side. Zelda Mae's neighbors could see her every coming and going. They even knew when she went to the outhouse, Borrowing from Grandma Lillie, she carried an item of clothing to hang on the clothesline with each trip to the little house with a throne. The item didn't even have to be wet. If it appeared that her trek was unobserved, she would carry the piece and continue to the privy. Should it be evident that someone was watching, she would hang the item on the clothesline and return to the house without consummating the original move. The ritual could be repeated to retrieve the item as needed.

The Bishop family couldn't have been any friendlier. But, due to the closeness of the houses, they now became a part of the Ledbetter's everyday existence. The closeness was more than Cal had desired. Oh how he longed for days gone by, days when it was often hard to see the smoke lifting from the neighbor's chimney. Would those times ever return? If so, the return would most likely culminate with a return to Hominy Corners, and that couldn't happen too soon for him.

For awhile after moving into town Cal was lost. Zelda Mae wished that she could help him, but she figured that he just needed time alone to grieve, much like experiencing the loss of someone dear. He really didn't enjoy being off of the farm, so that first year he went with a wheat harvest crew working its way north into the Dakotas. Calling on his experiences in earlier years while serving in a Civilian Conservation Corps Camp during the depression, he worked as a cook preparing meals for the men.

This was a short lived trip, as he burned his hands helping put out a fire and had to return to Las Animas. Actually his burns were frostbite from attempting to unhook a propane tank in order to remove it from the fire area. The extremely cold temperatures of the bottled gas could have caused an even worse injury. He knew that luck was with him.

"God didn't intend for a man to live in town. That's why the world was invented," said Cal. "There were no towns in the beginnin'. Man's misguided efforts have jammed people all together."

"We won't always live in town. It's our only choice right now," said Zelda Mae.

"Well, I hope it's only a short-term solution," retorted Cal.

Due to being a World War I veteran, it was easy for Cal to become employed at the United States Veteran's Administration Hospital at Fort Lyon, only seven miles east of Las Animas. This impressive fort built as an army outpost named Fort Wise during the early days of Indian skirmishes had been converted to a psychiatric hospital for military veterans during the early part of the century.

Therefore, in order to keep his family fed, Cal accepted employment requiring him to work inside. He was no longer to earn his livelihood from tilling the soil. He was a city dweller earning his living in an occupation where one had clean hands at the end of a day's labor. Many were the times Cal yearned to be back on the farm. No longer did he work in close harmony with nature, where God's very presence could be felt at any time. No, at every turn people needing his attention could be found in plenteous supply. He was now a nurse's aide in a setting where solitude or peace was non-existent or bought at a very high price. It was a highly regimented life lacking in the freedoms associated with being a farmer.

Cal knew, though, that farming did not grant complete freedom, either. Yet, he also knew, there was a feeling on the farm of being more in control of one's own destiny. Yes, even with the gamble associated with farming, one still had more control over his own life than being an employee in an organization employing hundreds of people.

Sometimes working the "graveyard shift," midnight to eight o'clock in the morning, gave Cal some of the solitude he so yearned for. Only when all or most of the patients were asleep could he feel most comfortable working in this setting. At the same time other benefits were gained as well. There was the night differential, extra pay for working hours nobody else generally wanted.

Better yet, this shift gave him time off during the day to watch his beloved baseball team, the Cleveland Indians, on television. The years when the Brooklyn Dodgers and the New York Yankees played each other in the World Series, however, found him temporarily switching his allegiance. The "Bums of Brooklyn" could count on him rooting for their side. Life was beginning to hold more joy for Cal. He didn't want for much, just the simple pleasures of a pastoral existence would do fine. Also, having the daytime hours free allowed Cal time for fishing trips or working in the garden. Both activities left opportunities to meet the family's need for a large grocery supply.

Maintaining a huge garden was a must for the Ledbetters. These gardens always contained corn, tomatoes, peas, black-eyed peas, green beans, potatoes and okra to name a few items. While the children did a large part of the spading and hoeing, Cal always supervised the work. As the produce matured, Zelda Mae was making preparations to can hundreds of quarts of vegetables. Peaches, pears, apples and berries were then purchased or picked on shares for canning as well. Without these extra provisions, the family would not have been able to survive. At no time did the family receive public assistance to help meet their needs. Going on the welfare rolls was a sure sign of failure. Cal never considered it an option at all.

Such an enormous supply of food was essential for a family like the Ledbetters. Zelda Mae spent many hours preparing meals for her husband and children. There was not a lot of variety in how the meals were prepared, however. There couldn't be. Almost all meals contained the basics, high in starches. Bread, potatoes and beans, such as pinto beans, were a part of most meals.

A typical breakfast included biscuits, pork sausage, eggs and gravy. Cal enjoyed mixing up streaked gravy, named because of the streaks caused by the coffee he stirred into the grease, milk, and flour base. Adding additional quantities of flour and milk until it looked just right, Cal was unsurpassed in the ability to make good gravy. While others called their similar product “poor man’s gravy,” their product never offered as much pleasure to the taste buds as the milk gravy prepared by Cal.

Homemade biscuits were standard fare at breakfast. Zelda Mae spent considerable time mixing the dough for these tasty morsels called “bullets” if they didn’t raise right. Light bread, sliced bread from the bakery, was sometimes used at dinner and supper times. It was best for sopping up the juices left on the plate at the end of a fine meal.

“What’s it like to eat in a cafe?” asked Abe.

“Well, they have this piece of blackboard on the wall with all of the prices written on it in chalk,” answered his father.

“It’s called a menu,” his mother broke in.

“Yes, it’s a menu. Anyhow, they give you choices on what you’d like to eat,” said Cal.

“Why don’t we eat in a cafe?” asked Cole.

“We can’t afford it,” answered his mother.

“Besides,” returned Cal, “nobody cooks as well as your mother. You’ll never eat food as good as she can cook.”

“Why thank you Daddy. I appreciate a compliment now and then.”

“I’d still like to find out what a cafe’s like for myself,” said Abe.

“You will soon enough,” responded Cal. “But to get the real benefit of the experience, it’d be best if you paid the bill yourself. That way you’d truly appreciate your mother’s cookin’.”

Red beans were a frequent meal at the Ledbetter residence. No more than one or two days would lapse without the red nodules being part of the family’s diet. Zelda Mae would cook up a large pot of the tasty dish, as her husband and children never seemed to tire of this fare. The meal was always simple.

Along with the beans there were always large helpings of cornbread and raw onions. While the onions could be cut up and added to the beans by the individuals, some had the ability to eat them like apples. There was one problem with meals like this. These beans were sometimes referred to as whisper berries. They had a tendency to talk behind your back when you were least prepared for the interchange. Being good friends, the Ledbetters loved them anyway. Then on Sunday all of the kids looked forward to Zelda Mae's specialty, a dinner roll she called buns that no one else seemed to make quite as well as she did.

Water was the main drink at meals. As a treat, the kids would sometimes be served iced tea. Cal didn't like this drink at all. He liked his coffee, especially if it was saucered. As hot coffee burned his tongue, he first poured it in a saucer so it could cool and then sipped it while holding the container level before his face. Saucering coffee was an art, as the opportunity was always present for easily spilling the strong liquid.

Sunday dinner in the summertime called for iced tea served in Zelda Mae's special goblets. Meal times saw everyone being quite prompt. If you were late to a meal, there might not be anything left. Genuine leftover foods were a rare commodity indeed. No words were needed; the family had raised their own cure for tardiness to the dining table.

Nineteenfiftyone saw further changes in the family. Mattie Jean was to marry. She was then fifteen years old. Knowing the young couple would be unable to get married in Colorado, Cal and Zelda Mae accompanied them to Raton, New Mexico, for the wedding. Much to their surprise they were unable to get married in Raton as well. Mattie Jean needed to be sixteen in order to get married. The decision was quickly made to continue on to Clayton, New Mexico, about seventy miles away. It was a long trip. Mattie Jean aged several months on the way over.

While Cal and Zelda Mae did not like living in town and working this way, the benefits were readily visible. They were setting a few dollars aside now and then. In 1952 another milestone was reached for the family. They were finally in a position to buy their own home. Checking their financial condition, they discovered that with the money they had saved, they would be able to borrow enough money to purchase the Sam Olson residence on Second Street in Las Animas.

For the first time in twenty-seven years of marriage, Cal and Zelda Mae would own their own home. It wasn't much to look at. Certainly *Better Homes and Gardens* would not be awarding any prizes for this dwelling. It only cost them about two thousand dollars, but it could be theirs, as surely as the sun came up every morning. Home ownership's time had come.

CHAPTER XXI

Home ownership can be a wonderful thing. Had Cal and Zelda Mae finally realized their dream? Certainly it wasn't like owning a farm, but it was a piece of property with a deed. The writing placed on the piece of paper with official looking words said that Caleb Ashton and Zelda Mae Ledbetter were the owners of 502 Second Street in Las Animas, Colorado. Of course they didn't own the property outright. The couple had to get help with the financing, so the bank owned more of the small house than they did. But, let there be no question about it, if they wanted to alter the property in some way, they could. These homeowners didn't need anyone's approval, not even the okay of the bank. The house was theirs.

"It's awful small, Cal," said his wife.

"Yes, but there's potential. The walls are solid on the outside, and they don't need to be changed. This house has seen a lot of change before, anyway."

"What do you mean? It looks like it has always been this way. It generally shows up when you've moved a door or window. A stucco house never looks the same afterwards."

"Well, for one thing, this used to be a two-story house. They've done such a good job that you can't see the alterations," replied her husband.

"Then how do you know it happened?" she asked.

"I've talked to Mr. and Mrs. Phillips across the street. They said that this house was once part of the property of the Sunbow Bottling Company. Furthermore, there was a second story removed many years ago."

"Why would you remove a second story of a house?"

"They never said. I suppose it could be if there was extensive damage from a tornado, or maybe a tree fell on the roof. There're lots of reasons to lower the roofline on a house. The important thing is that the workmen did a good job."

Alter the house the new homeowners did to no small degree. Actually, a lot of work was needed to make the simple structure meet their needs. While many people would only have seen a little house with four rooms of approximately the same size needing extensive work, Cal and Zelda Mae saw a home, their home, hiding inside that small stucco cottage. It merely needed an opportunity to emerge and be recognized, not unlike the work performed by a sculptor on a piece of stone. The remodeling work was reminiscent of the alterations done a few years earlier to the Crisafulli house out in the country.

This abode on Second Street was too small for such a large family as well. Modifying the structure was easier this time, however. The Conways, the previous owners, had already attached a long garage the full width of the back of the house on the north. Cal, Pearl, Belle and Abe worked long hours together to convert this single room with a concrete floor into two bedrooms by adding the necessary studs and sheetrock in appropriate places. With this extensive remodeling, the rooms were beginning to look like bedrooms instead of a place to overhaul automobiles. One room was for girls, and the other one was for boys. Granted these rooms were not laid out by an interior decorator, but they were highly functional in their design. That is, they maximized the number of occupants they would hold. Frills were for other families, not the Ledbetters. The windows were covered with the simplest of print curtains, while the lights had pullchains with no shades to cover the porcelain fixtures. Best of all, the bay window on the south side of the living room had a special promise.

"I can grow flowers here," said Zelda Mae. "Facin' the south will provide plenty of sunlight for most anything I want to grow. I might even grow some petunias indoors. Best of all, though, will be Easter lilies in the springtime."

"Flowers are special to you, aren't they?" asked Cal.

"Yes, and they become even more special with each passing day. But lilies represent life everlastin' like out of the Bible. They represent the fact that life doesn't end with the grave and we can hope for life after death."

"Well, they're special to me, too," said Cal. "They're named after my mother."

"I reckon your mother is named after the flower," said Zelda Mae. "But it's alright to think the order may be reversed. I won't disagree with you."

"Good. Because it's all settled in my mind. Now, is there anything we need to fix or do right off that you feel is important to the betterment of this house?"

"We really don't have any room for storage here, Cal," said Zelda Mae. Is there any place you could add a pantry? It certainly would be appreciated."

"I'm glad you spoke up when you did. The dividing point in the middle of the two extra bedrooms is made up of two closets opposite each other, one for each new bedroom. In the process of adding the closets, I was going to close up that grease pit in the middle of the original garage. If it was partially covered, while leaving an opening sufficient for human access, you could have your pantry. Of course you can't go down too often, because there's no room for steps or stairs."

This pit, not only lacking stairs but lighting as well, had shelving added to hold hundreds of jars of food Zelda Mae and the girls would can each summer from the garden with a pressure cooker. There were both fruits and vegetables of every kind on these shelves bowing from the weight of a most precious cargo. The larder was never empty. It was a joy to enter this dark cave with a flashlight and see a wide array of goodies much like a grocery store. It was a joy, that is, if you didn't mind spider webs or a cold, damp, dirt floor. Without the shelves of food it would have compared with the dungeons of the most exotic castles in ancient Europe. Better yet, it would provide almost perfect concealment in a game of hide and seek for the soul unafraid to occupy its eerie presence in total darkness.

One item sorely missing in this house was privacy for all but the girl's bedroom. To gain access to the new bedrooms, a window was removed from Cal and Zelda Mae's bedroom just off of the dining room for conversion into a door. Because of the hardness of the stone and concrete used in the old outer wall, it was impossible to remove the remaining stone below the window level. This meant a threshold about one foot high for anyone using this door. Use of this entrance only put you in the vicinity of the boy's room, though. A walk down a short hallway by the protected entrance for the canned goods storage area ended up in the girl's room. The problem for anyone desirous of entering either back bedroom was that they had to go through Cal and Zelda Mae's bedroom, which meant the couple had the least amount of privacy of all. But it was their very own home, so they rarely complained. When you own the castle, it's harder to find fault with how it was built.

These bedrooms and beds were community property for the children with ownership being established by occupancy. The boys had one room, while the girls had the other. This arrangement was crowded, but it had certain advantages. These rear rooms had no source of heat other than body heat. Therefore, on cold winter nights these youngsters found that snuggling up against a brother or sister was the order of the day. Also, they once again found themselves standing outside of the house trying to soak up the sun's rays on cold mornings while awaiting the call for breakfast. This time spent enjoying the benefits of solar heating was not spent in vain, though. At least the eastside of the house provided a good view of the neighborhood.

The similarities to the house on the Crisafulli place amounted to more than just the crowded conditions. The new home lacked the luxury of an indoor bathroom as well. The traditional short walk down the path for relief was still a requirement. At least toilet paper was now in fairly common usage with the Ledbetters. There was no choice; the house lacked a corncob pile across the fence. Catalogs were still kept in the small privy, but they were generally for conjuring up wishes and daydreaming, nothing else.

Before a year was to go by, however, Cal took his family into a world they had often dreamed about but never enjoyed before this. He built an addition for a bathroom on the northwest side of the house. Such an addition was not only possible now, but it was a requirement, as the city had just added sewer lines to this part of town and mandated their usage.

"I told you we'd someday have indoor plumbin'," said Cal. "Well, that time has arrived. This bathroom represents the latest in modern comfort. Of course only one person at a time can go to the bathroom, but they won't have to walk in the rain to get there."

"Oh, Cal, you think of everything. I don't know where this family would be without you. No sooner do we get one new convenience but what you're already thinkin' of the next thing. You don't suppose you could build us a telephone?" said Zelda Mae.

"Now you've exceeded my capability, woman. I don't have the foggiest notion how a telephone works. Perhaps we'll have one someday, but it won't be because I build the contraption."

The new bathroom truly was the last word in being modern for a family never before possessing one. The relief station even had a bathtub along the inner wall. Also, there was a hot water heater eliminating the need for heating water on the stove for baths. Needless to say, all of the family marveled at this most wonderful of inventions. Of course it would be harder for Abe to wash his feet now, because the length of the tub allowed him to stretch his legs so far out in front of him. But this was a problem he could quickly learn to accept. Besides that, some people claimed the white seated contraption with a tank on the back and lids on the functional part was for washing feet, anyway, so the long tub posed no problem for him. Most important, though, Zelda Mae didn't have to leave the house to go to the toilet. Just to be safe, however, Cal left the two-holer standing for some time.

As more people in this part of town acquired indoor bathrooms, the city further mandated that the little shacks from days gone by be removed. The authorities didn't even want citizens storing chicken feed or lawnmowers in what appeared to be a most likely place. What was once considered a modern convenience had already acquired the status of a public nuisance. Even the fun had gone out of the outhouse; it was no longer possible to advertise that your house had "three bedrooms and a path."

The days of rainwater dripping on Cal's head while he sat and contemplated his future had become a part of history as well. Hereafter, he could read the local newspaper, the *Bent County Democrat*, without getting the paper wet. Of course he no longer had someone sitting beside him in the toilet, either. The loss of the time-honored privy was much more than just the giving up of the smallest building on the premises. The consequences were so far reaching as to limit the number of conversations in the Ledbetter family. Also, the loss of this small castle with a throne built for two took away the hiding place for girls wanting to get out of doing dishes or boys desirous of not being found to mow the lawn with a reel-type push mower. However, you could now go to relieve yourself without someone trying to push the building over or throwing rocks against the wall while you were tending to personal business. Progress did have some advantages. It no longer felt like sitting on top of the San Andreas Fault, when you went to relieve yourself.

There was more than an outside toilet out back of the family dwelling. A chicken house was situated close by the back fence with tall poultry wire forming a pen to try and prevent the chickens from achieving their freedom. The children welcomed an occasional escape attempt by these white cluckers, as chasing the escapee sometimes broke the boredom of an uneventful day. Generally everyone would join in the chase for an errant chicken, as the pursuit produced a tremendous amount of excitement. Sometimes the yard looked like a circus with all of the yelling and running around. Fewer chasers probably would have shortened the time of the chase, but the fun was in the pursuit, not in the catching of the errant fowl. Entertainment was where you found it.

"Quick!" said Cole. "Don't let him out the gate. We'll never catch him."

"Your arms ain't broken," said Collette. "You close the gate."

"Well, at least head him my way, so I can grab him."

"If you'd move faster, I wouldn't have to force him your direction. I declare. You're the slowest movin' boy I ever saw."

"You can bet that I'm faster than you are," answered her brother.

"Will you two quit arguin'," said Zelda Mae. "The water will be cold before you catch that chicken. I believe you two could catch a cold faster than I've seen you get your hands on that chicken. Now get a hurry on you two."

The chickens provided food for the Ledbetters' table in three ways. The eggs gathered each day were most evident. They became part of a meal Cal referred to as "moo juice and cackleberries," when milk was added to the menu. Sometimes a chicken would be fried, as only Zelda Mae could fry it. Finally, a chicken escaping being fried, but becoming too old to lay eggs, faced a definite future in becoming the mainstay of a meal of chicken and dumplings. No matter what method was used in the cooking, preparing chicken to be eaten as meat was not a pleasant task, especially for the chicken. As a matter of fact, it was downright gruesome.

After being caught, the guest of honor would find its head held on the ground with the catcher's foot, while its legs were pulled until the head came off. The chicken would then be allowed to flop around the yard until its life was spent. This frantic last effort for life was usually of short duration. Next, the chicken would be dipped in scalding water to loosen the feathers for removal. Chicken plucking was the activity in this whole process most likely to be shunned if at all possible, as the person doing the plucking was likely to end up with wet feathers plastered all over him or her. It was not a pleasant task.

The lengthy task of preparing the unlucky critter for human consumption ended with fried or stewed chicken on the table. The aroma of fried chicken alone made the preparation task worthwhile. There was nothing quite like the smell of chicken frying in lard made from the fat of a butchered hog to make the saliva glands over-react. Cal could never resist Zelda Mae's cooking. Second helpings weren't even debated; they were required. The lady of the house took great pride in cooking for her family. While the children might not have received as much food in amount or variety as they wanted, their daily nutritional requirements were always met.

The remainder of the Ledbetter property closely resembled a farm. Part of this resemblance was due to being located adjacent to the last house at the edge of the town proper and next to the farm of Mr. Williams, who often had cornfields across the fence. Just moving into town was a monumental concession by Cal. When they had lived at the Bishop's house prior to moving within the city limits, their home was adjoined by farmland. Now their new home was similarly situated as well. Cal and Zelda Mae weren't sure they could assume the trappings of true city dwellers. They so much wanted to be able to look off into the distance without their view being obstructed by a cacophony of city type structures. If they couldn't live on a farm, owned by them or otherwise, they'd come as close as they could. Much of the resemblance of 502 Second Street to a farm, however, came about because of all the livestock kept by Abe and Cole.

"Could I talk to you, Dad?" asked Cole.

"What do you want son? You're not old enough to drive a car, and I don't reckon you're datin'. Well, let's hear it, and I hope it's not goin' to cost me money."

"No it's not money," said Cole.

"Praise the Lord," said Cal. "I don't need to get my wallet out."

"I want to be a farmer, too, Dad. Just like you and your pa."

"I have no problem with that, son. What's the holdup?" asked Cal.

"Well, I've signed up to take agriculture classes at high school."

"You want to be a book farmer, then?" said Cal. "Actually there's not as much wrong with that as I used to think. Mr. Crisafulli changed my mind on the subject. He was a book farmer, and a right good one at that."

"I'm well aware how good a farmer Mr. Crisafulli was. One of the best in these parts I've heard you say so many times. No, in order for me to take agriculture classes, I have to have a new project each year. Generally you're expected to continue the project from the previous year as well."

"Exactly what do you mean by project?" asked his father.

"Well, like a field of corn or some livestock."

"And who is going to pay for these projects, might I ask?"

"Me, Dad. I have to pay for them."

"I'll agree as long as they cost me and your mother nothin' in money or time. Otherwise, no deal."

"Fair enough, Dad."

At one time Cole had a brindle cow and two large calves along with a sow and twelve little pigs as Future Farmers of America (FFA) projects. Cal later added his own pigs as well. One thing was for sure. On a warm summer day with a breeze blowing toward the house, it certainly had the aroma of a farm.

To help feed these animals, a stack of hay and other sources of livestock feed were always present beside the pens and sheds used in this agricultural endeavor. The management of these animals was the total responsibility of the owner. While Cal made sure that the boys tended their livestock, he always found reasons to go out and check on things, and his motivation often wasn't supervisory. He felt more at home with the animals and the adjoining fields of corn and alfalfa hay. Sometimes he would sit on a bale of hay and rest his eyes while daydreaming of when he would be able to return to a "real farm." His dream never went away. It always lurked in the back of his mind waiting for an opportunity to emerge. Someday, his home would once again be in Hominy Corners.

It was not unusual to see Cal sitting on one bale of hay while leaning back against another. When Zelda Mae looked out of the girls' bedroom window, she saw him there with a stem of hay in his mouth. She had a good idea as to what was taking place. After all of these years she could sometimes read his mind. She knew that his dream for another farm in Hominy Corners had never gone away. While she had no complaints about their life, she didn't feel right knowing he wouldn't find real happiness until he returned to soil of his own in his beloved homeland. She couldn't count the times she wished he could be at peace with himself, but she also knew that farm ownership was still in the realm of possibility. After all, owning their own home had become a reality when they least expected it. No, if her husband wanted to allow his dream to linger, she certainly wouldn't discourage it. A man without a dream, she knew, was a man without hope.

"Look at your father, Mattie. I'll bet we know what he's thinkin' about," said Zelda Mae.

"It's Hominy Corners, ain't it Momma?" asked Mattie Jean.

"Yes, child. It's Hominy Corners. The older your father gets, the more he thinks about the old days."

"Should he be so preoccupied with something like that? It doesn't sound healthy to me."

"Well," said Zelda Mae. "It's really harmless. A man has to have a dream. Someday you'll get married, and your husband will have a dream, too. Anyway, he's too old to change now."

"You mean he'll never realize his dream?" asked Mattie Jean.

"No, child. I mean he's too old now to give up his dream."

One of the benefits of Cole owning a milk cow was having an opportunity for the Ledbetters to make their own butter. Churning butter was simple but not easy. Whole milk straight from the cow was placed in a gallon jar after foreign objects were removed through straining. The jar was not completely filled, with some air space left for the milk to move around. Then all that was needed was for someone to shake this jar back and forth diligently for what seemed like an hour. In the process small bits of butter would gradually cling to each other until large, golden chunks could be seen moving through the mixture. Looking for these globules of gold was like looking for goldfish in a horsetank. It was not unusual to see someone with a dishtowel draped over his or her lap to absorb spillage, churning away while listening to the radio or watching TV.

"I need a volunteer," said Zelda Mae.

"Run for it," said Abe. "Either she wants someone to wash dishes or churn butter."

"Those are girls' jobs," said Cole.

"Churnin' butter," his older brother told him, "is the job of whoever gets caught first. Maybe we can slip out a window."

"I hear you boys talkin'. Both of you better get in here right now."

"Now you did it," said Abe. "It's all your fault."

Everyone seemed to have a rhythm or motion they would use while churning. Some would rock the jar back and forth on the dish towel placed on their knee, while someone else might hold the jar up and shake it vigorously, as though they were punishing it. While these methods were not as easy as using commercial churns, they certainly were as efficient. Eventually these efforts paid off for the persistent churner and always consisted of a nice collection of butter for use on the table. Zelda Mae's good flour biscuits or homemade breads were made just with this butter in mind. Freshly churned butter has a unique way of melting and spreading on homemade bread. It was so soft that it was no chore getting it to spread uniformly over an entire biscuit before adding jelly.

It was hard, though, for Zelda Mae to get her family to wait for mealtime when they knew there were hot biscuits and butter waiting to be consumed. Delaying seemed to be letting a golden opportunity go by. These two commodities were best devoured within minutes after they were ready, not later. Prolonging the inevitable consumption made things worse, not better.

"I hate to be botherin' you Cal, but could you take me over to see Mrs. Dean tomorrow?" asked Zelda Mae.

"I suppose it's possible. Actually, Zelda, wouldn't it be better if you did more drivin' yourself?"

"I just can't get the hang of the gearshift or the clutch either one Cal. It's bad enough on level ground, but it's a real problem stoppin' on a hill."

"Well, I'll take you now, but we need to be thinkin' about gettin' better transportation one of these days," said Cal.

As time passed, the family of Cal and Zelda Mae did see more conveniences in the transportation they acquired. The last two cars they had owned, a 1935 and a 1947 Plymouth, were eventually replaced by a two-tone blue, 1951 Pontiac, considered quite new in 1955 when the Ledbetters purchased it. This four-door car had conveniences that would have been deemed impossible to devise or possess in the years the Ledbetters first acquired motorized vehicles. The Model T came close, as it had no clutch. This "new" car, however, had an automatic transmission, which enabled Zelda Mae to improve her ability to drive this "luxury" automobile. She didn't like being reminded about backing over the little elm tree on the Crisafulli place when first taking driving lessons with a stick shift, so she had rarely driven prior to this. Now she could concentrate on where she was going instead of worrying about shifting. With those earlier stickshifts it sometimes appeared that she intended to drive on the sidewalk at that moment a shift was being completed. Her driving, though, improved immediately with the ownership of that Pontiac. Better yet, she was no longer limited to the mercy of others in going shopping or driving over to Pearl's.

With the new car, Zelda Mae's world expanded significantly. Yes, she thought to herself, she was one lucky woman for having married such a good provider in that Cal Ledbetter. She didn't really want for much. Oh, she did want to see Cal realize his dream of farm ownership, but she herself didn't want for much. Surely she could use a new cookstove, who couldn't? But did she truly need a new stove? Well, actually, no. Zelda Mae was at peace with herself.

This newer car was not as nice as the older cars in some respects, however. Technological advances do not always bring about improvements. The windshield on the '35 Plymouth opened forward to allow good airflow through the car. Also, the two windshield wipers on this car were independent of each other, because they each had a little handle just inside the windshield for hand operation. Not many cars, Cal boasted, had different speeds for each wiper. The addition of luxuries for the Ledbetter family was not to end with the addition of this "new" automobile, either.

In 1955 the family purchased their first television set, a Sylvania console model. Up to this time they had been content to walk over to the neighbor's house, Wade and Wilma Longfellow's, to watch TV. The Longfellows had owned a set for about a year and enjoyed watching the Ledbetter's favorite programs, "I Love Lucy," "Maverick," and "Gunsmoke," with their neighbors. Even though black and white TV left a lot to be desired, there was no doubt the world had entered a new era. Sometimes the programming on Channels 5 out of Pueblo or 11 from Colorado Springs appeared to be an on-location news update on a snowstorm in the summertime, but you watched anyway.

TV antennas sprung up on the tops of houses all over Las Animas. Occasionally it looked like some of the houses were not sturdy enough to even support an antenna, but TV's were purchased, anyway. America was in the midst of a gigantic love affair with the television set. The Ledbetters were no different; they, too, looked forward to the next episode of Gunsmoke to see Chester limp as he went about his duties, or to see Matt as he tipped his hat to Miss Kitty at the Longbranch Saloon.

During the day, Cal could watch "his" Cleveland Indians to his heart's content. Often when Zelda Mae would peek in to see how he was doing, he seemed asleep on the couch. Hoping to give him more rest, she would proceed to turn the TV set off. This was his signal to immediately say, "Who's a messin' with my TV?" How he could be asleep and know the exact score of the game defied explanation to her. At least his method of watching TV left him rested and readied to go to work when the time came.

Working the evening or graveyard shift at Fort Lyon was a real boon to the marriage of Cal and Zelda Mae. They now had uninterrupted time alone, as they had never had before. If ever an example of two people in love was needed, here it was. A kiss or a hug between the two was rarely seen. But an observer could tell the love was there in the way they each paid attention to their mate. They responded to each other's needs without being asked.

The problem with Cal going downtown for a drink rarely occurred anymore. It was a surprise to him to discover that that which he had sought in pool halls and bars for so many years, he already possessed; it actually resided in the bond between him and Zelda Mae. The search was over. Cal and Zelda Mae's marriage had now blossomed into a deeper love. The measure of true love can not be graded like the answers on a test. No, the measure must be on the quality of the love, sometimes an ephemeral entity defying quantification. Only these two individuals would know the true depths of their love. Like electricity, others would benefit from its existence without fully understanding how or why it worked, and the nuclear family would continue to grow.

The Ledbetter children seemed to respond like Abraham's family, when he was told by God that his descendents would someday be greatly numbered, much as the grains of sand on the beach or the stars in the heavens. Cal and Zelda Mae couldn't have been happier. Their joy would grow with the addition of new grandchildren. By the end of 1956 Cal and Zelda Mae had sixteen grandchildren still living. Half of the dream shared by this couple was now a reality, even if they never had another grandchild. They accepted the pain encountered as they marched toward their goal. They didn't like it, but they accepted it. It was part of the natural order. They suffered in silence.

Grandchildren were not the only thoughts occupying the time of Cal and Zelda Mae. Concerns generally demanded equal time along with their joys. Hopefully the concerns weren't greedy, insisting on using a disproportionate amount of their time. Cal and Zelda Mae were still raising children of their own while enjoying the special treat that accompanies grandchildren living under another roof.

Fishing trips were more frequent now. Cal especially loved to take his whole family out to Rule Creek south of Las Animas on an outing. Sometimes the trip was overnight, and it wasn't exactly a camping trip. There were no tents or sleeping bags; the family didn't own any. Instead, each person had one of Zelda Mae's homemade quilts to break the chill of the summer's cold night air. Otherwise, the night was spent with a fishing pole cut from a tamarack bush or from the bamboo pole found in the center of a new roll of carpet, which the local hardware dealers gladly gave away.

The dozing fisherman would usually be awakened when a fish was caught on his line or he was the recipient of a bite by a mosquito. Pearl or Belle frequently went along on these trips. They kept a hot fire going to take the chill from the night air or to heat a pot of coffee. The kids never partook of any of the coffee, however. Cal always said it would stunt their growth. If he had been right, it's a good thing they followed his admonishment. Otherwise, of his boys would have grown to seven feet tall.

"Daddy, I haven't had a bite with this fishin' pole in hours," said Cole.

"Hush, boy. The fish will never bite with you talkin'. You'll scare them away. Besides, your line has only been in the water for ten minutes now. Your worm hasn't even had a chance to drown yet."

"The fish can't hear us. They haven't got any ears, and who cares if the worm drowns?"

"Hush, boy! I don't want to hear another sound right now!" said Cal.

Fishing and hunting certainly helped bring the boys and their father much closer together. Also, Cal and Zelda Mae continued to become more involved with the girls as well. More and better outings occurred as time passed. Then, in the summer of 1955, the decision was made for a family vacation in Oklahoma. Cal and Zelda Mae had stayed away far longer than they ever had hoped would happen. By now, the automobile would more easily contain those remaining at home. The year was 1955.

The long awaited journey began at midnight when Cal got off of work at Fort Lyon. The twins were still pretty much awake due to all of the activity when the departure occurred. Soon, though, the excitement of the big event was replaced with the reality of a long day and the lateness of the hour. Besides that, it was difficult to see much of the darkened countryside at two in the morning. A full moon didn't even help. The five children were ready for sleep. Therein was a problem. How was everyone to sleep on one seat?

"One of you could stretch out on the floor," said their mother.

"There's a hump here in the middle," said Collette.

"Well, pile something on each side to level it off. I'm sure you kids can solve that problem. Then, one can sleep on the shelf by the back window. The other three will have to sleep sittin' up on the seat. You can change places later." Turning to her husband, she continues, "Now if you get tired, you tell me, Cal. I'm willin' to help with the drivin'. Besides, I took a nap this afternoon for that very purpose."

"There's no way I can sleep at a time like this," retorted Cal.

"You're pretty excited, aren't you?" asked his wife.

"Well, I haven't been back in a long time."

"Yes, we've waited altogether too long for this vacation. Well, we're on our way now," said Zelda Mae.

"You can say that again," answered Cal.

Cal's precious vacation time could not be spent in sleep. He had awaited this opportunity far longer than anyone realized. He drove through the night, but he did not retrace the steps of that 1947 journey when the family moved to Colorado. Rather, instead of going east out of Amarillo, Texas, on Route 66, he continued driving south on US 287. Then, in the early morning hours, he picked up US 82 south of Wichita Falls by Henrietta and followed it east across the northern plains of Texas. He was anxious to get to Bokchito, and this was the quickest way to get there, even if it meant driving into a glorious yet blinding sunrise for much of the morning.

Turning north on US 75 at Sherman, Texas, he crossed the Red River quite close to where the old Colbert's Ferry had been located. He tried to see evidence of the long abandoned ferry from his vantage point atop the bridge. None was to be seen. He knew where it had been originally located, as his father had pointed it out to him when they went to Myra, Texas, in 1908 to pick cotton. You could see Cal's anticipation continuing to build as they entered Oklahoma. It was not unlike the reawakening of the spirit of a man reviving from a coma. He could hardly contain his joy.

Now they were in Bryan County, the original home of all his hopes and dreams, dreams later to be expanded even more when he and Zelda Mae married. His thoughts went back over his leaving here. Was leaving a mistake, he thought to himself.

Realizing the danger of such thoughts, he forced himself to think, what's past is past. After all, this journey was only for a visit, and he intended to savor it to the fullest.

Zelda Mae's mind silently questioned herself as well. Do you suppose J.H.'s grave is still marked? She would at least like to go by and see. She would do it alone, she reckoned, when she had some time to slip away for awhile. Maybe she could do it while they were at Clevon and Olive's. The old farm where she had lived with Papa by the community of Wade wasn't too far from there. None of the Cantrells lived around these parts anymore. Her only roots in the area were in that grave in the pasture. She knew it was too much to hope that the small, wooden cross was still there. But, how she did pray that the gravesite wasn't all grown up in weeds. Maybe there will be wild flowers growing there, she told herself. It would be so fitting.

Cal wanted to go to his brother Clevon's house first. This meant going right through Durant passing the homes of friends from days gone by. Driving along the thin ribbon of concrete connecting the communities of heavily wooded eastern Oklahoma, they passed through Blue and Bokchito before following the narrow dirt road leading to his brother's house. Cal felt his emotions arising as he drove amidst the thick stand of scrub oak lining the road. Sometimes the right of way narrowed due to the growth needing trimmed. Fond memories of a barefoot boy trudging down a rural, dirt road carrying his lunch in a syrup bucket on his way to a small country school made his eyes glisten. All was well. Cal could even smell the magnolia trees, even though they were no longer in bloom.

When the entourage arrived at Clevon's place, they found Myrtle there as well. This was the first reunion of the two brothers and their sister since their mother's, Grandma Lillie's, funeral in 1950. The noise soon reached a crescendo, as everyone wanted to talk at once, and the excitement level was not soon to die down. By now it was the middle of the afternoon. Olive had already prepared a big meal with Myrtle's assistance while awaiting Cal's arrival.

The victuals spread on the table were akin to the feast prepared by the father for the return of the prodigal son. There were sliced tomatoes, cornbread and butter, black-eyed peas, and fried okra and buttermilk for starters. Then they got down to some real serious eating when Olive brought in some ham and red beans, along with mashed potatoes and gravy, to add to what was already on the table. The feast appeared complete even before fried chicken joined the choices. She then admonished them to save room for some blackberry cobbler afterwards. And eat they did. A pall of quietness fell over the group as they used their mouths for something besides talking. There was nothing like good food to shut up a talkative bunch like this. A longstanding Ledbetter tradition was not about to be broken. Occasionally, however, the silence would be broken by, "Would you pass the taters, please?"

"Don't wipe your mouth on your sleeve, child. It ain't civilized."

"Yes, but it's quicker," said Cole.

"I declare. I don't know what the children today are a comin' to. Lord have mercy on us," said Zelda Mae.

What Cal was now experiencing was one of the main reasons he hated to leave Oklahoma in the first place. No, it wasn't the food he missed. Zelda Mae had done a good job of providing in that area. It was the feeling of kinship that he missed. He had always been close to his family, especially his sister Myrtle, as they had gone through so much together as youth. Even worse, Clevon now owned the very land he had tried to farm in 1934. He didn't begrudge Clevon for owning that farm; as a matter of fact, he was happy for his younger brother. No, it made him wonder what he and Zelda Mae would have owned if they had remained in Oklahoma. Maybe it had been a mistake leaving in 1947. But Cal wasn't one to dwell on what might have been. He and Zelda Mae were doing rather well in Colorado. Their turn would come. He just knew it would. No questioning about how much better off they now were, when compared to 1947, he thought to himself.

Little refrigerator space was necessary after that meal. A place to lie down was, however. Large meals require large naps, and no one wanted to violate the remainder of the time-honored Ledbetter family tradition concerning family feasts. While the men and children napped, Zelda Mae and the other women cleared the table and washed the dishes. The nap requirement often did not extend to the womenfolk. Instead, their highest priority was to make the house look like a dinner hadn't even occurred for a long time. Only a slothful woman would do otherwise. While men were often identified with their line of work, Ledbetter women were better known by their families and how clean they kept their house or how they pitched in to help do dishes at someone else's home.

The next day Zelda Mae was able to slip away in the car for awhile. Even though they had only been there about 24 hours, she felt called to visit a certain cow pasture. Cal knew where she was going, so he asked, "Do you want company?"

"No," she replied, "this is somethin' I have to do alone."

Driving past the old house where she and Cal had started married life, Zelda Mae was troubled to see it so run down. No one was living there, its emptiness and the front screendoor hanging by one hinge haunted her. It didn't help that the kitchen window was broken, exposing a tattered, rainsoaked curtain stirring in the wind. Furthermore, she knew that they would never have abandoned an old car by the front gate when they had lived there. The unkempt look of the rundown structure challenged her numerous memories of what had once been a happy place for her and Cal.

Continuing on to the field indelibly imprinted on her mind, she spied an opening in the fence. Pulling over to the edge of the narrow dirt road to park, she contemplated how best to get to the gravesite. She was thankful for the barbed wires being down in this place, as she knew she'd tear her new dress if she tried to climb over a fence. In no time she found herself across the barrow pit and into the pasture overlooking the creek. There were no signs prohibiting trespassing, so it didn't bother her too much to be on someone else's property. Actually, she told herself, she had as much right as anyone to be there. Her eldest son was buried in that pasture. As a matter of fact, she had more rights than even the owner himself to visit that hallowed portion of God's country.

As she slowly made her way to the small knoll with the best view of the creek, Zelda Mae's eyes gazed towards heaven. It was such a beautiful day; she wouldn't have wanted it any other way. A few rare clouds were stacked up like snowdrifts off in the distance with a pale blue sky as a backdrop, the same color as the dress she'd made special for this occasion. She shielded her eyes with her cupped hand, as the brightness of the sun was beginning to blind her.

There was a feeling that Zelda Mae couldn't deny; God was near as she walked alone. A gentle breeze at her back helped to lessen the warmth of the sun on her shoulders. She stopped to pick three small, yellow wildflowers, as there were none in bloom on the spot she knew to be the exact location of J.H.'s gravesite. She didn't know the name of the flowers, but they smelled like a mystery perfume, a fragrance she couldn't identify. She would place them on her son's grave. No longer would she associate the picking of flowers with the taking of a life. Now these beautiful gifts from God represented the link between the living and the departed, the renewal of the beauty of nature.

It was a difficult trip for Zelda Mae, as this pilgrimage was serving more than one purpose. J.H.'s grave would have to do triple duty. That knoll, lightly covered with vegetation, would represent both Momma's and Mattie Fern's grave as well. She doubted that she would ever get to return to Holly Grove Cemetery, but that small cow pasture dotted with an occasional purple thistle would serve quite well. Nothing, though, could be as depressing as seeing the bare ground where the simple cross over J.H.'s grave once stood. After almost thirty years, nature had taken its course. She was taken back at the bleakness of the setting. Now Zelda Mae knew what "ashes to ashes and dust to dust" really meant. While memories of the three loved ones that went on before her would always be in her heart, the earthly ties were now broken. It was useless to look for the simple cross left there thirty years earlier.

Zelda Mae didn't even try to hold back the tears as she gingerly laid the delicate flowers on a barren portion of the ground. It was appropriate that the gravesite was located at the highest point of the small knoll, as it had represented closeness to God for her when the burial location was chosen. Nothing had changed; the closeness was still there.

"Mama," she said aloud among sobs, "I hope you know that I think about you and Mattie Fern all of the time. It'll never change. I'll always be thinkin' of you. I hope you've met J.H. I think about him a lot, too. He's my boy, you know. I'll bet you like each other. Isn't he a nice grandson? I'm sorry I haven't been to your grave in a long time. Cal and I just can't afford such a long trip. It's not that we don't love you Momma; we just can't get back there. I wish you could meet Cal. I know you'd like him. He's a lot like Papa. Papa misses you, too, Mama. We talk together about it sometimes. His life has never been the same, since you died. Mine neither. Why did you have to die? Mama, take care of J.H. and Mattie Fern. J.H., you mind your grandma, now. You hear me? I have to go now, Mama. I love you all so much. Don't forget me, because I know I won't forget ya'll."

Zelda Mae knew that this would be her last visit to that bleak cow pasture for some time, possibly forever. The lack of a cross marking the grave just didn't seem right. Putting a new marker to commemorate the sacredness of that spot wouldn't help, either. No, the memories of those three loved ones would always be carried in her heart, where they really belonged. While she might share those precious memories with others, it would only be on rare occasions. They were too private for just anyone to know. It was hard to get up from her knees without someone's help, but with unseen assistance she arose. A lingering separation was not to be. With her shoulders hunched over and her head bowed in a look of reverence, Zelda Mae slowly made her way back to the car. She never looked behind her, as the tears in her eyes wouldn't have permitted her to see, anyway. Besides that, it was hard enough dodging the prickly thistles and the occasional meadow muffin that she encountered. Her drive home was equally as slow; she didn't trust her own driving right now. It seemed her glasses kept fogging over. At least there were drops of moisture on them.

On one rare occasion when Cal wasn't visiting relatives, he found time alone to wander in the woods behind Clevon and Olive's house. In among the heavy foliage of the trees it was hard to be quiet, unless he stood completely still. The leaves were so deep that it was like wading in snow; sometimes he would stumble upon a surface root hidden beneath the leaves. Looking up, he sensed being in a dark tent with an infrequent hole in the roof. A shaft of sunlight sometimes found its way down through the canopy of limbs revealing fine particles swirling lazily in the air or the cobweb of a spider awaiting its unsuspecting prey. On those times when he did stop and listen, Cal could hear a twig drop or the gurgle of the water flowing in the nearby creek. The air smelled musty from the dampness; the earth dried slowly after rainfall in these protected surroundings.

Occasionally he would come upon a Bois d' Arc tree (pronounced bo-dark, but often called a horseapple tree). From a distance they resembled a regular apple tree. Up close, though, he knew he wanted nothing of the fruit of that tree. There was no pleasure to be derived from eating the bitter, distasteful fruit it produced. He especially liked pecan trees, and they were everywhere. He picked up a few pecans and put them in his right, front pocket. Once in awhile the undergrowth was so thick that he had to change the direction of his travel. Sometimes, even at midday, it was almost dark from the heavy vegetation he encountered. There was no need for fear, however. He had an inner knack for finding his way back to Clevon's house based on a keen sense of direction that had served him well over the years.

Pausing for a brief while, he listened to the rustle of a gentle breeze winding its way through the trees. On a nearby sycamore tree was a bluejay with its head cocked to one side. It seemed intent as it quietly watched something Cal was unable to discern. Memories of another time flooded his thoughts, like when as a boy he so enjoyed chasing squirrels through similar countryside. But he was a man now. There would be no more chasing squirrels. There were thoughts of his father and mother, also. He missed them, especially his father who had died forty years earlier. Realizing the danger of getting lost in such thoughts, Cal hurried back to rejoin his family. He was getting dangerously close to losing his composure.

"When do you think you'll be a comin' back here?" asked Clevon.

"We're hopin' to live here again someday," answered his brother.

"Oh, really," said Clevon. "Tell me about it."

"Well," said Cal, "Zelda Mae and I've talked about it. She agrees we should live out our retirement years here around Hominy Corners."

"Most of the buildin's are gone and few people remember where it's located if they didn't grow up here."

"The buildin's ain't important," said Cal. "More importantly, it's where I grew up. This soil is special to me. I never owned land in Oklahoma before. When Mom and Dad were alive they owned all of the property. I just worked there. Of course I always expected to own it someday, but Grandma Lillie sold it before I got back from overseas."

"She thought you were dead in the war," said Clevon.

"I know. It was an honest mistake. Everyone makes those. I hold no grudge against anyone. I just want things made right now."

"I could give you a piece of my land. Part of my farm is in Hominy Corners."

"No, that isn't right. A man can't have pride if he hasn't earned what's his," returned Cal.

"Now you're soundin' like our father did so many years ago. He'd have said the same thing."

"Dad taught me most of what I know about farmin' and just about everything to do with getting' along with others. Can you watch for land comin' up for sale?" asked Cal.

"Well, I'll keep my eyes open. It sure would be good to have you and Zelda Mae back here. Say, there is one other thing I'd be a likin' to ask ya about."

"And what might that be?" replied Cal.

"You ain't run into old 'Fire and Brimstone' Thomas up there anywhere, have you?"

"Can't say as what I have. Why do you ask?"

"I hear he's mellowed a lot from the old days. I guess he changed after his service in the war."

"I didn't know he was in World War One like me."

"He wasn't. It appears he served as a chaplain in World War Two."

"Well, I'll be switched. And you say he's mellowed. I hope it's a change for the better."

"Me, too. That's why I asked. I hear tell he's up Colorado way somewhere now."

"Colorado's a big state," answered Cal. "Chances are I'll never run into him again."

That Oklahoma vacation was far too short. After spending a few days in Durant and Bokchito, the travelers went on to Hobart by way of Waurika and then up through Frederick into Kiowa County. Here, there were relatives everywhere. The descendants of Papa and Lillie Cantrell had been much more prolific than the Ledbetters had been. Cal and Zelda Mae's younger children found aunts and uncles and cousins to enjoy on every turn. Seeing recognizable landmarks was thrilling as well. Hobart had memories of earlier years for the Ledbetters. Not all were good memories, but they were memories to be treasured.

That was to be the last vacation taken by the complete family. Now, there was work at home waiting on Cal, so the return trip was a blur. Certainly the travel was long and hot, but they weren't going to someplace exotic or intriguing. They were just going home. Also, Cole and Collette had summer employment waiting on them, so they weren't exactly anxious to get back to Las Animas. Too quickly they would be in the fields hoeing sugar beets or stacking hay for some farmer. As soon as a Ledbetter child was old enough to earn money, he was expected to work and help pay for school clothes in this family. Also, the earnings of the children would help support the family in other ways as well. The luxury of having a summer off was not even considered as an option. Ledbetters were born to survive by the sweat created by their labor. Joy was oftimes ephemeral. They partook of life's pleasures when they could.

In time Martha Sue would no longer work in the fields. She had employment in downtown Las Animas as a waitress in Eddleman's Cafe. Zelda Mae loved picking her up at 9:00 p.m., when she got off work. Collette, knowing her mother loved hamburgers, would order one for her just before quitting time each night. Zelda Mae would then eat it in the car before going home. She knew it helped to prolong her weight problem, but the thrill of eating a hamburger was a joy unknown to her in her earlier years. Better now than never, she rationalized to herself as she slowly savored each bite.

Leaving Oklahoma had never cut off the Ledbetter ties from their southern relatives. Papa Cantrell could be counted on to spend vacations at Cal and Zelda Mae's. His grandchildren very much loved him and his visits, which occurred during the summer. He was one of the friendliest people they knew, even if he always wore a big black hat. Papa could generally be seen at any time any place cutting a chew from a plug of Red Man Chewing Tobacco with his Barlow pocketknife. He was most deft in doing the cutting. As the cut was completed, he would end up holding a chew using only the knife and his thumb. After putting a goodly portion in his mouth, he would wipe the blade of the knife on the side of his trouser leg before folding and putting it away.

Papa kept quite different hours from his hosts. After going to bed during the early evening hours, he would get up about daylight to walk downtown. Sometimes this would be as soon as four in the morning, when the dew was still on the roses. He and some of his newly acquired friends would then sit on a park bench soaking up the warmth of the early morning sun and swapping tales about the days of old. The kids always wondered if he talked about their grandmother, as he never said anything about her around them. Zelda Mae and Papa seemed to enjoy each other's company so much. Maybe they talked about Grandma in their private times together. The kids never knew her name while they were growing up.

Papa's vacations never lasted long enough to suit the Ledbetters, especially Zelda Mae. His staying there permanently would have been received with open arms. It always seemed, though, that Papa wanted to get back to Oklahoma. His was a restless spirit. It could not be contained in Colorado.

"Do you think we'll ever get to the West Coast?" asked Cal.

"It isn't likely," answered his wife. "We never went during the depression, and it ain't likely we're a goin' now."

"Why's that?" asked Cal.

"Well, we don't have the money for one thing. And if we did have the money, we'd be savin' it for our farm someday."

"It's your dream now, too, isn't it?" asked Cal.

"It always has been," answered his wife.

CHAPTER XXII

Dwight Eisenhower was inaugurated for his second term as President of the United States in January of 1957. The country was in a period of relative peace, as the Korean Conflict was now relegated to historical status. Cal and Zelda Mae had celebrated their thirty-second wedding anniversary on January seventh; the marriage looked as if it could go on forever. The Democratic Party wasn't happy with the political scene, but the year had every appearance of being off to a good start as far as the Ledbetters were concerned.

Yes, it certainly looked like an excellent time to be an American. Granted, there were a few problems around the nation and in the world, such as federal troops being sent into Little Rock, Arkansas, to enforce integration of the schools. Negroes were increasing their demands for equal access to the blessings of a bountiful nation. They, too, wanted their share of the American dream.

Also, the United States and Russia were in a "cold war" brought about by two nations developing huge arsenals of military weapons, yet simultaneously being fearful of each other and how these stockpiles might be used. But by and large it was a time for the country to assess where it was and what it stood for, before moving on to a new or different level of existence. Put another way, it was a quiet era in American history. These were the best of times to be alive for the individual content in his/her achievements. With one major exception Cal and Zelda Mae found themselves in this category.

Cal was 62 years old while Zelda Mae was 50. Cal had already made the decision to retire in December of 1957, when he would be 63. Serious plans for after his retirement were being discussed between him and Zelda Mae. They had debated more than once returning to Hominy Corners to explore the real estate market. Clevon had written to notify them of several small acreages that might just meet their requirements. Actually, he had been out more than once looking for a plot of land that would enable Cal to resolve the issue of whether he was to be a city dweller or a gentleman farmer. Cal's return to an agrarian way of life could only be achieved through the purchase of a small acreage in the country for a retirement home, and Clevon had every intention of helping to bring the reformation about.

"If you retire Cal, I'm not sure we have enough money to live on," said Zelda Mae.

"I know that we can't get by adequately on my retirement pay, and that has worried me a lot. My income will have to be supplemented with some earnings from a part-time job or the raising and marketing of a huge vegetable garden. Possibly we'll raise a hog or two. In any event, we should be able to sell what produce and meat that we don't use ourselves. As a matter of fact, I'm intending to grow far more than what we need to be sure of raising additional income. No, you're right. My retirement income by itself won't meet our needs."

"Also," said Zelda Mae, "I've got a part to play in this enterprise as well. You know I could make and market the colorful quilts that I've won all the blue ribbons with at the Bent County Fair. Why the people in Las Animas know how good they are. The judges always mention their beauty and intricate design."

Yes, Zelda Mae's quiltwork had brought her praise from friend and stranger alike. The product of a functional art form rarely practiced anymore was now regaining a cherished status for those knowledgeable of their construction and value. Achievement of a lifelong dream carried since the end of World War I was now a possibility for two simple souls willing to share the responsibility for its success. Better yet, the unreachable dream had now moved within range of being touched. Any closer and it would be a reality. Selling their current home on Second Street, though, was essential. The funds generated might even pay the entire cost of this new venture, a venture destined to resolve a dream.

"I suppose we should list the house with a real estate agent," said Cal.

"What if they sell it right away?" asked Zelda Mae. "What do we do then?"

"Well, property is sellin' real well right now. It may take a long time to sell it. On the other hand, if it does sell soon, we can try and negotiate a later possession date," answered Cal.

"And what if they want immediate possession?" asked his wife.

"Then we'll give it to them. We certainly know how to rent a house. Heaven knows we've had enough experience in that category. The important thing is we need the sale of this house for the purchase price of the acreage in Hominy Corners.

"Who's a good agent to handle things?" asked Zelda Mae.

"I was thinkin' of Hank down at Heritage Land Associates."

"Yes, I hear he's good at what he does."

One piece of property mentioned by Clevon appeared the most promising to the Las Animas couple anxious to relocate. Ten acres south of Bokchito clearly was ideal for Cal and Zelda Mae's purposes. The passing of Hominy Corners did not mean that their dream died as well. He knew the location and remnants of foundations could be found where White's Mercantile or Hominy Corners General Store once stood so stately in the wind. Clevon's description meant the available property was on the opposite corner from the store. Actually, it would be on the site of the old school house. Clevon said you could even find an occasional brick from the once regal chimney adorning the small structure. Immediately Cal could invoke memories of warming by the potbellied stove as he awaited his turn to read for Mrs. Cragen.

Yes, to Cal there was no doubt that here was a chance to realize that portion of his dream of returning to Hominy Corners. The fact that no original buildings now stood on the site was immaterial. It was the location that appealed the most to him, and everyone knew that the land was fertile. Then, too, the second part of the dream could now become fulfilled as well, the dream of once again being able to see his livelihood maintained by the fruits of his labor from soil that he and Zelda Mae owned and cultivated. The someday they had been dreaming of was almost at hand. Now Cal knew that they wouldn't need to own a full-scale farm to return to those days when he and his father worked side by side as a team tilling the productive soil of Oklahoma. He and Zelda Mae now made up the new team on the gridiron of life. They had finally realized that they didn't even need a son working beside them to make this new enterprise happen. It would be a real asset to have the extra help in this endeavor, but it wasn't essential. He and Zelda Mae would be able to accomplish so much together after all of their offspring were on their own. This couple lacked for nothing. Motivation was at an all time high; the time was at hand. Total commitment to an objective can take the place of so many ingredients, when the options have been narrowed to one.

Acquisition of this small acreage would now fulfill the long sustained hopes and dreams carried by Cal and Zelda Mae since their wedding in 1925, thirty-two years earlier. The other half of the hopes and dreams had already been realized. The love of eleven children had now been increased by the love of sixteen grandchildren. There would be more, Cal and Zelda Mae knew, calling them Grandma and Grandpa as the golden years went by. Cal didn't know how he would continue his practice of going around on weekdays and picking up the increasing number of grandchildren for time with him, however, with the pending return to Oklahoma. He would somehow manage, though. He certainly had no intention of discontinuing a practice bringing so much joy to a person deprived of many of life's "pleasures" of the 1950's. Maybe he could get the children to move to Hominy Corners. Surely they would love that corner of God's world as well as he and Zelda Mae did.

As the plans for Cal's pending retirement progressed, he and Zelda Mae discussed things needing done before the long awaited break from city dwelling actually occurred. The retirement years would be so much more enjoyable, Zelda Mae reasoned, if Cal felt better. While he was able to continue in his work at the hospital at Ft. Lyon, he found himself awakened more and more at night with an urge to go to the bathroom. After getting there he found it was not only difficult to urinate, but he experienced considerable pain as well. Yes, if there was an obstacle blocking the achievement of a much-earned return to a simpler way of life, this medical condition was the culprit.

As Cal was a World War I veteran, he had free use of the services offered by the hospitals maintained by the Veteran's Administration, an agency of the federal government. Therefore, he consulted doctors right at Fort Lyon about his urinary problem. Their tentative diagnosis was that he had prostatic hypertrophy. This problem with the prostate gland was not uncommon for men Cal's age, and the VA offered free surgery to correct the ailment. Ft. Lyon was a neuro-psychiatric hospital, however, so the surgery could not be performed on the site. Instead, hospitalization at the VA Hospital in Denver would be necessary to perform the surgical procedure.

Cal and Zelda Mae saw this operation as one more goal needing attained to insure access to a happier life in their post-retirement years. While Cal was apprehensive about the surgery, there was no choice; he needed some relief from the excruciating pain he found occurring on a more frequent basis with each passing month. Neither he nor Zelda Mae wanted to see him going through life knowing the pain would get worse. Therefore, Cal was admitted to the VA Hospital in Denver in April of 1957. Thereafter followed considerable correspondence between two individuals deeply in love. Even though he only had a fourth grade education, Cal was always good about writing letters when he was away from home, more so than Zelda Mae was. These handwritten letters were the main links most of the time between two people sorely missing and needing each other's company.

Cal rarely missed a day in using the mails to keep his loving wife informed about his situation. The actual correspondence was not in the words used by this deeply caring couple, though. Instead, the real expression of endearment was in the simple statements or questions asked, which carried a hidden message of "I care about what you're doing, and I want you to know what I'm doing." Even with an inability to use more sophisticated grammar, these two conveyed their hopes and dreams most accurately.

"April 19

Dear Zelda Mae,

How are you all? Fine I hope. For me just fine. I don't know what they are going to do. They still haven't told me anything yet. I'll let you know as soon as possible. I would phone, but we need to save as much as possible for Hominy Corners. Plus, it's easier to handle this separation knowing we'll soon be together for a long, long time. Waiting for answers from the doctors is the hard part. It seems at times like they don't want me to know what is going on. I hope this changes soon.

By by with love.
XXXXXXX
Caleb A. Ledbetter"

Cal and Zelda Mae often added "X's" to their letters to emphasize the depth of their love. Though the quality and meaning of their relationship was never in question with each other, a visible sign was vitally important during a separation that was bearable only because of the future rewards it would bring.

In recent years Cal had also experienced an ongoing problem with his teeth, which required the wearing of dentures. Leaving the false teeth soaking in a glass of water overnight on a countertop while he slept was not unusual, as this gave him some relief from the pain caused by an improper fit. The VA in its array of services offered yet another opportunity to improve his retirement years by making him a new set of false teeth. All of this attention by a government agency gave Cal and Zelda Mae cause for great optimism. Retirement would open the doors to an unbounded joy with him feeling so much better.

The letters to Zelda Mae continued to come on a regular basis. All contained news of additional medical tests to better pinpoint the exact nature of the problem her husband was experiencing and how it might be corrected. Also, Cal's letters contained concern about his family along with a certain uneasiness about how long his stay was becoming. He was anxious to get home. Was his hospital stay an omen of what was to come? The feelings that were easily recognized as optimism in the beginning of his hospital stay were slowly giving way to a sense of fear pictured in his mind as a dark and foreboding being which lurked just beyond his concept of understanding.

Making matters worse was the fact that Cal was sometimes left in the dark by the hospital staff concerning what was going to happen during his stay in the hospital. It was disconcerting not always being sure about what was going to occur next. Due to a lack of knowledge and understanding, the hospitalization was rapidly losing the promise of better times to come.

Zelda Mae knew of Cal's intense loneliness and a need to keep informed about all that the family was experiencing. No need making his Denver stay worse by a lack of information from home. Hospitalization was now posing a real threat to their sense of wellbeing.

At least letters weren't the only source of contact between Cal and Zelda Mae. Sometimes she would catch a ride with Mrs. Morrow, whose husband was in the same hospital. On other occasions family members would drive her to Denver, as she was too scared to even attempt to navigate the heavy city traffic by driving herself. Besides that, the two-hundred mile trip exceeded her experience level in driving; she rarely had driven herself more than five miles from home, and that was in the small town of Las Animas with only one traffic signal light to help the infrequent driver across the intersection.

Cal enjoyed Zelda Mae's visits immensely. While he was always glad to see the children as well, he missed his Zelda Mae so much. His life was not complete with her being so far removed from him. She felt the same way about being separated from the man who had for decades been the inspiration of her life. This team could not function as intended unless each member was in close proximity to each other. By now they knew that only the shortest of separations could be tolerated.

The closer the time approached for the long awaited surgery, the more apprehensive Cal became about it. While he tried to hide his concern, he was not always successful. He hated to upset Zelda Mae with his worry. The only way, however, that he could prevent infecting her with his worry was to not see her, and that was asking just too much of him in his increasingly anxious condition. She understood and shared his concern.

Sometimes at night, when he didn't have visitors, and he felt good enough to walk, Cal slowly made his way up and down the halls of the largest building he had ever stayed in during his entire life. The immense size was almost overwhelming to a countryboy longing to be outside and free, breathing the untainted air of the countryside. Of course, he thought to himself, the smell associated with a barnyard might not be seen as so invigorating by others, but little did they know that the smell of animal by-products could just possibly help rejuvenate his life as much as the lifesaving ingredients in an intravenous injection.

Late at night the halls were often empty and dimly lighted, reminiscent of his being in the woods alone as a boy during a full moon. Thankful for a robe to cover a most inadequate hospital gown, Cal sometimes paused as he made rounds to glance into the dimly lighted rooms with silhouettes of strange objects dancing on the walls. The quiet shuffle of his hospital issued slippers was occasionally masked by the rhythmic pumping sounds of life support equipment needed by the patient struggling to maintain the slim thread keeping him part of the living. Cal's trips always took him to the darkened waiting area late at night, where he could enjoy a cigarette without bothering anyone. As he inhaled on the small white container of tobacco leaves, he often allowed his mind to wander back to an earlier period, when he and Zelda Mae were first married. Those were happy times, they enjoyed every minute of their lives. The worries of the newlyweds were small ones until J.H. passed away. Maybe, just maybe, the soon to be performed surgery would allow him and Zelda Mae to return to a time of contentment. But then again, what if the surgery failed? After all, the doctors couldn't assure any onehundred per cent success rate.

Because of his apprehension, Cal decided to visit with one of the Protestant chaplains during those few days preceding the surgery. He knew Zelda Mae would have wanted him to do exactly that. This was a new experience for Cal; he really didn't know what to say. The chaplain, however, knew what was bothering the troubled man arriving unannounced at his office door. They discussed the possible outcomes of the upcoming surgery. Yes, they even discussed the worst possible alternative. Cal might not survive the operation. The chance of such a drastic outcome was remote, but it was possible. Cal had not been much of a churchgoer during his sixty-two and one-half years of existence.

The chaplain was a patient man as he helped Cal to allay some of his deepest fears. He even taught this novice in religious matters how to pray, which was a welcome experience for Cal. He now accepted the fact that the matters bothering him were out of his hands. Afterwards, then, he felt a level of peace as he had never known before. It was as though the ocean waves pounding on the rocks by the shore in his mind were no longer hitting with such ferocity. This gentle farmer at heart was at peace with his maker.

"Say," said the chaplain in closing, haven't we met before?"

"Can't say as we have," answered Cal. "What did you say your name was again?"

"Chaplain Thomas."

"Not Fire and Brimstone Thomas?"

"You obviously know me. I haven't heard that term in decades."

"It's me, Cal Ledbetter from Hominy Corners."

"Not Sinner Cal as I recall?"

"One and the same," said Cal. "But you've changed. You're not yelling at me like ya used ta do alla the time."

"I owe you an apology," said the chaplain. "I was pretty aggressive in my younger days. Yes, I've changed. A lot for the better I'm sure."

"What happened?"

"I guess the Good Lord let me know that even though I was trying to win converts, my way was not his way. Something about not hitting with a stick when a gentle pat on the back will do. I'm glad you won't hear me yelling at anyone anymore."

"I for one am right glad to hear that," stated the patient.

"There is no Fire and Brimstone Thomas anymore," said the chaplain.

"There's no Sinner Cal anymore, either," replied Cal.

"Glad to meet you, Caleb," said his counselor.

"And I'm pleased to meet you, Ishmael," replied Cal.

Later Cal was to share with the chaplain his lifelong dream of returning to the tilling of the soil he and Zelda Mae hoped to own in Hominy Corners. "I can't wait for this operation to be over. Zelda Mae and I have a new life before us. We need to be gettin' about it without delay."

"And why is that?" asked Chaplain Thomas.

"Zelda Mae and I have this property all picked out in Oklahoma. We're a goin' to be farmers once again. Just as soon as I get outta' this here hospital."

"You mean back where you lived on a farm before?"

"Absolutely, and not just lived, preacher. My daddy and I had our own place once, and I intend to own one again, I reckon. Zelda Mae and I have it all figured out. My brother has already found the place. It's not more than a mile from where I grew up, and it's right on the very piece of property where I went to school fifty years ago. We'll be a signin' them papers afore the year is out."

Sensing a joy soon to be fulfilled, Chaplain Thomas read Cal the 3rd chapter of Ecclesiastes, verses 1-8:

1 To every thing there is a season, and a time to every purpose under the heaven:
2 A time to be born, and a time to die; a time to plant, and a time to pluck up that which is planted;
3 A time to kill, and a time to heal; a time to break down, and a time to build up;
4 A time to weep, and a time to laugh; a time to mourn, and a time to dance;
5 A time to cast away stones, and a time to gather stones together; a time to embrace, and a time to refrain from embracing;

6 A time to get, and a time to lose, a time to keep, and a time to cast away;
7 A time to rend, and a time to sew; a time to keep silence, and a time to speak;
8 A time to love, and a time to hate; a time of war, and a time of peace;

"Yes," reasoned the chaplain, "if it is time for you to have that farm, you will have it. Are you sure, though, that you want to be that far away from your kids and grandkids?"

"Well, it's time for me to have a nice plot of ground, preacher. And, it doesn't have to be too big, either. You're right about one thing, though, preacher. You've touched a point I've been ignoring all alone."

"What's that?"

"I really can't be away from the family like I've been sayin'. I don't really want them away from us like Zelda Mae was from her mama and me from my daddy. Maybe Hominy Corners is a dream that was never meant to be. Maybe my roots are now in Colorado. There's land for the takin' here, too."

"Then you shall have it, my friend, God willing. Remember, there's a time and a place for everything."

On the morning of Wednesday, May 8, 1957, Mattie Jean and Zelda Mae visited with Cal before he entered the operating room.

"Could you give us a minute alone, Mattie?" asked Cal.

"I'll be right outside," she answered, as she gently closed the door.

"They tell me that I might not be able to have a deep physical relationship with you after this, Zelda Mae."

"How can that be?" she asked.

"Well, this surgery sometimes changes the way a man's body works inside. I'm worried that you might think I'm less of a husband to you. Lord knows I don't want things to change, but the doctors say that may not be our choice."

"Listen to me, Caleb Ledbetter. I'm bein' absolutely sincere with you," said Zelda Mae. "Let me assure you that you're my husband no matter what happens in that operatin' room. We have a love built on a bond and commitment to each other. Remember when we married in Bennington back in 1925?"

"Well, yes. We said it would be forever and let no man break us apart."

"Well that includes surgeons," she said. "Furthermore, our ceremony said in sickness and in health. Well, Cal, I intend to uphold those wedding vows. Our marriage is also based on mutual needs and feelin's. It goes deeper than a physical relationship, so you're mine no matter what happens."

"There is one other thing Zelda Mae."

"And what might that be?"

"We really can't move back to Hominy corners, what with the kids and all bein' in Colorado."

"I've known that all along, Honey, but it had to be your decision Cal. Remember the story I told you over thirty years ago about Ruth and Naomi in the Bible?"

"I've never forgot it."

"Well, your people are my people, and your home is my home. Actually, it's our home no matter where it is. It's better, though, with our family around us. I always knew you'd come to this conclusion. God works in mysterious ways."

"Why didn't you say somethin'?" asked her husband.

"I was bidin' my time, and now it's time."

"We'll plan on a new plot of land soon as I get out of this place," said Cal.

Cal squeezed his wife's hand as Mattie Jean reentered the room. The relationship of these two in love had achieved a degree often denied to mere mortals until they totally and mutually give themselves to each other. The show of affection between the two in this hospital room prior to his being wheeled away to surgery was more than was ever seen by one of the children before. It wasn't that they did anything wrong, either. It was just that they had never exhibited their physical love in front of others this way in the past. Was there something different about this time? Did Cal and Zelda Mae sense what was taking place?

After a long ride down the gaily painted hallway on a cart, and just as he was to be wheeled into surgery, Cal for the first time in his life also hugged and kissed Mattie Jean. Then, at the last moment possible before the operating room doors would close like a vault and leave his beloved wife and daughter standing in the hallway, Cal gave Zelda Mae's hand one lingering last squeeze. It seemed to say farewell.

On that same morning in one of the surgery rooms at that great hospital of mercy in Denver, Cal's soul departed this earth for worlds unknown. The heart of a gentle man filled with so many undone deeds stopped beating on the operating table due to a loss of life-sustaining blood for which the surgeons were acutely unprepared. The hopes and dreams carried for a lifetime and so close to being realized by two people deeply in love departed with this loving man at 10:50 A.M. The love remained behind, however.

Death has never possessed the power to take away a deep abiding love. As mentioned in the scriptures and sung about by one of Cal's favorite singers, Roy Acuff, the "great speckled bird" swooped down from heaven to take on yet another reluctant passenger bound for the promised land. The swift yet graceful bird was presumed to be heading west into a glorious sunset which really doesn't set but slowly makes its way on its never ending westward journey while providing moments of awe and inspiration for those who must remain behind. One of Cal's favorite songs contained the line: "If I had the wings of an angel, over these prison walls I would fly…" Earthly boundaries would no longer be a concern for him. He was now looking at the sunset from the other side.

EPILOGUE

Surely heaven must be somewhere west of earth. Cal's lifelong journey had always been in a westerly direction, and the only way he might have left earth voluntarily would have been to better his condition. Heaven was the only place meeting this standard. If he could have made any move with a free choice, however, it surely would have included his beloved Zelda Mae. Therefore, Cal must have left against his own free will.

When a partner in a loving relationship like Cal and Zelda Mae had dies, part of the survivor goes into that lonely gaping hole in the earth awaiting the deceased. Not only did a wealth of hopes and dreams get committed to eternity with Cal, but an irreplaceable part of Zelda Mae's heart shared that six foot repository of last remains as well. She was never to totally recover from her sweetheart's death, though she lived 25 years after his passing.

After all of her children passed the threshold of adulthood and moved on to experience their own lives without her daily guidance and direction, Zelda Mae was a lonely woman. She had never realized the bleakness of unshared surroundings before. As a matter of fact, she had always been encompassed by and assumed responsibility for children from the time she was ten years old. This was a new and different existence for which she was not prepared. In her own unselfish way she didn't want to be a burden on her children, either, so she declined offers to move in with any of the flock she had so lovingly nurtured through the trials and tribulations of childhood on to the rewards of adulthood.

The evening hours were the hardest for Zelda Mae. During the day she could visit her children or call old friends on the phone. Without these contacts she would surely have lost her sanity. The telephone was a godsend for those in similar situations to Zelda Mae. It was not unusual for her to spend hours on this marvelous invention she had never used until she was over forty-five years of age. But at night with no light streaming in the tall windows of a now spacious home, she felt the loneliest. Seeking to keep busy and hoping to ignore the dreaded feelings of being alone, she became even more active in making quilts than she had ever been in her entire life. A huge quilting frame, necessary for holding the fabric taut while the delicate stitches were made one at a time, could almost always be found set up on the large dining room table, a table rarely needed anymore. The time worn frame would remain there until she could no longer see well enough to make the finest of stitches. All of her grandchildren, eventually numbering over forty, would receive at least one of these most precious reminders of a grandmother with failing eyesight painstakingly making the delicate stitches one by one ever so slowly, sometimes into the wee hours of the morning. Eventually she would get to make these colorful quilts for great-grandchildren as well. Not only that, but she made them on special order for others who became aware of her talent for making these treasured keepsakes. The extra income was welcome for a widow on a limited income. Then after she passed away, over thirty beautiful quilts she had made were found lovingly wrapped stored in an upstairs closet. Not even her own children knew they were there.

Even with the many visits of her family at all hours of the day and evening, Zelda Mae could never totally cope with the realization that she was alone. It allowed too much time for memories of happier times to re-emerge. For a few brief years she took in Belle's daughter, Jeannie, to live with her. Adoption papers were even drawn up, but in time Jeannie would graduate from high school and move on. In 1967, then, over 10 years after Cal's passing, Zelda Mae married David Engelbreckt Wilson, a widower with no children. This didn't mean she loved Cal any less, nor did it mean David loved his first wife, Iva Gladys Wilson, any less, either. David and Zelda Mae were two loving, caring people who didn't want to live their final years out on earth without the shared existence found only with the mutual benefits of living with a fellow human being.

When Zelda Mae died on October 25, 1982, she was buried in the Las Animas Cemetery beside her beloved Cal. The tombstone made of granite was simple; it said Zelda Mae Ledbetter on the right side and Caleb Ashton Ledbetter on the left side. When David Wilson passed away onehundred days later, he was buried at the side of Gladys. The bonds of two different couples were once again united as though they had never been broken. The fertile soil on the lush green hilltop overlooking a small serene town that once promised a new future now rejoined what it had once separated. In response to the song, “Will the circle be unbroken?” the answer had to be yes, but only for a brief interlude. Never would they be separated again. Reminiscent of Zelda Mae’s earlier comparisons of departed loved ones to the beauty of flowers, the colorful bouquets on the mantel of that golden palace behind the pearly gates were now arranged and a part of eternity. Oh, what a glorious sight they must be when beheld in all of their beauty, growing even more exquisite with each loving addition. Love does conquer all, even death.

Rest In Peace

Hallowed Ground

Final chapter a will to close

Quiet Sentinels

Granite gray and marble rose

Silent, Calm

Stillness of a proud repose

Erect, unyielding

Chronicles of a time on earth

Reminders Etched

Testaments denote eternal worth

Divine, Inspiring

Monuments to a second birth

About the Author

O. Ray Dodson is a retired school psychologist. Previously he had served as a teacher, college instructor and principal before becoming a school psychologist. Ray received his B.S. degree from Eastern Montana College, his M.S. degree from Eastern Washington State University and his Ph. D. from the University of Oregon in psychology. Currently, Ray and his wife, Kathleen, travel this great country in a motor home doing genealogical and historical research. Because of a special interest in the Civil War (Ray's great-grandfather served in this great conflict), they have spent considerable time visiting battle sites where Joseph was engaged in combat. Ray's own military service consisted of serving as an aircraft mechanic in the U. S. Marine Corps prior to the Vietnam Conflict. At one time Ray taught American History, so he makes a special effort to insure the accuracy of the history in the stories he writes. Future endeavors will include writing more in-depth accounts of his great-grandfather's unit in the Civil War.